Learn the words.

Learn the Song of the Swords, for only then will you know your path.

~The Goddess Daknys to the Darennsai

BOOKS BY TAMERI ETHERTON

Song of the Swords*

The Prince of Dragons

The Stones of Resurrection

The Temple of Sacrifice

The Ruins of Betrayal

The Veils of Deception

The Keeper of Stars

The Fatal Fae*

Fatal Illusion

Fatal Assassin

Fatal Legacy

Fatal Forever

Fatal Destiny

Court of Stars*

Sunset in Shadow

Chronicles of Eidyn*

Child of Fire

Dragon Mage

Daring Ever Afters*

Enchant

*Books that are part of the Aetherverse: The fantastical realms of Tameri Etherton. Characters and storylines intersect within the books with magical consequences.

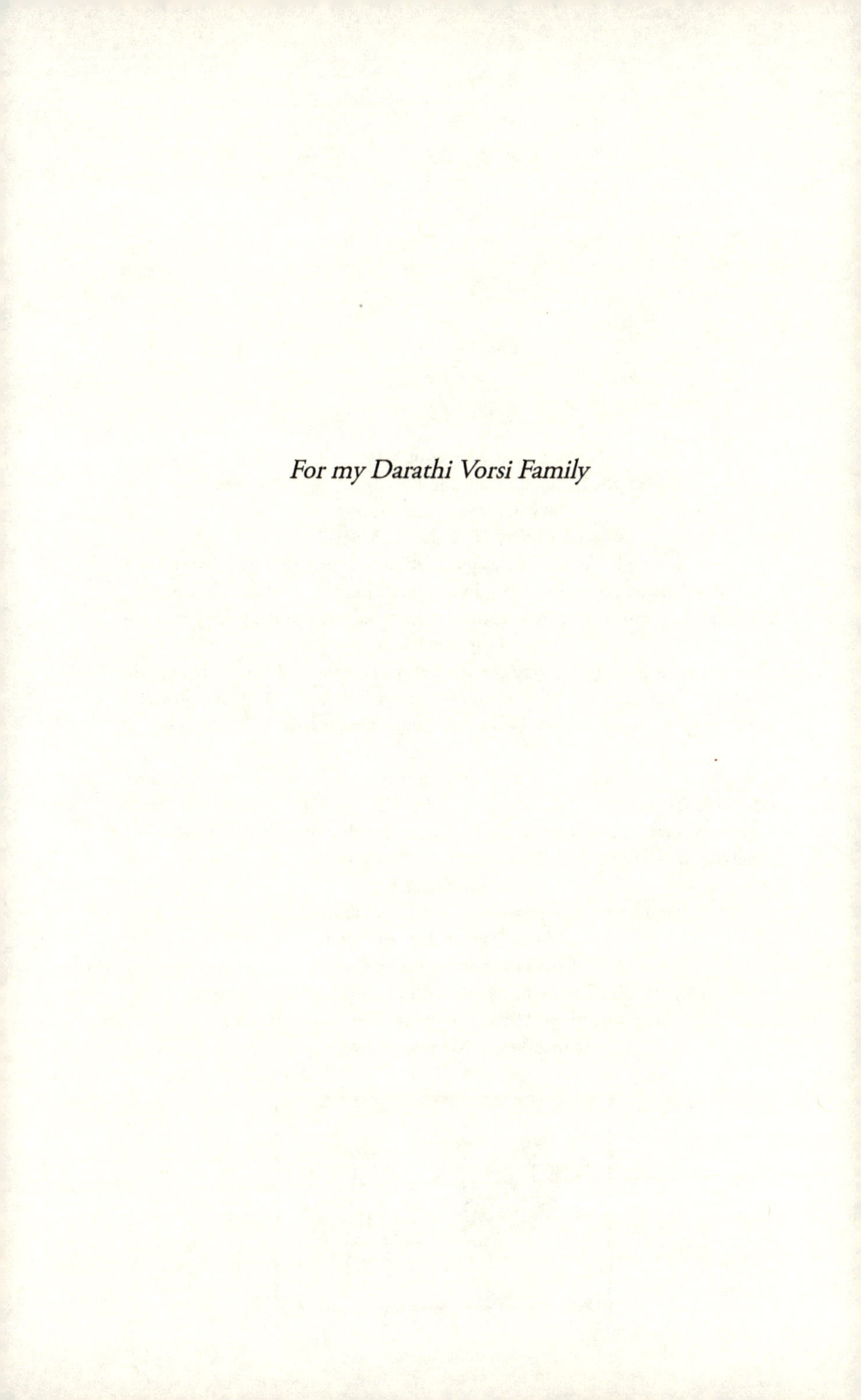

For my Darathi Vorsi Family

TEACUP
DRAGON
PUBLISHING

THE KEEPER OF STARS

SONG OF THE SWORDS

TAMERI ETHERTON

AELINAE

WORLD MAP

N
THE WALL
THE NARTHVIER
LAN GYLLARELLE
MIDVALE
PADERAU
THE TELMARAN ISLANDS
SEA OF JADEN
THE ULLAN DESERT
JADEN FLATS
SILVER R
ROAD
HIDDEN VALLEY
GREAT BARREN GORGE
ELDERS PASS
JANSEN STRAIT
WASTES OF SLOE
JANSEN PLAIN
THE EASTERN SEAS

Pendrian Wastes
Western Seas
Denk Scarbos
Caer Idris
Spine of Ohlin
Isle of Ardyn
Caer Danuri
Mount Nadrene
Danuri Provence
Gaarendahl
Celyn Eryri
Lake Oster
Talaith
Ahkae
Summerlands
Stones of Kaldaar
Sitari
Summer Seas

The Narthvier
The Weirren
Lan Gyllarelle
The Ullan Desert
Telmaran Islands
Sea of Jaden
Paderau
Jansen Strait
Wastes of Sloe
Eastern Seas

THE TWO KINGDOMS
The Wall
The Narthvier
The Ullan Desert
The Telmaran Islands
Sea of Jaden
Great Barren Gorge
Jaden Flats
Hidden Valley
Elders Pass
Jansen Strait
Jansen Plain
Wastes of Sloe
Eastern Seas

THE SUMMER SEAS
MEKIAE
SRINIVAS
THATIRAKA
MNABAIE
SCIABARRA
DETARRE
ANTHOS
AHKAF
SUMMERLANDS
NYLS
SALDANNA
MENURRA
WINE FIELDS
PIRATES COVE
SITARI
The Sea Kingdom

CHAPTER ONE

*I*t is time.

The tips of Taryn's scuffed boots dangled precariously over the cliff edge as she stared into the vastness of destruction that stretched out before her. She knew, deep in her heart, she'd caused this. But how? And when? She'd been here before. But had it been real, or in a dream? She touched the spot beneath her left breast where the vorlock had poisoned her all those months ago. The poison was finally gone, and now only a scar remained—she could recall the events of *that* day with absolute clarity.

Why could she remember the attack, but not this wasteland? It was there, buried deep in her memories, but she couldn't grasp the how or why. The answer was the key to everything. Or was it? Perhaps she was asking the wrong question. Always more questions, always another problem to solve. Seldom were there answers.

A frustrated sigh drifted on a breeze, and she rubbed her temples. Her life had become a series of riddles—of tests that she was woefully unprepared for. Like the demon in the void. Was it dead? Bloody hell, she hoped so. Gods knew she'd nearly died fighting it. If it was a test, had she passed? Or failed? Regardless, she was alive, as were Rhoane and Kaida. They'd found the exiled darathi. For now, that was all that mattered.

She stretched her hands in front of her and watched with curious fascination as stars twinkled beneath her skin. With a single thought, the stars blinked out, and with another, they grew stronger. Nadra had called her Keeper of the Stars. Yet that didn't feel right. The title sounded more like a caretaker role, someone who *watched* the stars, but was otherwise apart from them. She was the *keeper* of stars. They were as much a part of her as the blood that flowed through her veins. Infinite. Vast. Vital to her survival.

What did it mean? What did any of this mean? The demon, Kaldaar, Myrddin, even Nadra—what path were they leading her down, and how many more casualties would she have to suffer before the end? Whatever or whenever that was. A vision of two swords—hers and Rhoane's, crossed not in anger but in unity— seared her mind. Two swords. Two hearts. Two deaths. A single heartbeat. More riddles. Just fucking great. Didn't she have enough to deal with without having to imagine her imminent demise? That was for another day, hopefully far, far in the future.

Today, she had more pressing concerns.

Below her sparkling hands the canyon cut a deep chasm into the cliffs from left to right as far as the eye could see. Across the ravine was mist and more emptiness. More death.

They'd found the darathi vorsi, but too many had perished in the time since their exile from Aelinae. Far too many. What were once majestic creatures with wingspans to rival her mother's great hall were now skeletal beggars, scrimping what they could from the hostile landscape.

Still, they had hope. The dragons had never stopped believing the Darathi Vorsi Prince would come and their exile would end. Rhoane was here at last, but he couldn't return the dragons. Not yet. Not until he could be certain of their future, and at the moment, neither Taryn nor Rhoane trusted the rulers of Aelinae.

The darathi vorsi's survival mattered most. They had to find a secure location to hide them until they could return—but where? Who could they trust to care for the beasts? The dragons needed nourishment first and foremost. Their skinny bodies broke Taryn's heart every time she saw them. Again, that sense that she'd caused this crawled across her skin.

The question of *how* echoed in her skull. The darathi were cast into exile four thousand seasons before she ever existed. How could someone cause such horrific destruction before they were even born?

Her gaze traveled from the misty veil that kept the wasteland separated and hidden from Aelinae to where Kaida lay sprawled on the dirt, her fur once more a gleaming white. Beside her, a golden dragon lifted her face to the sun. It was Ahmbra's tears that had cleaned Kaida's fur and mended all the wounds she'd suffered in the void. Since then, she hadn't left Kaida's side. She was the first dragon born in the wasteland. Would she thank Taryn for taking her away from the only home she'd ever known? Or would moving her and the other dragons cause distrust? Mallaqai's betrayal hung heavy in the elder darathi's thoughts.

Taryn kicked at a clod of dirt, her mind even more unsettled than it had been a moment before. A dry breeze lifted her hair and she imagined herself falling into the ravine, silver scales glittering along her skin. Roiling blackness infused with lightning sparks rose from the ground to embrace her as she accepted her fate. She had caused this. It's what she deserved.

Icy pinpricks shot up her spine. She knew this vision—or was it a memory? A dream, perhaps? Or a warning? Again, those same questions pelted her skull. Why? When? Where? She stared at her boots and tried to force the vision to continue, but it remained stubbornly elusive.

Taryn darling, it is time.

She tilted her face to the ever-present sun and chuckled. "I hear you, Nadra. Believe me, I know. Any chance you could help a girl out and give a hint as to what I should do next? There's no shortage of priorities at the minute." She brushed her hand against her pocket where the vial with the trapped faerie rested. They needed to return him to his home at some point. After the dragons were settled.

Then there was the problem of Kaldaar and Zakael. And what about Myrddin? The list of priorities seemed never-ending. How the hell were she and Rhoane supposed to solve them all?

A soft cloud of dust rose to tickle her nose and she sneezed against the intrusion. Gilchrist settled his large body beside her and gazed toward the sky.

"I know that troubled look. Am I interrupting?"

She stroked the greyish-blue scales on his muzzle. "Nadra is insisting it's time for us to leave."

"And yet you have doubts?"

"I don't trust the rulers of Aelinae. Not yet. I fear if we return you too soon, in your weakened condition, you'll be manipulated and overpowered." A traitorous thought brushed her mind that perhaps Mallaqai hadn't sent the darathi to their deaths, but had tried to keep them from exactly what Taryn now feared—being used by Rykoto or Kaldaar for nefarious purposes.

Gilchrist nodded slowly, his eyes trained on the misty wall across the canyon. For the past four days she'd watched him as he stared moodily into the distance for bells on end, never flinching from his sentry post, never sharing his thoughts or what he might've witnessed. According to Ahmbra and Jinnipher, he'd done the same every day for centuries, always holding onto hope that Rhoane would save them all.

Even after Rhoane's mother Aislinn came to live with them, Gilchrist continued his silent vigil. How lonely it must've been for him to be the only darathi who could glimpse beyond the veil.

"I'm sorry for your exile." She stroked the scales along his jaw, flinching at the memory of the snake-dragon-demon of the void. While Ahmbra had healed Kaida, Gilchrist and Jinnipher had healed Taryn and Rhoane. Physical injury was easy to mend, but the heart and mind weren't so easily repaired. The events of the past season had left scars that she carefully tried to ignore.

Gilchrist sighed with the heaviness of someone who held too much responsibility as he gazed over the canyon. "You do not understand the relationship between darathi and their homeland. The Eleri are our caretakers, but we are the caretakers of the world. Without darathi, there is unbalance, and with that upset in equilibrium, chaos breeds."

Taryn's hand stilled upon his scales. "Kaldaar is creating chaos on Aelinae." She traced a ragged scale with her fingertip, her mind racing with darkened thoughts. "I saw the same on several other worlds. Wars, people who stole ShantiMari from living beings, magical creatures being held captive in glass prisons, it was horrific. On one world, there was a ruler who slaughtered not just darathi, but those with darathi souls like mine. How do you prevent chaos when there are people with evil in their hearts?"

A lone tear leaked from the corner of his eye and rolled down her hand. In its wake, a trail of stars brightened beneath her skin, and she felt the invigorating zing of his power. His healing power. Her fingertips brushed the pocket holding the vial, an idea forming. What if darathi tears could free the magical beings imprisoned in the glass pendants? It was mad to even think it, but a little bit of the impossible was exactly what she needed. She stifled a thrill and focused on his words.

"As long as there is greed in one's heart, there will be war and chaos. It is inevitable. The darathi cannot prevent it, but we remember all so that it might be avoided the next time."

"Do the darathi have a shared consciousness like the Eleri?

Are your memories passed down from one generation to another?"

"Aye. It is one of the ways we have a special bond with the Eleri."

A second dragon joined them on Taryn's left. Jinnipher's ruby-hued snout stretched to nuzzle Gilchrist's face, making an arch above Taryn. Their love emanated from beneath their scales and she was bathed in its warmth.

"You have not told her the most important part," Jinnipher said as she rubbed her head along Gilchrist's long neck.

Taryn had watched this particular display of affection several times but didn't understand the meaning behind it. When Jinnipher's snout reached Gilchrist's wing, she blew a soft breath of fire where the wing joined his body. He lifted his wing and flapped it several times, causing Taryn's hair to blow into her face.

She tore her gaze from the intimate gesture and peered at the wavering wall across the canyon. If she squinted, she could see Eleri moving among the trees, but not the Weirren itself. That was too far from the wall of powerful ShantiMari that kept the wasteland separated from Aelinae.

"What hasn't he told me?" she said, distracted. Deep in the gorge, a tar-like darkness bubbled and beckoned. It hadn't been there a moment ago, but now suddenly she felt the need to dive headfirst into the pit. She inched forward until only her heels were rooted to the cliff.

"About the darathi." Gilchrist shifted his weight and sent out a burst of sand in a spiral, blocking Taryn's view of the canyon. "We are more than history keepers of our world; we maintain balance by keeping ShantiMari stable. We have little to no true power ourselves, so we act as conduits for those who do. Without darathi, ShantiMari will die."

The shocking confession startled her. The implications were vast, but what really struck her was how wrong he was. Darathi had vast amounts of ShantiMari. How was it he couldn't tell how powerful they were? Even standing a foot from him, she felt the pull of his power. It was muted, yes, but it was there. Her mind went to dark thoughts, and she shook her head against them. Why would someone ward the dragons? And was it to protect them? Or control them?

"You should also know, the darathi guard the portals." Jinnipher's whisker embraced Taryn. "Only a select few are granted the knowledge of how to create them from nothing. We make certain that information does not fall into the wrong hands."

"I'm afraid in your absence, it has." A pit soured Taryn's gut. No wonder Zakael could explore unchecked. "Did exile cause you to lose that ability?"

"We did." Her heavy sigh blew warm across Taryn's cheeks. "This chaos you speak of... I would guess the other realms' portals are equally disturbed."

"They are." Thoughts of having to travel the void darkened Taryn's mood. Instead of dwelling on the inevitable, she asked the question that pinged against her skull.

"Your tears, how is it they heal?" She glanced again at Kaida, and then to Rhoane. The three of them should've died from their wounds from the void.

"A darathi tear, freely given, has the power to heal all that is broken, be it a bone, or a heart," Jinnipher said. "But if our tears are milked without our consent, they become caustic and amenable to nefarious purposes."

"Who would do such an awful thing?" Yet Taryn could name at least a dozen unscrupulous people who would commit such an offense. Her mother and half-brother topped the list. "What would happen if someone with evil intent gained control over the darathi?"

Gilchrist snarled low and deep and terrifying. "They would have access to vast quantities of power."

"Enough to kill a god?"

"Enough to kill *all* the elder and younger gods, though I am not sure that is possible. Only a god can kill another god and as you know, darathi are not divine. But we could cause vast amounts of damage if commanded." He snugged his head alongside her body, and she draped an arm protectively over his horns. "That is a long way down."

The blackness continued to roil deep below them. Inky tendrils crept up the ravine's walls.

"It is." She inched her boots back until they no longer teetered over the edge. "I think they're looking for me. But whoever is compelling me to fall into the darkness won't be satisfied today." The sun beat down on her, relentless in its heat. "Kaldaar would know exactly how powerful the darathi are. That's why he's so eager to have you returned, and why Cashiel tried to steal our dragon souls. He wants to use you to murder all the other gods, or at least help him do it. I promise I will not let that happen."

Jinnipher rubbed her snout along Taryn's back, in much the same way she'd caressed Gilchrist, but gentler. "We know you will not, darling. It is why we have waited all these long seasons for our prince. We believe in you."

Taryn nodded and stroked her scales. "We need to move you somewhere safe. I know of a place, but honestly, I don't know the caretakers well enough to guarantee you'll be treated well."

"What does your heart tell you?"

"That you'll be loved and honored as you are meant to be. They are not of the old ways, but Eleri of another world."

Both Jinnipher and Gilchrist gasped and a puff of wind lifted her hair. The silver strands drifted around her as if suspended in space, creating the image of a galaxy, and she glanced at her hands. Stars brightened beneath her ghost tattoos.

The Keeper of Stars.

She took a breath and patted the elder darathi. "Nadra's right. It is time. Time for a new Aelinae. Time for peace."

With the dragons' help, she and Rhoane would change the balance of Aelinae, hopefully forever. But first, she had a promise to keep. Only then would she face the unknown of the void where, with any luck, the snake-demon-dragon was either dead, or no longer wished them dead.

Either way, her options sucked.

CHAPTER TWO

One more try. It had to work this time. Taryn's legs cramped as she sat cross-legged on the clifftop with her eyes closed, hands resting on her knees. One more try, and then they'd leave. Desperation scratched at the base of her skull, but she wouldn't give in to the despair that so desperately tried to claim her sanity. They should've left a bell earlier, but she had to know Hayden and the others were safe.

Hayden. She sent the thought toward the Summerlands, and then to Talaith. He'd promised to stay in Menurra, but she knew better than most that situations changed and new plans must be laid now and again.

Taryn? a sleepy sounding Hayden answered, and she nearly sobbed to hear his voice.

Why weren't you answering? I've been trying to reach you for ages.

Because it's the middle of the bloody night and some of us sleep?

Oh. Sorry. I just—it's so good to hear you, sweet cousin. How are you? How is Sabina?

We're well. Worried about you, but nothing new there. Taryn heard shuffling and then, *Give me a moment to put on a robe.* Familiar sounds and scents came to her, not of the Summerlands, but of the Crystal Palace.

Are you in Talaith?

We arrived a few days ago. And before you ask, the baby is fine.

Taryn breathed a sigh of relief at the news. She focused her energy and materialized on the balcony outside his rooms. As she'd hoped, he stood alone. A sliver of guilt coursed through her when she saw his hair disheveled, robe haphazardly tied. She hadn't meant to disturb his sleep. A spark of surprise lit his eyes when he saw her, and then a slow smile lifted his cheeks.

"Where are you? *How* are you? You've been gone nearly a moonturn and so much has happened. Myrddin betrayed us— you especially. We only just found out, but the others have known since their return to Talaith." Tightness wound around his words.

She took his hands to comfort him, happy for the warmth she felt from his skin. "We know. We learned of his treachery on the Sitari Islands. We also believe he's trying to help us, but are loathe to trust anything he says or does."

Hayden withdrew his hands and tightened his robe. "Just after Myrddin told everyone you were dead, Zakael came to see us. He said you were alive and gave me the strangest rose. He made me promise to keep it safe, and to hide it until such a time as I would have need of it. Do you know what that's all about?"

"Not a clue." What the hell was Zakael playing at? Her mind pinged with possibilities, but also doubts. "What did the rose look like?"

"Clear, with opalescent veins." Hayden watched her closely for a hint of recognition, but she kept her expression bland.

How the fuck had Zakael gotten one of the roses she and Rhoane created in Elvenwood? A shiver of something dark wound its way down her spine to entangle her heart. Whatever game Zakael was playing, she knew who was behind it, and that terrified her. Were they able to follow her and Rhoane? They'd have to be extra cautious moving forward, just in case.

She briefed Hayden on what she and Rhoane had been doing —excluding any mention of far-off worlds or the dragons—and he filled her in on what the others had been up to in her absence. It appeared they'd been busy spying on Myrddin until he went missing the morning after Zakael informed them Taryn wasn't dead. It also appeared that while in the Summerlands, Lliandra contracted a mysterious illness and suffered from it still, much to Eliahnna and Faelara's consternation. By the strain in Hayden's tone, Taryn guessed it had something to do with Kaldaar, but he couldn't be certain. He only knew that the empress was erratic and impulsive with short stretches of clarity and focus. The entire court were on edge because of her behavior.

He informed her that Fae and Baehlon were traveling to Ulla to return Loghan to his homeland, but his brother Gwainne had stayed at the Crystal Palace. She hid her surprise that the Ullan prince had traveled from his homeland to Talaith. The last she'd seen of him, he'd been in Ulla and quite vocal about what he thought of her and her family. From Hayden's telling, he didn't know why Gwainne was in Talaith, nor had Loghan shared with those in Talaith what happened to Rhoane while they were with the Sitari. For that, Taryn was grateful to the Ullan healer for keeping his promise.

Of them all, Taryn worried most for Tessa. She more than anyone suffered from the events that were constantly tossing her life about like a ragdoll in a rabid dog's maw. She was still so young, too young really to be caught in the schemes, and Taryn feared her baby sister would be forced to grow up and face the reality Kaldaar threatened to bring about. Not if she could help it. For Tessa's sake, yes, but for everyone on Aelinae.

"Let the others know we are well, and that we'll return within a fortnight. But keep it to those you can trust. And please, spend extra time with Tessa. She needs you and Sabina right now." Taryn hugged her cousin tight, wishing for all the universes that she could have truly been with him.

She closed the connection and melancholy wrapped around her heart. For a long moment she sat still, letting her emotions drift while she processed everything she'd learned. Concern for her mother edged along her thoughts, but that would have to wait. They'd deal with her, along with Myrddin and Zakael, after they settled the darathi.

Soft steps approached, and Rhoane's warm hand pressed upon her shoulder. "Mi carae, we should go."

She nodded and stood, her gaze fixed on the horizon where Aelinae was hidden behind the wall of ShantiMari. Whose power was it that kept the worlds separated yet connected? One more bloody riddle to answer.

Rhoane's lips brushed hers and she held him against her. It had been too long since they'd had a moment alone. With the sun not yet risen and the darathi sleeping, this was the best chance they'd get. Her lips parted to take his tongue into her mouth, and she savored the taste of him. Apples and mint. No matter where they were, no matter what he'd consumed, he always tasted of apples. Her personal candied apple stand, available anytime, day or night, for the low, low price of a kiss. The thought made her giggle, and she wrapped his long hair around her fist as her body sparked with need.

With a groan, he pulled away, his eyes darkly lidded. "You temptress. Later, I will slake your hunger. Until then, we have a duty to perform."

"Your duty is to me—or have you forgotten your vow?"

His lips quirked in a saucy grin. "I have forgotten nothing. And when next we are alone, I will prove it to you." He traced a thumb over her mouth and bent to leave a trail of kisses along her jaw, making her knees wobble with each one.

"Now who's the tease?"

"I cannot help it. You are enticing." His grin slipped and eyes hardened. "Is everything well with your cousin?"

"He's in Talaith. I'll fill you in on the way. I also have an idea or two of how we might free those imprisoned in the vials. Right now, it's just a gut instinct involving darathi tears—freely given— and possibly that rose we created in Elvenwood.

He rubbed a finger along his jaw and she practically saw his mind working. "One heals, one restores. I think you might be onto something, but we must be careful. Either could harm as much as heal."

"Desperate times, my friend. Sometimes you have to dive into the darkness and trust there is a safe place to land. Like now."

She noticed the sky had lightened and reluctantly released his hair. Kaida padded to them, her snowy fur illuminated in the pre-dawn light. Her drowzy steps were adorable and Taryn was glad she'd let her friend sleep. The Gods only knew when they'd get another chance to rest.

Why did you not wake me? She sat with a huff, her ears drooping.

I wished to contact Hayden before we left. I thought it best not to disturb you until I was finished.

I appreciate your thoughtfulness. She looked over her shoulder to where the darathi slept. Aislinn stood at the doorway to her little cottage, a wistful look on her pretty face. *I will miss our new friends.*

We'll see them again. Gods, but she hoped they would.

It was now or never. She knew which she'd prefer, but she couldn't avoid this any longer. Scrounging up her courage, she made a circle with her hand and said the words to create a portal.

Silence cloaked them as they stepped into the swirling darkness of the void. Taryn gripped Rhoane's hand tight enough to cut off circulation, but she wouldn't lose him. The same for Kaida, who panted to her left. None of them relished the thought of revisiting the void so soon after their fight with the snake-dragon-demon, but it was the only way to accomplish their tasks.

The only way to save the darathi.

Breathe, Darennsai, Rhoane whispered in her mind, and she took a long drag of stale air.

"The void doesn't feel different." A flickering to her left drew her attention and she steered the little group in that direction.

"Are you sure?" Rhoane's slight tug toward the faint light at the end of the long tunnel of nothingness gave away his apprehension.

"If that thing is still alive, we either need to rehabilitate it, or kill it for good. We don't know if Myrddin or someone else set that thing loose in here, but someone put the seal into it, and we can't be certain it was consensual."

You would save the demon that tried to kill us? Anger spiked Kaida's words.

"I have to say, I agree with the grierbas."

"Since when can you hear Kaida?" She thought the grierbas only spoke in her mind. She wasn't jealous, just, confused.

"I honestly do not know, but it seems to me since Menurra?"

Since the runyon poisoning, Kaida said matter of factly. *Before then, you had a block preventing you from understanding me.*

Taryn was about to ask what she meant when a shadowed lump loomed in front of them, blocking their way. A swirl of uncertainty and dread tugged at her gut. They approached with caution, the memory of their fight too fresh, too raw. When they were close enough to see the demon's half-lidded eyes, Taryn released her death-grip on the others and sent a thread of Shanti-Mari toward the creature. It shifted, and her heart stilled for a moment, then beat ferociously against her chest. She took in drags of air to calm herself, but there was nothing she could say or do that would remove the sheer amount of fear swirling through her blood.

Rhoane touched her arm and she jumped as if he'd electrocuted her. She clenched and unclenched her fists before shaking them out. She could do this. The snake-dragon-demon thing was alive, but only just.

They moved forward as a unit, cautiously approaching until they were an arm's length from its stub-nosed snout. She and Rhoane simultaneously stretched their fingertips until they touched the smooth scales of the creature.

Release me, please.

The thought came to her softly, with a sad pleading in the words. His history rushed through them, from his creation ten thousand years earlier to this moment, and Taryn wept for the poor thing. Created for death, always alone, always seeking, he'd never known the light, only the infinite darkness of the void. His only nourishment had been those he killed and their suffering. Beneath the memories, she sensed deep remorse.

Taryn glanced at Rhoane and nodded. Kaida placed a paw on the creature, and she heard the grierbas whisper in the demon's mind that it was time for him to rest. Taryn opened her power, all four strains of her ShantiMari, and eased them into Rhoane's body. His power entwined with hers until it was difficult to tell her threads apart from his. Together, they coaxed the creature's heart to stop beating while soothing his troubled mind.

Regret washed over her—from the demon. He'd never understood his purpose, nor had he enjoyed his task. He had slain many over the millennia, and he remembered them all. One by one, she and Rhoane absolved him of the killings.

Of who had created him, or profited by those murdered, there was nothing. If the creature had ever known his maker, that information was wiped from memory. When Taryn put an image of Myrddin to the demon, there was no reaction. Same with Kaldaar. If the creature knew them, he'd been compelled to forget. Yet his master made certain he recalled every last grisly detail of those he slaughtered. What an asshole.

When at last the demon's memories were emptied, he breathed a final elongated breath and his weakened heart stilled. The three of them stood back for a moment of silence.

"We can't just leave him here." She placed her hand on his snout once more. "He was never able to see the light, but now, he can be the light. In his death, he can become useful and guide those who travel these pathways."

Rhoane shook his head, his cheeks shimmering with tears. "You never cease to amaze me, Darennsai." He returned his hand to rest beside hers.

Kaida yipped and placed her paw atop their fingers. The grierbas didn't have ShantiMari, at least not in the way Taryn and Rhoane did, but there was something coming from her that made the hairs on Taryn's arm quiver. Muted, like the darathi, but there.

Their power swirled and shifted, turning the demon's scales into glittering motes of dust that drifted above their heads like a sparkling cloud at midnight. When nothing physical was left of the creature, Taryn focused her attention on the billions of particles they'd created from his body. These she infused with light and sent them scattering throughout the void to act as beacons of hope for anyone who found themselves in the endless darkness.

From somewhere far, far away, she heard a roar of rage and knew Kaldaar was not pleased with what they'd done.

Taryn stroked Kaida's soft fur. "I guess now we know who created the poor thing."

"This was always Kaldaar's realm. You have shown that you are not as weak as he once believed." Rhoane ran the backs of his fingers over her cheek and tucked a strand of hair behind her ear. "You are gaining in strength, but I fear, so is he."

"That's a worry for another day." She indicated the portal opening and urged them forward. "We have more pressing matters to attend."

They stepped from the darkness into twilight near the pond

that Taryn had found on her last visit to the faerie kingdom. She'd half-hoped Tug would be there waiting, but the area was empty save for a few swans who languidly paddled across the glassy surface.

As they neared the gardens where Taryn had stolen one of Queen Eirlys's roses, a very familiar voice came to them from beyond a tall hedge. Rhoane pulled up with a jerk of his head toward the sound and Taryn nodded she heard it as well. What the fuck was Zakael doing here? Bloody hell and bagpipes.

She slipped a shadow over herself and Kaida, but the grierbas shook her head against the cloak. Taryn stared in wonder as Kaida shifted from a large canine to a sleek white cat with golden eyes.

She shared a look with Rhoane, who was equally as gobsmacked as she. Kaida yawned and stretched, looking for all the world like an ordinary cat.

Are you going to tell us how you turned into a cat? She shared the thought with both Rhoane and Kaida.

The cat sat on its haunches and blinked. *Lady Faelara might have given me a tip or two.*

Taryn suppressed a laugh. *I love you, furball.*

The cat hissed, but not very convincingly.

She and Rhoane made certain their shadows were in place and they couldn't be seen before stepping lightly around the hedge. There, standing not more than four strides from them, was Zakael and Eirlys, the Seelie queen.

Kaida meowed and strolled to the pair, entwining herself between Zakael's legs. To Taryn's utter surprise, he crouched low and scratched Kaida beneath the chin. At the very least, she'd worried he would kick the cat away. Never in her wildest dreams did she think he'd show a creature kindness. Kaida's tail arched and stroked along his jaw. Images skittered through Taryn's mind: Zakael at Elvenwood stealing one of the roses she and Rhoane created when they healed the great tree, Zakael giving the rose to Hayden, and finally, Zakael begging Eirlys for one of her roses.

Beneath everything, she sensed her half-brother's desperation —and fear. Not just casual anxiety, but deep-seated terror. He was afraid of Kaldaar, yes, but he feared for *her* as well.

This was unexpected, and she wasn't certain she liked this new game. As she watched him absently stroke Kaida's fur, an unsettling thought overcame her that perhaps her brother deserved a second chance. Or even a first chance since she never had the opportunity to get to know him. Yet…there was history between them not easily forgotten nor dismissed.

Rhoane's invisible hand reached for hers and she clasped it. *Are you getting Zakael's images as well?*

It must be from Kaida's connection to him. What do you think it means?

I do not know, but I sense great apprehension in him. Conflicted emotions as well.

Me too.

She studied Zakael from the safety of her shadows. It would take more than petting a cat to convince her he wasn't the vile, deranged man who'd threatened her life on more than one occasion. This was performative. Had to be.

And if it wasn't, what could've happened that would cause him to shift his behavior so radically? He was Overlord of the West now, as powerful as Lliandra—only a god was more powerful. For one heartbreaking moment, she allowed herself to feel hope for her half-brother. Hope that this wasn't just an act and that he had truly changed.

CHAPTER THREE

They waited several minutes after Zakael left before dropping their shadows. Queen Eirlys didn't shriek when she saw them, but she did gasp and grab at her chest. Taryn felt a tiny stab of guilt that they'd appeared out of nowhere without warning. They were probably lucky the queen didn't call her guard to have them executed on the spot for trespassing. She had no idea if the queen would such a thing, but it was a stark reminder that caution should be taken in these situations. It had become habit to pull shadows over herself or traipse through the endless void, but to most everyone else, these were anomalies. She'd do well to remember that.

Despite Taryn and Rhoane revealing themselves, Kaida remained a cat, a fact that amused and confused Taryn. One of these days, she and the grierbas were going to have a long talk about what, exactly, a grierbas knew about anything and everything. She didn't like surprises, and there had been too many of late. The irony of which was not lost on her.

"Apologies for appearing without notice, Your Majesty." Taryn inclined her head. "It was necessary."

"I assume the gentleman who just left is no friend of yours?"

Eirlys took in their less than courtly attire, a frown pulling her lips into a bedraggled state. "It seems he was in need of one of my roses, though I can't help but wonder how he would know they exist when he's not a citizen of Cilachaem. Care to explain?"

"I honestly have no idea." Although, this helped explain Hayden's query. Taryn flicked a glance at the stunted stalk where she'd stolen a rose only what? A few days earlier? A week? How long had it been? Hayden said they'd been gone nearly a month, but that was from when he last saw them on Menurra.

So much had happened since his wedding, too much, really. It felt like they hadn't stopped since she blew up her mother's ship. She rubbed her temples and mentally ran numbers through her mind.

One day on Aelinae was four in the wasteland, but how long had passed since they'd been here on Cilachaem? They'd left Elvenwood and went to Nasus, and then…and then they'd fought the snake-demon-dragon. That must've been at least a week. Or was it longer? Shorter? Her head ached trying to sort out the different realms and their flows of time.

"Strange, then, that he seemed to know about another rose, one crystal clear with healing properties. The description sounded oddly familiar to my rose. Have you any knowledge of that mystery?"

Rhoane cleared his throat and inclined his head, his hand over his heart. "We healed the Elvenwood tree and when we did, the rose Taryn stole from you was absorbed into the bark."

If Zakael knew about the flower at Elvenwood, which one did he give to Hayden? It must've been the Elvenwood flower judging by the description—but why would Zakael need either? And why was he on Cilachaem in the first place? So many bloody questions.

The queen harrumphed and glided toward the palace. "We shall continue this conversation in my rooms. The world has become a little too open for my liking."

They followed her in silence, ignoring curious looks from the courtiers and servants. Some might've remembered them from their previous visit, or not. Nearly all of them seemed to have no idea who they were. Taryn scanned the faces for Esme or Meg and was disappointed when she found neither.

At the doors to the queen's rooms, two guards regarded them with narrowed lids, but allowed entry without a fuss. Food appeared on a small table and the queen waved a hand toward it.

"You look like you could use some refreshments."

Taryn's belly growled loudly and she placed a hand over her abdomen. It had been four days of tubers or whatever the hell it was that Aislinn grew in the wastelands. Taryn had thought it best not to ask, nor look at what she was eating. It was fuel, nothing more.

As she passed the table, she grabbed what she hoped was a turkey leg and took three huge bites before sitting. Eirlys watched her with a curious expression, which Taryn ignored. She was too busy sucking every last drop of juice from the delicious bird.

A servant appeared from seemingly nowhere and took the bone, surreptitiously handing her a cloth napkin in exchange. Another appeared with a tray filled with various foods, and two beverages. She gave him a grateful smile and tucked in like the starved bilge rat she was. Even Rhoane lacked his usual neatness as he set to devouring his plate of delightfully cooked food with gusto.

Once their bellies were satisfied, which probably took all of three minutes, they both gulped a glass of elderflower tea, and wiped their mouths in perfect unison.

Eirlys studied them as if they were new creatures she wished to dissect. "And they tell me you are gods. Hard to believe after watching that rather vulgar display. Don't they feed you on your world?"

"Long story, but it's been a helluva few days since we last saw you."

"We destroyed the demon in the void," Rhoane said plainly. "And then found ourselves on a wasteland without the luxuries you are so generous to offer us here."

Eirlys leaned forward. "The thing is truly gone? Rori told me what happened when she fought it, and I'll tell you true, I believed there was no escaping its wrath. I nearly closed all my mirrors for fear it would come through seeking vengeance."

"The demon was created to terrorize the void, not the worlds outside the darkness. It has been eradicated for good. You and your people are safe." Taryn wiped a hand across her brow, surprised when it came away damp. Even talking about the demon stressed her the fuck out. It had been a harrowing experience she hoped to never repeat. She'd nearly lost Kaida and Rhoane to not just the demon, but the void itself. Rhoane reached for her hand, and she gripped it tightly.

"We brought you another vial. This one was purchased in the south of Cilachaem, but we found it elsewhere." Rhoane paused, and Taryn retrieved the amulet from her pocket. "We ask that you give us the vial with the dragon symbol in return."

"You're bargaining with me?" Eirlys held her hand out for Taryn and wriggled her fingers when she hesitated.

"This isn't a quid pro quo, Eirlys. We can take care of the dragon whereas you cannot. Tell me"—Taryn curled her fingers around the amulet and met Eirlys's stubborn stare—"Have you found a way to release them? All of those trapped in their glass prisons, have you freed them?"

A flicker of sadness crossed the queen's eyes, and she slowly shook her head. "Rori learned of a spell that should have freed them, but something is missing. I've tried a hundred times, but it hasn't worked. My daughter still slumbers, and the others remain encased in their glass coffins."

"Not coffins, Your Majesty. Not yet." Taryn handed her the amulet she'd taken from the woman on Nasus. "Please, let us

have the dragon. I have a plan how to release all those imprisoned, but can't risk it here."

Eirlys peered into the glass vial for a moment before she sat
back and motioned to a servant. A pretty girl brought her a
frothy drink without offering any to Taryn or Rhoane. When the
glass was empty, the queen nodded as if a decision had been
made.

"Bring me one of your Elvenwood roses—the one they call
Gllanaed—so that I can plant it in my private garden—and I will
give you what you want."

"What did you call the Elvenwood rose?" Rhoane asked, his
face scrunched in optimistic confusion.

"*Gllanaed,* although I might be pronouncing it wrong. My
spies are not fluent in the elven language."

"Your pronunciation is correct. It means star and is from a
language older than you could imagine." Rhoane glanced at
Taryn and she blushed at the realization they'd named the rose
after her.

Rainne must have had something to do with that. She'd be
sure to thank to woman the next time they met.

"I don't care what it's called. I want one. Get it for me," Eirlys
demanded, sounding every inch a spoiled queen. They'd dealt
with enough of those for several lifetimes.

Kaida the cat hissed, and Eirlys saw her as if for the first time.
"What is that cat doing here?"

Despite her tone, she reached to stroke the cat's fur. "She's
quite unusual, this cat. I feel I know her…" Her voice trailed off
and for a moment, Taryn thought she might give them the
darathi. "Bathe before you go to the elven kingdom. I might
tolerate your stench, but Queen Helena will not. When you've
returned with my rose, I'll grant you whatever you wish."

"Why is this rose so important to you?" Kaida moved from
the queen to her and Taryn absently stroked the cat's sleek frame.

"I don't know. I guess I feel it's part of me since it evolved from my rose. There's a need to have it, to understand its healing properties, that I can't deny." She gazed at Taryn, and for the first time since meeting her, Taryn saw the woman behind the crown. A woman with hopes and dreams, fears and disappointments. A mother desperate to help her child. Love. Pure and simple love shone through her eyes. "There are whispers of war, and anything I can do to help my people, I have to at least try."

"Where can we freshen up?" Rhoane asked as he stood, and Taryn joined him. "We will leave within the bell and return as quickly as possible. Then you shall have what you require, and we will be on our way with the darathi."

Eirlys sent them away with the servant who had brought the drinks. He led them to a smaller room down the corridor from the queen's suite. Close enough to keep an eye on, which shouldn't have been a surprise.

The double baths already filled with hot water that awaited them was not only unexpected, but much appreciated. Taryn nearly swooned when she saw the tubs. Before the servant handed them over to four waiting faeries, Taryn stripped off her torn and dirty clothing. She might've squealed a little when she entered the luscious honeysuckle-scented water.

The stress of the past few days—months, really—washed away as she relaxed into the gentle scrubbing of the servants. What a change from her first day at Paderau when she'd been shy with Lorilee and Mayla. Her thoughts drifted to her friends on Aelinae, and a pinch to her heart reminded her that though the bath was a luxury, time was not.

"You need to relax, mi carae. That is the purpose of the hot waters, yes?" Rhoane spoke Eleri and sounded a little too much like his sister, which made the ache all the more harsh.

"I keep thinking of our loved ones and what we need to accomplish."

"We cannot save the world unless we restore our energy."

He was right, of course, but her mind wouldn't settle. She lay back, eyes closed, and focused on the little spark of ShantiMari she kept hidden so that no one would ever be able to block her power again. Instead of helping, all that did was bring forth more memories of when Zakael had kept her from her power, and again when Cashiel had taken over Lliandra's ship. At least that time she'd been prepared, but it did little good when the asshole had her loved ones held prisoner.

She shifted in the water and tried to clear her mind. Strong hands smoothed over her shoulders, rhythmically kneading her muscles.

"I believe I told you to relax," Rhoane commanded.

His hands slipped over her collarbone to her breasts and she inhaled sharply with need. It was then she noticed the room had grown quiet. She peered through one half-open eye to see they were alone in the windowless bathing chamber. Even Kaida had wandered off someplace else.

It would be a shame to waste the opportunity for privacy.

She raised her chest until her nipples crested the water, and Rhoane understood her invitation. His hot mouth covered her breasts, by turns licking and sucking on her hardened nipples. A low moan came from the depths of her and her desire built. Instead of joining her in the tub, Rhoane lifted her from the water, his Shanti encircling them in a cocoon of warmth that dried their skin with each step.

She clung to him, eager for the touch of his lips on her body. He laid her on a velvet divan she'd not noticed before and hovered over her. The glint in his gorgeous eyes shone with desire. She arched against the sofa, a silent invitation.

"Not yet, you vixen." He left a trail of kisses from her jaw to her sternum, stopping for a short nuzzle at each breast.

Her overheated skin scratched against the velvet and her still-damp hair clung to her, but she paid them no mind. Her entire focus was on Rhoane and what his devious mouth was doing to her.

"You smell and taste divine, my love." His tongue lashed against her clit and she squirmed as a buzz of lust traveled through her veins.

Again and again he flicked and sucked. Again and again she arched into him, willing him to suck harder, to go deeper. When he slid two fingers into her, she gasped and her body vibrated with desire.

"Release for me," Rhoane whispered, and she felt the first stirrings of an orgasm tightening in her core.

Gods, she needed this. Needed his breath and his touch and his wicked stroking against her most private of spots that only he knew. Only him. Always him. Forever her Rhoane.

Cool air brushed against her skin, adding to the delicious torture of the moment. She didn't want it to end yet was unable to stop the rivulets of lust that spiraled through her veins. One swipe of his tongue more and she would be lost to her climax. A low needy moan came from deep within her, and Rhoane redoubled his efforts.

His lips, his tongue, and his fingers danced across her skin, eliciting more moans and soft whimpers as her release came hard and fast. She gasped and panted into her orgasm as her body convulsed. He greedily sucked her juices as his fingers kneaded her ass.

"More," she begged, and he grinned as he lifted himself to hover over her.

"Oh, there is much more to come."

She giggled at the unintended pun and arched to meet his eager cock. As he entered her still pulsating pussy, she wrapped her legs around him and welcomed his thrusts. Nothing else existed in that moment. Only them.

They didn't make love in the stars, nor were they absorbed in a healing cloud, suspended above the floor. In a way, their lovemaking was ordinary, which was unusual in its own right. A strange calmness came over her that they didn't need space sex or magic sex, but damn if it wasn't hot. So was this. All they needed was each other, and a scratchy velvet divan.

Of course, that divan just happened to be in a bathing chamber on a magical world in the kingdom of an Unseelie queen who may or may not have ulterior motives. As they lay on the divan, both thoroughly satiated, Taryn's gaze took in the bathtubs and for one long moment, she wondered if Eirlys had manipulated the situation to make them stay longer. The queen couldn't have known they'd delay their trip to Elvenwood to make love, but then, Taryn wouldn't put it past her to hope for exactly that. Possibly even hoped they wouldn't go to Elvenwood at all.

Or maybe the request for the Gllanaed rose was all a ruse? But if so, why?

She ran a lazy finger along Rhoane's naked chest and traced the tattoo on his shoulder, smiling when he moaned at her touch. They could delay their trip a little longer, couldn't they? But she knew she was being selfish.

It didn't bring her joy that she questioned motives. Once she'd been too trusting, and now she was far too distrusting. They'd been running for far too long; she was exhausted, as was Rhoane. Even so, Eirlys was a faerie queen with her own agenda. Taryn would be wise to remember that fact.

A faerie queen who had given Zakael a rose that brought up memories. What else was special about the rose? Hayden's words came back to Taryn with chilling clarity. Both the Elvenwood rose and Eirlys's rose had healing properties. They'd left Zakael close to death at Mallaqai's ruins. Was the rose for him? Most likely not, since Kaldaar could've healed him easily enough. Which left one other option. She didn't have to try hard to imagine why a damaged god like Kaldaar would need such a thing as a magical, powerful, curative flower. Flippin' bollocks.

CHAPTER FOUR

King Zakael—not Overlord, not boy, KING—strode through the castle, constantly reminding himself *he* was the lord here, not Kaldaar. The rose given to him by the delightful faerie queen rested in his pocket, and he gently brushed the petals with his fingertips, wishing it was the queen's flesh he caressed. Now there was a morsel he'd not object to visiting again soon. She'd denied him this time, but no woman could say no more than once.

Well, no woman except his half-sister.

He shunted thoughts of Taryn to the back of his mind and focused on the task at hand. A speck of something shimmering caught his attention and he flicked it from the black cassock he wore. Another four clung to the fabric. For every one he flicked off, more seemed to appear, as if they populated of their own accord. He pressed his fingertip against the silk and studied the sparkling motes that stuck to his skin. He knew this dust. It was present in the void on his recent return from the faerie lands.

Had it been there prior to that? He scratched his head, trying to recall. None of his previous trips through the emptiness had the subtle rainbow of light that seemed to follow him home. What had changed? He'd been distracted those past times, perhaps. It was a nasty habit he'd picked up, and one that would see him punished if he wasn't careful. He was already skirting the limits of rebelliousness with his recent indiscretion.

When Kaldaar had unceremoniously cast him out of his rooms, he'd been enraged and traveled in haste to Talaith, where he had confessed everything to Lord Valen. Was it rash of him to do so? Yes. Would he do it again? Also yes. Kaldaar was getting out of control and the last thing Zakael wanted was to lose Aelinae to the unhinged god. Especially so soon after becoming King of the West.

On a whim, he'd given Hayden the special rose he'd obtained from the strange Eleri tree that grew inside a palace that was built into a mountain. As hard as the it was to believe what he saw, the palace was even more stunning than the Crystal Palace in Talaith. And that tree? Nothing short of a wonder. Growing through the floors and ceilings, with branches spread above the room, he would never forget the sight. If he hadn't been in a rush, he would've loved to see more of the enchanting kingdom of Elvenwood.

Leaving the rose in Talaith had been another rash decision, but he sensed Taryn in the rose and for reasons he'd never understand, had decided whatever Kaldaar wanted it for would hurt his sister. By the end of this—whatever *this* was—she'd be the death of him. Or his salvation.

The frightening thing was, he couldn't say which he longed for more. At the moment, death looked like the least terrible option.

He cautiously opened the door to his rooms, relief sweeping over him with a chilling rush at the empty space. After a momentary pause at the threshold to the room Kaldaar used as his private study, Zakael entered with forced confidence. For two heartbeats, he debated leaving the rose atop the desk his father had used to conduct business for the West. Business Zakael should now be attending, but the lunatic Kaldaar insisted didn't need his attention.

He couldn't leave the flower here or Kaldaar would know he'd been in the room. His gaze swept the furnishings, stopping at the portrait of his mother for a moment. Her dark hair flowed over her bare shoulder in a graceful curl. Her brown eyes held a softness he long ago stopped searching for. There was nothing soft about Caer Idris. His father had taught him that before his mother's body had even gone cold. Rarely did he let himself miss her, but recently she seemed to invade his thoughts daily. It was most likely Kaldaar's doing, unsettling his mind to make him more pliable. It was a trick Zakael himself often employed to great success. He'd have to be diligent in not allowing the god access to his thoughts, and certainly not his emotions.

Without a further glance at his mother's portrait, his gaze continued to the corner where the shadow had lurked when Kaldaar grew incensed and threw him out of his own castle. Who had it been? Who would cause the god to panic and act spuriously? Whoever it was could be an ally. If only they'd show themselves.

"Come out, you of the shadow folk. Show your face to the king of these lands."

He could've sworn he heard a woman's cackle. Or giggle. A *caggle?*

"I won't harm you." He placed his hand over his heart. "This I swear as King of the West."

This time a snort answered. Someone *was* hiding in the shadows. Unlike when Kaldaar used to conceal himself in the ceiling of his mother's rooms, he didn't sense malevolence from this presence. Yet they'd upset the god.

He closed his eyes and sent a subtle stream of his power

through the room. Several wards snapped against his Shanti—Kaldaar's, most likely, or remnants of his father's power. The caggle sounded again, this time closer to the balcony. He circled the stone balustrade, hoping to catch whoever it was, but the air was empty. A moment later, a breeze rustled papers on the desk and the air was nothing more than the familiar scents of sea water and the ancient stones of Caer Idris.

Blasted spirits.

The sound of Kaldaar approaching sent a chill through his veins and for one mad moment, he contemplated turning into a levon and flying out of the room. Instead, he pulled his features into consternation and hunched into a semi-simper.

"I told you never to enter my room without permission. Do you have a death wish?" Kaldaar's bony finger pointed at Zakael's chest and he visibly flinched for dramatic effect.

"I heard laughter, and knowing your penchant for privacy, thought it best to investigate lest it be an unscrupulous visitor. I'm sorry if I overstepped, my lord."

Kaldaar's beady little eyes narrowed in his gaunt face. A face that had filled out greatly since arriving in Caer Idris.

"Laughter, you say? Male? Or female?"

"Definitely a woman. Are you expecting company?" His immediate thought went to Lliandra, but he'd not seen or heard from her again since her last impromptu visit, and if he had to guess, her absence was Kaldaar's doing. Everything came back to the lunatic god.

"That meddlesome trickster changeling." He glared out the window to the cloudless sky. "Come here again, and I promise it will be the end of your miserable existence. No one, spirit or flesh, shall defy me. Tell that to your master." Beneath his breath, he sneered, "Whore witch."

Changeling. Witch. Who in Ferran's hell was he talking about?

"A friend of yours, I presume?" Zakael quirked his lips in a flirtatious grin, hoping it would loosen Kaldaar's tongue.

Kaldaar regarded him a moment before stroking his jaw with fingers only recently covered in flesh. The grin remained plastered to Zakael's mouth, but internally he fought the urge to vomit on the god's putrid face.

"You are so beautiful, my darling boy. Where is that exquisite creature we brought back from Mallaqai's ruins? I fancy a bit of fun with the pair of you." He looked toward the bedchamber, his eyes lighting with a greenish fire that twisted Zakael's stomach.

"Amanda? You killed her a sennight past." The image of him feasting on her like a starved wolf devouring a baby doe echoed in his thoughts and he tried to block the memory, but it was seared into him like a scar that would never heal. The sounds Kaldaar had made that night were all too familiar to the moans he himself had often made in the torture chambers.

"Did I? Pity." Kaldaar waved his hand as if it mattered not. "After a while you all look the same—male, female, dark, pale, you're simply snacks for my growing hunger."

"I brought what you requested," Zakael said, changing the subject, and pulled the exquisite rose from his pocket. It was white with black veins, the likes of which he'd never seen before. He only hoped the god hadn't either, for Zakael had brought not the rose Kaldaar had specifically requested but a similar flower from the fae lands. "What will you do with it?"

Kaldaar's hand hovered above the flower. "I'm told it has healing properties if made into a tea, even more so if an elixir."

Zakael's mind churned with possibilities. "It's rumored Taryn and Rhoane created this rose. Are you certain you can trust that it will heal you? What if, instead of restoring your physicality, it destroys you instead?"

Kaldaar's hand snaked back into the sleeve of his dark robe. "That is a concern I share." He strode to the balcony and hissed at something Zakael couldn't see. "She has blocked me from my own realm. How is this possible?"

The rhetorical question went unanswered. Zakael had learned these queries didn't end well if he tried to supply the god with reason, and so he stood silently waiting. A tiny thrill warmed his blood that Taryn had thwarted the god.

"She will be punished for this insubordination," Kaldaar seethed, and Zakael braced for the physical blow intended for his sister. It wouldn't be the first time the god took his wrath for others out on him.

Kaldaar turned away from the balcony, a sneer on his thin lips. It was still disconcerting to see the musculature beneath a thin layer of flesh, yet not as upsetting as seeing rotting bone. One more purge of victims and his form would be nearly complete. Perhaps then he would leave the castle and Zakael could have a moment's peace.

"Tell me, what does the rose smell like?" The sneer lifted into a macabre smile and warning alarms sounded in Zakael's mind.

Although, how a rose's scent could be a trap, he had no idea. Yet the glee in Kaldaar's eyes made him wary. He lifted the petals to his nose and inhaled. The sweet, torturous scent of heathered honey came to him, and tears burned against his eyes.

"Well? What do you smell? Tell me now, boy."

It was most certainly a trap and he'd played right into Kaldaar's hands.

"My mother. The scent reminds me of my mother." He flicked a glance at the portrait, feeling somehow that he'd betrayed her.

"Yes, I thought as much." Kaldaar drifted close enough to smooth a hand over his cheek, wiping away his unshed tears. "Do you know how she died? My beautiful boy, do you truly know?"

He didn't want to know. Whatever lie Kaldaar was about to tell, he didn't want to hear. Not now, not ever. "She died in her sleep, peacefully."

"A young, healthy woman? Now, now, we both know you're not that stupid. She was murdered."

Stop it. Stop the lies. Stop the pain. Stop making him remember that awful day. "My father had several doctors examine her and they all concluded she died naturally."

Kaldaar's fingers traveled up Zakael's cheek to his temple and finally through his hair. It was meant to be seductive, but the touch left him feeling repulsed. The god leaned closer, his rank breath an assault to his nostrils. A slimy tongue trailed along his lips and he had to keep from jerking away. At his ear Kaldaar paused, his breathing ragged, as if he were excited and about to climax.

"Rhoane al Glennwoods ap Narthvier murdered your mother."

The world stopped for one terrible moment. Zakael was once more eight seasons old, standing very near where he stood now, sobbing at the loss of his beloved mother. He and his father had been on a trip and returned to find Troyanna dead. His father had allowed him a few minutes of mourning before taking him to the dungeons and giving him his first lesson in torture.

Time moved backward until Zakael saw Rhoane, disguised as a low-level courtier, sneaking into his mother's room. In the vision, Rhoane crept to the bed where Zakael's mother slept between her ladies-in-waiting. Rhoane carefully placed one of the women's hands over Troyanna's. He rested his fingers atop the innocent woman's and bent his head. Neither Zakael's mother nor the lady-in-waiting stirred, their faces peaceful in sleep. A few minutes later, Rhoane checked for signs of life, and then left the room.

Anger like he'd never known brought an awful clarity to his thoughts.

Rhoane had murdered the one good thing in Zakael's life. The one person who loved him unconditionally, killed by his greatest foe. Rhoane was responsible for every horrible thing that had happened to him since his mother's passing.

He curled his nails into his palms and breathed through his nostrils to control the raging storm that grew like a tempest in his heart. Blood oozed over his skin and he delighted in the pain. The need to slowly and methodically destroy Rhoane pounded against his skull. Was that Kaldaar's intention? Anger him so ferociously he'd scour the void to find the Eleri and strike him down?

To slaughter both Rhoane and Taryn in one fell swoop?

Yes, of course. Kill them both. That would benefit Kaldaar far more than it would assuage his need for revenge.

He forced his breathing to slow, his rage to temper. Several seconds ticked by before his mind settled, all the while the god studied him like an insect pinned to a board. Kaldaar had already sent Myrddin on his murderous task. There had to be another purpose he couldn't see.

"Why show me this now?"

"You were getting too soft. I needed to remind you who you are."

It worked. Curse the lunatic god, but damn if he wasn't ready to slaughter Rhoane and all his Eleri kin.

"Does Taryn know?" Somehow, he hoped she didn't. Hoped she wouldn't support such an atrocity.

"Yes." The sibilant whisper drove like a pike through his heart. "Your loyalty of late has been erratic. You made a covenant with me, or have you forgotten?"

He'd forgotten nothing. Especially not how Kaldaar had threatened and abused him. There was no willing covenant made at Mallaqai's ruins when Kaldaar found him wounded and half-dead. What choice did he have but to agree to serve the god? Knowing what he did now, death might've been preferable.

"Are you ready to do my bidding, my beautiful boy?"

"What would you have me do?" Resignation lingered in his words.

Kaldaar's tongue forced its way into his mouth and he sucked on the god's power like a babe his mam's teat. No words were spoken, but through the revulsion and acrid taste of the lunatic's rotted mouth, Zakael understood what needed to be done. Rhoane would pay for his crime in time, but first, there was fun to be had.

Devilish, murderous fun.

CHAPTER FIVE

The small group of travelers were quiet as they trod along the old Royal Road toward Paderau. How many times had she made this trip? Faelara gazed at her surroundings, naming plants to keep her mind busy. Her companions' excitement and consequent chatter about the trip had long since passed and now Baehlon, Loghan, and Fae rode in comfortable silence.

They were three days out from Talaith, just south of Lake Oster. From there, they would travel east to Ulla. Despite Faelara's trepidation about what they might find there, her enthusiasm for learning quelled any misgivings she might have had. She patted the hidden pocket in the bodice of her dress that held a vial of elixir she'd made from the mysterious rose Hayden had given her. Despite not knowing precisely where it came from, or if indeed Taryn or Rhoane had anything to do with its making, Hayden had been confident when he told her it might have healing properties.

With such crude provenance, she'd been wary of the pretty thing, but her inquisitiveness won out. To start, she'd taken two petals from the strangely clear flower and infused them with one of her own concoctions she used to ease troubled minds. Loghan had assisted with the process, curious about her tinctures and potions. Baehlon had stood a distance from them, but she had felt his annoyed gaze with his every twitch and grunt.

Dear sweet Baehlon. She cast a sidelong look at him and smiled when she found him watching her. Their love was decades old, but newly professed. He would adjust in time to this newfound need to protect her. Not that she minded, but it did become rather tiresome.

"I love you, Sir Knight." She reached to hold his hand.

"And I you, my lady." He lifted her fingers to his lips and a giddy little thrill ran the length of her. "Are you well? Are you comfortable?" His gaze went to her abdomen, and she suppressed a sigh.

"Yes. Just as I was five leagues back. And five minutes past. I am well, my love."

"Do all Aelans behave this childishly when they are in love? Ullans would be humiliated for acting in such a soft manner." The look on his face—not quite of disgust, but close—gave Loghan an ugly countenance.

Faelara's curiosity pinged. The Ullans had a fierce reputation for being brutal, but she thought that only applied to intruders on their land. She had no idea it was acceptable within their own people. "How would an Ullan court a lady?"

"We don't. Courting is for sappy people like you two. Ullans declare their intention, and that is all."

"I assume there is a conversation about what happens next. Or, is it that once the intention is stated—and again, I'm assuming here that women can make a declaration same as men —there is no further discussion and a partnership is formed? Do Ullans marry? I have so many questions."

"If you're not careful, you won't get a moment's rest until we reach your lands." Baehlon's smile belied his gruff words.

Loghan squinted into the distance. "There are riders ahead. Eight to ten, if I'm not mistaken."

Both Fae and Baehlon turned their attention to the road where indeed, a small party of travelers approached. She could barely make out a single blob of travelers, let alone a precise number. But then, she wasn't half Eleri as Loghan was. His vision —and hearing—was far more acute than her Aelan limitations. More questions rattled her brain, but they would have to wait, as would the answers to those she already asked. Silently, she cursed the group of riders and their unfortunate timing.

"It would be rude not to wait for them, but we are due to turn just up ahead. What do you think is the best course of action, Baehlon?" If they could avoid the approaching riders, then she would get her answers sooner.

"Lady Faelara! Sir Baehlon!" one of the riders called out, and she recognized Eoghan's voice—but that couldn't be, surely. He was in the Narthvier and the last she'd heard, had never been out of the vast forest. What in Ferran's hells was going on?

A lone rider pulled away from the others and galloped toward them. A few moments later, the rest of the group sped their mounts to catch up. Faelara spotted not just Eoghan, but the young lords Tinsley and Aomori as well. Three of Duke Anje's guard rode with them, with another two men whom she didn't recognize. By their clothing, she would guess they were the lords' personal valets.

"Well met this glorious morn." Eoghan beamed as he greeted them. "I have seen many wondrous things on our short journey thus far, but truth told, the sight of you has gladdened my heart." He kissed his thumb before placing it against his heart. "Tell me, what news of you from Talaith?"

Despite his flowery greeting, she was fairly certain he was only truly interested in hearing about the crown princess.

"Talaith is well, Your Highness." Faelara hoped he understood her meaning. By the grin he wore, she was confident he did.

Though it was not yet midday, they dismounted and let their horses graze while the two groups sat beneath a broad-leafed tree for an impromptu meeting. Eoghan told them about his harrowing departure from the Narthvier, and King Stephan's closing of its borders. Faelara half-expected to find Eliahnna taking notes, but she was in Talaith. A bitter sadness wedged between her thoughts that too many of their friends were scattered across Aelinae, herself included.

Even if Eoghan's flight from the Narthvier was rash, Eliahnna had been wise to alert the Eleri king to Myrddin's deception. Warmth spread through Fae at the image of Eliahnna sitting upon the crystal throne. She would make an exemplary empress.

And, with Eoghan by her side, they would be a mighty force for good.

Such was the hope she nurtured in her bosom.

Eoghan mentioned seeing Anje in Paderau, which surprised Fae. He'd been in Talaith since they returned from the Summerlands, but somehow found the time to travel to Paderau and back without anyone the wiser? She made a mental note to ask him about the conundrum when next she saw him. With a sigh, she realized that wouldn't be for several moonturns. Patience was sometimes an ally, but right then, felt more like an irritation.

When Eoghan finished his story by recapping the past few days of travel with his new friends Tinsley and Aomori, he looked to her group with excited expectation.

Baehlon didn't disappoint. He gave a highly edited version of events that had transpired in Talaith, beginning with Lliandra's unexplained malady and ending with the news Hayden had shared with them the morning they left for Ulla. The latter still sat uneasily in her gut, but Hayden had sworn his cousin lived, even though Kaldaar himself had instructed Myrddin to kill her and Rhoane. The mage's deception ran even deeper than any of them had thought possible.

Aomori grunted and crossed his arms over his chest as if trying to protect himself from the truth. "You're saying Zakael, the man responsible for much of what is wrong with Aelinae right now, told Hayden that Taryn and Rhoane are alive? What proof did he give? Why are we to believe him over Myrddin, a man until recently we all considered honorable? Are you absolutely certain your information about the mage can be trusted?"

"I wish we could discount it, but our sources are solid." Baehlon scrubbed a hand over his face. "I don't want trust Zakael, but he spoke true. Whatever game he's playing, this time his schemes benefit us. Be warned, however, the empress does not yet know about Myrddin or Taryn and Rhoane. She's not right in the head and we thought it best not to burden her further.'"

This far from the palace, speaking the plain truth wouldn't get him punished, yet Fae was surprised to hear him say it so plainly. Though concerned for Lliandra, the Eoghan's party agreed to continue the farce when they reached Talaith. The meeting had taken much of the morning and with the sun now directly above them, Faelara suggested they at least enjoy a meal before bidding farewell.

Baehlon strode to his horse and grabbed a leather-wrapped pouch of cured meats from his saddle bag. A few strides in, he scrunched his face and glared into the distance. Fae looked to the north and gasped at the sight of three strange creatures lumbering toward them from the eastern shore of the lake.

"What the blazes are those?" Baehlon shoved the pouch into the saddlebag and shouted for Loghan to secure the horses. "Eoghan, you help keep our mounts safe." He withdrew his sword and planted his feet on the ground.

By now, the others saw what she and Baehlon saw. The two guards rushed to join the knight while the two servants ran to help Eoghan with the horses.

"I have seen those beasts before, in my father's arena. They call themselves Mohram." Loghan's face scrunched with confusion. "Taryn fought one after Rhoane healed her."

Fae choked on a gasp. "Taryn fought one of those? Alone?"

Loghan nodded. "And won. It was a remarkable sight. Then

she battled my brother, a guard, and my father. This was only hours after she was nearly dead."

"Bloody hell."

"Indeed."

The three creatures lumbered toward them, and soon Fae could clearly see their ram-like heads' curling horns, complete with ape-like chests and sturdy man-like legs. What in Rykoto's name were these hideous beasts? More importantly, where did they come from? These weren't any species she knew of that called Aelinae home.

She and her traveling companions formed a line, Baehlon and the guards flanking Tinsley and Aomori, with Faelara in the middle. The two young lords both held swords, but she felt their ShantiMari swirling in twin tempests around the pair.

"Halt!" Baehlon shouted. "State your business before approaching further."

The beasts looked to one another and snarled. As answer, they loped forward, one brandishing a mace, the other two raising wickedly curved axes. Nadra be blessed, they didn't seem to possess much, if any, ShantiMari. Unless they cloaked it, in which case they were far more dangerous than just simple brutes.

"Blast it." The knight took a protective stance and held his sword ready for battle.

A loud cry went up from the creature-men as they rushed forward. Faelara swore at their recklessness and held back, moving cautiously closer to Baehlon.

The first sounds of clashing weapons tore through her hearing. With each subsequent clang, her heart hurt and her nerves jangled. The only battle she'd seen before was on the moors south of the Narthvier, when Taryn killed the vorlock to save Rhoane's life. It had been a terrifying afternoon of carnage and fear. She'd hoped to never have to smell the blood of wounded soldiers again, but it seemed the Fates did not intend to be so kind to her.

The metallic scent of blood assailed her senses, and she raised her hands, her power spinning into a fireball.

With a mighty heft, she hurled her Mari at the beasts, directing the ball to separate into three smaller bolts. Each found their target and the creatures wailed against the attack. Tinsley took advantage of one brute's momentary confusion and swiped at his thick hide with his sword. A fur-clad paw reached for him, and thick talons ripped his tunic. He cried out and dropped to the ground. Without sparing a moment's hesitation, the Mohram strode over the stricken man and looked for his next victim.

Aomori rushed to Tinsley's side and tried to stop the blood that spurted from his wounds, but it was too great. Faelara shared a look with Baehlon.

"Get him out of there." She ordered.

"On it." Baehlon raced forward and grabbed Tinsley by the collar. With one swift jerk upwards, the young lord was unceremoniously draped over the big knight's shoulder. Aomori stared after him, bereft for only a moment before he turned his rage on the creature that had wounded his beloved.

Baehlon jogged to where Loghan and Eoghan waited with the horses and set the man on the grass. "Look after him. But, no Ullan healing. Stay here, Eoghan."

The Eleri prince grimaced, but obeyed.

While Loghan bent to inspect Tinsley's wound, Faelara dragged her attention back to the attackers and studied their stance, the way they swung their weapons, and mostly, their dark, twisted—now completely unhidden—ShantiMari. Rykoto's balls, it would take more than a fireball to stop them, and possibly more power than she possessed, but she had to try.

Baehlon rushed the creature on the right and swung his sword at the last minute, slashing a deep gash into its thigh. A scream rent the air and the brute lashed at Baehlon with erratic swipes of his mace. Undaunted, Baehlon ducked and gave him several more gashes. The Mohram appeared untrained, a fact to which the highly skilled knight would most certainly exploit.

Faelara closed her eyes and pulled her Mari in tight. She pictured in her mind where their hearts might be located, securing the beating organ in her thoughts. With a whispered spell, she flung her arms outward, her fingers splayed, and sent shards of power at the beasts. A dozen dagger-like flares of white-hot Mari impaled the creature-men, digging deep into their thick hides to find their internal organs.

Their howls were a macabre mixture of animal and man. There was no time for sympathy. Whoever they were, or wherever they came from, they were bent on destroying those she cared about.

Her gaze slid right and then left, looking for something large enough to catapult at the beasts. If she could knock them over like skittles, Baehlon and the others could finish the fight. She spotted a large boulder that would work. Just as she was pulling her power in, she flicked a glance at the trees where a man stood half-hidden behind a thick trunk. Her heartbeat quickened, and her Mari faltered for one awful moment before she regained control and hefted the stone at the attackers.

When she looked again, the man was gone. But she was dead certain it was Zakael she had seen there. More than passing strange he was at the exact place at the exact time they were besieged. If it was mere coincidence, then why didn't he help?

Her belly buzzed with the one fear she'd avoided for weeks. They now knew Myrddin had betrayed them and was working for Kaldaar, but what about Zakael? Was he responsible for Taryn and Rhoane's extended absence? He might've convinced Hayden he was trying to help Taryn, but Faelara wasn't buying it. Zakael had something to do with that morning's events, but what exactly, and how deep did his treachery go?

CHAPTER SIX

It wasn't the void that caused Taryn to hesitate before opening a portal for what felt like the squillionth time that day. She no longer feared Kaldaar's presence, and with the snake-dragon-demon gone for good, there was nothing preventing them from traveling to the kingdom of Aerithilyn. Except a major case of imposter syndrome.

You can find us if you search your heart.

They'd met Princess Cassia and her ferocious swordmaidens in the palace at Eidyn, and she'd helped them retrieve the last seal. She was Eleri, and yet not. Taryn hadn't had time to puzzle out how, on another world, they'd met even more Eleri who called themselves elves, but were so very like the Eleri on Aelinae. Moreso even than those at Elvenwood. Rhoane had once mentioned that the first people the gods sent to new planets were Eleri; maybe that had something to do with it.

One day, when she wasn't busy running from one place to the next, she would have to research it. She mentally added it to her growing list of shit she needed to get done, though it wasn't a high priority at that very minute. She rubbed her temples and shuttled thoughts of gods and new worlds to the back of her mind. Her priority right then was finding the elven kingdom on Nasus. If it was even on that world.

Cassia's words echoed in Taryn's mind. Search her heart. Fine. She concentrated on darathi, on Cassia, on hidden dragons, but there was…nothing. Kaida nudged her hand, and she stroked the grierbas. Rhoane stood a distance away, surveying the area for anyone who might interrupt them.

It shouldn't be this difficult. After all, getting the rose from Elvenwood had been painless. They had seen only Rainne and her enchanted cat Pora. With a sweet apology, Rainne had confessed that it wasn't her who had named the Gllanaed Rose— that honor went to Queen Helena, who knew that gllanaed meant *star*—even though she wasn't sure why it was important the rose had that name. Taryn knew, though, and secretly believed the rose was named after her. "Gllanaed" was Eleri for *star* and "Galendrin" was Elennish for *gllanaed*. Helena would certainly know Eleri, or bits of it, but Taryn doubted she'd know Elennish. Although, nothing should surprise her anymore.

Rainne had promised to keep their visit secret, then shared that instead of recalling memories like Eirlys's rose, the Gllanaed Rose could be used to purify and restore not just someone's physical health, but their mental acuity as well. They'd made a tea for King Thane that seemed to be working, bringing him out of whatever darkness had overtaken him. The similarities between Thane's ailment and Amdi's didn't go unnoticed by Taryn or Rhoane.

On the one hand, she was pleased the queen not only knew Eleri, but had brought some of the old ways back into custom. Conversely, it was not fucking great that Zakael possibly had one of these powerful restorative roses. It didn't take a genius to figure out what he might need it for, but she couldn't focus on that. Not yet.

After their quick trip to Elvenwood, they'd given the Gllanaed Rose to Eirlys without any fuss, and she'd given them the amulet with the dragon inside as promised. Taryn also shared with the queen her suspicion that Rori's spell to open the amulets wasn't working because she was missing one critical ingredient. Since Cilachaem didn't have dragons, she suggested a drop of Rori's blood might be the key. Eirlys had challenged her, but Taryn refused to say why Rori was necessary, or why her blood in particular was needed. It wasn't her place to share that Rori had a unicorn soul. It was up to the faerie to decide who to tell and when. But if a darathi's tears could heal, didn't it stand to reason that so would a unicorn's blood?

Taryn shook out her hands and exhaled. It had all gone so well in Faerie, so why wasn't opening the damn portal equally as easy?

Rhoane drew his sword and anxiety twisted her belly. She glanced around but saw nothing alarming.

"Our swords, Darennsai. We must use them to help find the hidden kingdom."

Of course, why hadn't she thought of that? She withdrew Ynyd Eirathnacht and crossed it over Claidholm Solais's blade. A song started, gentle as a hum at first, and gradually grew in tempo and volume until they were surrounded by the melody.

"Search your heart, mi carae," Rhoane whispered in her ear, his lips brushing her cheek. "I can see the mountain kingdom in my mind, but you must see it as well."

Great. He could see it. Probably knew how to get them there.

Feel, Taryn. In here. Rhoane's hand pressed upon her chest where her heart was beating a rapid staccato.

She closed her eyes and let her mind drift. Stars blinked in and out of her thoughts until one shone brighter than the rest. Nasus. Other names came to her: Savinael, Cilachaem, Esiurc, and several more. As each one drifted through her thoughts, she caressed them as if they were her children, and in a way, they were.

They were all worlds she and Rhoane would one day create. Worlds that would cease to exist if they failed Aelinae.

Yes, but they are here, now. Our worlds. Our legacy. We will save them all, mi carae, together. He gripped her hand and opened the portal without a word.

Show-off.

His cheeky half grin made her belly tighten in all the best ways.

Together, the three of them stepped into the void, and a few minutes later stood in a small room that could've been inside the Weirren. Only, this wasn't the Weirren. The ash-hued branches were too light, the architecture similar but also vastly different. The room looked as if it were part of a Gothic cathedral made from a living tree. The high ceiling arched above them, its branches entwining to make not just a window, but what looked like stained glass with myriad colors depicting an Eleri landscape not unlike Lan Gyllarelle in the Narthvier. It was truly remarkable.

"Gorgeous."

"Yes, you are." Rhoane kissed her fingertips.

A warm flush swept across her chest and cheeks. "I love you so very much." She squeezed his fingers as if to seal the words.

"You are my heart, Taryn ap Galendrin. Never doubt that." His eyes bore into her and in that split second, he relived the pain his betrayal and breaking had caused.

She cupped his face in her hand. "Mi carae, you are my world." And he was. Gods help her, she would forgive him anything.

"Are you ready?" His gaze flicked to the door and the unknown.

"Yup." She hoped she sounded more confident than she actually was.

A long hallway led away from the small room in both directions, and they hesitated only a moment before Rhoane stepped to the right. More of the light-ash walls surrounded them, but she never felt claustrophobic. Kaida padded along the empty hallway, her ears perked forward, her eyes intent.

"Strange that no one has approached or tried to stop us, don't you think?"

Rhoane cocked his head before replying, "They know we are here, but do not fear us."

"Did the ancients tell you this?"

"No, I heard them. They are two floors down and waiting for our arrival."

She hadn't heard anyone. A ping of annoyance pelted her belly. Maybe it was because she only recently became Eleri, but still, it wasn't fair she wasn't able to hear everything Rhoane could.

The childish thoughts brushed through her mind and she shook her head at her own impertinence. Fairness, she had to remind herself, wasn't giving everyone the same thing, but giving them what they most needed. At least, that's what Brandt had always told her. Right then, she wondered what it was she needed if not to hear the others.

Kaida turned them down a corridor to the left and loped down a grand spiral staircase, only stopping when she reached a landing. As soon as Taryn and Rhoane caught up, she hurried down the next flight of stairs, causing Taryn to give Rhoane a curious look.

"Something's got her excited. I hope it's good and not an army of swords pointed at our necks."

"Where is your plucky optimism?" Rhoane teased. "It is not like you to be so suspicious."

He was right, but she was tired of not knowing what was going to happen the next minute, or if they'd survive the day.

To her great relief, they descended the stairs to a large room that was bright and airy. Similar to the first room, branches arched above them to create a beamed ceiling of sorts. Rose-hued marble covered the floor and delicate furniture sat atop fur rugs. Despite the size, the room felt intimate, homey. Taryn's gaze went to the center of the room where a distinguished-looking couple stood watching them with curious yet guarded expressions.

As far as she could tell, they were alone in this space, though she sensed several guards near enough they could be called forth instantly. The way the couple held themselves, she guessed they were the rulers of the elven kingdom. Both had rich brown skin that glistened in the candlelight. Both regally slim, the man was nearly Rhoane's height with greying black hair and eyes that held a lifetime's worth of worry. Beside him, a lithe woman with ebony braids that reached her buttocks wrung her hands, giving away her nerves.

Rhoane approached first, his fist over his heart. "Your Majesties, please forgive our impromptu appearance in your kingdom, but we come on a matter of supreme urgency." He spoke Eleri, and from the looks the king and queen gave him, they understood if not all, then most of what he said. "I am Rhoane al Glennwoods ap Narthvier, Surtentse of all Eleri, and this is my betrothed, Taryn ap Galendrin, the Darennsai."

Their eyes widened as they took in Rhoane first, and then her. She only hoped they understood what Darennsai and Surtentse meant. Despite calling themselves elves, if they were truly Eleri, they would not only recognize the titles, but the obligation they owed Taryn and Rhoane. It was certainly a gamble she hoped paid off.

The queen glanced at Kaida with a tilt to her head. "And what is this beast you bring into our home?" She replied in broken Eleri, her words sharp despite the stumbles in pronunciation.

"She's called Kaida and is a grierbas." Taryn stroked Kaida's head. "She is passive unless provoked, but please know we mean you no harm. We have come at the behest of your daughter,

Princess Cassia, and wish to ask a favor that will mean the difference between life and death for our darathi vorsi."

The monarchs exchanged a glance that needed no translation. It spoke of alarm, and hope.

"I am King Ezra and this is my wife, Queen Ingrid. We are intrigued by your appearance, this creature called Kaida, and mostly, your purpose. You speak of darathi vorsi, in a language similar to ours, but antiquated, and you say you know our Cassia? Explain yourselves so that we may better understand."

Taryn took a long drag of air and glanced at the ceiling. "To fully understand, you'd need our entire story, but there isn't time for that." She looked directly at the monarchs. "Our darathi were exiled thousands of seasons ago, or years if that's your measurement of time. At a crucial moment in a devastating war, they were cast out by a devious witch to a wasteland where they withered until we found them a few days ago. We need a safe haven where they can heal and strengthen. Not forever, just for a little while, until they're needed once more on Aelinae—our world."

"Your world?" Ezra glanced up the stairs. "You come from the stars?"

"In a manner of speaking," Rhoane answered. "Our world is connected to yours in ways you cannot yet understand. We ask you to trust us, Your Majesties, and to care for our darathi as if they were your own." He bent to one knee, and Taryn followed. "I give you my solemn vow as Surtentse that our only concern here is for the darathi. When our business on Aelinae is finished, we will repay your kindness however you see fit."

"A bold promise to make. You do not know what is in our hearts or that we will not abuse your darathi."

Taryn stood and met the king's even gaze. Kindness lurked in his deep brown eyes, and also worry for his dragons. He clearly wanted to help, but feared by taking in their dragons, his would perish. A concern she shared, but was overshadowed by her own desperation.

A commotion at the other end of the room drew their attention away from the stalemate and Taryn turned to see a small group of people enter the room.

"Cassia, darling." The queen rushed to greet her daughter and the king followed.

They didn't speak Eleri, but another language similar to Elennish. The familiarity made Taryn all warm and gooey on the inside. The palace was foreign to her, but it also felt like home. A home she might've made with Rhoane one day, if their path had been different. She flexed her hand with the ghost tattoos and bit against the sadness that lurked just behind her duty. If they survived whatever was to come, perhaps she and Rhoane would have the opportunity for such things as a cozy night snuggling together by a warm fire. Maybe. But first they had to survive.

He will betray you twice and then he will kill you.

Taryn fought against Xianqin's foreboding warning. If Rhoane was prophesied to kill her, there had to be a reason.

As introductions were made, Taryn recognized the woman they'd met on a street in Eidyn, the same one she'd taken the amulet from. Cassia called her Lady Amaleigh and her partner King Gwilym of Eidyn. The name stirred a memory in Taryn, but she couldn't quite grasp it.

Behind them, Cassia's four swordmaidens—her Fianna Bel'en —stood casually, but Taryn could tell they were wary of her and Rhoane's presence. One of the women shifted slightly and looked askance. It wasn't overt, but enough to intrigue Taryn. She was about to send a thread of her ShantiMari to the woman when one voice above the others caught her attention.

"What are you doing here?" Amaleigh asked as she approached.

Taryn touched Rhoane's sleeve and indicated the woman. It couldn't be coincidence that she was here, in the elven kingdom on the same day Taryn and Rhoane arrived. From the wide smile that broke across his face, she guessed he felt the same. What it all meant, she hoped to uncover sooner rather than later.

The others quieted when Amaleigh bent to one knee and bowed her head. Kaida took a step and sniffed the woman before dragging her tongue over her face in approval.

"Kaida senses your dragon, as do we." Not just sense it—Taryn could feel its presence as if it were in the room with them. Yet something was off with the dragon. No, not off, but conflicted. She'd been through hell recently, of that Taryn was certain.

Amaleigh rose and faced them. "Did you return the faerie to his home?"

Taryn nodded, but it did not fill her with gladness to relay the news. "He is with his queen." Not quite home, but as close as she could manage. If her instincts were right, she hoped all the imprisoned beings would soon be free.

"How is it you're here?" Amaleigh asked with a wave to indicate the elven palace.

Taryn opened her mouth to speak, but just then she saw something she didn't quite believe.

"Rhoane, look." She pointed toward King Gwilym, but it wasn't him that made her heart gallop with excitement.

Two scaled faces with snouts and newly sprouted horns atop their heads peered at them from between Gwilym's legs. Their little bodies, about the size of chubby border collies, were covered in scales right down to their wing tips and talons.

Two baby darathi. Tears stung her eyes at the sight of them. At the perfect, remarkable, absolute miracles they were. For the first time in far too long, her heart swelled with hope.

CHAPTER SEVEN

Two darathi faces gazed at Rhoane from where they hid behind the young king's legs. What had they called him? Gwilym, yes. King of Eidyn. The name was familiar to him but lost in the thrilling buzz he felt over the baby darathi. Never in his lifetime did he expect to find Aelinae's darathi, prophecies be damned, but that miracle had happened. And now, a second, more profound wonder stood not ten paces before him.

Rhoane sucked in his breath. "So it is true." His gaze went first to Taryn, then to Amaleigh, and finally to the king and queen. "You were right, *mi carae*. We have at last found a home for the lost *darathi vorsi*."

Despite the king and queen's reticence, he knew in his heart this was where the darathi were meant to be cared for and, with time, recover their strength.

King Ezra clapped for silence, and indicated his wife had something to say. In an imperial tone Ingrid explained to the newcomers how Rhoane and Taryn had searched many realms looking for a home for their darathi. A bold lie, but he didn't correct her. Let the woman have dramatic license if it meant her people would care for Aelinae's darathi vorsi. When she finished her tale, Rhoane inclined his head to the elven monarchs.

"With your blessing, Your Majesties, we would like to bring our *darathi* to live here, with you." He kissed his thumb and placed it to his forehead and then his heart, in the Eleri tradition.

King Ezra grasped Rhoane's hand. "We would be honored, *Surtentse*. They will be cared for and loved by all our elven brethren now, and in the future." He looked to Gwilym and Amaleigh. "Now that peace has returned to Nasus, the dragons will once more flourish."

Taryn shifted where she stood and Rhoane sensed her discomfort. Their stewardship over the darathi was only temporary, but they could hash out the details later. He gave her a look that said patience, and she nodded.

King Gwilym took Amaleigh's hand in his and the wee darathi approached with cautious steps. Taryn knelt and held out a hand. "Come here, my beauties. Kaida won't hurt you." She inched forward until a little snout touched her fingertips. "That's a good girl."

Rhoane watched, a little surprised Taryn has sussed out one was female, but she was able to intuit things he was not.

The other dragonling sniffed the air and sneezed a little fireball in Kaida's direction. The grierbas shook her head and pawed the ground.

"You are home, little one." Rhoane bent down and stroked the dragonling's scales. Tears stung his eyes, but he didn't wipe them away. They were tears of celebration and happiness. "*Dearth lach nothrin de las vendrigas, der darathi vorsi*. You are home." No more hiding. No more running for these darathi. And soon, Aelinae's would be home, too.

"That one is called Mali"—Amaleigh pointed to the darathi Taryn was stroking—"and this is Shen."

"Shen is a formidable name, you wee beastie." Rhoane nuzzled the dragonling and placed his forehead against Shen's scales. "You will grow strong and protect these lands." His own darathi longed to stretch his wings, but Rhoane doubted the king and queen would appreciate a full-grown darathi in their sitting room.

By the grin on Taryn's face, he suspected she'd had a similar thought. It has been so long since they'd felt the wind across their snouts. Soon, he hoped. Very soon.

Shen snorted and snuffled against Rhoane's tunic, nearly knocking him over. The crown he'd shoved into a tunic pocket earlier that day fell out and softly clattered to the floor. With a whispered recrimination to the overly enthusiastic darathi, he regained his balance and reached for the piece of twisted silver.

"Darling, look," the queen said softly to her husband. "Do you suppose it's true? That he's…that I'm…could it truly be?" Ingrid's voice caught and a moment later, she stood before Rhoane as he crouched, her hand outstretched. "May I?"

Rhoane hesitated a moment before clasping the crown and rising to face the queen. He did not, however, give it to her. "Do you know what this is?"

Her grey eyes were wide with suppressed emotion. "I do, as do all elves. Forgive me, I mean Eleri. It's been so long since we've called ourselves the ancient name." She inclined her head and curtseyed low. When she stood to full height, her eyes were full of tears. "When I was younger, just a child really, I had a vision that one day I would be tasked with presenting the true Crown of Awakening to our Surtentse. I admit, I was not prepared to accept that you and your lady are who you said you are, but you have the crown. I cannot deny what I see before me now. I would be honored if you would allow me to alter it to its rightful state."

Rhoane looked to Taryn, but she shrugged as if she didn't know what to make of the situation either.

He handed Ingrid the slightly dinged crown with trepidation. If she meant him or the darathi ill will, he had just given her the weapon she needed. Yet he didn't sense malevolence in her or the others. He sensed calm. A sort of peace she'd been longing for ever since she'd had that vision.

Ingrid clasped her husband's hand and together they held the silver piece. The elven queen whispered words only the four of them heard, words Rhoane knew from Verdaine's prophecy, and his heart stuttered its beating. Chills raced through his blood, but he did not snatch the crown from her. Trust went both ways, and right then he needed to trust the elven monarchs would not betray him or every living darathi on this world and beyond.

Taryn reached for his hand, her touch a warming balm.

The twisted silver crown Nadra had placed upon his head not all that long ago transformed into a bold golden crown with several peaked finials rising from the band. Scrollwork traced along the edges of each finial, but what caught Rhoane's attention were the five gems embedded into the gold base.

"As I said, your crown was incomplete." Ingrid raised the crown as if to place it upon his head but stopped short. Instead, she handed Taryn the magnificent headpiece. "These are not gems, but they are far more precious. They are darathi eggs. Are they actual eggs containing baby darathi? I cannot say, but I do know that each represents an element: Air, Water, Fire, Earth, and Space."

Space? What was a space darathi? Was space also considered time? He would have to research the meaning of the darathi eggs, and why Nadra had only given him a partial crown. He thought of the snake-demon-dragon in the void and suppressed a shudder. A moment later, warmth washed away his apprehension. If he controlled all darathi, even those between time and space, then he could make certain nothing again ever ravaged and terrorized those who walk between worlds.

Taryn watched him with solemnity in her eyes. Her fingertips idly traced the gem-like eggs. "Are you ready?"

He nodded, his hands shaking as she placed the crown upon his head. He hadn't been nervous when Nadra had done the same thing on Dal Tara, but now his insides were in a turmoil. The enormity of his responsibility nearly crushed him. Nadra had to have known his oath went beyond the confines of Aelinae's darathi and seen him worthy of the duty. Then why, suddenly, did he feel unsuited to the task?

You are more than worthy, mi carae. Taryn squeezed his hand, and he smiled gratefully at his love. She knew more than most what it meant to wear a mantle as grave as this.

"Thank you. Truly." He brushed her lips with his own.

The room quieted and darkened as if he had stepped outside of the reality the others were in. Taryn and the monarchs were oblivious to what was happening to him as they spoke quietly about how best to get Aelinae's darathi through the portal and where exactly they would stay. The others, too, held conversations without seeming to notice that anything was amiss.

Perhaps nothing was wrong. Perhaps this was simply the crown wishing for him to see something important. His heart beat strong and calm without a hiccup of concern. Only once did Taryn flick him a glance, and in that quick look, he understood she knew he was present, and yet not. She would protect him until the crown finished whatever it was it was doing.

He glanced around the opulent yet comfortable furnishings. This was not a room meant to dazzle or impress, but one where family gathered to share memories. Love lived here in every portrait, each pillow. He saw Cassia's childhood and that of her parents in the span of a breath and his heart warmed knowing these were good people. They would honor their promise and care for Aelinae's darathi.

His gaze drifted past the king and queen to the women standing inconspicuously toward the back of the room. Cassia's swordmaidens. One in particular caught his eye even as she sought to avoid his perusal. A darathi soul struggled inside of her, warded so it could not escape, but desperate to do so. His breathing quickened and sweat dotted his forehead. She'd been warded to spare her from the slaughter that had happened in the not-too-distant past.

Several paces in front of her, Amaleigh stood with Gwilym. Their newly discovered darathi souls hovered protectively over the couple. In a blink, he saw their pasts—the murder of Amaleigh's parents, the killing of darathi in Eidyn, and the aftermath that the purge caused. He looked to Gwilym with sorrow in his heart. It was his father who had caused the misery that had only just ended. They didn't know it, but together, Gwilym and Amaleigh would forge a new future for the city of Eidyn, with the kingdom of Aerithilyn as their strongest ally.

He saw it all clearly as if it were happening right then and he was a part of it. So too, did he see the despair Amaleigh had over a missing darathi egg. It had belonged to her parents, but someone cruel had destroyed it. In their culture an egg signified fertility of the parents and Amaleigh feared that without it, she would be barren. Rhoane sent a thread of his Shanti to both Gwilym and Amaleigh with an entreaty to not give up hope. They would have their own egg soon enough.

Next, he looked to the dragonlings. A tremor of rage ran through his blood and he slid his gaze to a pocket in Taryn's trousers. When he looked back to the wee beasties, Shen and Mali both watched him with wide, worried eyes. Then, as one, they nodded as if they understood his unspoken question. The darathi in the amulet was their sire. They recognized his scent even though he was imprisoned in the glass.

I will free him and you will once again be a family, Rhoane told the twins.

How, though? He and Taryn would sort that riddle in due time.

A darathi tear, freely given. Ah, yes, he saw it now—saw how to free not just the sire in the vial they had, but all those imprisoned. Taryn was right; a mixture of the right words, and either a darathi tear, or Rori's blood would restore those taken against their will. Another face came to him, of a man he remembered in the throne room of Elvenwood—Rori's brother. What he had to do with this mystery, Rhoane couldn't be certain, but he would play an important role in Cilachaem's future.

His awareness traveled beyond the room in which he stood to the mountains of Ingrid and Ezra's kingdom where darathi lived in harmony with their caretakers. Further still to the far reaches of Nasus, and then to other realms. With each breath, more history, more memories were shown to him of worlds where darathi had been hunted to extinction, and happily, worlds where they thrived.

He saw Gilchrist settled on the cliff where he'd sat sentry each day, watching the Eleri through the mist that blocked them from returning to Aelinae. The Wall, Taryn had called it. A great barrier of strong ShantiMari. Who had made it? Mallaqai? But why? The darathi were not on Aelinae. At least, there wasn't a desert that far north as far as he could recall. Or had the Wall made the wasteland when Mallaqai exiled the darathi there? If so, she was even more cruel than previously thought.

Gilchrist snuffled the air and looked toward Rhoane. With a solemn incline of his head, Rhoane understood that Gilchrist approved of their move to Aerithilyn. The darathi vorsi would alert the others and be ready to leave by the time Rhoane and Taryn returned. His mother Aislinn stood beside Jinnipher, her hand protectively on the lovely darathi's neck. With a sting of sorrow, he realized his mother would stay with the darathi until they returned to Aelinae.

Their eyes met through the hazy vision, and he saw tears in his mother's eyes. She longed to return to her loves at the Weirren, but it was not yet time. Rhoane nodded slowly, acknowledging he would honor his mother's wishes, though it did not make him happy to do so. Aelinae needed Queen Aislinn of the Eleri, but the darathi needed her even more.

He saw the entirety of the last sixty seasons she had spent in the wasteland in a blink of an eye and understood his guilt had been for naught. She hadn't died that awful day in the Weirren when she'd been engulfed in blue flames, but she'd come close. The darathi had saved her, just as they'd saved himself, Taryn, and Kaida when they'd arrived unannounced after their fight in the void.

A thought nudged at the back of his mind, but flitted away before he could grasp it. The darathi were so much more than they seemed. He had to understand their place in Aelinae's balance. It was crucial to his and Taryn's survival.

Lastly, he saw Therron of Elvenwood not sitting upon a throne but wearing the Crown of Awakening. His crown. The one Ingrid had only just enhanced. Therron's midnight blue darathi turned his gaze on Rhoane.

"Two truths and one lie."

But it wasn't the darathi who spoke the words. It was Mallaqai.

CHAPTER EIGHT

Smoke drifted to the cloudless sky and Eoghan followed its path to keep from having to see the charred remains of the creatures that had attacked them. *Mohram*, Loghan had called them, but he knew of no creatures with such a name. They might've been from the swamplands near Haversham, but if so, how did they get here? His gaze slid south toward the Stones of Kaldaar. No one lived in those marshy, swampy lands. But again, he'd never encountered the Mohram race in all his studies. Stars, but he hated inconsistencies.

Almost as much as he hated feeling useless. He gripped the hilt of his sword with all his pent-up anger. He was trained in swordsmanship—it wasn't right that Faelara had forbidden him from fighting.

It wasn't hard to guess her reasons, but that did nothing to assuage his hurt feelings. With each step he took away from the beasts, his ire rose. Had he left the vier and his family to sit idly by and watch? No. He'd forsaken everything to help.

And to see the woman he loved. But also to help.

His gaze swept the forest where earlier, during the fighting, he'd sworn he saw a man standing between the trees. He'd looked as if he didn't want to be seen and had disappeared once Faelara swung a large boulder at the attackers. Admittedly, Eoghan was impressed with her use of ShantiMari, and the breadth of her power.

Not only had she disabled the beasts, but then to witness her healing Lord Tinsley had been a marvel. The Ullan had helped, of course, weaving his Shanti between Faelara's Mari and Eoghan's Eleri power. Loghan was gifted, no doubt, but he lacked the nurturing that Faelara brought to her healing.

There was something about her that Eoghan couldn't name, but it was there, in everything she did, the words she spoke. Her very being set her apart from the other Fadair he'd met. He'd noticed it upon their first meeting at the Weirren more than a season past, and was just as baffled then as he was now as to what it was. Eliahnna had noticed it too, but even together they hadn't solved the mystery. Then life became complicated and they'd forgotten all about it. Until now.

A shiver cut through him at what he'd found while healing Tinsley. A new mystery that had nothing to do with Faelara, but someone else far more familiar to him. He shoved the discovery to the far depths of his mind. The day was already too chaotic; he didn't need to dwell on that just yet.

His gaze flicked to where Faelara and Loghan sat beside the ailing Tinsley. They'd healed him as much as they could with limited resources, but he'd need potions and tinctures found in Talaith to fully recover. Whatever the beasts were, their weapons left horrendous wounds that wouldn't stop weeping. It would be slow going for the next few days, but Eoghan was determined to see the man safely to the Crystal Palace.

Sitting quietly to Tinsley's left, Lord Aomori wiped his eyes on the cuff of his traveling cloak. Confusion rattled though Eoghan's mind and belly.

Two men in love.

It was a revelation. One that intrigued Eoghan, but also

worried him. That sort of relationship was forbidden to the Eleri. So much so that he'd never given a thought to two people of the same gender loving each other romantically. It was almost treasonous to do so.

He knew why, but even so, that didn't settle the emotions swirling through him. It was becoming more and more difficult for Eleri to procreate and since Eleri only had one partner they mated with all their life, each pairing was precious. He rubbed his head trying to recall when that custom had become official, but even the ancients were quiet on the matter. Perhaps they didn't agree with the edict.

Or maybe they refused to speak to him because he'd left the Narthvier without his father's permission. A fresh shiver sliced at his nerves. Would he become sheanna? Would he, like his brother Rhoane and sister Carga, have to cut his hair and live as an exile?

Neither of his siblings had talked much about their time outside the vier, and now he understood why. Life beyond the vier was unpredictable and dangerous. Again his gaze drifted to the smoldering bodies of the slain beasts. Loghan had said Taryn fought one in his father's arena—alone—and lived. He also mentioned that Rhoane had been forced to fight in Amdi's arena many times. What other horrors had Rhoane faced in his many seasons of exile?

What would Eoghan's future bring? He looked toward Talaith with determination. Whatever punishment his father gave, he would fully accept. To see Eliahnna, to feel the touch of her skin beneath his fingertips, to smell her scent would be worth it.

"Tinsley will make a full recovery once he reaches Talaith. Let him rest today, and at first light tomorrow move as swiftly as you can, but with care to his injuries." Faelara flicked a glance to the trees. "I doubt there will be any more attacks, but we should be cautious."

Eoghan quieted his racing heart. He'd not heard the woman

approach, and that left him feeling vulnerable. If he didn't wish to be surprised, he needed to be mindful of his surroundings, and his thoughts.

"Where do those creatures we fought dwell? Are we close to their homeland?"

Faelara squinted into the distance, her lips flat. "I don't think they are from Aelinae." She turned to him. "Do not repeat my concern to anyone except Eliahnna. Baehlon and I have decided to continue our journey to Ulla, though our focus has now shifted. I still wish to learn from their healers, but their laird has some explaining to do."

"Loghan can offer no answers?"

An angry flush mottled her neck and throat, stopping at her tight jaw. "I will tell you this in confidence, so do not share it with the others. He says Zakael is responsible for the strange creatures Amdi procured for his fighting arena. Loghan claims no knowledge of where Zakael got the beasts, only that he's been sneaking them into Ulla for many seasons. There is an arrangement between Zakael and Amdi that reaches beyond the creatures, and I am determined to learn all I can about what, exactly, Zakael is planning in the desert lands." She met his gaze, and the intensity of her stare knocked the breath from his lungs.

"Should Eliahnna know of this development?"

Faelara rolled her bottom lip between her teeth. "On this, Baehlon and I are divided. He says no, I say yes. Trust your judgement whether to say anything or not to your beloved."

His cheeks warmed with embarrassment. "I do not believe we are at a stage to consider one another beloveds, not yet."

"Pish." She shook her head with a grunt. "Life outside the vier is wildly different than what you've been led to believe. Perhaps it's a good thing you left when you did. Now you can see the world and decide if Rhoane was right, or if your brother Bressal and his steadfast grip on tradition is best for the future of Eleri."

His mind whirled with her words. Rhoane and Bressal had argued their entire lives, it seemed. There was nary a moment of peace between the two men. What Faelara was hinting at, he could only guess. Then, like the dawn of a fresh day, he understood.

"You are talking about the *Darennsai*. Will she destroy the Eleri, or will she save them?"

"It goes much deeper than that, but Taryn is a good place to start." Faelara placed a hand on his heart and he felt her warmth. "But it also has to do with you being here, right now. Your beliefs will be challenged, the Eleri teachings you've been taught will come into question. And in the end, you will have to decide your own path, not just for your life, but for the Eleri as well. This is an incredible opportunity."

When he'd left the Narthvier, none of this had been a concern, but now, he realized Faelara was right. He could learn from this experience, not just to grow as an Eleri, but for the benefit of all Eleri. Possibly even all of Aelinae. It would help immensely if he knew what the lessons were that he was to learn.

His gaze traveled to where Aomori sat vigilant beside Tinsley, their hands entwined. "There are dangers in this world I have been purposely kept innocent of, like those creatures we just encountered. But when I see the tenderness between Aomori and Tinsley, I refuse to believe *they* are a threat to the Eleri. I admit, it is strange for me to see, but only because it is new." He pressed his hand over hers. "In here, in my heart, it gladdens me to see two people in love. I care not what pairing it is, or what plumbing they have beneath their clothing."

Witnessing the affection between Tinsley and Aomori for the past sennight had been delightful. He begrudged no one their love.

He just didn't understand why the Eleri forbade it. Even with the declining number of births per couple, denying another's love seemed wrong. His gut twisted with the truth he'd tried to hide from himself. The truth his father would never admit.

To keep the bloodline pure.

Though, how two men or two women in love would taint the bloodline, he wasn't certain. Ah, yes. To keep the Eleri population strong. With declining births, each coupling was important, every child precious. But those children were only valued if they were of Eleri bloodlines and not contaminated with Fadair blood.

He shook his head and tears stung his eyes. "Taryn is a threat to everything my father and Bressal believe to be true because she is not Eleri, not truly in their eyes. She was born Aelan and became Eleri. To them, she is an aberration." The words gave him no comfort to speak aloud.

"What do you believe, Eoghan? You healed Tinsley, you must have sensed what was in his blood?" Her eyes softened and he saw in them the depths of the ocean. When she blinked, it was gone.

Not only had he recognized the Eleri in Tinsley's blood, but the source of his parentage. Whether Faelara had guessed at his origins, he couldn't say—but if the secret became known, the Eleri throne itself would be threatened.

CHAPTER NINE

The portal opened in a small copse of trees just north of the Temple of Ardyn. Taryn stepped through with Kaida a half-step behind. She paused to listen, aware that she could take nothing for granted this close to Rykoto's lair. The air misted with her heavy breaths and she willed her rampaging heart to calm.

Even though she and Rhoane had decided together that he and Aislinn would return to Aerithilyn with the darathi while she and Kaida came to the temple to return the seals, she wished he was still here with her instead. They were better as a team.

That is true, Darennsai, but you are also capable on your own. It is important for the Surtentse to care for the darathi, especially now, in this time of adjustment. They have suffered much and need their Darathi Vorsi Prince now more than ever.

I know, Kaida. I miss him when he isn't with us. She scratched the top of Kaida's head. *Same as I miss you when you're not around.*

You are too sentimental.

But there was warmth and affection wrapped in the recrimination. "You love me too, but are afraid to admit it. That's fine— I know, and now you know I know, so it's all good."

Kaida shook her head and growled, but there was no threat in the sound.

"Enough stalling. Time to seal a god in his temple forever and hopefully not get our asses scorched for the effort." Taryn took a deep drag of cold air and straightened her shoulders.

They'd popped into Gwyneira's rooms in Paderau to grab the final seal and then headed to the temple without anyone in the palace the wiser. As much as she loved the instantaneousness of making portals, there was always the risk that she'd open one in the wrong place at just the absolute worst time. Thus far, she'd been lucky. As she trod lightly toward the front of the temple, she prayed her luck continued.

A lone standing torch burned brightly near the altar, but otherwise the temple was empty. She couldn't remember if the torch had been there before or if it was a recent addition. Flames from the simple metal grate cast shadows on the pillars that circled the room and she suppressed a shiver. Even after she'd cleansed the place, it still creeped her the fuck out.

Before she could stop herself, she glanced at the pristine altar, relieved it was as she'd left it. The memory of Eliahnna lying prone on the marble with Valterys standing above her, dagger in hand, buckled her knees. A few minutes later, and her father would've killed Eliahnna. All for what? Immortality? Or, more precisely, the promise of everlasting life. She highly doubted Rykoto would've kept any promises he might've made.

Your father was a fool to bargain with an imprisoned god. But you are no fool, Darennsai.

Thank you. She buried her hand in Kaida's fur and reminded herself that just because her parents were power-mad psychos didn't mean she had to be horrible, too. Tessa and Eliahnna were proof that kindness could thrive even in dire situations.

She strode to the columns that were missing seals and pulled a silver disk from her bag. When she tried to place it in the empty spot, a jolt that felt far too similar to being electrocuted snapped against her hand. She jumped back, nearly dropping the seal.

"Fuck." She shook out her hand with a grimace. "That hurt."

Maniacal laughter came from deep beneath her feet.

"Shut up, Rykoto."

His answer came in the form of the flames from the standing torch growing bigger, the shadows more menacing. Since she'd sealed the temple floor, the brazier must be Rykoto's connection to the temple. She'd deal with him after she figured out the puzzle of the seals.

The pillars were either warded, or something else. Or both. After replacing the seal in her bag, she made a ball of drossfire to better see. Tiny inscriptions wove around the empty slots of each pillar. She tentatively placed a fingertip atop one, expecting another shock, and was relieved when it didn't come.

With the pad of her fingertip, she traced the inscription. Words came to her, ancient spells spoken by the gods who imprisoned Rykoto. They were powerful spells woven into the marble pillar itself. Somewhere in the words was the answer to which seal fit into which pillar.

The laughter died down and an eerie silence followed. Rykoto was watching her, probably from the fire in the torch. The sensation of a million insects crawling beneath her clothes, pinching her skin, eating at her flesh made her almost shriek, but that's what he was hoping for. The insects were only in her imagination. And even if they were real, she could deal with them. She had to stay focused. Rykoto wanted her to fail. Needed her to and would do everything he could to stop her.

She took a step back and blew out a long breath. It was important to get this right. She arched her back and stretched, looking up to the ceiling as she did. Her sword hummed a tune she didn't recognize, but she listened for clues. Daknys would've had the sword with her when she imprisoned her lover. She withdrew Ynyd Eirathnacht from its scabbard and grinned at the hiss that came from deep underground. The mad god feared her sword. Good to know.

Pushing thoughts of Rykoto to the far reaches of her mind, she compared the writing on the blade to the inscriptions on each pillar. But they were different languages, or else written backward, because there were no similarities between them.

With a frustrated grunt, she sheathed her sword and stared at the pillars. Rykoto chuckled, but she ignored him. One by one, she took out a seal and went from pillar to pillar, holding the seal close to but not quite touching the marble. Once she'd repeated the process with all five seals, to no avail, she sat on the cold floor with her head in her hands. The mad god was worryingly silent.

What was she missing? The seal she held was perfectly blank on both sides, but the one she'd found in her belongings on her first day in the cavern had had markings that only she could see.

Only she could see. Her heart skipped a beat and giddiness tangled her belly.

She ran her thumb over the seal the same way she had on her first visit. Words appeared in the same ancient script found on the pillars. But that wasn't all—an image of a cliff or mountaintop etched itself into the silver before disappearing.

Excitement bubbled in her veins, and she hopped up to examine the pillars again. This time, she stroked the inscriptions with her thumb. On the third pillar, the seal in her hand glowed and a zing of power raced up her arm from the disk. An image of Daknys flitted across her thoughts as she placed the seal carefully into its slot.

For one brief moment, the pillar and seal pulsed with powerful ShantiMari, and then settled to nothing more than stone. Rykoto hissed and shrieked at her from the depths of the temple. The flames in the torch grew to stretch toward the ceiling and fiery tendrils struck out at her. Taryn withdrew her sword and held it aloft.

"Hush, now. I'll not have you disturbing my work." She

stormed toward the torch and slashed at the wild flames. Instantly, they shrunk until only a small wisp danced in the steel frame. "That's better. Be a good god and let me continue."

"I could kill you now, Betrayer. I could slaughter you and drink your blood. I am a god. You are nothing." Rykoto's slurred words echoed in the empty temple, but they held no true threat. Even so, that didn't stop her insides from churning.

"Shhhh." Taryn put a finger to her lips. "If you could have done anything, you would have by now, yet I live." She knelt and placed her hand on the tiles that made a labyrinth on the floor. Her ShantiMari swirled in her veins, but she kept it controlled. No sense in letting Rykoto know how much strength she'd gained since she'd last stepped foot in the temple. "Do not speak again or I shall be quite vexed with you."

She waited a heartbeat for him to argue, but there was only silence. She swallowed hard, tasting acridness on her tongue. It wouldn't do to show fear now, even though she wanted nothing more than to run from the temple and shit herself in the woods.

"Good boy." She stood and held Ynyd Eirathnacht in her left hand while she took a seal from the bag with her right.

Having discovered the solution, she quickly replaced the remaining seals. When finished, she stepped to the altar and gazed at all thirteen pillars flanking the edge of the round temple. A sense of accomplishment washed over her and for one brief moment she was proud of herself for not giving in to her fears or quitting when the task had seemed impossible.

Kaida's growl came at the same time Taryn heard a slow clapping coming from the shadows of the temple. She gripped the hilt of her sword and turned to face the intruder. Even before seeing him, she knew who it would be, though honestly she would have rather sparred with Rykoto than deal with her half-brother's traitorous, whinging bullshit.

CHAPTER TEN

Gods, but Taryn hated being right. Zakael's face emerged from between two columns, the shadow cloak he wore sloughing off with each step. Dressed all in black, only his pale face illuminated in the dim light, he could've been a shade himself. Probably imagined himself sexier with his goth attire and permanent sneer. It didn't make him mysterious or alluring to her, but she was certain there were others who drank from his dark well like starved beasts. People like Cashiel and Marissa. For them, he offered danger and excitement. For Taryn, he was an annoyance to be pitied.

The slow clap continued and with every slap of his hands together, Taryn had to stop herself kicking him upside the head with one well-placed roundhouse kick. What a deceitful, conceited shittgibbon.

Kaida sat beside Taryn, her tail flicking with annoyance. She stroked Kaida's neck and settled her hand atop her head, more to ground herself than to comfort the grierbas. If Zakael was spying on her, then Kaldaar would soon know what she'd done and there would be hell to pay. And she was fresh out of fucks to give. Just being in the temple was unsettling enough, but then with the ordeal of the seals, and Rykoto…she was shattered. If only she'd waited until the dragons were settled, then Rhoane would be with her.

When exactly, had she become so dependent on him that she believed she couldn't do anything without him? It wasn't dependence, she argued—no, they were better together, stronger. He lifted her when she was low, and she did the same when he needed a boost. If that was dependence, then fine.

Only she knew it went deeper than that. An old insecurity wormed its way into her psyche and she struggled to not let it take hold. The last time she and Rhoane were separated, things hadn't gone so well for her, especially where her half-brother was concerned. He'd not only orchestrated Rhoane's breaking, but then he'd held her violently her against her will and blocked her power. She checked to make certain her ShantiMari was protected. If Zakael tried to block her again, she'd teach him a lesson or three.

Taryn kept her expression neutral, bored even, as she watched him approach. Finally, the clapping stopped, and he stood three paces in front of her. Close, but not so close she could slice him with her sword.

"Well done, sister. Although, you lost me a bet. Kaldaar thought you might return sooner rather than later to replace the seals, but I had you down for another fortnight before you'd return to Aelinae." He waved a hand to indicate the temple. "Rykoto isn't happy with the changes you've made to the place."

"I don't give a fuck what Kaldaar or Rykoto think." She sheathed her sword and crossed her arms over her chest. "But you care a whole lot, which makes me wonder—whose bitch are you? Kaldaar must've healed you in Mallaqai's ruins, so you owe him for that, but why cling to a mad god? Rykoto is imprisoned. There's nothing he can do for you."

"That's where you're wrong." He snarled at Kaida before returning his gaze to her and grinning wickedly. "Where's your lover? It's not like you to travel without him. If I recall correctly, the last time you left his side was after he betrayed you. Was it another woman again? Such a shame he can't be trusted, but those Eleri are incredibly seductive. It must be the pointed ears and silky hair." His voice had a dreamy undertone and she pressed her nails into her palms to keep from shaking. "I've fucked my share of their kind to know exactly what makes them alluring."

"What do you want? I've got things to do that don't involve your games." Her heart beat in her throat and a buzz started in the back of her mind. Taryn knew of at least one Eleri he'd fucked and also knew that once he was done with her, she'd been exiled from the Narthvier. Rage boiled in Taryn's veins, and she took a staggering breath to calm her nerves.

He was baiting her to get a reaction, nothing more. She wouldn't fall for his tricks, not this time. She'd trusted him once too often and had the war wounds to show for it.

Zakael strolled around the altar, his fingertips dragging along the surface. "I wonder how well you know your betrothed. I mean, truly." He passed the torch and wriggled his fingers in the flame before licking them as if they were covered in honey. "Delicious."

"You're a sick fuck, Zakael. I don't have time for this." She turned toward the doorway but was blocked by her half-brother. How the hell had he traversed the space so quickly? And silently? Her interest piqued, her attention snapped to his every move, every expression, every word.

Zakael loomed over her, attempting to intimidate, but all it did was annoy her even more. His glare cut into her, through her, like a sharpened blade through butter, and she suppressed a shiver.

"Rhoane murdered my mother. Your sainted betrothed killed an innocent woman—and you call *me* sick." His steely eyes turned to hardened bits of hatred. "She was the only good thing in my life and he took her from me when I was just a child."

The power of his emotions rocked her and she staggered backward a step. For one tiny moment, she saw past his defenses and felt the love he had for his mother. She withdrew quickly before the enormity of his loss swallowed her whole.

"I'm so sorry." And she was. She understood what it was to lose a loved one and be left bereft on a churning sea of uncertainty.

Burying her anger, she changed tact and cupped his cheek with her hand, surprised when his tears tracked over her fingers. Whether real or not, his heartache couldn't be faked.

Instead of pulling away, he placed his hand over hers. "Did you know?"

His grip tightened and she fought to control her own emotions. She would never be held captive by him or anyone ever again. She was Taryn Fucking Galendrin.

Shall I bite his arse? Kaida asked with a little too much enthusiasm.

Not yet. If he gets violent, then have at him, but I'm curious what this is truly about.

The grierbas sat with a low snarl, her eyes trained on Zakael.

With a long, slow breath to release her rising apprehension, Taryn nodded. "Yes, Rhoane told me. None of us are innocent, Zakael. Not Rhoane, nor me, or you. We've all done things we'd rather not have done." She turned from his grip and pointed to the ceiling. "Just up there you ran a sword through our father's heart." He made a sound of objection, and she held up her hand. "Don't deny it or try to say I killed him. We both know you were responsible for his death. I was simply the instrument of his beheading. Which, saying it out loud, is pretty damn awful."

"You killed him, and then you killed Marissa. Your own sister," Zakael insisted.

Taryn faced him and forced herself to remain calm. "Yes, I

murdered Marissa. You and I both know why, and it had nothing to do with her raping Rhoane. Don't pretend you weren't in league with her to steal my powers. You, Valterys, Marissa—hell, even my own mother—all of you would've killed me if you'd had the chance and stolen what only I possess. So, no, don't cry your crocodile tears and expect me to feel sorry for you because Rhoane did what he had to do for Aelinae. For me. Is he a saint? Hells no, but he's the only one who's ever protected me. Fought for me. You've only ever fought against me."

Zakael scoffed and shook his head. "Maybe if things had been different, we would be allies like you once said."

"'If things had been different?'" It was her turn to scoff. "You chose your side before I was even born. Maybe that had to do with your mother's death, maybe not. All I know is, if Rhoane hadn't killed your mother, I wouldn't be here. Or maybe I would. For all we know, Valterys was scheming to do what Rhoane did for him. Your mother was an obstacle he needed removed." She met his eyes and saw the hurt and confusion in them. "He knew of the prophecies long before Rhoane snuck into Caer Idris to do the unspeakable."

"He wouldn't. He loved my mother."

She took his hands in hers. "I'm not going to diminish your memories of your mother. I only ask that you look at this without emotion or judgement. No one could be married to a man like Valterys and be completely ignorant of what he's doing." She stepped away and resisted the urge to wipe her hands on her tunic. "I've seen you in the dungeons, Zakael. I know the horrific things you've done. Don't try to tell me your reasons were just. Those people you murdered? They had family, too. There are people out there right now mourning their loss just as you mourn your mother. None of us are innocent—but we *can* choose to do better."

She strode toward the door and paused. When she turned,

Zakael was watching her with a curious expression. Not anger, not remorse, but something between the two.

"We can still be allies. You don't have to obey Kaldaar or Rykoto. You have the power within you to chart your own course, a path for good. But you have to want it. You must believe in yourself."

"All I've ever known is death and darkness."

"That's not true. As you just said, your mother was goodness. Look for her Light, Zakael. It's in you. I believe that with my whole being."

"Why?" He took a tentative step and faltered. "Why are you so fucking kind?"

She hesitated only a moment before she returned to him and put her arms around him in a bear hug like she always imagined a mother would give her child. His arms hung loose, and then wrapped around her in a cautious embrace.

"Because I choose to see the goodness in this world. There's grace in people, even you. You just have to look for it." She squeezed a little harder. "Life isn't fair, but sulking and rage don't solve problems. You're better than what you've become. Only you can choose your path. No one else, not even a god." She stretched on tiptoe and kissed his cheek. "Be well, Brother."

Then she left the temple with Kaida padding by her side. When she was certain Zakael hadn't followed, she leaned against a tree for support. Her breaths came in heavy drags and tears coursed over her cheeks like a river that burst its banks. She wouldn't have stopped them even if she could. The release of emotion was exactly what she needed; she just hated that it came at the expense of witnessing Zakael's pain.

She hadn't lied—none of them were innocent. That did nothing to assuage the guilt that cut her heart. In order for her to live, Zakael's mother had had to die. It was a simple truth. Yet no less devastating.

Who would Zakael have been if Troyanna had lived?

That was a slippery path to tread. Everything that had happened in the past led to this very moment. To change one thing would alter everything. Her mind spun the logic, but her heart still broke over her half-brother's mourning. He'd truly loved his mother, and for all Taryn knew, Troyanna had been goodness incarnate. Perhaps had even been the barrier between Valterys destroying Zakael and her son becoming a great ruler.

They'd never know. What's done is done, as they say. Zakael had a choice now to follow his path or forge a new one. Same as she.

Kaida nuzzled her hip and wrapped a paw around her leg in the sweetest damn dog hug she'd ever had. *I am here, Darennsai. You are not alone.*

The truth of Kaida's simple words hurt more than they soothed. Taryn wasn't alone—she had Rhoane and Kaida, plus an entire family, some by blood, some not, who loved and supported her. Who did Zakael have? Two deranged gods, each of whom joyfully wished for her death.

He also had her.

CHAPTER ELEVEN

Shadows crept into the temple with Taryn's departure as if she'd taken all the light in the world with her and left him alone in the darkness. He looked toward the spot in the ceiling where he'd thrust an obsidian sword through his father's heart and knew the truth of her words.

He, Zakael, had killed their father. Not Taryn, as he liked to believe. He'd convinced himself they had a connection through Valterys's death, but that was only wishful thinking. His gaze went to the pristine altar and then to the soft glow of flames in the brazier. After that fateful night when Taryn had sealed the opening in the floor of the temple, he'd brought in a standing torch as a means of contacting his god. Would it continue to work now that she'd replaced all the seals?

His fingertips trailed along the marble altar and through the flames. The most delightful burn against his skin reminded him he was still alive. He slid a hand beneath his coat to where Rhoane's blade had pierced him at Mallaqai's ruins, in nearly the same spot he'd stabbed his father. Ironic, really. Or perhaps justice of sorts. Rhoane was a skilled swordsman; he knew he would miss Zakael's heart by mere inches. Had he meant to keep Zakael alive? If so, why? They were never friends, he and Glennwoods, always adversaries.

Taryn's healing ShantiMari swirled beneath his touch. Even now, all these weeks later, he felt her power.

Her kindness.

A harsh laugh came from deep inside him to echo against the rounded walls of the temple. She'd said he had a choice, but if ever he had, it was long past. Kindness was anathema to him. He caressed the scar and grimaced against the scratch of pain his touch brought.

Why had Taryn sent healing power into his wound? It always came back to her weakness. Her goodness. In the end, that's how Kaldaar or possibly even Rykoto would win. Taryn's bleeding heart would be her downfall, and he'd be there to witness her ruination. Glennwood's, too. They could both eternally burn in Dal Ferran's fires for all he cared.

One by one, he inspected the seals on all thirteen columns, not just the ones Taryn had replaced. He sensed her wards on them, but others as well. Those, he didn't recognize. Myrddin, perhaps, or the elder gods, or even Lliandra. He could only guess who would need warning if the seals were tampered with. Kaldaar would know soon enough, but there was time yet before he'd have to face the temperamental god.

He strode to the altar and knelt, his fingertips touching the intricate tiles that made up the labyrinth in the floor.

"Oh great lord, hear me now. How may I serve you?" Zakael braced for the lash of heat that always came with Rykoto's rising.

Silence. Cold, dark silence answered.

"Great lord Rykoto, I am here to do your bidding."

A fissure of paranoia started in his mind. If Rykoto had heard his conversation with Taryn and thought him unworthy, he might have forsaken him, and that Zakael could not afford. He needed Rykoto to free him from the shackles Kaldaar had placed upon him. But he'd first have to strengthen Rykoto before he freed him so that together they could defeat Kaldaar once and for all. Zakael's life—and his sanity—depended on it.

The memory of what he'd witnessed seared his mind and his gut twisted violently. He coughed against the sickness that reached his throat. Taryn had shushed the god.

Taryn. Shushed. Rykoto.

Ohlin's balls, what did it mean? Had she somehow silenced the god forever? Was he now trapped in Dal Ferran and unable to reach into the temple even a little?

This wasn't good. Of that, Zakael was certain. Perhaps it was the only thing he was certain of at that moment.

It also meant Taryn was gaining in strength. His gaze flicked to the columns again. If she'd somehow managed to seal Rykoto for good, he'd have to come up with a new plan to be rid of Kaldaar.

But how? Who wasn't afraid of the god? Someone who might see profit in helping him?

The laughing figure Kaldaar despised. Who were they? And how could he coax them out of hiding?

Heart lightened by this new, albeit dangerous, plan, he rose and took one last glance at the temple before he practically ran out the entrance. Even before his feet were through the doorway, he transformed into a levon and flew toward the west.

He landed on the cliff where the runyon tree once stood. Only a charred area about the size of a carriage remained of the ghastly tree. Zakael flexed his hand automatically, and felt phantom pain from the many times he'd been forced to press his palm upon its thorns.

"So that the tree will know you," his father used to say.

But it was just another form of torture that he'd had to endure. Perhaps Taryn was right and Valterys had already set Zakael's path of darkness in motion before his mother's death. It was only a few bells after her passing when his father took him to the dungeons to get his first taste of what happened in those dank cells.

A stirring in his blood warmed his chilled skin and he cursed the eroticism that always accompanied even the mere thought of torture. He truly was a sick fuck.

There was no Light in him. There was no goodness buried somewhere in him ready to be discovered. He was who he was.

His boots ground against the gravel path as he hurried to the secret entrance to the dungeons that only he and his father knew about. There were other entrances used by informants and those not wishing to be seen at court, but this one was for his use only.

The door swung open at his touch and he glanced around to make certain he hadn't been seen or followed. Satisfied no spies marked his movements, he closed the door behind him and reinforced his wards just in case.

For several moments, he simply stood in the dark and breathed deeply of the stench. Death. Decay. Fear. These scents used to sustain him, but today they no longer held the same sweet aroma. Irritation plucked at his nerves. This was his place of calm, his sanctuary away from the troubles of the world. That something had disturbed his peace angered him mightily.

He stormed down one corridor and then another, his rage building with each step. The cells were empty. All of them. Kaldaar had taken his refuge and abused it for his own greedy needs.

It was time he stopped letting the god control his kingdom.

He rushed up the stairs to the castle proper and pushed past the courtiers who found themselves in his way. That there were any living souls left in the place was a miracle. Kaldaar's feeding frenzies had decimated his staff, as well as his kingdom.

His boots skidded on the slate floor with his abrupt stop. Those around him stared in shock, but quickly moved on before he could single any one of them out. His gaze took in the several dozen men and women who lingered in the sitting room where as a boy he used to hide beneath the tables and eavesdrop on his mother and her friends.

Why were these courtiers spared? Were they loyal to Kaldaar? Or to him? As he took in their appearances, he saw the haggard expressions, the furtive glances filled with fear. These were his subjects, not Kaldaar's, and it was time he protected them as the king should.

Once in his rooms, he opened the balcony doors in both his sleeping chamber and the room Kaldaar had claimed as his own. No more. This was his study and would be used as such from now on. He searched the desk for the diary he knew his father had kept for scheduling meetings and trips. What he hoped to find in the diary's pages, he wasn't certain, but anything to give him guidance on how to run state affairs or even a record of knowledge to fill in his own gaps would help.

First on his own agenda was to gather his privy council for an update on the state of the West. The diary was tucked beneath a pile of scrolls Zakael knew contained prophecies relating to Taryn. Which meant Kaldaar was looking for something in the prophecies—but what?

Being careful so as not to leave evidence, he unbound each scroll and read every page, but found nothing that he didn't already know. Several pages were missing that he knew should be with these. He ran a finger along his lips, circling back to when he last remembered seeing them.

At Mallaqai's ruins. They were the sheets that had instructions for opening the vortex. A violent jag raced through him, fused with a tiny thrill. Taryn must've taken them from him when she knocked him out. Clever girl. Kaldaar needed those papers to return the dragons to Aelinae and with them in Taryn's possession, Zakael hoped that meant the deranged god couldn't succeed in his plan to not only return them, but to force each one to obey only Telraicht Noir practitioners.

The diary forgotten for the moment, he searched the room

for signs the cackling trickster might be present, but found nothing. A gentle breeze drifted through the open doorway and he stood still for a moment to let it caress his face. The scent of roses floated through the room—a familiar smell he'd known since childhood. They were his aunt Gwyneira's roses that she planted when she and Anje were first married. He'd not allowed himself to indulge in their sweet scent in far too long.

They reminded him of happier days. Days of lightness and laughter. A time before the darkness consumed him and he became "Kaldaar's bitch," as Taryn had succinctly put it.

A door closed in the outer hall of his rooms and he took one long last drag of the sweet air. His mind raced with how best to play the game. How could he pretend obedience with a god who knew his every move, sometimes before he did?

"Ah, here you are, my beautiful boy." Kaldaar breezed into the room, his gaze immediately going to the scrolls before flicking to Zakael. "I have a gift for you. Come, you will be delighted with what I've brought."

Zakael held up the diary. "I should see to the business of running the kingdom. Can your gift wait?"

The god's eyes narrowed to dangerous slits and his wretched lips stretched over ancient teeth. "The kingdom will be here in the morning. This cannot wait."

"Very well." He set the book atop the scrolls as if they were unimportant sheets of paper.

Kaldaar's hiss followed him into the bed chamber where two women knelt beside his bed. Each was naked, except for a thin gossamer veil covering them from head to foot. The fabric vibrated with their quaking and his gut roiled—he could guess what Kaldaar would ask of him.

"These delicious young maidens are here for your pleasure. Take them hard and with violence. Their virginity is a willing sacrifice, isn't it my loves?" Kaldaar's bony hand snaked from the sleeve of his robe to stroke each woman's head. "Yes, you will make exquisite vessels. You will want for nothing. Your every wish, satisfied. Once you're with child, of course. Until then, King Zakael is your master. Do you understand?"

The women sobbed quietly and nodded.

Zakael hated Kaldaar in that moment but hated himself more. There was a time when their tears would've excited him, their cries spurring him to greater violence. But now? His heart pinched with conflicted emotions even as his cock enlarged.

The women rose in unison and began undressing him. He refused to look at their faces beneath their veils, instead staring out the window at the blue of the sea. An ocean the same color as his half-sister's eyes.

Don't think of her. Focus on the moment, on the women and their lovely soft mouths that wrapped around his cock. Yes, better. There, just there.

His attention dragged from the sea to the nubile waifs fondling his balls with inexperienced yet tantalizing hands. He could teach them many things. And he would.

Kaldaar drifted behind him and Zakael tried to remain relaxed, but he knew what was coming. The god didn't disappoint and a moment later, several strands of power violated his orifices. This was how Kaldaar preferred to fuck him—from behind, as if he wished to remain anonymous. A participant, and yet not. Despite the strangeness of the god's preferences, damned if Zakael's body didn't respond to the brutality of his ShantiMari.

"I am all things to you, Zakael, never forget this. Without me, you do not exist." Kaldaar's sibilant hiss scorched Zakael's hearing.

A bony finger traced down his torso. Upon reaching the scar Rhoane's sword inflicted, Kaldaar flinched and swore curses in the ancient tongue Zakael barely understood. He glanced down and saw that where flesh had once been, only bone could be seen. The scar had damaged Kaldaar, but how?

The women ignored what was happening between him and

the god. They were too busy taking turns sucking his cock with a zeal that made him question their virginal posturing. His attention pinged between their mouths and what Kaldaar would do next. Anxiety tore at his thoughts, making him mad with worry. Would Kaldaar punish him for something he couldn't control? How was he to know his scar would burn the god?

"Your blood is impure, my beautiful boy. Your sister has tainted you with her healing, but I shall remove all traces of her from your body."

The violation deepened until Zakael was gasping with pain. The more he bucked and flinched from Kaldaar's assault, the harder the women sucked his cock. Almost as if it had been planned.

His body burned with fever as if the god were literally burning Taryn's ShantiMari from his blood. When at last Kaldaar wheezed his rapturous climax and pulled away from Zakael, he was panting and sweating as if he'd been the one fucking an unwilling participant.

"We will destroy her together," Kaldaar whispered for his hearing alone. "We shall dine on her corpse for eternity." The ragged exposed bone of his finger caressed down Zakael's face from his temple to his lips. "Never forget, I own you and I am forever in your mind."

"Yes." Zakael heaved with his own release.

Kaldaar was in his mind, but so was his sister.

CHAPTER TWELVE

The water of Lan Gyllarelle buoyed Taryn as she stared up at the stars. Flickers of ShantiMari streaked above the tree-tops and she watched them, idly curious if Stephan had put a veil over the entire forest. To do so would've taken at least one hundred Eleri strong in the power. The sky darkened as she watched the flickering lights, reminding her she'd been floating for so long her fingers and toes were puckered like dried plums. Yet no matter how long she stayed in the sacred waters, she feared she'd never be rid of Rykoto's filth.

Fresh tears tracked down her cheeks to the water. She'd given up wiping them away and let them flow. The shock of realizing how much pain Zakael held inside himself kept churning her belly. None of them were innocent, but she would do well to remember that no matter what led someone down a path of darkness and destruction, they were still capable of feeling. She hoped Zakael would take his pain and rage and turn them into something positive.

She curled into herself and fought off the flood of icy pinpricks across her skin that came with her own remorse. For Marissa, for Brandt, for the poor vorlock she slayed to save

Rhoane's life. She would forgive herself in time, but at that moment, the guilt was too raw. It was easier to forgive Rhoane his betrayal than it was to forgive herself. Forgive herself for what, exactly? Not being enough? Not being worthy? Not being perfect? She knew it was all her own bullshit, but nevertheless, it rang true.

Ever since she arrived on Aelinae, she'd been trying to be the perfect friend, the perfect sister, the perfect daughter, and more recently, the perfect whatever the fuck she was. Balance-bringer? Savior? She didn't like the titles of Eirielle or Darennsai. Each brought with it the possibility that she could just as easily destroy Aelinae as save it.

Sometimes, she wished she could just be a girl who loved a boy. As simple as that. No threats from mad gods, no complicated family dynamics that made her doubt and question everything that made their love pure. No enchanted swords that would be the instruments of their deaths.

She let herself drift lower until the water completely submerged her and stretched her entire body as far as she could. Her fingers splayed outward, and her toes pointed to reach into the warm depths of the lake. She pushed to hold the position and then relaxed to release all the tension she'd built up. The crying had been cathartic, as was letting her emotional crap float away into the healing waters.

Feeling a tiny bit less terrible, she swam toward the surface reminding herself that she was a good person who sometimes had to do bad things. She didn't have to be perfect.

A flash of red—an angry and burning liquid—crossed her vision and she looked to the treetops, but it wasn't the veil of ShantiMari that she saw. Her gaze swept the shore where Kaida sat with another grierbas. They nuzzled each other's necks similar to how Jinnipher had stroked Gilchrist's, and Taryn realized with a start that this was how animals hugged. Warmth tugged at her belly. The second grierbas, more drab in coloring, turned toward her with eyes the same golden shade as Kaida.

Another flash of red followed by a vision of a rift in Aelinae's core stabbed at her head. She grabbed her temple with a soft whine. The vision came and went, too quick for her to make sense of it.

She swam to the shore and placed her feet on the sandy bottom of the lake. A third flash brought her to her knees. In this vision, she clearly saw rivers of molten lava, and again the burning fissure.

"What does it mean?" she asked aloud, hoping the lake or the Eleri could help her make sense of what she saw. Her fingers dug into the soft sand and she whimpered against a slash of pain that felt like she'd been seared with a hot poker. A new rune appeared on her marked hand. Unlike the other images, this one wasn't a ghost tattoo, but a burning mark in the shape of a volcano, complete with flowing lava. She sucked in a breath and blinked back tears.

Darennsai, my mam wishes to meet you. Kaida's voice pulled her out of the pain the vision brought.

Taryn struggled to her feet and sloshed to shore. Her long silver hair clung to her wet skin like an uncomfortable wool blanket on a hot summer's day. With a flick of her wrist, she used her power to dry not just her hair, but her skin as well. Another flick and several Eleri braids twisted to hold her hair off her face in a complicated pattern that Ellie had often used. Thinking of her maid brought an unwelcome pinch of homesickness, and another healthy glug of guilt. They'd been gone too long this time. She could only hope Hayden had told everyone that she and Rhoane would be home soon.

Home.

Talaith was as much her home as the Narthvier, but at least at the Crystal Palace she had her own room with a comfortable bed. She tugged on her trousers and a shift, leaving her feet bare. Stars, but she missed a bed, and regular meals. The ties of her trousers had a little too much extra length on them.

She knelt beside Kaida and waited for her to introduce her mam. The dun-hued grierbas placed her paw on Taryn's knee and inclined her head.

It is a great honor, Darennsai.

Surprised, she looked first to Kaida, and then to her mam. *Do all grierbas communicate with people?*

Only those we find worthy. You are my first.

Taryn placed her hand over her heart and bowed her head. *I am honored.*

You have cared for our pup and treated her as an equal among the two-legs. We owe you much gratitude. If not for you, she would have been lost to the forest.

Immense sadness clung to her words. A memory of meeting Aislinn at a wavering wall of ShantiMari cut through Taryn's thoughts. Hazy around the edges, she focused on the words spoken that morning, and remembered Aislinn telling her it wasn't yet time before she kissed her. She touched her lips, recalling the coolness of air that had slipped down her throat. To allow her passage through the wall. After the kiss, Aislinn had commanded her to forget their meeting, but she remembered everything now. If it hadn't been for the Eleri queen, Taryn wouldn't have found Kaida.

She is family. She stroked Kaida's neck. *We were meant to find each other.*

Kaida's mam licked Taryn's chin before doing the same to her daughter. *As Verdaine wishes it, so it shall be. I hope we meet again.* She turned to run off, but stopped. Her golden eyes met Taryn's. *Please tell the leader of the tree-things to release his hold on the forest. There are many who will perish if they cannot leave the trees.* And then she bolted into the dense foliage as if startled.

Taryn glimpsed a pure black grierbas not more than fifty feet from where they sat. His blue eyes regarded her as he sat perfectly still. Then, ever so slowly, he lowered his head.

That is my sire. He does not yet trust the two-legs. Kaida's gaze didn't leave her sire and Taryn sensed her sadness. She missed her family.

I hope in time he will.

He knows what you are—not in your present form, but who you will become—and it confuses him.

"What do you mean?"

When you were in the in-between after the Surtentse was broken, Verdaine came to see me. She told me of your future— your fate to become a goddess. I never doubted her word, or that you were worthy of such a feat. Even when you stumbled, I believed. My sire, however, is of the old ways like King Stephan. He does not know yet if you will benefit the forest, or destroy it.

Taryn's gaze traveled to where the black grierbas had been sitting. The spot was empty now, but she felt his keen stare from the forest.

"I promise to do all in my power to bring peace to Aelinae, and all the creatures who live here." The words were spoken not only to reassure the sire, but as a promise to herself. She settled onto the sandy bank and stroked Kaida's impossibly soft fur. "Are you happy? I mean, really? You didn't ask for this life, or all that we've been through. Would you prefer to stay here with your family?"

As you said, you are also my family. I have experienced too much to live a gentle existence in the Narthvier. I would get bored within a day. Her tongued lolled to the side and Taryn scratched her behind the ears where she knew Kaida liked it best.

"Do you think I'll make a good goddess?"

Kaida dipped her head, and Taryn wasn't sure if it was out of respect, or contrition. *What does a grierbas know about being a goddess?*

Taryn chuckled at the not unexpected answer. "You've been

the best friend I could ever hope for. How can I ever repay you? Is there anything you want or need? I mean, besides a hot meal and comfortable bed." Her stomach growled and she placed a hand over her abdomen.

Wings, Kaida answered without hesitation. *I do not like to be held between your talons. They are most uncomfortable.* She lifted her face to the night sky. *I should like to feel the wind in my face without the fear of being dropped.*

I would never drop you! She positioned herself so that she faced the grierbas and looked her dead in the eyes. *Is this truly what you want? I'm not sure if I can undo it once it's done.*

It is. But, I would like my wings to be hidden when I am not flying.

You've thought about this a lot, it seems.

Every time I was clutched in your talons, and for a while afterwards.

Taryn chuckled at her serious tone. *Then wings you shall have my dearest friend.*

She could do this. How hard could it be to give a grierbas wings? Pffft, anyone could do it. Except, she wasn't just anyone, and Kaida was far too important to fuck this up. She wiped her hands on her trousers and imagined wings that a Pegasus would have. Strong with sturdy feathers.

Slowly and with focused calm, she smoothed the fur over Kaida's shoulders and used her ShantiMari to grow wings befitting an esteemed grierbas. Kaida yipped in surprise, and Taryn reassured her she was fine despite the fear nagging the back of her thoughts.

When the wings were complete, Taryn hugged Kaida and kissed her muzzle. *You are glorious, mi carae.*

I feel funny.

Your balance is off. Give yourself some time to get used to them. Walk around, run, skip, whatever you need to do to feel like they've always been there.

Kaida wobbled a few steps, her wings dipping this way and that. Every time she fumbled, Taryn was tempted to rush to her side and help her, but she knew Kaida needed to do this on her own.

When I am a cat, will I still have my lovely wings?

I don't see why not. They're part of you now, whatever shape you take. You decide when they're visible or not.

Kaida nodded and wobbled a few more steps. Finally, she tucked in the wings and loped along the shore. A short distance away, she ran back, her wings extending the faster she went. When she was a few paces from Taryn, she beat her wings and lifted to just above Taryn's head before tumbling to the ground.

"Give it time. It's unnatural for a grierbas to have wings. It will take some getting used to."

Kaida sat with a huff and growled at the lovely feathers. A moment later, they tucked in and disappeared from sight. Taryn smoothed her fur, surprised she couldn't feel anything. Kaida looked and felt like her old, wingless self.

"See? You've already mastered disguising them. Tomorrow, we'll work on flying." She yawned and glanced at the flickering ShantiMari. "We're too far from the Weirren, so it's sleeping under the stars for tonight."

"I am sure we can find a bed for you at the temple," Carga said, and Taryn spun around to find her sister-in-law standing several paces away near the tree line. She wore a simple burgundy shift, her long dark hair loose. She'd never looked more at peace, and a swell of love overwhelmed Taryn.

She and Kaida rose to greet her. Two steps in, another vision flashed in her mind. Stronger than the others, this time accompanied by a piercing pain that tore at her skull. She crumpled to the ground and grabbed her head with a moan.

"Taryn, what is it?" Carga's voice came from far away even though Taryn felt her firm grip on her shoulder.

"Destruction. Death," she managed between gasps of air.

The burning landscape was littered with bodies. Faces of those she loved stared blankly up at her from crushed skulls darkened by fire. In the center of the carnage stood a lone figure, cloaked in shadows.

The figure turned and faced her.

Bloodstained silver hair matted with pieces of flesh, the woman raised her sword in victory. To her right, a lump of what was once brilliant white fur was a bloody mess. At her feet, a body, barely recognizable, lay shattered. Rhoane's dead eyes stared at her with recrimination.

Taryn screamed, her voice disturbing the forest and setting birds alight. The woman laughed and pointed her dragon-hilted sword at Taryn's heart. It wasn't Kaldaar, or Rykoto, or even Zakael who had caused the carnage.

It was her.

CHAPTER THIRTEEN

Novices and priestesses alike gaped at Taryn as she and Kaida followed Carga through the maze of halls in Verdaine's temple. She nervously tugged her sleeve over her arm to hide the burn mark. It might've been they'd never seen a grierbas up close, or realized how large they truly were, or it could've been Taryn herself that drew their stares. Whatever the case, she tried not to dwell on what their opinions of her might be. All of them, novices included, had most likely read Verdaine's prophecy and knew precisely her role in it.

She was the gyota of their nightmares.

Not true, she reminded herself. The visions had shaken her, but this pity party just wouldn't do. She wasn't a destroyer. Whatever she'd seen in that horrid illusion, it wasn't real. Right here, right now in the temple with Carga and Kaida, this was real.

And Carga had promised she'd have answers to the mystery of the Jansen Strait. After a good meal, of course. Kaida panted at her side, and Taryn buried her hand in her white fur to give comfort. She was nervous, too.

What is it, girl?

These men, they remind me of Gian. They, too, are physically altered.

Taryn glanced at the dozen or so woodland faeries that busied themselves with various tasks, paying her and Kaida little mind. Odd, certainly that they didn't stare or make a sign above their heads. It brought uncomfortable questions of what, exactly, had been altered.

"Are men allowed to study at the temple?" Taryn asked quietly.

"Traditionally, there have only been priestesses." Carga answered. "These woodland faeries have dedicated themselves to Verdaine and serve her by serving us."

"Willingly?"

Carga slid her a glance. "Of course. We do not force anyone to stay. Our way of life is peaceful; we are here to study so that we can be of help to others. These faeries, they have voluntarily been castrated so that they are not tempted by the novices and priestesses. They see us as holy extensions of our goddess, Verdaine."

"They're eunuchs?" An involuntary pinch to her nethers made her cringe. "Ouch."

Carga waved her hand. "The procedure is painless. We use ShantiMari and have been told it is a rather pleasant sensation for them."

"If you say so." Taryn wasn't convinced, but who was she to tell someone they couldn't worship in the way they chose. "They don't seem bothered by us."

"Oh, they are quiet excited by your presence, but they will not disgrace themselves by showing their giddiness. They know you helped one of their brethren and hope to honor you with service."

Taryn smiled to a eunuch as they passed and her heart beat slowed. He could've been Gian's brother, they were so similar in coloring and size. It made her miss her faerie friend. The eunuch's thought brushed hers and Carga hadn't misspoken—he was grateful to be at the temple, but seeing her and Kaida gave him a peace nothing at the temple ever had.

It was nothing more than a fleeting touch of her mind, but profound in its scope and importance. He and all the faeries believed in her. Believed in the prophecy that said she would restore balance on Aelinae and usher in a new era of peace.

She felt his hope and expectation like a granite slab that had been laid upon her chest. So many lives depended on her and Rhoane not fucking it up.

They turned a corner and entered a large dining hall. The moment Taryn stepped inside, the room quieted. Carga continued walking as if nothing had happened, but Taryn felt every pair of eyes as they scrutinized her. Did they think her worthy? The granite slab turned to a boulder and weight of responsibility seemed too much. She and Rhoane were just two people, and yet somehow they had to bring balance to Aelinae.

At the head table, Carga took the center seat and indicated Taryn sit to her right. Kaida, too large to squirm beneath the table like she used to do as a pup, sat quietly beside Taryn. Even without a chair, her shoulders reached the table height. It was comical but considering the gravity of the stares Taryn continued to receive, she kept her expression placid, as if a grierbas sitting the high table with Verdaine's high priestess was an everyday occurrence.

Novices and faeries brought in plates of food, serving Carga first, and then Taryn. Kaida was given a huge bowl full of something that smelled delicious. One of their tummies rumbled, and Taryn stifled a bout of giggles.

"Something amuses you?" Carga asked above her glass of wine.

"It's been so long since I've sat down for a proper meal, I'm not sure I remember how to eat with utensils."

"Use your hands if you like." Carga motioned to the others in the room who now tried not to stare. "If they have a problem with your manners, they can eat elsewhere."

"That won't be necessary, but I appreciate the sentiment." She toyed with a fork. "This is for soup, right?"

Carga's laughter tolled like a joyous bell through the room. "I have missed you, my sister. More than you will ever know."

Tears stung Taryn's eyes as she took a long sip of a rich red wine that felt like silk flowing down her throat. "I'm pretty sure I have a good idea. There's much to tell, but it can wait until later."

Carga nodded and took a delicate bite of what Taryn hoped was steak. The sound of cutlery and conversation filled the dining hall, and she relaxed knowing the focus was no longer on her. If they had been expecting Carga to make a speech, they were left wanting.

Later that evening, after a satisfying meal of not steak but something close, Taryn joined Carga in her private rooms. Kaida stretched in front of a fire and snoozed loudly while Taryn told Carga a highly edited version of what she and Rhoane had been up to since they last saw the high priestess. In return, Carga told Taryn about Eoghan leaving the Narthvier and Stephan closing the vier's borders. With so much to share, they talked late into the night, barely noticing when the drossfire dozed lazily in their sconces.

"Are you ready to tell me what caused you to collapse at Lan Gyllarelle?" Carga gently prodded.

"I wish I knew. One minute, I'm floating, the next, these visions besieged me with vicious intensity. They showed a burning land. Not just burning but made of lava. Death was everywhere. In the final vision, I saw myself standing at the center of it all." She rubbed her eyes and yawned. "I don't know if it's a warning, or a portent to something else. I do know there's no way in hell I'll slaughter everyone I love. Not willingly."

Carga sat with her legs folded, her chin resting on her knees. Her intense gaze didn't leave Taryn. "I know you will not, but there are malevolent forces here now that were not present a decade ago. Perhaps you will not have a choice."

"I *always* have a choice." She might've put a little too much emphasis on the word more to convince herself than Carga.

"Hmmm." Carga's eyes narrowed, lips thinned. "What is this mark you keep trying to hide?"

Taryn's cheeks flushed not from the wine, but embarrassment. She'd thought she was being sly in her constant tugs of her shirt.

"A gift from the visions. It won't heal, and it's unlike the others. Some of those burned a little upon receiving the image, then settled. This one is angry, it seems."

Carga held Taryn's wrist and studied the crusty black outline of the volcano. She held a hesitant finger over the skin. "Shall I try to heal it?"

"I don't know what will happen to you if you do. Usually, the runes come after I've completed something. This might mean I have a task unfulfilled."

"Does it hurt?"

"Like I'm being constantly burned."

"Tomorrow, we will find some herbs and tinctures for your wound." She swirled her fingers above Taryn's skin and a soothing settled into the fiery rune.

"That helped, thank you."

A frown marred Carga's pretty face, and her brows drew tight. "So much unrest. I fear what is on the horizon." She held her cup to her lips for several seconds before drinking. "Did you know about Myrddin's betrayal?"

Taryn shook her head slowly. "Not fully. I never truly trusted him, but I wanted to because of his friendship with Brandt. I was close to giving him that trust when Kaldaar violated Hayden in the Summerlands on his wedding night. Then Rhoane and I left, and when we returned, Hayden told me about Myrddin's assholery. I'd like to say I was surprised, but I'm not. Disappointed, yes. Rage-inducingly so. He didn't just betray Brandt and those we care about, but all of Aelinae. For thousands of seasons. He's on my list of those I'd like to see punished violently."

"Perhaps violence isn't the answer."

Taryn's chuckle was full of contempt. "What? You want me to hug it out with Myrddin? No thanks. He deserves, at the very least, a brutal dick punch."

Carga stretched and yawned, her lithe body unfurling like a bloom opening to the sun. "It is getting late. There is something of great importance I need to discuss with you, but it will have to wait until tomorrow." She placed her hand on Taryn's forearm. "It is something I can only share with you."

Taryn hesitated a moment before replying, "If it's something I must keep from Rhoane, then maybe you shouldn't tell me. We promised each other no secrets."

Her face fell for a split second before she nodded. "If Verdaine wills it, then I shall unburden myself to both you and my brother. When can we expect him?"

Taryn had been vague on where he was and what he was doing, saying only that he was taking care of something and would be with them soon. In truth, she didn't know when he would return, or if he'd know she was in the Narthvier.

"Soon. A day, maybe two."

"That will give me time to discuss with Verdaine the best path forward." Carga rose and beckoned her to follow. "It is late and we need rest."

She led Taryn and Kaida to a room that could only be described as ethereal. The temple proper was built into a grand tree, not as large as the Weirren, but similar in structure. But these walkways and rooms looked to be made of spun silk. The airiness was belied by the stability of the path and walls. At a large door that resembled a maple leaf, Taryn sucked in a breath.

The door not only looked like a leaf, complete with veining and variegated coloring, but curled in a bit as if it had just fallen from a tree. Inside was even more magical. Sturdy walls in shades of green kept out sounds of the temple and forest while keeping in warmth. A large bed dominated the space, its canopy made up of flowering vines. She had the impression everything within the room was alive. Except for possibly the copper tub tucked away in a large alcove.

"Breathtaking."

"I am glad you like it. We are especially proud of our home." Carga kissed her on the cheek and promised to collect her later that morning, after the sun was up and she'd had a chance to rest.

Kaida jumped onto the bed and curled into a semi-circle before Taryn had her boots off. She couldn't blame the girl. Warm bed, soft downy mattress, hells yeah. Taryn stripped down to her small clothes and snuggled beneath the blankets. Despite her exhaustion, unease rippled across her body. She stared at the canopy, cycling through her thoughts to what was causing her distress.

Carga's cryptic warning about sharing something important was a vague annoyance, but Taryn didn't get the sense it impacted her personally. Only that Carga felt the need to tell her. But why only her? And why would she need to discuss it with Verdaine? Maybe it did involve her, and she wouldn't like where the information led.

Stressing about it wouldn't help. She snuggled deep into the blankets and closed her eyes. Just as she was drifting off to sleep, she thought of Myrddin and his betrayal. But that wasn't what caused her heartrate to spike and cold sweat to break out on her forehead.

She bolted upright, her gaze bouncing off the walls of the strange room. No strands of ShantiMari could be seen here, which gave her small comfort. What caused her great distress, however, was the realization that although Stephan had closed the Narthvier's borders, both on land and above the canopy, she had been able to portal in without any issues.

If she was able to, so was Myrddin. Where the hell was that traitor? And how could she keep the Narthvier safe from him? Her heart pinched as she thought of Brandt. What had her grandfather thought of Myrddin's betrayal? He must've been devastated. Even in death, it would've hurt to learn your best friend had not just duped you, but everyone you loved.

Myrddin would answer for his sins, most definitely.

CHAPTER FOURTEEN

Glass fragments and a mysterious dusting of black glitter covered most of the desk. Papers strewn haphazardly covered the rest. Myrddin reached for the broken looking glass and hesitated. A faint trace of Taryn's ShantiMari remained, enough so that it made him wary of touching the thing. He scrubbed a hand over his face and mourned the loss of his beloved looking glass. That Taryn had discerned what it was vexed him to no end.

No one in all his long seasons had ever discovered he was spying on them through the little glass baubles he'd given as gifts. Yet somehow, she had.

He'd underestimated her, as had everyone else. Everyone except Brandt and Rhoane. His two dearest friends. His two fiercest foes.

Soft snores came from the lone bed in the chamber and he slid a withering glance to Kane. The stupid boy had gone and gotten himself killed by the Eleri prince and now Kaldaar thought he would make an excellent Shadow Assassin. Once again, Myrddin was called upon to babysit the would-be lethal enemy.

Bugger. The boy went by Cashiel now. He'd do well to remember this fact for it made Kaldaar angry to hear his given name. Although why, Myrddin couldn't understand. Whether "Kane" or "Cashiel," he was a weapon to the god, nothing else. A dead weapon that snored when he slept. Bloody fucking hell, how had it come to this?

Kaldaar knew a Shadow Assassin was best utilized once they'd gone through all the stages of death. Cashiel had still been warm when Kaldaar claimed him and brought him back from the first stages of death. The stupid boy still craved food and rutting. What was he supposed to do with an immature weapon such as this?

He planted his fists on his hips and arched backward to release the cricks in his muscles. He'd been cooped up too long in this blasted cavern. Yes, fine, he was hiding from Kaldaar, but still, a man needed fresh air, good food, and the sun every so often. And possibly the company of a lively partner for play of a sexual nature.

Even as the thought crossed his mind, his cock stirred and an image of Lliandra scraped across his skull. His Lliandra. His Light. His Love.

She was the only woman he'd ever loved, and now he'd lost her for all time. He placed a hand on his heart to steady its rampant thumping. It was a small relief to know his heart wasn't completely broken. Never in his life had he believed himself capable of loving someone as much as he'd loved Lliandra. Still loved her, if he was honest with himself. Would always love her.

Kaldaar had tricked him, seduced the one woman Myrddin thought would never betray him. Everyone was for sale, it seemed. What had Kaldaar promised her? He scoffed at the answer. The god most likely told Lliandra she would have everlasting life and the beauty of her youth. The empress was vain enough to believe the god's lies.

Had Myrddin ever believed Kaldaar? Yes, most certainly. But

not for many, many seasons. Instead, he'd believed his own lies.

His gaze went again to the sleeping form. They couldn't hide here forever, and now that Taryn had replaced the seals in the Temple of Ardyn, Kaldaar would be even more desperate to see her dead. He'd been wise to set his own alarms into the pillars at the temple, a fact that brought him very little solace. They'd alerted him to Taryn's actions, but he was impotent to stop her. And now, Rykoto was even more removed from Kaldaar's plans than before.

Oh, Kaldaar must be fuming. It was for the best he was blocked from the god in this cavern. There was a time when he might've gleefully done his god's bidding, but now his heart was conflicted. Chaos and manipulation were always part of him. He lived for it, thrived on it. Never the one in charge, but always the one whispering in the leader's ear. Always in the shadows, never the spotlight. Stirring the pot once brought him the same kind of euphoria as an orgasm. It was his drug. His addiction.

Perhaps he was getting old, or the game was no longer fun, but he tired of the constant anxiety that came with keeping track of his various schemes. It was akin to juggling a dozen or more balls, some glass, some stone, but all of them equally important. If one fell, all the others were in jeopardy. It was taxing not just on his physical state but on his mental and, apparently, emotional well-being. Four thousand seasons old and he was finally understanding what it meant to care for others.

The scent of cigar tobacco wafted to him and he hid a wry smile.

"I never pegged you for a coward, Alswyth Myrddin. Yet here you are, cowering from your god with a broken boy as your only plaything."

Myrddin turned to see Brandt gliding across the small pool of water that was the only entrance to or from the hidden cavern. His corporeal form waned in and out of solidity and for a moment Myrddin wondered if he'd been sent by Nadra, or if his old friend was breaking the rules by visiting him. He suspected the former, but hoped for the latter. Despite everything he'd done, he missed Brandt's company.

Brandt picked up a shard of glass and turned it over in his hand. "Doing some redecorating?"

Myrddin was about to warn him to be careful, then realized a ghost had no need to worry about slicing a palm.

"Taryn destroyed it when she was here with Rhoane rooting through my things, stealing my notes on portals."

"Which, if I recall, was exactly what you wished for. Pity, though. It was such a lovely looking glass. One that could've been used for good instead of your nefarious purposes."

"Did you come all the way from Dal Tara to chastise me, or is there a reason for this impromptu visit?"

Brandt glanced at the sleeping lad with a grimace that said he didn't approve of Kaldaar's latest project. "Cashiel will make a terrible Shadow Assassin, but who am I to tell a god he's wrong?"

"Believe me, I've tried. He no longer listens to reason." Myrddin straightened a pile of papers and sat his ass on the edge of the desk. "Tell Nadra she has nothing to fear from him."

Brandt chortled and looked him full in the face. "I doubt she's worried at all. Taryn replaced the seals—which, I might remind you, were heavily warded and spelled with a riddle you believed would take her much longer to solve. No, Nadra's concern right now is what you'll do. Whose side will you fight on when the time comes?"

Myrddin scraped a hand through his hair and sighed. "I've been an agent of dread for so long, who am I without my tools?"

"If by 'tools' you mean lying, betrayal, misdirection, manipulation, and deceit, then I would argue that without those, you might be a decent man. Your hiding here doesn't help Taryn, it only delays the inevitable." Brandt drifted closer to Cashiel and bent low to whisper in his ear. Whatever he said, Myrddin couldn't hear.

"And what is 'the inevitable?' Taryn's death?"

Brandt motioned for him to follow and walked to the far side of the cavern where Myrddin kept a trunk full of old clothes and trinkets from his travels. Nothing of value was in the sturdy leather box, but his anxiety spiked all the same.

"Taryn will die, it's true. But not by your hand, I hope. Come, I want to show you something." Brandt held out his hand for Myrddin to take.

The moment their skin touched, they were no longer in the cavern, but in a vast land of roiling rivers the color of blood. Geysers spewed orangish liquid that fed into cracks in the black ground. Myrddin knew this place, but had always believed it to be a myth. Sort of like Dal Tara, even though Brandt's presence could only mean the home of the gods was real. Which meant Dal Ferran was real, too.

"Why have you brought me here? Do you wish to show me a living hell so that I might become the man you wish me to be?" Myrddin scoffed, and waved his arm wide. "This doesn't frighten me."

"Then you're a fool." Brandt moved effortlessly over the terrain, ignoring the flowing lava that should've singed his shoes. "Look closer, my old friend. Tell me what you truly see."

He followed Brandt, being careful where he placed his feet, and did as asked. His gaze took in the blackened earth, the burning rivers, and the spray of the geysers—but beyond these things he saw misery and death. As he stepped over a shallow flow of reddish-orange, a face contorted in agony floated beneath him. Another followed, and one more until he could no longer discern individual faces from the hundreds of bodies that drifted from one flow to the next.

These were the trapped souls of those who followed Kaldaar, his Telraicht Noir Brotherhood. This was where he'd end up when he died. It didn't matter which side he fought for in the end —this was always to be his fate. It came with the oath he made to

Kaldaar when he was just a lad. Seeing the truth of his situation did little to persuade him to the side of goodness. A few moon-turns of doing the right thing wouldn't erase millennia of dark deeds.

He glanced up at the sky, but there was no sun, no stars, only charred roots that dangled through a blackened ceiling of earth. He rubbed his arms, suddenly chilled in the inferno of Dal Ferran.

"Are we beneath the surface of Aelinae?"

"For now." Brandt's grave stare gave Myrddin shivers.

"This is what Kaldaar wants all of Aelinae to become?"

His old friend nodded, sadness pulling his features low. "This is Rykoto's prison for now, but Kaldaar plans to slaughter his brother and eat his still-beating heart to gain his strength. When Taryn replaced the seals, she effectively weakened Rykoto and once Kaldaar realizes what she's done, he'll become even more desperate for revenge."

The shocking news stunned Myrddin, and for a few moments he couldn't find his voice. "He doesn't know? But how? I thought Zakael was his snitch."

It was inconceivable that the god wasn't aware of what had happened at the Temple of Ardyn. Had Taryn somehow warded the entire building to keep Kaldaar from seeing or hearing what transpired inside?

"He's otherwise occupied at the moment." Brandt led them over more rivers and past several mounds of what Myrddin hoped weren't bones but knew probably were.

A flickering caught his attention and he turned to the right to investigate the source. Ahead of him, perhaps one hundred paces or so, was what looked like a rip in blue fabric. A few steps further in, he saw it was indeed a tear, but had nothing to do with clothing. Steam hissed and rose in menacing spirals where the lava flow of Dal Ferran met the seas of Aelinae.

"Do you understand what this is?" Myrddin said, hesitant to

move closer. "To become fully realized, Kaldaar needs the blood and the blade of the one who is and who is not—Taryn and her sword, yes, but he also needs the tear of Aelinae. Is this the place where Kaldaar holds his power?"

Brandt floated to the steaming rift. There seemed to be some kind of barrier that prevented the seas from flooding the molten land, yet Brant reached out to place his ghostly hand into the water. "I hadn't thought of that possibility. I always thought the tear was something tangible—not as in an actual tear from Nadra's eye, but something physical to represent one? It's vexed me for ages and annoys me that I can't figure out the riddle." Brandt shook he hand to dispel the water that dappled his skin. "In any case, we should strive to keep Kaldaar far from this place until we're certain."

"*We?* We're a team now?"

Brandt returned to him, his face shadowed by sorrow. "I always believed we were." He flicked a glance toward the earthen ceiling. "Will you continue to hide in your cavern like a coward? Or will you face your god? The choice is yours, old friend."

Myriad emotions swirled through Myrddin's veins and he struggled to keep them in check. Remorse bubbled to the surface more than once, as did fear.

"After four thousand seasons of life, I admit I'm afraid to die."

Brandt nodded his understanding. In a way, it was because of Myrddin that Brandt was dead. If he hadn't taken Taryn away from Aelinae, he would still be alive.

"Death isn't so bad once you get used to it. Although, I suspect you wouldn't be invited to Dal Tara." His gaze went to the grizzly scene beneath the surface of a nearby river of lava. "Or maybe I'm wrong. Stranger things have happened."

Myrddin's snort served as answer. Kaldaar fed on misery and wouldn't stop until Aelinae was his own personal hell. Myrddin knew what his choice must be, but that didn't stop him from being terrified.

CHAPTER FIFTEEN

gain, Kaldaar whispered in his mind, and Zakael flinched from the word. They'd been at it since the previous day when the god had magnanimously gifted the virgins to Zakael for one purpose: to get them both with child. They would be Kaldaar's vessels and carry Telraicht Noir children in their wombs until the god no longer had need of them. But first, they had to conceive.

Whatever offspring they produced would belong to Kaldaar, including any male heirs that could inherit the Obsidian Throne. Zakael had never given much thought to an heir until Marissa made him believe her child was his, and now that he was being forced to beget his children with these two women, it made him realize how naïve he'd been about his future. Who would sit on his ancestral throne if he died? He had no heir, no partner, no one.

Focus, Zakael.

He snapped his attention to the women, to his own movements, and lost himself in the task at hand. If only he could abuse them a little, perhaps that would keep him interested, but Kaldaar had forbidden any sort of deviant play. His precious vessels were to be pristine, pure, even though everything Zakael knew of the women suggested they'd be equally as interested in his type of sexual activities.

Servants came and went, bringing food or running baths, but never under Zakael's command. The god had worn him down such that he stopped being angry that Kaldaar had taken control of his castle. Each time his mind wandered, Kaldaar would whip him with his power until his cock engorged enough he could once again fuck the young women.

He rolled atop one of them, having forgotten their names just as he'd tried to forget their faces, and plunged his abused member into the waiting pussy. Her cry was of surprise, not pain. A fact he was certain annoyed Kaldaar. Within two strokes, he felt the god's ShantiMari slithering along his cock, fucking the woman along with him. The first time it had happened, he'd been offended, but with each successive time, he came to expect it, almost welcomed the feel of Kaldaar's Telraicht Noir ShantiMari coiled around his cock. Now he understood what Marissa had meant when she'd begged him to wrap his Shanti around her naked skin. It gave him a buzz as if he'd drunk too much ale. If he wasn't careful, he'd become addicted to the feeling, which he expected was exactly what the god wanted.

While he grunted and rammed himself against his willing partner, the other woman writhed on the bed, either through her own self pleasuring or from something Kaldaar was doing, Zakael couldn't tell. The god had kept himself hidden from the women during their play sessions, most likely to keep from frightening them with his hideous appearance. Such a small mercy, but one Zakael was secretly grateful for.

The writhing woman's heavy breasts flopped toward him as she squirmed and bucked. Her eyes met him with an unspoken plea of need. Not one to ignore an invitation, he bent to suckle a nipple. Her moans grew louder, encouraging him to bite into her flesh. The lass beneath him giggled and fondled her playmate's naked breast before stretching her neck to give her a noisy kiss.

They might've been virgins when Kaldaar brought them to his rooms, but after more than a day and night of fucking, sucking, nibbling, and licking, they could easily work for Nena at her whorehouse in Talaith. At the thought of the madam, his blood raced and some of his old longings for pleasure mixed with pain resurfaced.

Thus far, he'd been humping and pumping as Kaldaar ordered, but if the deranged god truly wanted Telraicht Noir offspring, it would take more than this gentle lovemaking. Kaldaar had demanded violence, but then changed his mind once he'd broken their virginal seals. A fact that had confused Zakael, but when he questioned the god, he was met with a command for obedience and the matter was dropped.

The women continued to suck each other's tongues in a vulgar display of lust that was exactly what Zakael needed to spill his seed. He ground into the woman's slick channel, pulling Kaldaar's ShantiMari deeper into her with each thrust, and came with a groan loud enough to be heard throughout the kingdom. For several moments he hovered above her, his breaths coming in ragged drags. She ignored him as she twisted to better reach her playmate.

His arms shook as he rolled off her and sat on the edge of the bed. "I need a bath, food, and rest. Then I shall make certain you get what you desire." He spoke to Kaldaar, but both women made an excited squealing sound.

They had no idea what he was capable of, but soon would. After he was rested, he'd take them to the dungeons where softness was not allowed. Even before he lifted from the bed, the women were entangled in each other's bodies. The one he'd just fucked had turned herself to better accommodate the other's mouth, which was presently devouring the seed he'd just spilled into her womb.

For half a second, he debated joining them, but decided to give them one last afternoon of pleasure. Once they were in his hidden playroom, there would be no rutting between the two. They would serve him and only him until they were either with child, or dead.

He arched his back and cricked his neck on his way to the bathing chamber. It felt good to be himself again. Thinking clearly. Thinking for himself. He'd get the deed done on his terms. Deviousness was in his blood.

Hot water sloshed around him as he slid into the tub. The little nicks and cuts Kaldaar had given him burned for only a moment before the soothing warmth took over. Maybe he would take the women to Gaarendahl instead of the dungeon. There he wouldn't have Kaldaar constantly hovering, popping up at inconvenient times. The game amused the god, but Zakael was tired of the constant surveillance, the having to explain his every move. A trip to Gaarendahl was exactly what he needed. His body relaxed into the tub as he mentally made preparations for the trip.

"They are as yet barren. What is your plan for impregnating them?" The bodiless voice came from his left, jolting him out of his pleasant mood.

He wasn't ready yet to tell his plan to the unpredictable god. Not until he had an ironclad argument for leaving Caer Idris.

"Fucking them with violence, isn't that what you originally said? Perhaps you should allow me to do what I do best. Be a love and wash my back, will you? All that power you so enjoy scraping along my skin has made it tender." He knew Kaldaar couldn't refuse the opportunity to cause him more pain.

As he'd hoped, a sponge appeared from seemingly nowhere and vigorously scrubbed his back, neck, and nethers. Zakael moaned and ahhhed appropriately, all the while plotting his escape.

"You haven't told me what happened at the temple. I sensed a disturbance. Was there any issue with Rykoto?"

Blood and ashes. He'd completely forgotten about Taryn setting the seals and the way she'd shushed Rykoto into silence.

"Haven't I? Well shame on me. Oh, that's right, you interrupted me with your delightful gift." He settled further into the water, accustomed now to Kaldaar's scouring. "When I arrived at the temple, Taryn was there. She'd already returned the seals to their proper columns and when I confronted her about it, she said it wasn't my business and that I could fuck off. Then she left."

The sponge stopped midway up his thigh. "She replaced the seals? All of them?" An ominous tone cut Kaldaar's words and Zakael stifled a shudder.

"I believe so. I didn't count them. I was more concerned that Rykoto ignored my command to come forth."

"Did he?" The voice trailed off somewhere to his right, near the window. The sponge forgotten. It bobbed to the surface and Zakael casually took ownership of the wretched thing.

Kaldaar's hazy form appeared, much less solid than it had been previously. Zakael's interest piqued, he watched the god for signs of vulnerability. All the time spent in sensual play must've depleted his reserves, something Zakael was keen to remember.

"I made certain the torch was lit and had plenty of fuel, but he refused to answer." He shrugged as if it were a puzzle. "Should I return tonight and bring him a meal? It's been some time since he's fed, as per your instructions."

"I was hoping if we starved him, he'd be more compliant." A wispy finger rubbed Kaldaar's disgusting lips. "First Myrddin goes missing, and now Rykoto." The finger pointed at Zakael. "And you're sure this isn't the doing of your meddlesome sister?"

"Half-sister, and not even the good half." His chuckle was met with a stare. "What could Taryn possibly do? She's just a stupid Aelan girl." He repeated Kaldaar's favorite lie. Taryn was so much more than a girl, but he wasn't about to tell the god just how powerful she was. He could discover that on his own. "What do you mean Myrddin is missing? Didn't you send him to kill Taryn and bring you her still-beating heart?"

"Mmmm, yes, but he's vanished. All I can guess is that Taryn somehow controls the void and he's gotten himself trapped elsewhere." The god's translucent shape warbled like the ripples of water on a pond after a stone's been tossed against its clear surface.

Zakael buried his surprise and delight that Myrddin was at least for the moment not hunting his sister. The man had to be mad to try to hide from Kaldaar, so it must've been as the god suspected and Myrddin was off world. Or he was hiding and even more clever than Kaldaar gave him credit.

His mind spun with schemes and ideas, all revolving around using this information to his benefit. Once he was at Gaarendahl, he could think clearly. Kaldaar's oppressive presence obfuscated his mind.

He sank beneath the warm water as if to shield himself from the reality his life had become. He just needed to get away—to escape. But convincing Kaldaar would take finesse. If he made it look like it was the god's idea, even better. When he surfaced, Kaldaar's rank breath burned against his face.

"Your attack at Lake Oster was pitiful. We need more soldiers. Go to the other worlds and find dimwitted creatures to fight in my army. While there, look for Myrddin. If you see him, alert me immediately. Do not try to engage with him, and do not be seen. I will deal with the mage."

Alarmed at the prospect of losing his freedom yet again, he stuttered a barely audible reply.

"Stop mumbling, I can't understand your whimpering."

"How am I supposed to impregnate your vessels if I'm not here? I can't be in two places at once. Give me a fortnight with the women at Gaarendahl—alone—and if they aren't with child by the end of the two weeks, I'll happily go to any world you desire. While I'm gone, send the captain of my guard to the swamplands to study the beasts. They aren't accustomed to our style of warfare. Perhaps we need to learn their strengths to better exploit them." His mind whirled with possibilities, excitement building not just for his trip south, but for Kaldaar to finally understand that they couldn't just rip people from their home worlds and expect them to fight for the god.

Kaldaar's hand stroked Zakael's wet hair, his bony finger tracing along Zakael's mouth, pulling the lower lip at an odd angle. "My beautiful, deceitful boy. What scheme are you working now? You know I can't trust you on your own, and yet time down south might be just what you need to release your Telraicht seed." His crusted tongue swiped along Zakael's exposed gum, and he stifled a gag. "Your usefulness is waning. I would hate for you to disappoint me again."

Zakael endured the disgusting touch and belittling words. It was all part of Kaldaar's game to destroy his confidence, but the god didn't know that these were games Zakael had played since he was a lad.

With a sheepish nod, he waved a hand toward the door where the women could be heard pleasuring each other in the other room.

"You have no need to worry. I will do as you need. Now go so that I might recover my stamina to do your bidding since you so obviously cannot." The last was not meant to be spoken aloud. As soon as the words slipped past his lips, he regretted them and prayed the god hadn't heard.

A thread of ShantiMari wrapped around his throat and squeezed with brutal efficiency. Zakael panicked and tried to gulp in much needed air, but that only made matters worse. His head pounded as if it might explode. His heart spasmed in his chest, and his vision clouded. He clutched at the god's power but couldn't wrench away its grasp. From far away he heard Kaldaar berating him, calling him a child and cursing him to the depths of Dal Ferran.

Another thread of the god's power slammed up his rectum, and a third plunged into his gaping mouth. The twisted Shanti-Mari spread throughout his body, violating not just his orifices, but his veins and vital organs. The room reeled and his vision turned red as blood pooled in his eyes.

He'd gone too far this time. Been too concerned with his own plans and for one brief moment given his innermost thoughts a voice. He thrashed in the tub, sloshing water everywhere as he kicked and writhed to escape the hold Kaldaar had on his throat. On his very life.

What a terrible way to die, naked in the tub, alone. For one pathetic moment, he allowed himself pity that he truly had no one to mourn him.

As the light faded, he stopped fighting and let the water buoy his body. He drifted as if on a cloud, peaceful. A face came to him, not of his sister Taryn, but another. A face he'd not thought of in many seasons. A face he'd savagely forced himself to forget.

CHAPTER SIXTEEN

A soft knock brought Taryn out of a nightmare-fueled, fitful sleep. Aelinae being torn apart from blood-hued volcanoes and pregnant virgins featured heavily in her dreams, each ending in horrific deaths. Hers? Theirs? She wasn't sure, nor did she wish to linger too long on them. Strangely, she recalled seeing Zakael's terror-stricken face as he descended into the depths of a watery grave. For several heartbeats, she debated reaching out to him, but it was just as likely a trap as a dream. Still, she couldn't shake the sense that something bad had happened to him.

Another knock and she sat upright, blinking at the unfamiliar surroundings. Was she dead? The cocoon-like gossamer room might've been heaven, or hell if she was claustrophobic. It took a minute to register where she was, who she was, and what the hell she was doing there. She'd had too much wine the night before with Carga. Ah, yes, she was at Verdaine's temple.

She flopped a hand beside her and breathed a heavy sigh when she felt Kaida's form beneath the blanket. Rhoane was in Aerithilyn with Aislinn and the dragons. It all came back to her in a rush, including her final thought before passing out from exhaustion the night before. She'd puzzle through the portal situation later. It wasn't something she could discuss with Carga, but hopefully Rhoane would arrive soon and together they would find answers.

A throbbing on her arm drew her attention and she ran a finger over the rough edges of the blackened scab. Carga had promised to find an ointment for her, but she had a feeling this wound would require more than herbs and good wishes.

Another, more insistent knock sounded, and Taryn rolled out of bed. Brushing off her rising concerns, she shuffled to the door and pressed her face against the strange solidness of the leaf.

"Yes?"

"The High Priestess bade me wake you so that I could tell you all that Gwainne and I learned about the Jansen Strait."

Gwainne? High Priestess? It took her groggy brain a moment to realize she meant the Ullan prince and Carga.

"Give me a sec. I'll be right there."

She pulled on a soft flowy gown that hung near the bed. The fabric brushed against her skin in a silken caress. On the floor were a pair of short boots made of what looked like suede. Carga must've brought the clothing while Taryn slept. Or they were there last night, and she was too knackered to see them.

She gave Kaida a light kiss on her muzzle and wished her sweet dreams before she left the room to begin her day.

A pretty Eleri woman waited for her in the walkway. Her short spiky hair caught Taryn's attention first, followed by her height. As tall as an average human woman, she was quite short by Eleri standards.

"I am Khrystina. Please follow me."

Before Taryn could introduce herself, Khrystina turned and walked down the hallway. Taryn spied several streaks of color woven through her platinum locks. What an unusual, intriguing woman her guide was. She'd never met an Eleri who willingly wore their hair short, but she wouldn't be allowed at the temple if she was sheanna. Taryn tempered the questions that banged against her skull.

"We shall break our fast in the library so that we may start our work as soon as possible." Khrystina turned down several hallways before abruptly leading them down a spiral staircase that seemed to go on forever.

Taryn followed in silence, unsure if she'd done something to upset the woman, or if she was always this brusque. By the time they reached the final floor, Taryn's thighs burned, a reminder that she'd been lax in her training. Khrystina, it appeared, was in top form. Only a slight hitch to her breath gave away her efforts.

"This way. Please do not touch anything."

Taryn took a moment to look around the library, which was built within a cavern beneath the great tree above. Alcoves of neatly stacked shelves were tucked between thick roots, and the walls were a mixture of crystals, like those found in the cavern at Mount Nadrene, and limestone. Desks dotted the space, but there was no rhythm to their placement. In the center of the vast space was a small lake, its waters pale blue and clear, again like the one at Mount Nadrene.

Taryn took long strides to catch up to the woman. "Doesn't the water hurt the scrolls?"

"Quite the opposite. We use the water along with ShantiMari to control the temperature and moisture so that the books and scrolls are kept perfectly preserved. We will work here. This is pleasing to you, yes?" She pointed to a large desk already over-flowing with papers.

Khrystina's logic made no sense to Taryn, but she'd found with most things on Aelinae it was better not to question logic, or physics, or anything Earth would consider unnatural. She was a motherfucking dragon—what logic was there in that?

She nodded to the Eleri, a little surprised she'd asked after her comfort.

A much taller Eleri approached with a tray and Taryn swooned with giddiness even before she'd set it down.

"Oh, how I've missed you." She took a mug of grhom and held it close to her face to inhale the spicy chai chocolate scent. Her stomach gave an appreciative gurgle and she took a luxurious sip. "It's delicious. Please thank the cook for me."

"You can thank her yourself," Carga said from behind the woman. The servant left them and Carga came into full view. Dressed in a gown similar to Taryn's, but pale blue where Taryn's was white, her long dark hair framed her lovely heart-shaped face. "I thought you might appreciate a welcome start to your day, early as it is."

"You thought right. Thank you." Taryn took a longer drink, delighting taste and feel of the thick chocolate.

The warmth of the grhom filled her belly and flowed through her veins, invigorating her with renewed energy. Her mind cleared as the last bit of exhaustion left her. As promised, Carga dressed her burn with a salve before wrapping it in gauze. The pain remained the same, but she lied and told the high priestess it helped immensely. She wouldn't drag Carga into her nightmarish life more than necessary.

Carga eyed her skeptically, then gave a curt nod before indicating the papers on the desk. "While Gwainne was here only a short time, he and Khrystina found some intriguing information about the Jansen Strait. Once the prince left for Talaith, Khrystina continued their studies. I believe you will find what she discovered quite remarkable."

Taryn picked at her breakfast while Khrystina gave a recap of her and Gwainne's time together. She gave a brief history of the strait, originally called King Jansen's Strait in honor of the king who created it to keep ships from crashing on rocks, or something like that. Khrystina rushed through that part and Taryn wasn't entirely sure she understood how an Ullan king could create a divide in the sea. Nor did she sense King Jansen was pertinent to her path.

Something Gwainne discovered, however, was. He'd found a scroll with ominous scribblings in the margins. Khrystina pushed a page toward Taryn and she skimmed the contents, her blood chilling with each sentence.

Written in a deliberate hand without the flourishes of the main content of the page were the words, "Heed ye not to where travels are borne, but to the place where worlds are torn." Taryn ran a finger across them, but nothing came to her of the author or their meaning, although she could guess.

Then, farther down the page in the same tight handwriting were the words, "Travelers be warned, the witch queen be scorned. Only the one who is and who is not shall straddle the line."

She blew out a breath and closed her eyes. This she understood perfectly. They referred to her and Mallaqai—but what did it mean? Mallaqai was scorned by whom? Rykoto? Then that would fit with her suspicions that Mallaqai might've been trying to save the dragons. Which line did the words refer to? The void? The Wall? There were too many possibilities.

"Prince Gwainne and I also discovered one legend involving the Jansen Strait that had to do with a scar in Aelinae's terrarae. Though, we could never find more on this, nor did we understand what it might mean."

Taryn perked up—a scar echoed what she saw in her visions the previous night. "I think I might know. What else did you learn?" Fully invested now, she focused on the young woman.

Khrystina shifted under her scrutiny and twisted a lock of hair until it curled like a tiny horn. "After the prince left, I found another legend, this said to be from the merfolk." She snorted with a look of derision. "Which we all know do not exist, but I thought it intriguing enough to make a copy for the prince. We had a whole parcel ready to send to him, but then King Stephan locked our borders."

"I'm here now, so you don't need to send him anything. But I would very much like to know the merfolk story."

It wasn't so much a tale as a warning. Taryn listened intently as Khrystina recounted the legend of a sapling who lived on the terrarae and a star in the heavens. Day after day they watched each other, falling more and more in love, until one day the star dove to the terrarae and the sapling caught her. They tumbled into the sea, where a miracle happened. The sapling became a man, and the star became a woman. In the warm waters, they consummated their love.

When night fell, there was no moon, and no stars in the sky. The next day, the flora and fauna of the terrarae began to die.

The sapling and star were horrified to realize what they'd done. It was their duty to look after the terrarae and the heavens, even if that meant they couldn't be together. In great sadness, the star returned to the sky and the sapling the terrarae.

Taryn chewed her thumbnail, the story churning in her mind. "I take it Rhoane is the sapling, and I am the star, but we're together and the world hasn't devolved to ruin. Not yet, at least." She snorted a sad little chuckle. "Is that the end of it? Or is there more to the story? I'm trying to understand the metaphor but feel I'm missing something."

Khrystina pushed a stack of papers toward her. "There are perhaps a dozen endings. None of them make sense unless you believe in darathi eneari and seafolk."

Taryn's hand hovered over the stack, her eyes intent on the spunky woman. "Tell me, do you believe in the Darennsai?"

Carga frowned and gave a quick shake of her head, but Taryn kept her inquisitive gaze on Khrystina. She could guess the girl's answer, and suspected more than a fair share of the novices upstairs echoed the novice's belief, but she wanted to hear it for herself.

Khrystina didn't bat an eyelash, nor did she appear flummoxed. "I believe our goddess believes in the Darennsai. Do I believe you are or could be this mythical person? I am not convinced."

"Fair enough. What would it take to convince you?" Taryn sipped her grhom more to give her a moment to calm the rapid beating of her heart. If she could convince the sceptics, then she might have luck getting Stephan to release the protective wards on the Narthvier.

"Nothing."

Taryn choked on her drink. She'd expected Khrystina's answer to come in the form of a request—some grand gesture of power or turning herself into her dragon form, perhaps—not blunt denial. "If there's nothing that will convince you, then how am I to prove I am who Verdaine says I am?"

"You do not try to *prove* anything. You exist and do what is necessary." She twisted a lock of hair, giving her a second horn to match the first. It was difficult to be angry with a woman who looked like a devilish pixie.

"Well that's a fancy conundrum." Taryn took a longer gulp of grhom, puzzling through Khrystina's statement. "It's not about whether you believe, is it? It's about what I believe."

Khrystina nodded, the tiniest of smiles lifting her lips. "I am an academic. It is my job to study the evidence not to form an opinion of what I believe, but to find the truth in all the variables. I am sorry to say, we may only know the truth of whether you are the true Darennsai *after* you have made your choices. And even then, what if they are not the choices that benefit Eleri? Then are you not the Darennsai, but a pretender? If we place our trust in a fickle prophecy, we risk being disappointed."

"Whoa, that's some heavy logic you're throwing at me. But I can't fault it." Taryn leaned forward until she was mere inches from both women. "The truth is, I don't know if my choices will benefit the Eleri. When the time comes, I will do what's right for all Aelinae, without favoring one race over the other. In order for Aelinae to thrive as a cohesive world, all races need to live in harmony."

Carga smiled serenely and took Taryn's hand. "That is all we can hope for."

There was hidden meaning in her words, and Taryn was reminded of the night before when Carga told her she had something important to share. If her brain wasn't crammed with all she'd learned about the Jansen Strait, she might've asked if Carga wished to talk privately, but instead she excused herself. She had a belly full of grhom and needed to empty her bladder.

"Will you take me with you?" Khrystina blurted as Taryn stood.

She looked from the rogue Eleri to Carga, confusion drawing her brows low. "To use the facilities? I'm pretty sure I can do that on my own."

"No," Khrystina's cheeks pinked and it delighted Taryn to see that she did have emotions buried beneath her academic posturing. "To Talaith, if that is where you are going." She lowered her gaze, her hands clasped tightly in her lap.

"That's not my decision to make." Nor was she sure she wanted a young, inexperienced novice tagging along to the gods knew where. Taryn looked to Carga. "You should ask your High Priestess, not me."

Carga ran a finger along her jaw, her eyes distant. "Let me consider your request, Novice Khrystina. I will give you my decision in the morning, if I have permission from the Darennsai and the Surtentse." The use of their titles was deliberate and Taryn felt the importance of Carga's decision.

"If your High Priestess decides in your favor, we can take you as far as Talaith, but after that, I don't know where our journey will lead." To Carga, Taryn said, "She does realize outside the borders of the Narthvier is a wilderness full of danger, right? Is she in any way prepared for it?"

Carga shook her head slowly. "She is an academic who has never lifted a weapon, as far as I know."

"I am sitting right here, you know." Khrystina folded her arms over her chest. "I can take care of myself. Intelligence is far stronger than a dagger."

Taryn stuck her arm out and called forth her sword. A moment later it materialized in her hand and she lunged at the Eleri. The blade stopped just below her chin and Taryn stuck her face close to Khrystina's. The woman's visage lost what little color it had, taking on an ashen hue. Her eyes grew large and dark and filled with fear.

"Tell me, how will book learning save you when a blade is at your throat? You have zero seconds to think, you must react because trust me, whoever is holding that dagger or sword or knife doesn't give a fuck about how smart you are." Taryn withdrew and flicked her wrist to send her sword back to her room. "If you come with us—and that's a big 'if' at the moment—you will train with me and learn to defend yourself. That's non-negotiable. I won't be responsible for your death."

She stormed away before the others could speak. Why hadn't she outright said no? Hell no. Fuck no. She didn't need the woman slowing them down, and that's exactly what she would do. Then why?

Despite her reservations, she knew the answer—she understood the importance of the Eleri living outside the boundaries of the vier. And if a sceptic like Khrystina could see the value in that, then Taryn was one tiny step closer to world peace. Even if it annoyed the hell out of her.

CHAPTER SEVENTEEN

Mist shrouded the valley, but Rhoane knew that beneath the covering, hundreds of darathi were waking to a new day, a new future. He and his mother had brought Aelinae's darathi to Aerithilyn without any problems, a fact that gave him small comfort. The king and queen had been delighted to see so many come through the portal, their expressions one of joy until the reality of what Aelinae's darathi had suffered over thousands of seasons became too apparent to dismiss.

They were little more than scale and bones compared to Aerithilyn's healthy darathi. Princess Cassia openly sobbed as the last of the herd came through, as did Lady Amaleigh. Promises were made to care for the beasts, to feed them and nurture them back to health, which was all Rhoane could ask for. Yet the king and queen had surprised him when they offered their own darathi to help in the war if needed. He hoped it wouldn't come to that but accepted their offer.

His mother took his hand in her own and gave a slight squeeze. "I will watch over them. They are safe here, Rhoane, surely you know this."

He did, and yet it was hard to leave. His darathi soul ached to join the others.

"I have never seen your darathi, not fully. I would catch glimpses when you flew close to the Wall, but always as shadow, never in full sunlight." Longing filled Aislinn's words, and she made a little sighing sound that he recognized from his youth. It was the same gesture she'd make when trying to convince his father to do something.

Flying would certainly feel good, but it also felt like a betrayal to Taryn. He kissed his mother's hand and smiled. "You will see our darathi when everyone is returned safely to Aelinae."

Aislinn took a deep breath and nodded. "I thought that might be your answer. You said your farewells last night. You are needed elsewhere. It is time to join your beloved." She kissed him on each cheek and held his face between her hands. "I am so proud of you, my son. Be safe on your journey."

He hugged his mother tight, not wanting to leave and feeling guilty because he knew he must.

Too much of his life had been lived feeling guilty about one thing or another.

"What do I tell Father?"

"Nothing. Act as if nothing has changed. If he knows I am alive, and living on another world, he will tear apart the galaxies looking for me. Right now, his focus needs to be on Aelinae and our people."

More lies. More guilt.

She smoothed his hair as she'd done so many times when he was a child. Her eyes searched his and he worried for what she might find. So much had happened in her absence.

Finally, his mother said, "When it is time, I will return with the darathi and then shall I make amends to those I hurt with my leaving."

"You have nothing to apologize for." Rhoane held her face between his hands, his heart aching. "It was my fault you left that day. I was being a temperamental brat who would not listen to reason. I caused you to almost destroy yourself. I am solely to blame."

"No, mi carae, nothing was not your fault. Do not carry this responsibility with you. Verdaine and I had planned that morning for quite some time. It was always supposed to happen this way. My path was to care for the exiled darathi, but Stephan never understood this."

Rhoane stared at his mother in shock. For more than six decades he'd hated himself for seemingly causing her death, and to now learn it had nothing to do with him brought up emotions he couldn't even name. His hands shook and his heart stuttered. Words stuck in his throat—curses, apologies, recriminations— but then an odd calmness overcame him, and he realized none of that mattered. His mother was alive. She'd done what she must for the sake of the darathi. He couldn't fault her for following her path when that was exactly what he'd done ever since the moment Verdaine had taken her from him.

He released his guilt and betrayal and hurt feelings to drift on the breeze. They had never served him, only caused great strife. It was a relief to let them go. "I am sorry you had to live in exile, but I am not sorry the darathi had you to love and care for them."

Her shoulders slumped and she let out a long shaky breath. "I thought you would hate me for knowing the truth. I know you blamed yourself, but I was impotent to stop your pain."

"I could never hate you." He embraced her hard, putting all his love and longing and forgiveness into the hug. Her arms wrapped around him and squeezed until he couldn't breathe. He didn't care. His mother was alive and the darathi were safe. Almost all was well in his life.

"You must go to your beloved, mi carae. Do not worry for us. I will look after our precious friends."

Rhoane relaxed his grip and stepped back with a sad nod. It

was time to go. The wind swept up his mother's hair and for a brief moment, it looked like a darathi wing expanding behind her. The cobalt dress she wore fluttered like waves on the shore. It made him think of Xianqin, which in turn made him homesick for Taryn.

There was still much to be done on Aelinae before his mother and the darathi could return.

Aislinn placed her forehead against his. "When next we meet, may it be in sweetness and not sorrow."

"When next we meet," Rhoane finished the saying.

He stepped away from the cliff's edge and turned away from the valley where he longed to join the other darathi. His hands shook as he raised them to open the portal. The first few times had gone well enough, but he'd had Taryn there in case something went wrong. He was alone now and would be the only one in the void. No grierbas to keep him safe, no Taryn to calm his nerves. He could do this; it was part of his path.

Why, then, did he suddenly feel inadequate?

The words slipped from his lips and he moved his hands in a circular movement Taryn said wasn't necessary, but doing so made him feel more in control of the dark opening that materialized out of nothingness. With a final wave goodbye to his mother, he stepped into the void.

It was different now that they had vanquished the snake-demon-dragon. Not as harrowing, yet just as silent. He kept the Weirren in his mind while searching his heart for where Taryn and Kaida might be found. Aelinae was vast—they could be anywhere.

Speak to me, mi carae, he sent the thought through time and space. *Show me where you are.*

A light shone in the distance and he quickened his pace to reach it. He stepped from the absolute darkness of the void into twilight. A forest surrounded him. His gaze took in the trees and lake. He knew this place, knew these trees as if they were his siblings. And there, on the banks of Lan Gyllarelle, was his love.

Taryn stood with Kaida on the shore of the lake. The white gown she wore, a filmy sort of garment that looked like it was made of spun clouds, billowed around her. In her hands she held Ynyd Eirathnacht and looked as if she were seeking answers from the sword. Kaida, ever protective, sat beside her, ears flicking and alert to danger. A moment later, she turned to look at him, her golden eyes shining in the dim light.

Rhoane nodded to Kaida and returned his gaze to Taryn. His breath caught, and he took a moment to regain his composure. In his heart, he'd always known what she would become, but seeing her now, he realized her fate was ever closer. Stars twinkled beneath Taryn's skin, and her silver hair flowed to her buttocks in cascading waves. She was more than a goddess. She was ethereal. She was everything.

You will betray her twice, and then you will kill her, Xianqin's warning pinged against his skull, and he swore against the invasive words.

"Yes, and Mallaqai ominously said two truths and one lie. Explain *that*, you tricksy darathi eneari," he mumbled to the empty air.

An image of their swords covered in blood—his and Taryn's—seared his mind.

Remember the words, a familiar voice whispered, and he struggled to place who said this, whose voice he was hearing. *Learn the song, Rhoane. Trust the swords.*

It wasn't Mallaqai who brushed his thoughts. Nor was it Xianqin. Then who? Black hair, skin of deepest brown, sadness in her eyes. He knew her. Daknys. The hilt of his sword glowed, and he gripped Claidholm Solais with both hands and inclined his head to the unseen goddess.

It was a stark reminder that he and Taryn fought to bring balance to Aelinae not just for those who called the world home, but for the gods and goddesses who, for whatever reason, could not save the planet on their own.

A chilling thought slithered down his spine. Why couldn't they, with all their power, fix what was broken and bring peace to Aelinae?

Because we were the ones who unbalanced the world, my darling. If we tried now, we might well destroy everything. Sadness lurked in Daknys's voice. *There would be no more Aelinae.*

Is there more I need to know? He feared he already knew the answer and that it would involve his and Taryn's paths.

Learn the song of the swords. It is part of your path.

Bollocks and snickertits. When he glanced at Taryn, he could've sworn he saw not just Daknys, but Julieta and Verdaine gathered around her as if they were protective mothers guarding their young. When he blinked, they were gone.

So as not to frighten Taryn, he stomped through the underbrush to alert her to his presence. A bit much, really, but she looked to be deep in thought and the last thing he wished for was to startle her. She looked up from her contemplation and her entire face lit up in a smile. With a flick of her wrist, the sword disappeared, and she ran to him, nearly crushing his ribs with her embrace.

"Finally! We've been here three days. I was beginning to think you got lost in the void." She planted several kisses on his cheek before moving to his lips. Instead of opening her mouth and inviting him in, she pressed her lips to his for far too brief a time, and then pulled back. "You didn't, did you? Get lost I mean? The void—it's still safe, right?"

"I had no trouble traversing the portals. I stayed longer than I had intended to make certain the darathi were settled."

"And the darathi in the vial? Is he—did he—?"

"You were exactly right in how to free him. He was confused at first, but when he saw the younglings—which you correctly guessed were his offspring—he was overjoyed to be reunited with them. I am confident Cassia and Amaleigh will be wonderful caretakers."

"And Aislinn?" She glanced behind him, a frown pulling her smile low.

"My mother insisted on staying with the darathi, which means we must not mention her to anyone."

Taryn nodded and chewed her bottom lip. "I understand her reasoning, but now we have the burden of hiding her existence. It's just one more thing I need to remember."

He ran his thumb across her forehead. "I could ease those memories if you wish. Then you would not have to bear this weight as well."

"I'll be fine." She half-chuckled, half-grunted. "It's fine. We're fine. Everything's fine."

Her tone suggested nothing was, in fact, fine. Something had happened while he was away; he could see it in the shadows of her eyes, the slight shake of her hands.

Kaida nudged his leg, and he bent to scratch between her ears. "I missed you, too. Did you keep Taryn out of trouble?"

She sneezed and shook her head, which he took to mean no. He was about to ask what they'd been up to, but Taryn slipped her dress over her shoulders and stood before him naked.

"Swim with me." She held out her hand, an invitation to follow. "Ease my burden."

It took him a few minutes more than her to undress, but he made quick work of untying his Eleri boots and stripping garments from his body. They jogged to the lake and waded into the warm water hand in hand. The lake was sacred to the Eleri, and he couldn't in all his memory recall anyone entering the waters unless they were being purified, yet somehow being there with Taryn felt right. If Verdaine or Lan Gyllarelle didn't wish for them to be in the hallowed waters, he was certain they would know.

They swam to the center of the lake where Taryn dipped beneath the surface. He waited only a heartbeat before following. Unlike the ocean, this water was fresh, and a fissure of panic raced through him that he wouldn't be able to breathe beneath the surface.

Relax, mi carae, Taryn's soothing voice echoed in his mind. *Breathe.*

He searched the dark depths but could not see her. Then, like a silver darathi eneari, she swam into view, her hair fanning around her in a glorious halo. She reached for him and pulled him close, her lips pressing into his. The warmth of her mouth begged him to open for her, but he resisted. The anxiety and panic he'd had since a child resurfaced even though he knew he was safe.

Finally, her tongue wedged between his lips, and he closed his mouth around hers. Air bubbles escaped their kiss, taking his fear with them. He could breathe fresh water the same as salt. Their hair entwined around them, making a screen of sorts that afforded them privacy from any creatures living in the water— not that he cared if they saw him making love to Taryn.

She mounted his erect cock and a moan vibrated up his throat to their kiss. Her long legs wrapped around him, and he rocked into her with building need. They spiraled and drifted as their pace increased. He ran his hands up her torso to her extended arms, his fingertips brushing her ghostly runes. They sparked and shimmered as usual, all except one.

A vision seared his mind, of blood-orange lava rivers that tore through Aelinae's terrarae. He cried out, breaking their kiss, and Taryn arched, driving her pelvis against him. Another vision— this one of blackened ground, the faces of the dead staring up at him—made his heart race and body shudder.

Stay with me, Rhoane. This is important. Do not stop making love. Taryn ground against him, and he gripped her arse to pull her tight so that he could drive his cock deeper. Her warmth enveloped him and he felt the stirrings of his release.

Taryn gripped his arms, her face a torment of pleasure and pain. All around them the vision played out, of ghastly volcanoes and rivers of the dead. From somewhere beyond the visions, he heard a familiar melody and grasped at the words.

> *In a world forgotten, lost in shadows deep,*
> *A tale of redemption begins to seep.*
> *From ashes we rise, like a phoenix in flight,*
> *Embracing the Darkness, reclaiming our Light.*

He knew the song, had heard it many times from Claidholm Solais, but could never make out the words. Why now?

Because we are ready to hear them, my love.

He held her tight and they tumbled in the water. Around and around they spun, making a tiny whirlpool. Their hair twisted like watery cyclones as they held each other, their bodies tangled together. Her breasts pressed against his chest with her gyrations, teasing, tantalizing. His hand slid from her arse to cup one in his palm. Her moan echoed in the water and she arched into his touch.

A flicker drew his attention to the vision—just there where the lava flow met the sea, he saw the tear in Aelinae's terrarae. Where exactly? Where was it, and how would they fix it?

Now, Rhoane. Please, Taryn panted in his thoughts.

His release came hard and fast, spilling into her womb, and into the lake. The whirlpool exploded with Taryn's release and she screamed into the watery depths.

Are you hurt?

Oh gods, no. Just the opposite. That was fucking amazing.

Her pussy clenched and pulsed against his cock, stirring him to excitement. Her held her face and kissed her deeper than he ever had before. His breath became hers, his heartbeat hers. They floated as one, slowly rising to the surface.

From the edge of his vision, he saw beyond the rift to the seas where a solitary shadow drifted, its long tail swishing with great force.

Their heads breached the lake's surface and he released his kiss with great reluctance. Taryn watched him with eyes the color of midnight. Her pale face scrunched with disgust and he knew she'd seen the same vision he had.

"We need to heal Aelinae."

"And we will."

If only they knew how.

CHAPTER EIGHTEEN

The Temple of Gyllaren, or Verdaine's temple as it is colloquially called, was similar to the other two temples Taryn had seen on Aelinae, each round with thirteen columns supporting a domed ceiling. Unlike those two, with their cold marble and silent interiors, this temple was built into the great tree that also housed the priestesses and novices. It wasn't used daily, but the few times Taryn had wandered into the space, there were several people either in quiet meditation or walking the outer ring. Today it was empty, save for her, Rhoane, and Kaida.

Carga had asked them to meet her there, but either they were early, or she was late. It gave Taryn time to fully appreciate the beauty of the temple. Light and airy like Aerithilyn, with arched windows high above, thick trunks served as columns, rising to the ceiling like grand sentries. Smaller branches from each trunk stretched to make a canopy through which sunlight filtered to the floor.

It reminded Taryn of the Elvenwood tree and her heart skipped a beat with the memory of what had happened inside the ancient elven palace. They'd recovered the seal Myrddin had cleverly hid in the tree, but had nearly lost their lives in the process.

She placed a hand over her chest to calm her heart's rampant thumping and breathed through the panic. They were safe. The seals were safe. They'd defeated Myrddin's traps. It was the same each time she thought of the trials they'd been through.

They were safe.

For now.

Her gaze took in the serenity of the temple and her breathing leveled, her heartrate slowed. How could anyone be stressed in such a gorgeous place? Rhoane took her hand and gave it a gentle squeeze. Sometimes she forgot he was in her thoughts.

"Tell me, how was it you made Ynyd Eirathnacht appear and disappear at Lan Gyllarelle?" He was clever to pull her attention away from her anxiety.

She grinned sheepishly and snapped her finger. Instantly, her sword vanished from its scabbard. Another snap, and it reappeared. "Amaleigh showed me when we were at Aerithilyn. Cool trick, right? I call it space storage. You think of a place in your mind—mine happens to be a lovely cupboard with about a dozen locks—and you send your items there. It's going to be wicked convenient when I have to wear a gown, but need my sword handy, don't you think? Far less obtrusive than just hiding them with shadows."

He chuckled low in his throat and her belly tightened at the sound. "Let me try." He picked up a leaf and held it with a frown. She could see the concentration on his features, and feel his Shanti, but something was off. When he snapped, the leaf fluttered to the ground, unimpressed by his actions.

"What did I do wrong?"

"You have to truly believe your items will be safe. Fully visualize where you're storing your items. This is your space, and yours alone. Try it again."

Once more he scrunched his face and focused on the leaf. This time, when he flicked his wrist, it disappeared. He looked at her with a wide smile.

"I did it."

"Yes, you did. Well done, my love." She kissed his cheek. "Now bring it back."

It took several tries, but he finally got the gist of how to do it properly. Having space storage would make their lives so much easier. No more wearing a sword to formal events. Need a crown but don't want to lug it everywhere? Space storage. She was quite impressed with the novel idea and had her new friend Amaleigh to thank for it.

A light drifted from the ceiling; one Taryn recognized immediately. Bursts of rust, green, and gold feathered out in rays of light that coalesced into the womanly form of Verdaine. She wore a silk gown of palest green, her crimson hair floating around her.

Rhoane sucked in a breath and knelt before the goddess. After a beat, Taryn did the same.

"Arise, my children," Verdaine commanded, and they both stood. Kaida nudged the goddess and was rewarded with gentle scratching atop her head. "I like the change, little dragon."

Kaida barked and sat beside Taryn, a self-satisfied grin on her grierbas lips. Heat spread across Taryn's chest and up toward her cheeks. Of course the goddess would know she'd given Kaida wings, but she was hoping to keep it secret a bit longer. Just until she figured out how to tell Rhoane.

Verdaine took Taryn's right hand in her own and ran a finger along the underside of her wrist where the burned rune cracked and oozed. She'd given up on the bandage as all it did was itch her mercilessly. The goddess then took Rhoane's left hand.

"Your bonds have strengthened admirably. It would be impossible for anyone—including a god—to break them now. This, however, causes me great concern." She tapped Taryn's burn.

"I don't know what it means. Usually, a rune appears after we complete a task or challenge, but this came after a vision I had in the lake, and I can't shake the sense that it involves something I need to do."

"*We* need to do," Rhoane added, and she gave him a grateful smile.

Verdaine harrumphed several times before releasing their hands. "You must meet Xianqin at the Jansen Strait. She will know what you must accomplish to heal the scar in Aelinae's terrarae."

"You know Xianqin?" The moment she asked, she felt a fool. Naturally a goddess would know an ancient creature that'd probably been around as long as the first seed of the Weirren was planted. "Dumb question. Do you think she'll ever have a mate? She's all alone out there and I worry about her."

Rhoane took her hand and squeezed. "We found our darathi —I am certain we will find a mate for Xianqin."

"Or," Verdaine cocked her head with a wink, "you could find another solution. A more immediate one that involves something the two of you do rather well."

Taryn scrunched her face in thought. "Find trouble? I'm not sure how that will help."

"I do not think she meant that." Rhoane gave her a look full of meaning and she stared at him, knowing there was something she was missing, but it escaped her.

Then it dawned on her, and she gasped, a look of shock raising her brows. "Oh. OH. You mean *dragon sex*. Would that work? I mean, we've never been darathi like that. Could we? Should we?"

"Darathi, Eleri, celestial, they are all the same. I have no doubt you will figure it out." A small chuckle came from the goddess. "It is lovely to see you are still innocent, darling Taryn."

She bent and kissed Taryn on the cheek. Warmth infused her and she felt light as air. Any ailments or exhaustion she'd had evaporated and a renewed sense that the impossible was possible filled her lagging spirits.

Verdaine smiled a secret little smile and turned to her attention to the grierbas. "Now, if you do not mind, dear Kaida, I would love to see you fly."

"What?" Rhoane choked, and looked straight at Taryn.

She shrugged and gave him an apologetic smile. "She really wanted wings. Who am I do deny a grierbas?"

Kaida barked and raced to the other end of the temple. They'd tried testing her wings near Lan Gyllarelle before Rhoane returned, but with the trees and water, Kaida wasn't able to get the lift needed. Here in the temple, she had a little more space, and Taryn suspected Verdaine would lend assistance if needed. Kaida's nails scraped on the stone floor as she scrambled to gain speed. A few moments later, her wings spread wide and the three of them gasped in unison.

"Go Kaida, you got this," Taryn murmured beneath her breath, encouraging her friend to fly.

"'Tis a strange thing you have done, but a kind thing, mi carae." Rhoane kissed her knuckles, and her knees wobbled.

Dragon sex. Who knew? The thought had never crossed her mind—but anything to heal Aelinae, right?

Rhoane chuckled and she hoped he'd been in her thoughts. His wicked half-grin confirmed he had.

With a giant leap, Kaida soared into the air, her wings flapping like a rabid chicken. They shouted encouragement, all three of them offering a bit of ShantiMari to help keep her aloft. Taryn saw her strands of power wrapped in Rhoane's, and recognized Verdaine's fall-hued threads as they enveloped Kaida's wings. Within two beats, she'd leveled out and flew in circles above their heads.

It was a cramped space for flying, but Kaida did a remarkable job of keeping calm and maintaining her speed. Every so often her legs would kick as if she were trying to run to the beat of her wings, but otherwise, she did brilliantly. Taryn watched like a proud mama and wondered what Kaida's mam and sire would think of their airborne daughter. Pride swelled in her heart and she knew they would be just as happy for Kaida as she was.

"I am late a few minutes and you turn a grierbas into…" Carga paused, her face contorted with confusion. "What is that, exactly?"

"She is Kaida," Verdaine stated before giving Carga an embrace. "Welcome, daughter."

Kaida made a less-than-graceful landing and jogged over to their small group.

It is not as easy as you make it seem. She panted the words and Taryn sent several strands of her power to Kaida to make certain she hadn't hurt anything.

It takes practice. Once we're out on the moors, it will be easier.

Kaida licked her hand and she buried her fingers in her fur. Once Rhoane and Carga said their hellos, Verdaine straightened and looked at Carga as if she was expected to speak.

The High Priestess twisted a lock of hair between her fingers for a long moment before giving Verdaine a pleading look. The goddess shook her head, and Carga cleared her throat. Tears shimmered in her gorgeous jade eyes.

"Very well." She looked at Taryn and Rhoane, her features set with a seriousness Taryn had only witnessed a few times. "I would like it to be known, I am making this confession against my better judgement. Verdaine sees merit in what I am about to tell you, but I do not."

Taryn took her hands in her own. "If it brings you sorrow to tell us, then don't."

Verdaine glanced at her and her insides chilled. "You must know, Darennsai. And you, Surtentse. I urge you to listen without judgement or complaint until Carga has finished."

The goddess's tone sent shivers down Taryn's spine. What could Carga possibly tell them that would warrant such a warning?

"We are here for you," Rhoane assured Carga and took one of her hands in his. The three of them stood together, connected by more than physical touch. "There is nothing you can say that will ever change our love for you."

Carga took a long breath and let out a sad little chuckle. "If only that were true, dearest brother. I daresay this news will test you both."

The temple walls dissipated and Taryn felt as though they were floating in a realm just outside of Aelinae. Verdaine hovered nearby, her goddess light embracing the small group. For protection? Privacy? Whatever it was, Taryn paid close attention and braced for the unexpected.

"Twenty-one summers past I met a man and fell in love," Carga started, and a buzzing irritated Taryn's belly.

She recalled a day a season or so past when she had sat in the kitchens of Paderau talking to Carga about what made her sheanna, and exiled her from the Eleri.

"This man, he used me to glean information about Taryn, but I did not care. He was beautiful with his dark hair and even darker ShantiMari. I did not know of his reputation; all I knew was that he made me feel things I had never felt before. When I was with him, I was alive for the first time in my life." Tears spilled over her cheeks and she snuffled against her shoulder to wipe them.

"Is this man what caused you to become sheanna?" Rhoane asked, his voice tight.

"No questions. No comments until she has finished," Verdaine warned.

His jaw clenched, but he nodded for Carga to continue.

"Yes, he is what made me sheanna. Please know, our relationship was consensual. I knew it would not last, but I did not care. I had been so sheltered until that point, always directed to becoming High Priestess, and this felt like something just for me." She took another long breath and blew softly through puffed cheeks. "After I was exiled, I went to Paderau and spoke with Duke Anje, who gave me a job, and anonymity. He knew who I was but protected my secrets with his life."

Secrets. Plural. Even before Carga said her next words, Taryn knew what they would be, and also knew it would destroy Rhoane. Not just Rhoane, but Zakael, too.

CHAPTER NINETEEN

If Taryn could've protected her loved ones from the catastrophe that was about to unfurl, she would've. But she was impotent to stop it, just as Verdaine knew she would be. Damn the meddling goddess and her insistence Carga tell them her terrible truth.

The stirrings of tears accompanied her belly coiling with apprehension. Rhoane would lose his shit when he heard the name of Carga's lover. Taryn had had an entire season to process it—and forced herself to forget it because Carga had explicitly told her that she would deal with Zakael when the time came. How the hell were they going to keep Rhoane from rampaging off to do gods knew what to Zakael? And that was only a small part of Carga's tale. He'd go completely berserk when he heard it all, if Taryn was right in her suspicions. All she could do was vehemently hope she was wrong.

"Go on, Carga," she urged. "Tell us everything. We promise we won't freak out." She squeezed Rhoane's hand hard, and he looked sharply at her.

"A child was conceived of this union. Only the duke and I know about his existence."

There it was. It gave Taryn no joy that she was right. Her grip on Rhoane's hand softened even as the importance of what Carga said slammed into her brain.

"Your child is heir to both the Weirren Throne and the Obsidian Throne." Taryn whispered, too afraid to hear the awful truth too loudly.

Carga glared at her and Taryn regretted her words. "This child is now a man and innocent of his heritage, as it will stay. He is heir only to his own happiness."

Rhoane shook his head as if his understanding had only just dawned. "Heir to—? Is Valterys the father of your child? Did he rape you?"

"No!" Carga grabbed her brother's hand and shook her head. "I told you, the relationship was consensual, and something I desperately wanted. I am sorry for this, Rhoane, truly. I thought this knowledge would go to my grave, but Verdaine had other ideas. The father of my child is Zakael."

Heat blazed through Taryn from Rhoane's rage. He trembled violently and worked his mouth as if to speak, but no words came out.

"Temper yourself, Surtentse. There is a reason I wanted Carga to share this information with you."

"And why is that, you villainous goddess? To hurt me? To hurt my sister? Can you not see how much this pains her? And for what? What makes this worth it?" He stormed off several paces, his ShantiMari sending moss-green sparks into the dimness.

Carga openly sobbed and Taryn took her into her arms. Whatever reasoning Verdaine had for the confession, she wasn't seeing it. All she knew was that her heart broke for these two people and the anguish they suffered.

Kaida growled at the goddess, clearly as upset with her as the rest of them.

Verdaine followed Rhoane and wrapped a tendril of ochre-colored power around him in a sweet caress. "Rhoane, search your heart. What does it tell you once you delve past your anger?"

"My heart tells me I should go to Caer Idris this minute and shove my sword through Zakael's deceitful, lying, backstabbing, cold heart. I will not miss this time."

"Ah, but you did have the chance once, why did you not kill him then?"

Rhoane sneered at the goddess. "Bloody fucking kindness." His glare went to Taryn, and her knees quaked at the vengeance in his eyes. "Because I knew she would not forgive me if I murdered her brother. But now, now that I know what he has done to my sister, he will pay."

This felt strangely reminiscent of Zakael's threats at the Temple of Ardyn. Taryn stood at an intersection with many possible paths before her. Her gaze slid to Verdaine, and reading her expression, Taryn's apprehension rose. What Rhoane did next was only part of the equation—what she did next affected all Aelinae, and possibly the worlds beyond. The newly created worlds that she and Rhoane had made without even knowing what they'd done. One of those worlds might even be Nasus, where the darathi recovered at Aerithilyn.

The enormity of the situation rested precariously on her slim shoulders. If she got this wrong, they may well lose the darathi, yes, but Aelinae as well.

"Rhoane, mi carae." She took him in her arms and held him so tightly her body trembled with the effort. His body stiffened and she felt his anger as if it were her own. "This is not the way. It is not for us to punish Zakael for something Carga wanted. If anyone is to exact revenge, it should be her, but I don't think that's what she really wants." Taryn cast a glance to Carga, who shook her head.

"I want my son to live his life exactly as he is—happy in the knowledge he was raised by two loving parents who gave him everything I could not." Carga stepped closer, her hands raised as if to reach for Rhoane.

Taryn reached for Carga's and held her hand in her right, with Rhoane's hand in her left, making a bridge between the two siblings. "Now is not the time for more bloodshed, mi carae. Zakael knows you killed his mother. He too wants revenge. Shall I let you both murder each other for your own pride? There has been too much anger, too much hate between you. The only path forward I can see is forgiveness, even if that means you need to be too bloody fucking kind."

Rhoane startled out of his ire to stare at her. "He knows? But how?"

Taryn shrugged, some of her tension slipping away with the action. "Kaldaar probably told him so that he'd tear off and kill you. He tried to break our bonds on the ship and failed. As Verdaine said, we're too strongly connected now. The only way to break our bonds is to kill one of us. Or, maybe Kaldaar is bored and felt like toying with Zakael's emotions. It doesn't matter now. He knows the truth about his mother's death, and you know the truth about your sister's sheanna. Now we need to heal. We can't balance Aelinae if we carry this anger within us."

His body relaxed a fraction and he hung his head not in defeat, but understanding. He turned to Carga and said, "Who is your child? At least do me the courtesy of knowing my nephew."

"You already know him." Carga wrapped her arms around the both of them. "He is a brilliant young man who is wildly in love. But I sense darkness around him, and pain. So very much pain. I have had visions lately of fearsome beasts with the head of a ram and the body of an ape. They are terrifying and each time I see them,, I hear my son cry out. I fear for him." She pulled back and looked Rhoane square in the face. "Eoghan is with him. For now, I do not sense danger for him, only for my son."

Taryn shared a look of alarm with Rhoane. "You don't

think…it couldn't be the same beast I fought?" Her voice shook at the memory of that awful night in Amdi's arena.

The tension of Carga's confession vanished with the collective threat facing them. The walls of the temple came into focus and Taryn felt the stone slabs beneath her feet. If she had passed Verdaine's test, any celebration was hampered by the knowledge that Kragor's brethren were roaming Aelinae unchecked. Or, more likely, being directed by someone.

Rhoane held tight to Carga, his fingers digging into her skin. "Where did you see your son in these visions?"

Taryn gently prodded him to release his grip and he complied, but only just.

"Near Lake Oster. Tinsley and Aomori were traveling with Eoghan to Talaith when they were attacked. At least, that's what my visions tell me. I could be wrong."

Taryn looked at Verdaine. "Is she wrong?"

Sorrow pulled the goddess's features low. "She is correct. Her son Tinsley was gravely wounded and is currently enroute to Talaith with his beloved by his side. Eoghan, Lady Faelara, and the Ullan healer Loghan did what they could to heal him."

"An Ullan healer touched my son?" Now it was Carga's turn to be angry, but just as quickly as her outburst came, she calmed herself and said, "Will he live, Great Lady?"

"His future is not decided by me or the other gods. Only he can determine if he lives or dies."

Taryn bit her cheek to keep from cursing the goddess. Bloody riddles. She squeezed Carga's hand. "Your secret will remain as such. Both Rhoane and I promise we will protect Tinsley's identity, don't we?" She glared at Rhoane, who solemnly nodded.

"If that is your wish."

"It is. Thank you, Brother." Carga kissed him on the cheek and held him tight for a long moment.

Taryn had the sense a secret conversation was spoken between the two, but she didn't intrude. What they said in the privacy of their minds was for them alone.

"We'll go immediately to Talaith and do what we can for your son." She started to hug Carga farewell, but Verdaine stopped her.

"Not yet. You have business elsewhere first. And there is the other matter."

Taryn looked from Verdaine to Carga to Rhoane, and finally Kaida. "What other matter?"

Just then, Khrystina came rushing into the temple, her face flushed. "I tried to enter, but the door was jammed. Apologies for my lateness, High Priestess." Her gaze went to Carga, then froze when she saw Verdaine hovering between her and Taryn. "Holy mother of— Your Eminence, I did not realize you were here. Forgive me."

"There is nothing to forgive. You are exactly on time. I was just telling Rhoane and Taryn they are to take you with them on their journey to Talaith." Verdaine drifted closer to the girl. "You will see many miraculous things on your travels. Some of which you must never mention to anyone. Do I have your word as an Eleri and novice of my temple that you will keep these secrets locked in your heart?"

Khrystina gulped and swallowed loudly. "I do. I promise. I will, yes, anything you ask."

"Good, now go pack. I fear you will not be returning to your sisters for quite some time. Say your goodbyes but be brief about it."

Rhoane gave Taryn a What-The-Actual-Fuck look, and she in turn repeated the glare at Carga. The issue of Khrystina leaving wasn't mentioned again, so Taryn had assumed the topic settled.

"I trust you have your reasons for Novice Khrystina to travel outside our boundaries." Carga's tone implied she had spoken with Verdaine about it and she didn't agree with the goddess's decision.

"I do." To Taryn and Rhoane the goddess said, "Do not limit your travel, or the way you travel, because of Khrystina's presence. I cannot disclose my reasoning just yet, but trust that this is for the best. You only have to take her as far as Talaith. But first, you must see King Stephan and convince him to remove the wards over the Narthvier."

Rhoane crossed his arms and blew out a breath. "You are the goddess of these woods; my father would listen to you before me."

"Exactly, but this is a decision he must make without my interference."

Taryn shared an exasperated glance with Rhoane. Interference was exactly what the goddess had been doing all morning. Now they were saddled with a spiteful Eleri novice who knew nothing of the outside world, and the task of convincing the Eleri king he was wrong.

Just fucking great. She dreaded what the rest of their day would bring. Why Talaith? Then she remembered Carga mentioned that was where Gwainne was presently. It had been obvious to her Khrystina had feelings for him, but were they reciprocated? She had no idea what Gwainne was doing at that precise moment, but she doubted the pretentious Ullan prince was thinking of Khrystina. If Verdaine thought to matchmake the Eleri novice with him, Taryn already knew how that would play out, and the last thing she wanted was to be party to more heartbreak.

CHAPTER TWENTY

Sweat beaded the empress's forehead, either from the efforts of their lovemaking or from her illness, Gwainne couldn't tell—neither affair interested him at that moment. It wasn't that he disliked their naked time together, but it had become rote and, honestly, boring. The empress told him where to touch, how much pressure to apply, and anything else she felt he needed to know. It was always about her gratification, never his. Satisfying her had become more of a chore than about any sort of pleasure.

Despite his hope that he might glean some important information from her during their sessions, she kept her mind locked tight. Whatever secrets she safeguarded, whatever schemes she made, he hadn't the slightest inkling. A fact that worried him, because he sensed the others were losing faith that he was useful. They allowed him in their meetings, but each time he had nothing to share, he saw the looks of disapproval, the growing mistrust.

He couldn't blame them. Every morning he dutifully arrived at the empress's extravagant suite of rooms and performed as she dictated, and every afternoon he told Eliahnna and the others the same thing—nothing. Even he was getting annoyed with himself, but mostly the empress.

Today Lliandra had set a glacial pace, which allowed him to let his mind wander. It was when she got a little more…experimental, that he needed to keep his focus. But this rhythmic pumping in and out was about as unsensual as it came. There was something missing, and he knew exactly what, but he'd forced himself to put that part of his desires away.

No matter how much he needed the touch of another man, his father wouldn't allow it. Said it wasn't fitting for an Ullan laird. At times, it made Gwainne consider giving up the title to one of his younger brothers, but according to Ullan custom, to do so would be asking for death. No Ullan laird could rule with the true heir still living.

Birds frolicked outside the open windows, their cries and chirps so different from what he knew in Ulla. Everything in Talaith was new and exciting, and a little terrifying, too. Buildings not made of tents, but stone structures that squatted above the paved city streets. More water than he'd ever seen in his life, or had ever imagined existed, was but a few steps from where he now fucked an indifferent empress.

To distract himself from his own needs, and the duty he performed for the empress, he thought of the docks and how goods from all over Aelinae came and went through Talaith's harbor. Spices and wine from the Summerlands, fine glassware and darker, more intoxicating wine from Danuri, silks from Midvale—they all made their way to the capital. Ulla was surrounded by water; surely they too could have a port or two along the coastline? The Jansen Strait would allow goods to come all the way inland almost to the Sea of Jaden.

An excited thrill passed through him at the idea. Followed closely by a crushing sense of frustration. His father would never allow such a thing. No one would claim Amdi Agnar an easily frightened or superstitious man, but for reasons known only to him, the Ullan laird kept his people inland, far from the shores of the Eastern Seas. Gwainne promised himself that when he returned to Ulla, he would ask his father about the lack of harbors, and perhaps persuade him that trade would benefit their people. After all, wasn't it the laird's duty to not only protect his people, but to provide for them as well? And that provision went beyond protection from the elements—it meant providing opportunities for trade, for growth, for exploration.

And possibly, for love, in whatever form it took.

A slight *pop* sounded in his mind, and he searched Lliandra's expression for any discomfort. A curious smile curled her lips and a soft moan escaped her luscious mouth. He bent and kissed her, savoring the moment. Instead of lackadaisically humping her, he shifted so that he could reach the secret spot he knew Lliandra enjoyed. Another moan tickled his lips and he nudged her mouth open to explore with his tongue. It wasn't that he didn't enjoy women—the gods knew he did—but he also craved the curves and cocks of men. Another *pop*, this one he felt low in his belly.

A delirious, delicious lightheadedness came over him. His father had ruled their people with an iron fist, and until his trip outside their borders, Gwainne had reluctantly agreed with his efficient yet brutal way of leading. But now? Now he saw the merits of a privy council to discuss and debate what was best for the kingdom. One person deciding the fate of thousands might benefit the ruler, but what of the people? Were they truly happy? Were they satisfied with their lives? Did they yearn for more?

And what about Ulla's relationship with the other kingdoms? They'd always kept to themselves, but he was beginning to realize that wasn't the path to peace. The more secretive they were, the more other kingdoms envied or reviled them. Open borders meant open trade, yes, but it also meant allies, something Ulla could benefit from. A third *pop*, and then a fourth traveled up his sternum.

Lliandra's breathing deepened, her breasts heaved, an invitation to nuzzle them that he didn't ignore. Her quim, always ready for him, clenched against his cock, sending a buzz of desire through his veins.

"Whatever you're doing to me, don't stop. It feels…exquisite. Unlike anything I've ever known." The words came out slightly slurred, as if she'd been drinking, but he knew she hadn't touched a drop all morning.

Panic flared and his throat tightened. He didn't consciously know what was different, but he understood what she meant. This morning was indeed exquisite. He breathed into his movements, focusing now on her instead of random, meandering thoughts. He marked her pale skin and long, lovely golden curls that always seemed to arrange themselves in a half circle around her head. As if she were the sunburst that brightened his days. Perhaps she was.

They'd certainly shared enough time in bed for her to be, and yet he knew the arrangement wasn't permanent for either of them. Warmth infused his blood as he realized he loved the empress not as a passionate lover, but as a friend. Another pop and his throat relaxed with a gentle swallow. Lliandra gasped and licked her lips. A subtle glow came from her, and not from any ShantiMari that he could sense.

It came to him in a gentle whoosh of warmth and tantalizing thrills—he was healing her. Quite possibly healing himself as well. But how? He wasn't a healer like his mother and brother. He'd never studied the art of lovemaking to open energy channels. Yet that's exactly what he was doing. Ferran's tit, he was a healer. His father would be furious. His mother—what would she think?

A sense of euphoria, almost of rapture settled in his thoughts and he felt completely at peace with himself, the empress, with everything and everyone. The room grew hazy and his vision blurred as he thrust in and out, his movements tender yet confident. He blinked and was no longer in Lliandra's bed, but floating in a white space of nothingness.

"You are the son of the greatest healer Aelinae has ever known, and the brother of her heir. It is natural you would have this gift, but you are not meant for the healer's tents, Prince Gwainne."

He spun to find the source of the admonition and locked his gaze on the goddess Verdaine.

"What are you doing here?"

"You tell me."

"I am in the middle of, erm, something. This is highly inappropriate." He folded his arms, only slightly embarrassed that he was completely naked.

"I did not beckon you here. It is you who called to me." A twinkle lit her lovely eyes, and for a half second he almost covered himself. Instead, he stood taller to give her a full view of his manhood.

"I did no such thing."

She shrugged as if to dismiss his denial. "Forgive me, I must be mistaken. If you have no need of me, then I shall leave you to your endeavors." The twinkle left her eyes and her face became shrouded in sadness.

He knew he should return to Lliandra, but this goddess he hadn't believed in less than a moonturn past intrigued him. "Something distresses you?"

"The world is in turmoil and this hurts my heart. But you are close to bringing Aelinae one step closer to peace."

"How?"

Instead of answering, she made an elegant motion with her hand and a vision played out in the white space around them. He saw a war of great magnitude being fought with creatures he knew from his father's fighting arena. They roared and trampled the soldiers from Talaith and Paderau. Of the Eleri, he saw nothing. Behind the combatants, a shadowy figure lurked, his death-like shroud ominous and frightening.

He dragged his gaze away from the dark figure to Verdaine's Light. "What does this mean? Will Ulla go to war with Talaith?"

"If your father is not healed, this is the most likely outcome. The future is not known to us, but all signs point to war. It can be avoided, but only if Amdi Agnar is healed by the Gllanaed Rose."

"I do not know this flower. Where can I find one?" Desperation entered his voice.

"Lord Hayden is in possession of such a rose. And Lady Faelara travels even now to your father with an elixir made of its petals. She and your mother will heal your father before you return to Ulla." Verdaine's tricolored eyes watched him intently, and he squirmed under the scrutiny.

"Why are you telling me this now?" He waved to indicate the bed and empress, neither of which were in the strange nothingness.

The goddess ignored his question. "Pour the love you have for your father into your healing. You are close to ridding Lliandra of Kaldaar's taint, but his force is strong and she will not happily relinquish his touch. Give her tea steeped with a petal from the Gllanaed Rose. Only once she is fully recovered can Talaith and Ulla become allies."

Verdaine started to drift away, but returned, her brows drawn. "I should not tell you this, but travelers will arrive in a few days, one gravely injured. Without Lady Faelara here to heal him, I fear he may not live another fortnight."

"You wish for me to heal him?" Shock and curiosity swirled through his thoughts. Could he? Should he? How would that work? "But you just said I am not meant for the healer's tents." Lliandra's healing had been spontaneous; he wasn't sure he could do it again on command.

"Not you, dear prince. Go to Nena, she knows who can

help." For a long moment the goddess didn't speak, and Gwainne debated if he should go, but how did he leave the emptiness? "You will make a great king, but only if you forge your own path. Ulla has lived too long in the dust and heat of the desert. Your people are thirsty for more than water. As are you."

And then she was gone. The strange white nothingness as well.

Lliandra writhed beneath him, her brow soaked now. It took him only a heartbeat to gather his wits and focus on what needed to be done. Verdaine's words burrowed into his brain, but he would untangle that riddle later. Lliandra needed him, and he would not let the empress down. He smoothed her hair and whispered sweet flattery in her ear, telling her she was intelligent, beautiful, and strong.

He urged her to let go her fears and concerns and to drift deeper into the intoxicating bliss their lovemaking brought. For the first time since they began their affair, he opened his Shanti-Mari and let it travel the length of their bodies. It wrapped them in a protective cocoon before delving deeper, into their flesh.

Lliandra gasped and shuddered, but he continued with the healing. A stain pressed against his power, hard and dark and terrifying. It tried to consume his Shanti, but Gwainne slid his power past the shadow to travel up Lliandra's torso to her open mouth and deeper still into her mind. There, the stain vibrated and fought against the intrusion, but Gwainne was not daunted.

He envisioned his mother and father, their smiling faces beaming with pride. Loghan's image joined theirs, along with his half-siblings from Amdi's other wives. The love he felt for them channeled into Lliandra. The glow deepened until her curls really did look like rays from the rising sun.

"Yes, there," she panted. "More."

His pace quickened and he slammed into her balls-deep until she was shrieking with pleasure. The stain coiled and snapped, but with each attack, he infused more love into the empress.

Sweat ran down his shaking arms as he held himself above her. Her hands gripped his biceps tight enough to leave indents from her fingernails, but he didn't care. This was too important. The way she tossed her head from side to side, he guessed she understood what was happening.

One final *pop* sounded in his mind and his ShantiMari poured from him with more force than he'd ever experienced before. It flooded not just his veins, but the empress's as well. Her cry worried him, and he missed a beat, but her grip never lessened.

"Come for me, Your Majesty. Release yourself and the torment that haunts you." Gwainne pressed his lips to hers and sucked hard into her mouth.

Her legs wrapped around him and held him tight against her as she came in a shuddering climax that shook her entire body. Her pussy convulsed and contracted against his throbbing cock. His orgasm hit hard and fast, stealing his breath and making him dizzy.

The stain shrieked like a stricken vorlock, a sound that would haunt Gwainne until his dying day. It shriveled to nothingness. He felt rather than heard Lliandra's final energy store open, and she twisted her head to sob into the pillow. Kaldaar's taint was gone for good.

Her legs released him and she curled in on herself. She looked young and fragile as she continued to weep. His instinct was to hold her, to cradle her in his protective embrace, but he hesitated.

"Shall I go?"

"Stay. Please." She reached a hand to him and he snuggled against her.

A deluge of memories, thoughts, images, and emotions overtook him. They were hers, and he wasn't sure if she was aware she was sharing the entirety of her existence with him. This was what the others had expected him to find, but somehow it felt wrong to finally come about the information this way. He hadn't forced her to open her mind, but in a way the healing had done the work for him, unintentionally.

Instead of shutting her out, he held her tighter and took on her burdens as if they were his own. She turned and curled into him, her tears wet against his chest.

The display of vulnerability was enough to break his heart—that is, until the savageness of her life hit him full force. He saw it all: How she'd raised her first daughter to rule with treachery and deceit, to her hatred and fear of her second daughter—the Eirielle. Taryn was her only regret, and even now, with him, she sought to make another Eirielle that she could control.

More memories shuffled through his mind of the lovers she missed, most notably Valterys and Myrddin. She then dwelled on her sister Gwyneira, and a tinge of remorse pinched his heart. Lliandra missed her sister more than she'd ever admit. Behind that confession throbbed her pride in Eliahnna and the knowledge that her third daughter would be the empress she could never be.

Melancholy mixed with outrage as she shuddered against him, allowing her insecurities and flaws to pass into him. He took everything in without complaint, even when some of the images were hard to process. A few would leave him emotionally scarred, but this was important to her for reasons he'd never comprehend.

From what he saw, and what she'd shared, he should've hated her—but he didn't. Couldn't. In a bizarre way, he understood her more than she'd ever know. Being raised by Amdi Agnar, with all the expectations that entailed, gave him a unique perspective on the empress's outburst. She wasn't so different from his father. They ruled as they thought they must, with force and cunning, and all too often deception.

He planted soft kisses on her forehead and stroked her hair. As he drifted in and out of her memories, he made plans of his own. He wouldn't betray Lliandra's trust by telling the others what he'd learned but give them just enough to satisfy their thirst for knowledge. Then he would go to Eliahnna and confess everything he knew not just about Lliandra's dealings with Ulla, but Zakael's and Marissa's as well. The three of them had used Ulla to their advantage, but Gwainne would see to it that Ulla was never used by another kingdom again. Especially not by Talaith's rulers, including Eliahnna.

He was on the cusp of dozing when he remembered Verdaine's warning about an injured man. Something about finding Nena. Who the hell was Nena?

CHAPTER TWENTY-ONE

I f she had to hear one more insidious excuse, she was going to lose her damn mind. Taryn pushed from the table and clenched her fists to keep from annihilating the lot of them. Fucking Eleri and their ridiculous ideals. It was their belief that they were apart from the rest of Aelinae—the Fadair, their word for anyone not Eleri—but it was said in such a way that she took it as a slur. They believed keeping aloof and apart from the rest of the world would keep them safe from Kaldaar's treachery. No amount of explaining how wrong they were did any good. They were blind to the fact that Kaldaar had already insinuated himself in their lives.

She'd had enough. For two straight days they'd sat at the huge table discussing how the Eleri were safer in their forest and that the wards needed to remain in place. None of her or Rhoane's persuasion or counterarguments had helped convince them otherwise, and she was done. Just fucking done.

"Sit down, girl. We are not yet finished with our discussions," King Stephan's voice boomed from the other side of the room.

She turned slowly to give her a moment to calm her rage. "Girl? You dare call me *girl* after everything I have done for you, for your people?" Her legs trembled with suppressed anger and she had to remind herself that blasting the king to the far reaches of some planet she couldn't even name was probably a very bad thing.

"Father, we are trying to help. You must listen to reason." Rhoane reached for the king's hand, but Stephan snatched it away.

"Reason? You tell me the forest creatures are suffering and this is reason enough to lift the wards? Let them die if it means protecting the Eleri."

Taryn blew out a long breath and glared at the king. "Let them die. Fine. Let's let all the forest creatures starve so your, what, five thousand Eleri can live? Sure, great plan." She scraped her hair off her face and looked to the ceiling for answers. "Or, you could lower the wards, allowing your people to find shelter in their own homes instead of cowering in nooks and crevices of this great tree. They are scared, Stephan. You're frightening them with this nonsense."

"Nonsense? How very dare you!" Bressal rose as he shouted at her. "We would not have to close our borders if you were not here. Life was peaceful before you arrived. The Eleri were thriving."

"No, they were not, Brother." Rhoane glared at his younger brother before joining her. His hand slipped into hers and she felt his trembling. "The Eleri have dwindled in the last several thousand seasons and it is because we hold ourselves apart. Aelinae must be united to survive, can you not see this? They are not Fadair—but they are allies if we allow them to be. I have seen many miraculous things in my travels, things that would make you sob with wonder, and shudder with terror. But in all, I have seen those kingdoms who believe they are better than the others do not last. Eventually they fall due to their own hubris."

The room grew quiet and Taryn took in the other high-ranking Eleri who all sat stone-faced, backs straight. They had offered little to the discourse and she'd wondered more than once why there were there.

Janeira, the warrior woman who at one time had challenged Taryn and caused much consternation but was now a friend, crossed her arms over her chest. "I agree with the Darennsai and the Surtentse."

"You would go against your betrothed?" Bressal sounded astonished, which only irritated Taryn more. Of course he'd think "his woman" would go along with him.

"I wear the gold chain, but I have yet to give you my answer. Perhaps this is the test we were set." Janeira rose and went to Bressal. She stroked his cheek lovingly with a sad little smile. "You are my heart, but you cannot see that what you and your father are doing to the Eleri, to the entire Narthvier is harming not just our people, but the entire forest. This weakness will only serve to help our enemies." Her gaze went to Taryn and Rhoane. "The Darennsai and Surtentse are our greatest strength right now. I only wish you could see it as I do."

She kissed his head before leaving the chamber. No one spoke as she strode away, nor after the door closed softly behind her. Bressal lifted his chin defiantly, but Taryn saw the shimmer of unshed tears.

"I do not want to cause strife among the Eleri." She held her marked hand out, palm up. A vision played out as if on a screen, of Stephan and Bressal kneeling before her. They had both pledged oaths that day to follow her, to uphold her station, and to protect her if needed. "But you did give your word. All I am asking is that you allow living beings passage through the veils as you have always done. Place wards if you must to prevent anyone with ill intent from entering the vier, but allow those that call this forest home to thrive."

Stephan scrubbed a hand over his face and glanced at his second son. "Do you agree with this insanity?"

Bressal shook his head slowly. "I do not, but we gave our oaths."

The king cleared his throat. "Let the record show that neither King Stephan nor his Second Son Bressal agree with the Darennsai. If anything should befall the Eleri, it will further be known that the Darennsai and Surtentse are forbidden from entering the Narthvier ever again."

Taryn glanced at Rhoane with a look that said his father was nuts. Nothing could prevent them from entering the vier. Hell, they'd both entered via portal without Stephan even realizing it.

"Agreed," Taryn and Rhoane said in unison.

"And now, dear father, we must say our farewells." Rhoane bent low, his arm and leg extended in the formal Eleri bow.

"What? You are leaving so soon? But you just arrived." Stephan cocked his head and narrowed his eyes. "How *did* you arrive, exactly?"

Rhoane cleared his throat and asked for a private audience with only the king and his heir, which technically was still Rhoane, but this small courtesy would soothe Bressal's ego. Stupid prat. Taryn shook her head to rid herself of the unbecoming thought. They had to work with Stephan and Bressal, not against them. Calling him names, if only in her mind, would do no good.

Even if it was true.

The king granted Rhoane's request and the silent Eleri shuffled out of the room.

When Taryn heard the door shush closed she sent a thread of her power to each door, securing it from anyone entering uninvited. Next, she enclosed them in a bubble of privacy.

"Who are those people besides high-ranking Eleri? They say nothing, offer nothing to the talks." Taryn had been curious about them since they first started their discussion with the king.

"They are record keepers and witnesses. They only add commentary if asked, which I chose not to do. Now, will you tell me how you came to be in the Narthvier? Were you here before we raised our barriers?" Stephan stroked his chin, his eyes bright.

Before Rhoane could explain, Taryn beckoned Bressal to come forth. "You won't believe us if we tell you, so let me show you."

Bressal turned to his father for permission, and the king nodded with a short wave toward Taryn.

"Do not hurt my son."

"I promise, this will not hurt, though he will return changed." She held out her hand and spun a portal right there in the middle of the room.

Stephan jumped up, his eyes wild, his mouth agape. "What sorcery is this?"

"Not sorcery, Father, but Taryn's rightful inheritance. She is the Walker Between Worlds. You must trust us right now, though I fear that will be difficult. Please, do not interfere." Rhoane directed Bressal to stand between them. "Hold my hand and do not let go."

"Where are you taking me? Is it safe? Will I be harmed?" Bressal's shaky words spilled forth, and for a second, Taryn felt sorry for him.

"Step through and you shall see." To the king, Taryn said, "We won't be a moment. You have my word no harm shall come to him."

They moved forward with Bressal a half-step behind. Taryn felt Rhoane's tug on the man and together they all three stepped into the void. A sense of calm washed over her, so unlike the first time she'd encountered the all-consuming darkness. Kaldaar had controlled the passageways then, but now this was her domain. If she wished, she could envision every single path that led between worlds.

Where are you taking us? Rhoane asked in her mind.

Home.

A soft chuckle brushed her thoughts. *I thought as much. That is a good choice.*

Bressal held himself aloft, but she felt his trembling and placed a hand on his shoulder. A faint light shone in the distance and she led them toward it. When it grew larger, she adjusted the destination so that the portal opened inside the sitting room of her London flat instead of the cellar.

Clever.

Thanks.

A bubble of giddiness tickled her belly. She'd never adjusted the course before and was grateful to learn she could. Each time she used the mysterious pathways, she learned something new about them.

They stepped from the void into the little room and Taryn said the phrase that made all of her and Brandt's belongings appear. Bressal blinked against the electric lighting and glared at his surroundings.

"Where are we?" The sneer he wore dampened her almost good mood coming home had brought.

The portal popped closed behind them and he whirled around, his hand going to a sword that was not there. Rhoane put a hand on his arm to calm him while Taryn strolled through the room, her fingertips trailing on the back of the sofa. A scratching sound came from the roof and she glanced up as if to see what made the strange noise.

"I grew up here." She walked to the window and gestured for Bressal to follow. "This is where I was hiding all those seasons since my birth." She pointed out the window to the city beyond. "This is a world far from Aelinae. There are many worlds like this that exist without Aelinae's knowledge. To be fair, Earth has no idea Aelinae exists, either. They live in tandem to each other, a symbiotic relationship in a way." Hearing the sounds of the city made her at once homesick for London, and Talaith.

"Worlds besides Aelinae?" Bressal whispered as he looked out the window to the streets below. "There are many strangely dressed people—and what are those carriages?" He placed a fingertip on the window, a frown pulling his lips low. "This feels like glass."

"Because it is." She gazed out the window, relief spreading through her that the horrible vision she'd had the last time she'd been there with Rhoane had not happened. London was as she remembered. "Our worlds are not so different, and yet there are many things about Earth that I would not wish for Aelinae."

"What do you mean?"

The pounding of steps came to her, and a moment later, two men dressed all in black, their eyes dark with intensity bound into the room. Behind them, a shorter woman with dark hair and a stony expression glared at Taryn.

Bressal positioned himself as if to protect her, which she found adorably sweet since until that moment, she'd thought he hated her. It was also unnecessary of him.

"Dony!" Taryn edged around the Eleri and went to her friend. "Hey Gage, Silar." She greeted the two Stone Guardians as she went to hug Dony.

"Lady Donyatella." Rhoane inclined his head to Dony first, and then the two men. "Esteemed Guardians. This is my brother Bressal, Second Son of the Eleri."

Silar and Gage relaxed and the scraping sound retreated from the roof. It occurred to her that she should've had Khrystina research Stone Guardians at the temple. Dammit. An opportunity missed, or perhaps not. There might be information about them hidden in Talaith's library.

"It is our honor, Prince of the Eleri." Dony made a sort of curtseyish bow. "Long have our people guarded yours."

Bressal gave Rhoane a sharp look, and her betrothed replied, "It is a long story. One I shall tell you over a cup of grhom once we are returned to the Weirren."

"If you have no need of us," Silar turned toward the front door, "then we shall leave you to your business."

"We'll only be here a few more minutes. Thank you for your continued vigilance." Taryn took a step toward the small group. "Have there been any developments with Rori or Nikala?" The last she saw either of them had left her with too many unanswered questions.

"There is always something happening with them, but none of that concerns you. They follow their paths, just as you follow yours." Despite Dony's encouraging words, Taryn saw the tightness around her eyes, the worry that lingered there.

But like she said, it wasn't Taryn's path. Not right then, at least. Rainne, Rori, Nikala, even Cassia and Amaleigh—they were tangential to her, not directly related to bringing balance to Aelinae. She couldn't afford to expend emotional energy on them at the moment.

"Thank you. When you see them next, please let them know I am thinking of them."

"I will." Dony reached up and kissed her on the cheek, and Taryn breathed deeply of her odd scent of dust and citrus. "Come see us again when you can stay longer."

Taryn squeezed her friend in a tight embrace. "I would like that."

After Dony and her boys left, Taryn turned to Bressal, who stared at her as if she'd turned into an ogre.

"What the hell was that?"

"That was my past, present, and future." She slipped her hand into Rhoane's and heaved a heavy sigh. "While you were sitting around with your thumb up your ass, Rhoane and I have been traveling from world to world, nearly dying several times, to bring peace to Aelinae."

Bressal grunted and crossed his arms over his broad chest. "Why would I put my thumb up my ass?" He fidgeted and twisted, reaching an arm behind him. "Is that even possible?" His hand rubbed his bum and he harrumphed. "I suppose it is. But why would someone do that?"

"It's just a saying. I wasn't being literal." She bit her cheek to keep from laughing at the ridiculous man. "My point being, you and your father are hiding in the Weirren when there are others out there fighting—and now I am being literal—and *dying* for Aelinae. Rhoane wasn't lying when he said we've seen things that would make you question everything you've ever known."

She went to the window and beckoned Bressal over a second time. He stood beside her and watched the people going about their day. Several busses rumbled past, and on the Thames, boats sailed up and down the river. It was a typical day for London, but nothing like he'd ever known.

"Once, long ago, darathi called this world home, but they are no longer here. They only live on in legend. Tell me, can you sense any ShantiMari?" She looked up at him and studied the clench of his jaw, the flaring of nostrils. London made him uncomfortable, but her questions disturbed him greatly.

"With those peculiar people you called friends, yes. Within this room, I sense your presence, and Rhoane's. There is one other that eludes me, but out there?" He tapped the glass. "It is dead."

"Darennsai, we should go before Father gets worried." Rhoane stood away from them near the bookshelves, his hand outstretched and ready to make a portal. The tightness of his lips told her he was bothered by something, but she sensed no danger.

"We'll continue this conversation at the Weirren." She took Bressal's arm and together they stepped into Rhoane's portal.

If Bressal was impressed with his brother, he didn't show it. By the tightening of his arm muscles, he was still apprehensive about the void. Not that she could blame him; it was a terrifying place if you didn't know what to expect.

They stepped into Stephan's privy chamber and nearly

crashed into the king. He stood exactly where the portal had been when they left him.

"What just happened? One moment you are here, the next gone, and now you are back again." Stephan searched the empty air beside and around them. "What was that spinning hole?"

"It is called a portal, or a doorway depending on your preference. It is how we travel to other worlds," Rhoane said simply as he dusted specks of glitter from his trousers.

Bressal knelt in front of his father and clasped the man's hands. "Father, I have seen a marvel. Not just one, but several." His gaze slid to Taryn and she saw the confusion that clouded his features. "I am changed by what I have seen."

Stephan directed his son to stand, then looked to Rhoane for answers. "Explain."

A knock at the door startled them and Stephan swore at whoever interrupted their meeting. Janiera's worried voice traveled through the solid oak door.

"Darennsai, you must come quickly. There is an issue with Kaida."

Without waiting for permission, she yanked open the door. "Lead the way."

Bressal could tell the king about their adventures. It would hold more merit coming from him, anyway. Kaida was her priority now.

CHAPTER TWENTY-TWO

Taryn took the steps two or three at a time, practically falling down the grand staircase as she raced after Janeira. In her mind she called to Kaida, but all she heard was the peculiar sound of yips and squeaks. Her mind spun to the worst possible scenario of Kaida being tortured and she bit her lower lip to keep from crying.

If anything had happened to Kaida, there would be hell to pay.

She was already wound tighter than a band ready to snap.

"All will be well, mi carae," Rhoane huffed as he kept pace with her. "I feel your fear, your frustration. We will find her and do what is necessary."

Taryn focused on the slim gold chain Janeira wore around her midsection as it jostled above the gauzy pants she wore. For a moment, she wondered if the woman hid any weapons in the slightly see-through fabric, and if so, where? How?

That tiny detail, a gold chain and hidden weapons was the distraction from Kaida's emergency she needed to clear her anxiety and calm her heart. It would do no one any good to rush into a situation highly emotional. But this was Kaida they were talking about. Her friend, her love. Gods, she better not be hurt.

Janeira led them through the great hall of the Weirren and out through a doorway Taryn had never been through before. It let out near the kitchen gardens where in the distance Taryn knew the stables were located, and just beyond them, the kennels.

The yipping and snarling squeaks grew louder, and she increased her pace. The anxiety threatened to return, but she struggled against it. Though the tears did flow. Please, don't let Kaida be hurt. She prayed to whatever gods might be listening, even that asshole Kaldaar. If it helped Kaida, she didn't care who heard.

Past the stables, they slowed their pace as they approached the kennels. A moment of confusion swept over Taryn. Then a rush of relief followed by more tears.

Janeira turned to grin at her, but the smile quickly disappeared. "I am sorry for the subterfuge, Darennsai, but I thought perhaps you could use a break from the king and his son." She pointed to where Kaida lay on the ground, covered in wiggling puppies. "I did not mean to cause you distress."

"That was a dick move, Janeira. Subterfuge or not, you scared the crap out of me." She half-laughed, half-sobbed as she crashed to the ground and clutched Kaida to her chest. Within moments, several pups claimed her fingers as chew toys and she winced against the pain their sharp baby teeth inflicted. If it meant Kaida was safe, she'd endure whatever torture the little scamps brought. She snuggled her head into Kaida's fur and silently sobbed in relief.

Just behind Kaida, Sheila, the bitch who had nursed Kaida when Taryn first found her alone in the Narthvier, kept watch on her playful pups.

Rhoane gripped Taryn's shoulder to let her know he was there if she needed him and then knelt beside Sheila to scratch between her ears. Her tongue flopped to the side of her open mouth and she rubbed her muzzle against his arm.

Janeira had good intentions, but goddamn, what a horrible way to get her attention.

You are too emotional, Darennsai. One day I will die. This I cannot avoid, but you can prepare yourself for that day.

Don't talk like that. You're not allowed to die. Ever. She hugged Kaida tighter.

You are being foolish. Everyone and everything dies. It is inevitable.

Kaida's words hit harder than she'd have liked. Perhaps Taryn was being foolish, but it felt like she'd had so little time with those she loved as it was. Still, she resolved not to dwell on the inevitable.

Taryn's emotions are what make her the Darennsai, Rhoane interjected, and she glanced at him above Kaida's fur. *We were worried you were in peril, so if she is a little emotional right now, there is good reason for it. Even if there was not, you surely must understand that her kindness, her love is what Aelinae needs right now. You give her strength, Kaida, whether you understand this or not. So please, do not belittle her affection.*

Kaida whimpered and licked Taryn's face in apology. Taryn gazed at Rhoane through her tears and mouthed the words, "Thank you." Maybe her emotions weren't a weakness, but her superpower.

Janeira knelt beside her and stroked one of the pups. "I truly am sorry to have deceived you, Taryn. I meant no harm."

Taryn gave her a grateful look. "I know. Thank you for caring enough to give me a heart attack."

Janeira grinned at her dramatics. "I do think you are right to insist we lift the wards. I see the Narthvier, unlike my betrothed. He is too concerned with governance and what is best for the Eleri, but I see what the forest needs as well. Not just Eleri, but the fae folk, the creatures that call these woods home, the flora and fauna. We exist in harmony, but we are not separate from the rest of Aelinae."

"I think Bressal might have a different perspective now. Whatever he tells you, it is in confidence and must not be shared outside of your bond." She gave Janeira a meaningful stare, and the warrior nodded.

They would finish their conversation with Stephan later. Janeira was right—they needed this happy distraction. The kennel master arrived and shook his head at the shenanigans, but he didn't criticize or complain, merely stood by and watched with curious interest as a hunting dog and her pups accepted a grierbas as one of their own.

Khrystina approached from the forest and asked to join them. Soon everyone had a pup or two snuggled in their arms. Taryn watched the quiet woman and wondered again why Verdaine would insist they take her to Talaith. It wasn't her place to question the goddess, but it certainly piqued her curiosity. They'd traveled to the Weirren on horseback from the temple, but the rest of their journey would be by portals. Verdaine seemed to understand this, even encouraged it, and again Taryn wondered why.

She'd find out soon enough. Or not. That seemed to be the way of the gods. Damn riddles and games that drove her mad.

She picked up a wriggly pup and held it against her face, breathing in the milky sweetness of its puppy breath. It reminded her of when Kaida was little, and she longed for the innocence of those days.

"Ride with me."

She blinked up at the hand that extended to her, then at the shadows lengthening over the courtyard. Janeira was gone, as was Khrystina, Sheila, and the other pups. The one she cradled snoozed happily against her chest. How long had she zoned out?

"Taryn?" Rhoane asked, his tone concerned.

"I'm fine. Just…not sure where the day went."

"You were so peaceful, we thought it best not to disturb you." He indicated two saddled horses. "Let us clear our minds in the vier."

She worked herself out of the pretzel she'd been sitting in and stretched to relieve her cramped legs. The kennel master came to take the pup from her and she gave him a grateful smile. Kaida roused herself and sniffed the air, her slow blinks echoing Taryn's confusion at the passing of time.

The three of them rode out of the palace grounds and into the vier in silence. Eerie silence. Taryn looked from one tree to the next, neither seeing nor hearing birds. Her gaze swept the ferns and underbrush that always seemed to be twittering with scampering critters, but was now dead quiet.

"Where are all the animals?"

Rhoane cocked his head as if listening.

Kaida sniffed the air, her ears pinned back. *They have taken to nest and burrow. There is a presence in the woods they do not recognize.*

Kaldaar? The dark god was always her immediate thought when it came to danger, though there were other things that might frighten the forest dwellers.

I do not think so. The presence is this way, whatever it is. Kaida loped away, and they turned their horses to follow.

Taryn shared a concerned look with Rhoane as they rode after Kaida. She recognized this part of the woods and her heart lodged itself in her throat the closer they came to the shimmering wall of ShantiMari she'd discovered the day she found Kaida. The wall she'd never told Rhoane about.

Crap on a cracker. She'd have to confess to him that she'd known about the wall for the past season. But did she need to? Really? It wasn't like she remembered the wall or seeing Aislinn. Those memories had come back to her after they stumbled into the wasteland where the Eleri queen was hiding. Although accusing her of hiding was a bit cruel. Whatever reasons Aislinn had for staying with the darathi and not returning to her family were her own, and it wasn't for Taryn to judge her.

Kaida barked for them to hurry and they kicked their horses to a gallop. When the path ended, they dismounted and ran to where Kaida growled at the wall, her tail a bottle brush, her ruff huge.

"What is it, girl?" Rhoane searched the area, his gaze going past the wall as if he couldn't see it or feel it.

Taryn surveyed the shimmering strands of ShantiMari and saw, just there, a rip in the webbing of power. She gasped and put a hand to her heart. What did it mean? Had someone tried to break through? She searched the surrounding forest, her Shanti-Mari stretching out like feelers for anyone or anything untoward, but she sensed nothing.

Even as they stood there, Taryn saw several more threads unravel. She stepped closer, curious now that she didn't feel nauseous as she had the first time she'd encountered the wall. Hand trembling slightly, she reached out to touch the undulating power.

"What are you doing?" Rhoane placed his hand over hers, and she looked at him with an apology in her eyes.

"I've been here before, the day we found Kaida." Her fingers laced with his. "Can you see the wall? It's just here." She flicked a glance to her right.

He looked from her to the wall and shook his head. "I see only more forest, more trees, more Narthvier."

Why the fuck couldn't he see it? More importantly, what did it mean?

CHAPTER TWENTY-THREE

Rhoane, First Son of the Eleri, lifted his face to bask in the warmth of the sunlight filtering through his window. His father had lifted the wards the previous evening after yet another strenuous argument with him and Taryn. If it hadn't been for Bressal reversing his decision on the matter, he was certain the vier would still be closed. He owed his brother a deep debt of gratitude for swaying their father to do the right thing.

It had been risky, but ultimately a stroke of genius for Taryn to take Bressal to London. Her reasoning that he needed to see the void to believe them had been sound. Rhoane doubted his brother would've changed his opinion if he hadn't experienced a new world for himself. It took some time to convince their father —with Taryn offering more than once to take him to London as well and being soundly denied—but he'd eventually relented.

Janeira had been privy to their closed talks, with all of them agreeing the information was not for general knowledge. Of that, he was extremely glad. Knowing others like Dony could use the void to travel where and when she pleased disturbed him for reasons he couldn't articulate.

A series of three knocks on his door brought him out of his

musings and the sunlight. He moved to his desk and leaned against the heavy wood. "Enter."

Khrystina peeked her head through the doorway and glanced around. "Are you alone?"

"I am." He beckoned her inside and she hurriedly shut the door behind her. "Have you found something?"

"About a wall? No. About the other matter, only a little." She pulled several scrolls from a canvas bag and handed them to him. "I borrowed these from the palace library, so please do take care in your handling of the paper."

He swallowed a chuckle. She sounded far too much like Taryn. "I promise I will. Thank you." She started to leave, but he stopped her. "Are you packed for travel?"

"Yes, Your Highness. Whenever the Darennsai is ready, let me know."

He nodded, and she left the room without a sound. Such an odd woman. She wore her hair short as if she were sheanna, but by choice. Never in his life had he known an Eleri to wish for short hair. Except for Kaleigh, but then, she was sheanna—well, technically still was, even though Verdaine had told her she'd served out her exile. Yet she'd stayed with Amdi and kept her blonde curls short.

His own hair hung to the middle of his back with several braids securing it away from his face. Did he miss the freedom of shorter hair? It certainly took less time to ready himself in the morning, but otherwise, no. He was Eleri, and that meant he wore his hair long.

Although, that was partly what he and Taryn had argued about with his father—that Eleri needed to adopt more modern customs if they were to survive and thrive. He ran a hand through his silky strands. This was one tradition he would gladly uphold.

He seated himself in the desk chair and reached for the scroll nearest to him. There wasn't a quill on the desk, so he rummaged through a drawer to find something suitable for taking notes. It had been so long since he'd lived there that even if he found a quill, all the ink pots would be dried out. He pulled a stack of papers from one drawer, smiling at the stain of grhom on the top page.

When he traced the stain with his fingertip, an image of Carga came to him, followed by the memory of the morning Verdaine had told him the time was near when he'd have to leave the vier to honor his vow. It was the morning after Carga's grand ball to celebrate her becoming a novice and she'd made him breakfast.

Those were days of innocence and laughter for them both. But everything changed that day. Verdaine had given him the cynfar she'd crafted for Taryn, and then taken Carga with her to the temple. He'd been so angry in those days. Resentful of the vow he'd made to Verdaine as a child, but also for the life he'd have to leave.

It was interesting how life came full circle. Only the night before, he'd argued with Bressal that life couldn't remain the same if the Eleri were to survive. Not just survive, but flourish. He'd seen how on other worlds the Eleri had gradually weakened. Taryn believed it had something to do with the disappearance of those worlds' darathi, and he was inclined to agree. There did seem to be a correlation to the loss of ShantiMari and the absence of darathi.

His gaze went to the papers, and he carefully tucked the stack he held into his drawer. He'd not allowed himself to think of Carga's betrayal since they'd left Verdaine's temple, but he knew he would have to deal with those emotions sooner rather than later. They'd promised they would say nothing to their father about Tinsley's lineage—regardless of him being fifth in line to the throne, the Eleri would never accept an Aelan as king.

They had a hard enough time accepting Taryn as one of their own. No matter that her ears were pointed, her hair long and glossy, and she spoke Eleri fluently; to his kin, she would always be the gyota of Verdaine's prophecy. Remembering how the Eleri had first reacted to Taryn brought him up short.

He could forgive his sister for loving Zakael, and Tinsley was innocent, of course, but Rhoane would not forgive Zakael. The man had never loved anyone but himself and it would take some mighty convincing to make him believe Zakael ever held affections for his sister.

His hand shook as he reached for a scroll. He and Zakael had been adversaries ever since he could remember, although he couldn't recall what had set them on the path of enmity. Taryn would tell him forgiveness was in order, but how could he? How could he be expected to forgive a man who abused his sister?

Says the man who killed that man's mother.

His heart twisted with guilt and he set down the scroll with the other papers Khrystina had brought. He placed a hand over his chest and went to the window. The sun had moved on, but he sought its warmth all the same.

Carga had said she'd loved Zakael. Could it be possible the vile man had loved her in return? Would it change anything if he had? Or if he knew he had a fully grown son?

No.

The only thing that could come of that thinking was heartache for everyone involved. And yet Rhoane had once believed Marissa carried his child. Even though he knew there was the possibility it wasn't truly his, he'd vowed to love the child and raise him as an Eleri. And he'd known Taryn would accept this with grace as well.

She was far too good for this world. Too good for him.

"You look like a man with the weight of the kingdom settled on your shoulders."

Rhoane turned to see his father eyeing the scrolls on his desk. "Not the kingdom, but equally heavy responsibilities." He motioned to the papers. "I will return those when I am finished reading them."

Stephan picked up a sheet of paper and skimmed the words. "Stone Guardians? Is this another of your otherworldly encounters?"

"They are. I am trying to understand their connection not just to Aelinae, but to the Eleri. Have you heard of them?"

His father shook his head and set the paper down. "I confess I do not understand much of what you and Taryn told me last night, but I believe in you and therefore am willing to extend some grace to the other kingdoms. You spoke of a joint meeting."

"A summit."

"Yes, a summit with representatives of each kingdom coming together for the betterment of all Aelinae. Is this why you have a novice traveling with you? Is she to represent the Eleri?"

Rhoane chuckled. "No, Father. When there is a summit, either you or Bressal will speak for us. In all honesty, I do not know why Verdaine asked us to take Novice Khrystina to Talaith. I am only her guardian and escort until she reaches the Crystal Palace."

"Verdaine works in mysterious ways. If that is her wish, then you must abide it." He tapped his fingers upon the desk. "Your betrothed said she will be ready to leave by midday. I will have horses prepared and waiting for you."

"We will not be needing them, but I thank you for the offer." He gave his father a pointed look.

"Ah, yes. The mysterious way of the Darennsai. Bressal tells me you can conjure one of these openings, too." Stephan glanced at him, and Rhoane realized his father was nervous, but of what, he couldn't be certain.

"I can. There are…other skills I have as well. Skills that have been lost to most Eleri, and some that have never been known to us at all."

"So it is true then?"

"What is?" His heart buzzed in his chest. He didn't at all like the way his father was looking at him, as if he was some sort of misshapen creature that he'd found in the depths of a pit.

"You once told me Taryn would become a goddess and I argued it was not possible. But lately, I have had visions of not just her sitting at Verdaine's side, but you as well." He looked at Rhoane with tears shimmering in his dusky eyes. "Is it true? Am I to lose you to these other worlds you claim exist?"

Rhoane closed the gap between them and folded his father in a hearty embrace. The king stiffened for a moment before relaxing into the hug and wrapping his arms around his son.

"You will never lose me, Father. I am always here when you need me. Always have been. Even when I was exiled, you and the Weirren were in my heart."

The man Rhoane knew as the king of the Eleri, the strongest, most formidable person he'd ever known, sobbed quietly against his shoulder.

"When I lost your mother, I never blamed you, but I admit I harbored ill feelings toward you because I knew your choice to leave really meant you had chosen your destiny over me. It was selfish of me, I understand, but you were my first born. My heir. And I lost you the same day I lost Aislinn. It was too much to bear. I hope you can forgive me, my son."

Rhoane squeezed tighter and kissed his father on the cheek. "There is nothing to forgive. I have always loved you and always will."

"I love you too, mi carae."

It was perhaps the first time Rhoane heard the words and believed them.

His father pulled away from the embrace and looked out the window. "I see her sometimes."

An uncomfortable prickliness edged across Rhoane's skin. "See who?" He knew who his father meant, but hoped it wasn't her all the same.

"Your mother. Out in the vier, always through a misty veil, but I see her. It brings me comfort to know she is still with us, watching, protecting as she always did."

It would be easy to tell him the truth—that his beloved wife was alive and at that very moment on another world caring for their darathi. It would be a relief to ease his father's anguish. It would be nothing to break his promise to his mother.

But he'd broken another vow before, and this was the consequence of his actions. He wouldn't break his promise again, no matter how easy it seemed. Sixty seasons of living in exile had taught him that some lessons had to be learned the hard way. His gaze traveled to the south, toward Ulla, to where his punishment began all those seasons ago before Taryn was born.

They'd all suffered in some way for his beloved, his Taryn, but by his reckoning, it was she who had suffered the most. No one else knew what she'd been through—was still going through—and yet they all questioned and doubted her very existence.

Rhoane knew. He'd memorized every scar, every bruise, every crease of worry on her brow. He knew what she'd been through for these people who doubted and derided. There was a time he was no better than them. He'd argued with Verdaine that his life was too important to throw away on the gyota of her prophecy. That was when he was a selfish youth, too full of himself to see reason.

His gaze went to his father. "Do you believe who she is? Truly believe with all your heart that Taryn is the Darennsai?"

The king turned to him with clouded eyes as if he'd been lost in memory. "I had a dream last night of your mother. She rode a crimson darathi, her dark hair trailing behind her like an ebony river. It was quite the sight to behold. Behind her, the other darathi blew fire from their snouts with roars of glee. They were home. Your mother brought our darathi home. When I woke this morning, I went to the place in the vier where I would sometimes see her, but she was not there. Do you know who was?"

Again, that creeping sense of discomfort pricked his skin.

"Your Taryn. She sat with that great beast of hers, staring at nothing. I told her of my dream, and do you know what she said to me? She stood tall, her long silver hair like a flowing stream down her back, her ears tipped as with all Eleri, and she placed her hand over my heart. Then she said, 'Aislinn never left you, Your Majesty. I feel her love in here.'" His father tapped his chest and tears slipped over his cheeks. "She told me that some miracles are tiny, barely perceptible by those that need them most, but that some are grand and frightening."

The king held to the desk and shook with sobs. Rhoane helped him sit in a comfortable chair then knelt before him.

"Do you need anything? Shall I call for someone?" He'd never in his life seen his father so much as blink back tears and this flood concerned him.

"I have been a fool, Rhoane. I thought if I could keep the Eleri separate from the rest of Aelinae, I could protect you—all of you. But your sister, and you, were right. The Eleri will only survive if we open ourselves to the rest of the world. Mingle, interconnect"—a grimace marred his handsome features—"mate with the other races. Will it thin our bloodline? Yes, but our quest for a pure bloodline is folly. That boy who showed up here, Gwainne, he is a prince of Ulla and half Eleri. How is this possible?" He held his head in his hands. "An Ullan prince of Eleri blood. And Taryn—an Aelan who is now Eleri."

"There are some mysteries in this world I cannot solve. I have learned it is best to have faith and trust in the seemingly unknown. In time, it may all make sense, and if it does not? What lesson could I learn from it?" Rhoane stroked his father's hair as if he were a child. "Taryn did not come to us with the answers. She is muddling her way through the same as we are. Sometimes she gets it terribly wrong, but more often than not, she is terrifically right."

His father nodded and wiped his face with a cloth he

produced from nothing. "She showed me her darathi vorsi. I tell you true, until that moment, I still had doubts, but no longer. She is magnificent." His eyes shone in the midday light. "Pure grace."

"She is." Rhoane wasn't at all surprised she showed the king her darathi, but he was concerned to hear she'd returned to the forest without him. "Did she say anything about a wall?"

"Not that I recall. There are no walls in the Narthvier, only our veils that act as barriers." Stephan rose and shook himself as if to slough off the emotions he'd displayed. A serene mask fitted into place over his features and Rhoane detected the subtle change in his father. "I did not mean to take up so much of your morning." He gripped Rhoane's forearms. "Travel with my blessing, my First Son. If you have need of us, we are here."

Rhoane watched his father leave with mixed feelings. Happiness that his father had finally accepted Taryn, sadness to be leaving his home again, and worry that Taryn could see something he could not. Whatever the strange wall was, he hoped it had nothing to do with the Eleri's safety.

CHAPTER TWENTY-FOUR

A dozen riders appeared from seemingly nowhere to surround her, Baehlon, and Loghan. Dressed all in black with only their eyes visible through a gap in the fabric, they were quite intimidating. Faelara adjusted her position, more to hide her anxiety than for comfort, and peeked a glance at Baehlon. He rode beside Loghan; neither of them seemed concerned they were now surrounded by possible rogues or highwaymen.

Loghan gave the slightest nod to one of the riders, and they in turn dipped their head. Perhaps he knew them, which meant they might be an escort sent by Amdi Agnar, but without any words exchanged, she couldn't be certain. She opened her mouth to speak, but Loghan flicked two fingers at her before putting them to his lips.

The cheek! She would not be silenced by him nor anyone. Once again she started to ask, but this time, it was the rider—the same one that had acknowledged Loghan—who cut her a quick glare that said she would do well to keep silent. Then the rider's startling blue eyes softened, and Faelara had the sense it was a woman who hid beneath the layers of cotton they wore.

She closed her mouth, and the rider inclined her head before spurring her horse ahead. The rest followed as if there was an unspoken command. Intrigued by this seeming power hierarchy, Faelara quieted the questions that swirled in her skull, at least for the moment.

For the next several bells, no one spoke. Loghan kept his focus directly in front of him, his jaw tight, and Baehlon rode with a silly grin on his stupid handsome face. Men. No doubt Loghan had already explained the protocol when visitors entered Ulla's borders, but no one saw fit to tell her they'd be ambushed by a bunch of mysterious riders.

She busied herself with studying the landscapes, but after a while, it was all the same. Dirt, rock, more dirt, maybe a reddish arch of rock, and more dirt. Although, now that she looked closer, it might've been sand.

Sand was new. She looked up with renewed interest. Yes, the ground was definitely changing from a dusty ochre hue to a beiger tone. The terrarae beneath their horses' hooves was leveling out after the mountainous terrain they'd traveled through, and in the distance she could've sworn she saw the faint glimmer of water.

"Are we near the sea?" she asked before remembering the no-speaking admonition.

Loghan cast her a withering glance, followed by a wink and a slight nod. The other riders ignored her completely. Baehlon held out his hand and she took it with a small smile. His strength flowed into her, and she gave a soft squeeze to let him know how grateful she was to have him with her.

The sound of singing came to her from the area to their right. She glanced at the sun to determine the direction of the singing, but it was directly overhead, no help at all.

My love, do you hear singing? she asked Baehlon. His sharp glance was enough to tell her he hadn't. Bugger. That meant the strange sea woman was near—but how would she know Faelara was in the desert and would be near the seas? She wouldn't, unless she was somehow tracking her.

Loghan, Faelara began, unsure if he would appreciate the mental intrusion. *I thought the Ullans stayed far from the water, yet I can see the seas from here.*

My mother insisted we bring my father closer to the seas to keep him cool. Even close to Harvest, the inland gets intolerably hot.

Do you hear singing?

I do not. Ullans are not known for their vocal prowess. Quite the opposite, I would imagine.

She held in a snicker. Whether he knew he'd made a jest, she couldn't tell, but the sincerity of his statement made her tummy flutter. She released Baehlon's hand and placed it over her abdomen.

Is there a problem? Do we need to stop riding? His concern was charming, but unnecessary.

The baby and I are fine. All is well, my darling. She retook his hand and rode on with an ear to the singing while scanning the horizon for threats.

A short while later, they rode into a camp of hundreds of tents. It was a dizzying array of color in stripes and harlequins, squares and spots. Each tent was distinct, yet similar to the others. The black-clad riders led them through wide openings between the tents with Ullans gaping at them the entire way. Some recognized Loghan and bowed or curtseyed to their prince, while others were more interested in Faelara and Baehlon.

When finally a group of youths rushed out to take their horses, she breathed a sigh of relief to be out of the saddle. It had been a stressful trip through the desert and she felt every anxious nerve in her body.

The hooded figure who'd motioned to her at the very start of their escort made their way to Loghan. Once they removed their headpiece, Fae saw that it was indeed a woman. A very pretty one with short blonde curls, tipped ears, and a complexion that was better suited to the Narthvier than the harsh desert. In her heart, she recognized the woman from Rhoane's stories of his time with the Ullans. She had to be Kaleigh, Amdi Agnar's first wife.

Loghan embraced the woman and put his forehead against hers. "Mother. It is good to see you. How is father? How is the baby?"

The baby? Faelara put a hand on her abdomen as if to protect it from an unseen threat.

"We are well, your father is no worse, thank Verdaine." Her gaze went to Faelara and Baehlon. "Who are your friends?"

"This is Sir Baehlon de Monteferron, and this lovely woman is his betrothed, Lady Faelara kaj Endion. They are both good friends of Rhoane and Taryn and offered to see me safely home." To her and Baehlon he said, "This is my mother, Kaleigh al Fyrnwood ap Agnar."

"So many names. Please, call me Fae. Or Faelara, whichever you prefer." Suddenly, she was nervous, which made no sense since she was accustomed to meeting royalty. Knowing Kaleigh's history with Rhoane, however, made her uneasy.

"I am happy to make both of your acquaintances. Let me show you to your tent." To her son, she promised to meet with him in a little while.

They meandered through the maze of tents, some barely wider than Baehlon's strong shoulders. Finally, they came to a deep green tent and Kaleigh held open the flap for them to enter. As Faelara ducked beneath the fabric, she noticed two guards positioned several paces away. Whether to protect Kaleigh, or to spy on them, she wasn't sure.

"I hope these accommodations will be adequate. We were not expecting guests, but I can arrange for a nicer tent to be prepared for you." Kaleigh held her hands clasped in front of her, eyes downcast.

"The tent is lovely. We won't need other arrangements." Fae

glanced at the sumptuous furnishings, surprised Kaleigh thought this tent unworthy. It boasted a solid wood dresser, two comfortable-looking chairs, several large pillows, cashmere throws, an alcove she assumed was for bodily functions, and a bed large enough for both her and Baehlon. What more could they possibly want? Besides, they wouldn't be staying long enough to outgrow the room.

After an awkward pause, Kaleigh wrung her hands and apologized in a rush that the laird was not well, it was a bad time for a visit, and she was sorry but they would need to remain in their tent most of the duration. At the end of her confession, she bit her lower lip and edged toward the door, but didn't leave.

Fae took Kaleigh's hand in hers, surprising the woman. "We are not here on a social call. I brought with me an elixir that may help your husband. Yes, I admit I am curious about your healing and would like to learn more—as an observer only—but our first and foremost concern is restoring your laird's mental faculties. I'm sorry if we gave you any other impression."

Kaleigh ran a hand through her short curls with a light chuckle. "I suppose I am nervous because of who you are, yes. Compared to Talaith, we live humble lives, but also you are close companions to the *Darennsai*. We spent so little time together when she was here a few moonturns back, but of you two, she shared a great deal. I feel compelled to make your stay as comfortable and memorable as possible so that I do not let you or her down."

Fae barely hid her surprise. "I am honored Taryn mentioned us, but since you did spend time with her, you know she isn't one to put on airs or begrudge someone for a missed cushion. I doubt she'd be worried for our comfort if she knew we were here."

"She does not know? But I thought she sent you?" Kaleigh's look of consternation made small wrinkles in her clear skin. "Her and Rhoane's visit was…challenging. And then when she took

Loghan without an explanation—I thought perhaps she meant to assert her authority or punish us somehow."

Took Loghan? Assert authority? This woman clearly didn't know Taryn as Faelara did. Or perhaps she knew her better. Jealousy and guilt swirled in her belly. She'd known Taryn as a newborn babe, and then again when Taryn returned from wherever Brandt had hidden her, but did she know her friend now? Truly? So much had happened in so short a time. It was possible Kaleigh knew a different version of Taryn than Fae did.

Baehlon grumped and shifted, his displeasure at Kaleigh's words evident. He was protective of Taryn, as they all were, but even more so of Rhoane. They'd been friends ever since he left the Ullans sixty seasons past. She thought she knew Rhoane well, but as with Taryn, perhaps there was another side to the Eleri she'd never seen. She placed a hand on Baehlon's forearm with a slight shake of her head. This was a time for diplomacy, not angry retorts.

The tent flap opened and several young servants entered with platters of food. Silver platters, no less. Fae spied sweets and breaded puffs she hoped held some kind of meat. Their portions on the road had been lean, consisting mainly of dried meats, cheese, and bread. Whatever Baehlon caught was added each night, but they traveled light, which meant a growly belly most of the time.

The servants placed the trays on a low table and Kaleigh thanked them as they left. Behind the rest, a young boy of perhaps five or six with sandy hair and clear blue eyes approached cautiously. Balanced on his chubby fingers was another silver tray with delicate cups of steaming liquid. He set the tray on the table and stood back, a wide, toothy grin on his little face.

"This is Michel. He is a foundling without a family or tribe. I am looking after him as the *Darennsai* requested. He was the one responsible for bringing Taryn to us when she was injured." Kaleigh stroked the lad's head, pride exuding from her in waves.

"He found her not far from where we are now, and made a litter out of scraps. Verdaine must've been watching over him because I often wonder how someone so small made the long and difficult trek to where we were staying."

Faelara and Baehlon bent to one knee in unison. "Dear boy, you have our greatest thanks for saving our friend." Fae spoke softly and kept herself from reaching for his hand. They were strangers to him and the last thing she wanted was to frighten him.

He looked to Kaleigh and she translated from Elennish to Ullan.

"Darennsai is safe now?" he asked Faelara in broken Elennish.

She smiled, her heart all warm and buttery. "Yes. Taryn is well." Gods, she hoped it was true. Wherever the girl was, she hoped she was safe and healthy.

Baehlon inclined his head to Michel. "We owe you a debt of gratitude. Anything you need, you just ask."

Again Kaleigh translated, and Michel looked at the pair of them with wide eyes. He reached a little hand out to touch the bells in Baehlon's braids. When they chimed, he giggled.

"Music shells."

"Bells," Baehlon corrected him.

Michel shook his head and pointed to the tent opening. "Shells. Music. Pretty." Then he did the most remarkable thing. He pointed to Faelara, and back to himself. "We hear music. We understand." He placed his hand over her heart and nodded. "Home."

Fae's face went warm and then cold as tears pricked her eyes. She shared a glance with Baehlon, but instead of curiosity, his features were clouded with alarm.

"No, Fae. I won't allow it."

She sat back and glared at the foolish man. "*Allow it?* I don't recall ever needing your permission, and I'm not about to start asking for it now."

Michel babbled to Kaleigh in Ullan, his face full of distress.

"I do not understand," Kaleigh said. She arranged herself on one of the large cushions and Michel crawled into her lap. "Michel worries he upset you, but that was not his intention. He says Xianqin told him of your arrival and he thought you would be happy. He brought you tea to show how honored you are." She shook her head, making the blonde curls bounce with her movements. "Who is Xianqin? What is Michel talking about?"

Faelara sat with an *oof* on a cushion, regretting it immediately. It was only slightly softer than the saddle she'd been riding in for the past fortnight.

"I thought Julieta would give us more time. Or, perhaps, was mistaken." She looked to Kaleigh, her face weighed down with sadness. "We truly did come to offer healing to your husband, but we were also tasked by the goddess Julieta to travel to the Jansen Strait and find this mysterious Xianqin. That Michel here knows of her is no coincidence."

"Who or what is a Xianqin?" Kaleigh wrapped her arms around Michel and he snuggled into her. "What does she want with you and Michel?"

"Of the former, I could only guess. Of that latter..." Fae picked up a cup and sniffed the delicious tea before downing it in one long gulp. It wasn't dreem, but it would do. "I believe she wishes for Baehlon and I to seek out King Baldev."

Michel nodded enthusiastically, and Faelara's heart sank. She'd really, *really* hoped Julieta had been jesting when she'd said King Baldev sought an audience with her.

What could the sea king possibly want with her? Her gaze slid to Michel, a pinging suspicion rattling in her skull. *Home,* he'd said. Which meant he wasn't a foundling or an Ullan. He was one of the merfolk.

He was her kin.

CHAPTER TWENTY-FIVE

Futnuckers and snickertits. Where had she heard those words before? Taryn cast her memory in search of the source, but too many names and faces crowded her mind. She glided behind Rhoane, her scales slick with rain, her talons half frozen. Whose great idea was it to fly from the Narthvier to Paderau? Oh, that's right, it was hers. Futnuckers and snickertits. Worst idea ever.

An image of blue hair and a sweet face came to her. Rori! The young faerie with unicorn blood and a penchant for getting herself in trouble. And a knack for making up silly swear words. Taryn's body warmed with the memory of the lass, but she couldn't allow her thoughts to linger on where Rori might be or how she was faring. At the moment, she needed to focus on not crashing into the copse of trees Rhoane led them toward.

He'd chosen the ridge above Paderau so they could shift into human form before entering the city, but with the sudden storm that had popped up, they probably could've flown right into the palace courtyard and no one would've noticed. If anyone was even out at this dreadful hour.

We'll be landing soon, hang on to my scales. She sent the thought to Khrystina, who squeezed her legs tighter around

Taryn's midsection and gripped her scales as if her life depended on it. Which, to be fair, it did. But Taryn would never let the girl fall. Not on purpose, anyway. Though she'd thought about it twice on the flight over. The girl could be annoying with her prickly attitude and pretentious airs.

Be kind, mi carae, Rhoane chuckled in her thoughts. *She is no threat to us.*

I'm not worried about her being a threat, I just wish she wasn't such a downer. I feel like I need to be extra peppy just to get her to smile.

Be yourself and let her be herself. You do not have to entertain everyone all the time.

He was right, of course, but the girl's surliness made her nervous.

Kaida barked twice and spiraled through the trees before making a perfect landing on a patch of grass. She'd been thrilled to fly, truly fly, and Taryn was beginning to think she'd created a monster. In the best way, of course.

She chuckled to herself and brought her dragon body through the treetops without issue. When her talons were firmly planted on the ground, Khrystina slid from her with a sigh.

"I do wish I had a saddle, but that was exhilarating. Thank you, Darennsai." She curtseyed low in the Eleri fashion and Taryn felt a pinch of guilt for thinking her annoying.

Taryn shook herself into her human form. "It's not common knowledge we are darathi, so please keep that to yourself." She arched and stretched her back. "But it is a quicker way to travel than by horseback, and I have to admit, it's a lot more fun."

Rhoane transitioned into his human form and nodded. "When the darathi are returned to Aelinae, perhaps you will be one of the riders."

Khrystina's face lit up, but then she frowned. "I do not think that is what Verdaine has in mind for me."

Taryn glanced at Rhoane and he shrugged. Neither of them understood Verdaine's insistence the girl travel with them.

"What path do you think she is steering you toward?" Taryn reached for Kaida, and they made their way to the road that led to Paderau.

"I am not fully certain, but I will know when we reach Talaith." She adjusted the bag she wore slung across her chest and set her shoulders. "I have no family, and very few friends. Perhaps she believes I am a good candidate for a traveling academic."

"No!" Rhoane cast her an alarmed glance. "That is a lonely life, and one chosen by those who wish to live it. Did you tell Verdaine that is your choice?"

Khrystina laughed a bitter chortle that made her face scrunch. "Since when do novices have a choice? We are told from an early age what our life will be, and when the time comes, we are shipped off to the temple."

Taryn blinked against the rain, anger rising at what she'd heard. "Everyone has a choice. If the Eleri are forcing young girls to be in Verdaine's cult, that must stop."

"It is not a cult, Taryn," Rhoane cautioned. "I am sure Khrystina's experience is not the norm."

By the way Khrystina clamped her lips shut and stared straight ahead, Taryn guessed that was totally the way things were. They let it drop for now, but Taryn would find a quiet moment to talk with her and suss out the truth. Then she and Carga would have a serious discussion about consent and obligation.

They cleared the trees and there, sitting between two rivers looking just as enchanted as the first time she saw the city, was Paderau. The sense of homecoming she always had when she returned to the palace washed over her and it took all her control not to race down the road to her uncle's home. Even though she knew he wasn't there, it was comforting to be in his space.

The rain let up by the time they reached the city gates, and the sun made a welcome appearance. Soaked clear through, they shivered as they passed from the old city into the new. Khrystina's eyes were large and full of wonder as she gazed at the surrounding buildings. It reminded Taryn of her first time walking through the streets of Paderau. They might've come from different backgrounds, and her thoughts and experiences of Paderau were vastly different from Khrystina's, but the city had been the first for both of them. In that, they shared something special.

She'd been raised in a world of technology; in comparison, Paderau seemed positively medieval to her. The Eleri, on the other hand, was raised in a forest—albeit with indoor plumbing and ShantiMari enhanced drossfire—but without buildings like those hunching over the streets, or the magnitude of people.

"Where do they all sleep at night?" Khrystina mused. "How do they produce enough food to feed everyone?"

Rhoane pointed to the timbered buildings with tenements above the shops lining the streets. "Most live in flats like those, but a good number live in houses we will pass in a few minutes."

"Paderau trades with many other cities in Aelinae. Some of those places produce wheat and grain, others wine or cheese. Trade makes it easy to obtain what you need without having to grow it all yourself." Taryn paid close attention to Khrystina's reaction to what they told her, pleased when she saw a spark of interest instead of condemnation.

They passed the square where the Shadow Assassin had attacked Taryn and a moment of panic slowed her steps. Rhoane tucked her hand in the crook of his arm and stroked her fingertips.

"Do you need a moment?"

She shook her head and strode forward, but her thoughts remained in the square. Gavyn had been a tool used by Kaldaar to destroy her. Feelings of loss, remorse, and guilt washed over her. She bathed in them for only a few minutes before reminding herself that he'd sacrificed himself for her not once, but twice. He was as much a victim to the god's evil's schemes as she was. She owed it to him to defeat Kaldaar, and Myrddin too if he continued to do the deranged god's bidding.

What about Zakael? Was he a victim? Or a willing participant?

"These homes are glorious." Khrystina broke through Taryn's musings. "Who lives here?"

"Paderau's wealthy merchants, courtiers, nobility—anyone who can afford to, I would guess." Rhoane glanced at Taryn, his concern making crinkles near his eyes.

"I'm fine." She kissed his cheek as they continued to the palace. "Just sad about some things."

Khrystina scoffed. Whether she meant to out loud or not, Taryn heard and chose to ignore the slight. Rhoane, however, did not.

"Explain yourself, Novice." His tone, deep and threatening, made little swirlies in her belly.

She'd never thought she'd like a protective man, but damn if it wasn't hot to hear the low growl in his voice, to feel the steel in his grip and know that if needed, he would destroy or heal a world for her.

"Look at her. She is perfection. Intelligent, funny, gorgeous. Tell me, what does she have to be sad about? It is not as if her path was chosen for her at birth all because of bad decisions her parents made." Khrystina kicked at a cobble and swore beneath her breath.

Neither Taryn nor Rhoane broke into laughter, but damn, she wanted to, and could feel him controlling himself to keep from unleashing holy hell on the poor girl. The novice had no idea how wrong she was, and at the same time how true her words were for Taryn as well.

"You never truly know a person by only seeing what you wish to see." Compassion cloaked Rhoane's words.

As much as Taryn yearned to lecture the academic, possibly

even show her the scar the vorlock had left, she chose to follow Rhoane's lead.

"Being bitter about the past never did anyone any good." One day Khrystina might regret her words, but Taryn had no ill will for the girl. "We're here." She pointed to the palace gates.

Thank fuck. At least the conversation would end before it got super awkward.

Two guards challenged them as they approached, neither of which Taryn recognized. When she told them who they were, they glanced at each other, but did not open the gate.

"Taryn ap Galendrin is dead," one of the men said.

"By whose authority do you make this claim?" Rhoane lifted his chin even though he stood at least half a head taller than either guard.

"By decree of Her Royal Majesty Empress Lliandra." The guard didn't sound as confident as he studied the three of them, his glance avoiding Kaida altogether.

Taryn chewed a cuticle, her mind spinning. Clearly, she wasn't dead. But for her mother to send a decree to the cities of the east meant she'd believed Myrddin's lies. Did her mother mourn her? The question burned against her skull, but she couldn't loiter on unpleasant thoughts. They'd have to be gentle in their appearance in Talaith if Lliandra truly believed she was dead.

That matter was for another day. Right then, her only concern was convincing the guards to allow them passage. Beyond the gates was her room with not only a comfortable bed, but a lush shower built for two, and her raggedy ass was tired of playing games.

"I am Taryn ap Galendrin, I am not dead, and you will open these gates or I will open them for myself." She took a step toward them and a guard withdrew her sword to block her.

She'd been expecting that. She waved a hand and the sword went limp. Another wave and the gates clicked open to allow them entrance. An alarm sounded, but she continued toward the palace. Behind her, she heard Khrystina make a sound—whether it was a whimper or grumble, she couldn't tell. Rhoane strode by her side, a wide grin on his face. Kaida padded to her right, her tongue lolling from her open mouth.

Two dozen soldiers rushed the courtyard and surrounded them, swords drawn. She and Rhoane ignored them and continued onward only to be stopped by a familiar voice.

"Are my eyes becoming so old they are playing tricks on me, or have two beloved friends risen from the dead?" Stanton, Duke Anje's Captain of the Guard stood inside the ring of soldiers, hands on hips, a wide smile on his handsome face.

Khrystina stood between him and Taryn and Rhoane, her eyes large in her pale face. Taryn felt a pinch of pity for her. She didn't understand what was happening and probably thought they were in trouble.

"I think I died once in Ulla, but as far as I recall, I'm not dead now." Taryn strode to the man and gripped his shoulders. "It's good to see a friendly face."

The smile slipped and he glanced at those around him. "There is much you need to know. Not here. Meet me in my office in a quarter bell." Then, louder, he said, "Back to work for you lot, nothing to see here. And I mean that—you saw nothing, you heard nothing." His piercing gaze went to each soldier, who nodded and shuffled toward the barracks.

"That bad?" Rhoane asked as he approached.

"Worse." Stanton's glare flicked to Khrystina before returning to them. "Much worse."

CHAPTER TWENTY-SIX

Gentle waves lapped upon the shore of the Kiltern River, the sound soothing to Taryn's worried mind. "Much worse" had turned out to be the understatement of the century.

She adjusted herself on the bench—the same one she'd sat upon numerous times during her first visit to Paderau. So many firsts had happened here: The first time she'd met her sisters, though she didn't learn they were her sisters until later. The first time she saw Lliandra and was entranced by her presence and beauty. Her first kiss. Rhoane had kissed her on her birthday just a few paces from where she sat. How innocent she'd been those first heady days on Aelinae.

If she'd known what her future entailed, she might've run screaming straight back to Nadra's cavern and demanded she return to Earth.

Would she have? Truly? No, she would've done exactly what she did when she learned her mother was the Empress of the East, and her father the Overlord of the West—embraced her destiny with as much courage and grace as she could muster.

She folded her legs and rested her chin on her knees as she watched boats cruise up and down the river, bringing goods to

Paderau. The Kiltern River flowed all the way from Paderau to the Eastern Seas, forming a natural border between Lliandra's kingdom and Ulla. Somewhere out there, creatures like Enghor gathered, an army of aliens hellbent on destroying Aelans. But did they come willingly? Or had they been forced?

According to Stanton, the ram-ape beasts roamed the countryside looking for something, but he couldn't ascertain what. Three of his scouts had confirmed sightings of the creatures. He'd received word only a few days earlier about the attack on Tinsley's group. He confirmed the lord was gravely wounded in the altercation and only survived because Faelara and Loghan had been there to assist. He relayed the news that Tinsley and his group, which included Eoghan, were traveling slowly toward Talaith. As to the man's condition, Stanton only knew he was alive.

Taryn made a mental map in her mind, placing Faelara and Baehlon in Ulla, and Loghan, Eoghan, Tinsley, Aomori, and Gwainne in Talaith with her sisters and cousin.

As concerned as she was for Tinsley, especially in light of Carga's admission, it was Stanton's report on Caer Idris that upset her the most. His spies had found the dungeons empty, but the graveyards full. Kaldaar was slaughtering people wholesale. No one was safe from the god's wrath—nobility, servants, peasants, they were all fodder for his increasing appetite. The only people he spared seemed to be soldiers, and even those he would randomly decimate if they displeased him.

Of Zakael, Stanton had no update. The new overlord, or king, or whatever Zakael called himself these days, had been silent for near on a sennight. Whispers hinted that the young ruler was dead, but no one could confirm those rumors.

Did they go to Talaith first and see to Tinsley? Or should they go to Caer Idris and confront Kaldaar? And what of the creatures? She was certain they were Enghor's kin and it broke her heart to know that Kaldaar meant to use them for his personal army. What if they could find where Zakael had hidden them?

They could return them to their home worlds and rob Kaldaar of fighters.

The gentle waves crashed a little harder upon the riverbank and she unfolded her legs to stretch. The boats she'd watched earlier were no longer on the water. The river was empty of craft, large or small. Either it was an odd moment of tranquility, or something else entirely—either way, there was definitely a ripple in the current. Enough to cause the water to move, as if a great force was pushing it farther up the shore. Intrigued, she shuffled to the river's edge and peered into the clear water. Sand and rock and little fishes darting in every direction gave no cause for alarm. And yet her belly buzzed with apprehension.

She knew this feeling. Had felt it before on a similar riverbank in the cold and rain and sleet. She stepped back to avoid what she knew was coming, and was powerless to stop, but it was too late. Rykoto's face emerged from the clear water. His red-rimmed eyes were angry bits of steel as he glared at her. His bloodied lips snarled with a grotesque laugh.

She tripped over her own feet as she scrambled backward. The mad god's hands thrust out and didn't grab her by the throat like she'd assumed he would—no, his hand tore through the fabric of her tunic into her flesh, leaving a gaping wound in its wake. Bony fingers squeezed her heart as he lifted himself fully out of the river.

Panic seized her, halting her breath, clouding her mind. She reached for her sword, but it was locked in a cupboard in her room. All she had on her was a small knife. Her fingers twitched above its hiding place tucked inside her trousers. She called forth her sword, but it didn't respond. More panic, this time Rykoto had done the one thing she swore never to let happen—he'd blocked her from her power. Yet she felt her ShantiMari swirling in her blood, could feel its need to be released. Once more she called for her sword and once more was denied. Why would Ynyd Eirathnacht forsake her in her time of need?

Another squeeze and the breath whooshed from her lungs, leaving her gasping. Her heartbeats thrummed against the pressure in her skull. Every inch of her screamed for her to attack him, to defend herself, but he literally held her life in his hand. Besides, even if she could kick out or throw a punch, it would be useless against his power. *Patience*, her mind whispered. Rykoto was a master of illusion. For all she knew, this wasn't real. Her flesh was solid, her heart still strong.

If she remained calm, she might learn something if she let him believe he'd overpowered her. As difficult as it was not to fight back, she hung limp and affixed a defeated grimace to her face.

"You worthless cur. You thought to silence me? To imprison me in my own temple? You are a fool. And now you will pay with your life." He moved his face to within an inch of hers and breathed in. "I will take all your glorious power for myself and enact revenge on those that thought—like you—that I could be defeated. Starting with my half-wit brother."

"My power is not yours to take." Taryn ground out the words between small breaths.

Rykoto's grip tightened around her heart and stars blinked on the edges of her vision. They'd danced this dance before, but that first time she'd been too afraid of him to think straight. Not that she wasn't metaphorically shitting bricks at the moment, but she'd be damned if she let him know how frightened she was. If he was after her power, it was for a reason, and she could guess why that might be—the same reason Kaldaar needed his, to become fully realized once more.

She tucked her power deep inside where he couldn't reach it. Or where she hoped he couldn't find it. Just to be safe, she checked that the little flame she always kept separate still burned. If he stole anything, he wouldn't get everything.

"Your power was given to you by the gods. It is as much mine as it is my brother's." Rykoto stood to his full height, a good head and a half taller than her, and her feet dangled above the ground. Black hair hung in greasy chunks, curling around his shoulders. High cheekbones accentuated the hollowness of his cheeks.

He was weakened. Despite his bravado, he wasn't nearly as strong as he once was. What had Zakael said? Rykoto wasn't happy with the changes she'd made to his temple. Her mind flashed to the pristine altar. It hadn't been used since she cleansed the place.

"You're weak, Rykoto. Hungry." She glared at him, ignoring the hiss and snarls he made. "Zakael did his best to feed you, but I made that near impossible, didn't I?"

The pressure increased on her heart and its beating slowed to a deathly pace, but she couldn't stop now.

"What did Kaldaar promise you? That you could have Julieta and Daknys first? Then you'd be free to go after Verdaine? Or would you skip straight to your mother and father? When will it be enough, Rykoto? When will your revenge be complete?"

"You know nothing, stupid girl." He drew a long breath and moaned in ecstasy. "I can smell your death. Even now, your heart weakens. Your mind is tiring. Your power…ah, you've hidden it quite well, Aelan. But I am a god, and you are not. There is no hiding from me."

"Tell me." She tried for a seductive tone, but it came out more like a croak. "Tell me of your wicked plans. Excite me with your deviousness. Enthrall me with your brilliance."

He leaned back, his face full of rapture. "With your power, and your sword, I will annihilate them all. The elder gods, and the younger. They will bow to me first, and then, one by one, I will take their power as my own."

"Yes," she cooed, more confident in her deception. "You are smarter than all of them. How will you do it? Don't tease me, tell me how it's done. How will you take their power?"

It was a dangerous game to play, but she hoped Rykoto was

too arrogant to see through her performance. With one twitch he could end her life, but she had to know.

"Eat their still-beating hearts." His sibilant answer burned her ears. A blood-soaked tongue licked his lips, and she swallowed the bile that stung the back of her throat. "Starting with yours."

"Like hell you will," Rhoane said from behind Rykoto.

Taryn looked at him in surprise. She'd been too focused on the mad god to hear him approach. With a hearty grunt, Rhoane thrust his sword through Rykoto's torso. "And now you die, you pathetic excuse for a god."

Claidholm Solais glowed with Rhoane's power, illuminating Rykoto from the inside out. His grip on Taryn lessened and she dropped to the ground gasping for air. She poked and prodded her chest, but there was no open wound, no sign he'd assaulted her at all. Even so, she placed a protective hand over her heart.

Rhoane held Rykoto around the neck with his left arm, and shoved his sword deeper until the blade came out the other side of the god's chest. His dark eyes glared at her in surprise, a question lurking in their depths. He hadn't counted on Rhoane or his sword interrupting them and was enraged that he'd prevented him from destroying Taryn.

She stood on wobbly legs and stared, not quite understanding what was transpiring before her. The flesh on Rykoto's face peeled back to reveal blood and bone. A moment later, that was replaced with a charred skull. She retched at the sight but did not look away.

Claidholm Solais's glow turned from white to golden light. Her gaze went to Rhoane and she realized it wasn't the sword that emitted the light, but her beloved.

Rays of light burst from him like a small sun. In that moment she saw him as the god he would become, and he was glorious. Righteousness and strength. Quiet yet lethal, just as he was in life.

Rykoto's shriek rent the air and a vision flashed in her mind

—the same as the one at Lan Gyllarelle, only this time she saw the mad god as the figure standing in the hellscape of flowing lava and death. She also saw exactly where the tear in Aelinae's terrarae was, and how to fix it. Whether Rykoto was intentionally showing her these things, she couldn't be certain. His mind was a chaotic mess of rage and disbelief.

She took the opportunity to embed false memories into his thoughts in the hopes he would forget what he'd discovered about her, and especially Rhoane.

Rhoane's brilliance began to fade and the charred body of Rykoto slid off his sword to land with a thump on the ground. Quicker than she'd thought possible, the lump wriggled into the water and disappeared beneath the surface.

Both she and Rhoane stared at the river for several minutes, half-expecting the god to reemerge. When he didn't, she slumped against Rhoane and he led her to the bench. He checked her neck and face, turning her head this way and that before delicately lifting her tunic to inspect her unmarked chest.

"Are you injured?" His healing wrapped around her like a warm blanket.

"I'll recover." She rubbed his hand, grateful for the solidness of him. The reality of him. She pressed a hand to her chest and breathed in several times. "I don't feel his presence, not even a lingering taint." She pulled Rhoane's ShantiMari deeper, into her veins and around her heart. His startled look quickly changed to wonder, and she felt his power strengthen inside and outside of her body. She could've stayed in his protective cocoon all day, but Rykoto's appearance was a cruel reminder they couldn't dawdle. "I let him think he had control of me."

"Did you learn anything of value?"

She stretched her back and took in a long drag of air as she nodded. "Loads. First, where the tear is and how to fix it. Second, he's terrified of us. He had no idea you were to become a god." She took Rhoane's hand in hers. "If he doesn't know, then Kaldaar might not know. We can use this information, I'm just not sure how. My brain's a little scrambled right now."

"Anything else?"

"He's using the waterways as a means of escaping his prison. Remember last winter when he nearly killed me by the river on our way to Celyn Eryri for the Light Celebrations? Water. Lan Gyllarelle when we both had the visions? Water. When we repair the rift, he can't escape Dal Ferran and this, more than anything, frightens him. But that's not the best part. He's weakened. Kaldaar was siphoning his power to restore himself, but now that Rykoto is sealed away, Kaldaar can't get to him. Not only that"—her heart raced with excitement and her words came out rushed—"I know how to kill a god."

Rhoane looked at her as if she'd lost her damn mind. "Is that what you wish for? To kill Kaldaar?"

From his tone it was clear he didn't approve, but wasn't that the only way to restore balance to Aelinae? If not, what the hell had the past season been about? All the suffering, the near dying and actual dying? The bopping from world to world to find the seals? Everything she'd done since she arrived on Aelinae had been moving her toward one specific outcome, and now he was making her doubt everything.

She watched the water ripple upon the shore and shrugged. "Do you have a better plan for balancing Aelinae?"

They sat for a long time with fingers entwined, each lost to their own thoughts. The sun slipped behind the horizon and a chill entered the air, but neither stirred. When Taryn shivered, Rhoane put an arm around her shoulder and pulled her close. His steady heartbeat sounded beneath her ear, the soundtrack to her life.

"No." It was barely a whisper, but she heard it as if it came from his heart.

She twisted to look him in the eye. "No what?"

"I do not have a better plan. Either Kaldaar must die, or we die trying to save Aelinae. I do not see another path."

She shifted completely until she straddled him on the bench and stroked her fingers along his handsome face. "There is another way, mi carae."

And it didn't involve eating a god's still-beating heart. In the throes of his mania Rykoto had shown her the meaning of Xianqin's warning, but it was what Rhoane just said that made it all make sense. Rhoane would indeed betray her, but as the wily water dragon once said, not all betrayals are bad.

CHAPTER TWENTY-SEVEN

They stood in the far corner of the garden where they were least likely to be seen, each tired from the day's events, but for different reasons. Kaida from worry and guilt she hadn't been with Taryn when Rykoto attacked, Khrystina from bell upon bell spent scouring Paderau's library, Rhoane from the amount of ShantiMari he'd used to free Taryn from Rykoto's deathly grip, and Taryn from, well, nearly succumbing to the mad god's rage.

Ynyd Eirathnacht hung at her side, a solemn melody playing from the sword. She understood now why it hadn't answered her call. Rykoto had said he needed her power and her blade. Her sword had stayed hidden in the cupboard she'd warded to keep him from gaining her power. She stroked the dragon winged hilt and silently thanked the sword for protecting her. Her fingers went to the cynfar she wore and she smiled. Ynyd Eirathnacht had always been with her, as had Rhoane. Rykoto couldn't steal what was rightfully hers.

She yawned and scrubbed her eyes, giving one last longing glance to the palace and her lovely bed with the delightful shower in the next room. One night, that's all she had to enjoy their pleasures, but she promised herself she'd return soon and spend an entire week cooried in with nothing to do but read, sleep, and soak in the tub.

"Are you ready?" Rhoane stood next to her, his eyes scanning the area for threats.

"As I'll ever be. Kaida, this will be a longer flight. Let us know if you're getting tired." She scratched the grierbas between the ears and sent a thread of her power to give her strength.

A wag of her tail served as answer. The silly girl was excited for the trip. Taryn couldn't fault her, though. She remembered her first flights and how exhilarating they had been. Still were, if she was being honest. But what lay ahead of them dragged at her heart.

She and Rhoane shifted into their darathi vorsi forms and Khrystina climbed atop her back. The Eleri was wearing gloves and Taryn noticed she had also fashioned some kind of padding to the inner thighs of her trousers. It was as close to a saddle as she'd get and would hopefully make the trip more comfortable.

A moment later, they were airborne and heading south toward Talaith. As tempting as it was to dash off to the Jansen Strait and repair the rip in Aelinae's terrarae, both she and Rhoane needed to be at their strongest before they faced that challenge. And with Rykoto wounded, he wouldn't be much of threat for a little while. That was the hope, at least.

They flew in silence with Kaida racing ahead to scout for danger and returning with a barrel roll or loop thrown in. Her long wings whooshed slightly with each beat, but otherwise she ghosted through the air. It was an incredible sight to behold.

Darennsai, there is something ahead at the southern end of the lake, Kaida warned in her mind.

Taryn peered into the distance, her darathi sight much better than even her Eleri vision. It took only a few moments for her to spot the lump of charred something on the ground. They descended slowly, aware there might be more creatures lurking in the woods to the west of the road, but the night was quiet. There was no threat in the immediate area.

Once shifted, she and Rhoane withdrew their swords and approached the heap with caution. The stench of rotting bodies came to them, making her gag. She saw a burnt horn and paused.

"This is where they battled the ram-ape beasts."

Rhoane nodded as he circled the pile of charred bodies. "I sense Faelara's ShantiMari." His gaze went to a large boulder that looked out of place. "She knocked them over with that rock." He bent and rubbed his fingertips along the ground. "Three beasts." With a startled gaze, he looked at her, eyes huge in the scant moonlight. *They are from the same realm as Enghor. I would guess they are kin.*

Taryn put a hand over her heart. She'd been afraid that's what he would say. She looked around them, at the emptiness and darkness. "Where is he keeping them?"

"Who?" Khrystina kept behind her, away from the remains. "What are they?"

"Mohram." Rhoane rose and wiped his hands on his trousers. "Their horns and talons are slathered with poison not easily found in this part of Aelinae." He looked at Taryn with a meaningful stare.

"Is 'Mohram' the poison? Or the creatures?"

"They are of the Mohram race. I recognized the name from Amdi's camp, but this one confirmed it." He shuffled a booted toe toward the one he'd been inspecting. "He was not yet dead."

Taryn and Khrystina gasped in unison. The novice gagged and raced toward the lake. There was a time when Taryn would've done the same. But now? Now she was not unaffected by the scene but had learned to parcel her emotions into a neat box when dealing with unpleasantness such as this. The realization drowned her thoughts in sorrow.

"Rhoane, they were burned. How was it he survived?" She crouched beside the poor creature.

"He clung to life long enough to ask that he be forgiven. We are the first to come upon them. I do not know if he would have lasted much longer." Rhoane's solemn tone held vast amounts of meaning that Taryn understood. It was as she suspected—they'd been coerced into service.

"Did you ease his passing?"

"I did."

"Kaida, take Khrystina to the woods so that she cannot see what we do."

Rhoane watched Kaida trot toward the novice. "What do you have in mind?"

"Return them to their home world." She chewed a thumbnail. "But not like this."

When Kaida and Khrystina disappeared in the trees, she opened a tiny portal only as big as a dinner plate. Rhoane joined her and together, they used their ShantiMari to disintegrate the bodies into motes of dust and glitter. Their shimmering essences drifted through the portal to their home world. Once the last of the beasts was removed from Aelinae, Taryn closed the portal with a silent prayer for those that were slain.

Their family members would never know what had happened to them, but she hoped by sending their heavenly forms home, their spirits might be at peace. It was all a guess, but it felt right.

"We will find the others, mi carae, and when we do, we will send them all home—alive." Rhoane rubbed her back, and she sighed, knowing it wouldn't be as easy as that but hoping she was wrong.

She called Kaida and Khrystina so that they could resume their journey to Talaith. Heaviness weighed on their hearts. Death was never easy—whether to mete out, or to observe—and it had become too much a part of her life of late. There had to be a way to bring balance to Aelinae without more death. Or destruction. Yet she knew, in the depths of her soul, there was not.

They took flight once more, and Taryn scanned the distant landscape looking for where the Mohram might be camped.

There is a tent up ahead. I cannot sense anything from it, can you? Rhoane asked, and she searched the ground beneath them, seeing immediately one lone tent.

She closed her eyes and sent feelers of ShantiMari toward the single structure. Someone had warded the tent not to be seen by others, but they didn't count on her or Rhoane's enhanced darathi vision.

It is warded, but there are people within. I sense the same strain of ShantiMari as the Mohram.

Do you think it is Eoghan and Tinsley?

Only one way to find out.

They spiraled slowly to the ground, far enough away that they wouldn't scare the shit out of anyone keeping guard. When they transformed, she no longer saw the tent. Curious.

Khrystina looked around with a question clear on her features. "Why did we stop?"

Rhoane strode toward the tent. "Keep up. We believe friends of ours are close."

A lone guard approached, his sword held loose, ready. "Keep walking, travelers. These woods are not safe at night."

"Are you one of Anje's men?" Rhoane asked by way of greeting.

"Who's asking?"

"Prince Rhoane of the Eleri. The duke and I are friends, and I believe we can assist with what you have in your tent."

The guard took in Rhoane's appearance, which for once wasn't bedraggled, and then glanced at Taryn. He ended his survey with Khrystina.

"How do I know I can trust who you say you are?"

That was twice they were challenged by Anje's guards. Taryn's belly buzzed with the uncomfortable realization that he'd had to conscript more soldiers, many of whom she'd never met even though she'd trained with most of the battalions for several moonturns over the last season.

"I am Taryn ap Galendrin, niece of your esteemed lord." At her introduction, the guard visibly paled, which was some feat in the waning moonlight. "I am here to heal Lord Tinsley and if you don't let me through, I will turn you into a fieldmouse. You look like you're a smart man, so please don't force me to make you a tasty snack for a hungry carlix."

"I have my orders." But his words had lost their conviction. "I really don't want to be eaten. Wait here."

He disappeared into nothingness, and Taryn whistled at the power it would've taken to hide the tent so thoroughly.

"Is this Eoghan's work? If so, it's mighty impressive." She stretched a finger to see if she could feel the tent, but it was empty air. "Damn, he's good."

"Rhoane! Taryn!" Eoghan appeared from nowhere with a wide grin on his face. "I am sorry for the bother." He cocked his head toward the guard who had reappeared behind him. "We were worried about being attacked and this seemed the best solution." His gaze flicked to Khrystina and then to Kaida, who sat at his side and smiled for the scritches he gave her. "How did you find us?"

"Darathi can see what others cannot," Rhoane offered. Very few had actually seen their dragon forms, Eoghan not among that small group.

"Ah, yes. I had quite forgotten. Please, come inside. Tinsley is in a bad way. Lady Faelara and I have done what we can for him, but something ails him that I am unfamiliar with." Again, his gaze flicked to the novice. "What you will see is alarming. Will you be alright?"

Khrystina lifted her chin in a surprisingly haughty fashion. "I am an Eleri and novice to Verdaine. I do not flinch from that which is unpleasant."

Taryn wasn't about to remind her that only a short while ago she was emptying her guts into Lake Oster.

"Eoghan, this is Novice Khrystina. Verdaine tasked us with seeing her safely to Talaith." To Khrystina, Rhoane said, "This is my younger brother, Prince Eoghan, Third Son of the Eleri."

"Forgive me, Your Highness." She curtseyed low, but the scowl on her face belied her apology.

"Consider it forgotten. And please, call me Eoghan." He motioned for them to follow and disappeared through the tent opening they still couldn't see.

Taryn caught Khrystina's look of surprise and smiled. "They're not all tight-assed pretentious twats. Eoghan's one of the good ones."

The novice had the good graces not to laugh, but Taryn saw the twinkle in her eye.

They ducked as Eoghan had and stepped into the warmth of a large tent. Inside, two braziers burned brightly, and half a dozen men snoozed close to where they'd entered.

In the far corner, crouched over a cot, Taryn saw the black hair and distinctive jacket of her friend Aomori. She rushed to him, but her steps slowed the closer she came. He lifted red-rimmed eyes to her, a look of hope chasing the despair that clung stubbornly to his features.

"Taryn, Rhoane. Thank the gods you're here." He stood and indicated the prone figure on the cot.

If Taryn didn't know it was Tinsley, she never would've recognized him. Black boils dotted his skin, and where the Mohram had scratched his flesh, long jagged lines of ochre-colored puss oozed to pool on the cot.

Khrystina coughed and fled to the other side of the tent,

which was for the best. Kaida whimpered and lay her head beside Tinsley's, her long tongue licking his face.

"We'll heal him, girl. I promise you that," Taryn said to the grierbas, but also to the others.

Just how the hell they'd pull off that feat, well—that was the conundrum.

CHAPTER TWENTY-EIGHT

Tinsley was dying. A slow decay into death that he couldn't prevent. Sweat dripped from Rhoane's brow as he concentrated his Shanti's flow into Tinsley's body. They'd been trying for bells to heal him, but the poison was stubborn. Almost as if it clung to his insides like a barbed fish stuck in a fisherman's nets. No matter what approach they made, or how invasive or gentle they were, nothing worked.

Aomori's head dipped and Taryn admonished him again to get some rest, but he refused to leave his beloved's side. She gave Rhoane an exasperated look, but he understood all too well how it felt to have a loved one drifting dangerously in the in-between. He'd healed her, but that was through lovemaking, which he wasn't comfortable asking Aomori to perform in front of them just so they could open Tinsley's energy stores. There had to be another option.

Rhoane looked to Taryn, hope flittering around his thoughts. "What did Loghan have you do in Sitari when I was poisoned?" He knew he was grasping at futile wishes, but it was all they had left.

"I know we're desperate, but I don't know, Rhoane. That was

dangerous. I had to merge myself with you. I didn't think about it, I just did it because you were dying." She looked at Tinsley, her eyes darting left to right, her brow furrowed. "I'm willing to try again, but your poison was from the runyon tree. This? I've never seen the like."

"It is insidious."

"Exactly." Taryn bit her thumbnail, and he gently removed her finger from her mouth. If she continued with the habit, she wouldn't have a thumb left by the time they reached Talaith.

Their swords lay beside Tinsley, making a protective shield of sorts. They'd already tried using them to withdraw the poison, but that hadn't worked. Nothing had worked to rid him of the poison. Rhoane's mind churned with impossible ideas.

"What if, instead of ridding Tinsley of the poison, we cleanse it—internally?"

Taryn's head tilted and her eyes brightened. Just as quickly, they dimmed. "That might kill him if we get it wrong."

Kaida whimpered and put her paw on Taryn's leg. His two greatest loves stared at each other for a long moment, but Rhoane was excluded from their conversation. Curious what Kaida would have to say to Taryn but not him, he was also a little hurt. The only explanation was that it had something to do with his poisoning in Sitari and Kaida wished to safeguard his feelings.

"She thinks we should try." Taryn glanced at Aomori. "If we don't, he might die anyway. But I'm not risking his life unless you give us your blessing."

Aomori blinked at them as if he only just realized how dire the situation was. Or he'd only been half-listening from sheer exhaustion.

"You have my blessing. Hells, give him my blood if you must. All of it, I won't need it if he dies."

Taryn's face softened and she stretched to kiss Aomori on the cheek. A ping of jealousy ran through Rhoane from the old wound Marissa's lies about the couple had left. He shoved it aside and reminded himself they were only friends.

"Rhoane? What do you think?"

He shook his head to clear the distressing thoughts. "Sure. Fine." He didn't know what he had just agreed to, but if it helped Tinsley, he had no objections.

"Right. Here we go." Taryn lifted the edge of her sword and ran her palm over the sharp surface. "Shitfuckcocksucker. That hurt."

"What are you doing?" Alarmed, Rhoane reached for her hand to stop the blood that poured forth.

"Exactly what I said I was going to do—use my blood to cleanse Tinsley's. You agreed."

He had. Bugger it, but he'd been lost in his thoughts. Instead of arguing, he repeated her action with Claidholm Solais, wincing at the sharp sting the cut brought.

Together, they placed their bloodied palms against the weeping wound in Tinsley's torso. Rhoane's Shanti swirled and shifted, spreading through the man's body as it swept through the veins like a dam bursting its bank. Taryn's power joined with his and they concentrated on cleansing Tinsley's blood with their own.

A lightheaded dizziness overcame him. From the other side of the cot, he heard Taryn speaking low to the man, coaxing him to open his power. Rhoane listened closer and realized it wasn't his ShantiMari she was asking him to open, but his energy stores. Was it possible to open them without the sexual component? He hadn't thought of that, but Taryn had. Because she was fucking brilliant.

He focused his power on cleansing Tinsley's blood with his own, giving more than he should, ridding the young lord's body of the poison. Bit by bit, they released the hooks and barbs that clung to his insides, but it wasn't enough. They needed Tinley's energy stores to open fully, for him to release his ShantiMari and burn away the last vestiges of the Mohram's contamination.

Through the dizziness and fog from blood loss, Rhoane's mind wandered. Thoughts he didn't understand drifted in his mind. He heard Taryn's voice, but it was echoed as if bouncing off a cavern wall. An image of Aomori straddling him naked flashed in his thoughts and he flinched from the realization he was in Tinsley's memories. In his mind.

Are you allowing this? He'd never been mentally connected to the man and didn't wish to intrude on his private moments.

There wasn't an affirmation so much as a feeling of warmth, of acceptance. Rhoane's heart quickened with the knowledge Tinsley was fighting just as hard as they were to save his life.

More images came, too fast to catch them all, but one slashed against Rhoane's skull as if it had been a passing dagger.

Zakael drifted in the in-between, just as Tinsley did. Unlike the young lord, Zakael was alone. Was he dying? Even now? Or was this sometime in the past? Rhoane couldn't shake the feeling this memory was recent. Not only that, but Tinsley felt compelled to help Zakael.

We cannot save everyone. He said the words to Tinsley, but also to assuage his guilt.

Would he save Zakael if given a chance?

"Rhoane, look," Taryn whispered, and he struggled to pull his focus to what she was talking about.

Just there, near Tinsley's privates, he saw a soft glow. Another opened near his belly button, and then a third beneath his sternum. As each successive glow brightened, Rhoane's mind cleared, and his heart rejoiced. They'd done it. They'd found a way to open Tinsley's energy stores.

A rush of blood coursed through Tinsley, cleansed of the poison and full of life-giving oxygen he needed. The man woke with a gasp that sounded as if he'd been held underwater and denied air. Immediately, he vomited a putrid blackish muck that made Rhoane's stomach recoil and twist. Wracking shudders followed, and both he and Taryn grabbed Tinsley to keep him from hurting himself with the thrashing. Moments later, he settled, his eyes wild, his face no longer ashen.

Aomori shouted and cried and hugged his beloved. The others rushed over to see what had happened while Rhoane and Taryn gradually pulled their power from the stricken man. As he was removing the last threads of his Shanti, he heard Tinsley whisper in his mind, *Thank you.*

He gave a gentle squeeze to Tinsley's shoulder and stood on shaky legs. Taryn took Rhoane's hand in hers and healed the wound he'd made to save Tinsley's life. When she finished, he did the same for her. They removed their swords from the cot before anyone cut themselves on the sharp blades and slunk to the floor a few paces from where Aomori continued to smother his lover's face with kisses.

It was sweet to see his affection boldly displayed. Until then, the men had been circumspect in their relationship. He held Taryn's hand and brought it to his lips. "You are incredible."

"*We* are incredible." She laid her head on his shoulder, a welcome weight after their tumultuous night. "He needs a proper bed and healers."

He nodded against her. "Give me a bell to rest and we will take him to Talaith." He chewed the side of his cheek, debating the wisdom of his next words. "I saw Zakael in Tinsley's memories."

She pulled back and looked at him, confusion clouding her eyes. "In the in-between? I didn't see him."

"He was there." He stroked her face, sorry for what he had to confess. "I think he is dying. And he is alone."

Wetness shimmered in her lovely eyes, but she did not cry. She searched his eyes, her teeth grinding against her bottom lip. "We can't save everyone."

It was his exact thought but hearing her voice it aloud did not bring him comfort. Because he knew it was true, and he also knew she wished she could. Not just save everyone, but in this instance, he felt her need to do whatever it took to save Zakael.

It was her decision, and he support her no matter which path she took, even though he selfishly hoped she would leave Zakael to his own fate. After a long moment, she exhaled slowly and shook her head. Her pretty face was drawn and too pale.

"We'll rest for a bit and then see to Tinsley."

Rhoane held her hand and put his other arm around her shoulders to draw her in close. It was the decision he'd hoped for but did not fill him with relief.

CHAPTER TWENTY-NINE

He drifted in the sweet nothingness between life and death. There were no mad gods here commanding him to do their bidding, no demanding fathers forcing him to do unspeakable acts at a tender, impressionable age. No beautiful sisters begging him to find the goodness in himself.

Silly Taryn—there was no goodness to find. Possibly never had been.

Zakael floated, begging for death, but it eluded him. Why? Why would he be forsaken now? Wasn't he worthy of dying? Even if his eternity was spent in the rivers of Dal Ferran, wasn't that better than the living hell his life had become?

Images raced through his mind. Faces he could barely remember sneered as they passed, and he realized they were all people he'd once known. All dead or near dying. Some by his hand, others not. One in particular caught his attention, though he knew not why. The handsome man was familiar, but he couldn't place a name to him. Had they been lovers? No, not possible. He recalled all their faces, even the ones who pleased him most.

It was those who displeased him that stayed in his memories like a grisly tick burrowed beneath the flesh.

But this man, he was neither. Yet he touched a part of Zakael that was as dank and dark as the dungeons—his heart. That dark hair and ghostly pale skin…yes, they shared some resemblance, but those greenish-blue eyes were nothing like his kin. Everyone in Zakael's family had the unmistakable grey eyes that resembled storm clouds. Even Anje, that miserable old man who had defied his father.

Zakael chuckled to the empty air. No one dared defy Valterys except Anje. The man had paid for his disobedience with the death of his firstborn, wife, and daughter. Served him right. Zakael had no time to mourn the loss of Anje's family. The man chose his path when he turned his back on the Dark and Valterys. He was lucky to be alive.

Life. Death. What did any of it mean anymore?

The nothingness began to tremble and Zakael felt himself being forcibly taken from the bliss of emptiness. He clawed at it, desperate to remain now that the decision was no longer his to make. Despite his earlier wish, he wasn't ready to die.

He sent a frenzied plea to his uncle to please forgive him. He'd never truly wished his family's death and in fact had mourned them when Valterys callously killed them.

It wasn't a complete lie. He had felt a shiver of regret over the senseless deaths, but if he was honest with himself, it was only because his father had done the unspeakable without him. Had left him home alone yet again. Was that it? He was angry his father had left him alone while he killed an innocent man's wife and child?

Gods, but he was a horrible man and deserved to die.

Zakael sent a second, genuine apology to his uncle. Not that he'd ever receive it, but it gave him a small sense of peace knowing he'd felt remorse in the end.

Bright lights flared against his closed lids and he braced himself for the worst.

"My beautiful boy, come back to me," Kaldaar rasped into his ear.

Not his mind, but his physical body. Which meant he wasn't dead, not yet. He struggled to open his eyes, to twitch even a finger. It was as if his brain had forgotten how to function in the physical world.

"I have missed you, my sweet." A fleshy hand stroked his hair. "That's it, I can feel your heart stirring, your blood swirling in your veins. Yes, come back to me."

It was true; his heart pumped harder and his thoughts became clearer. In the fading nothingness, he saw the handsome young man once more, but he had turned away, heading toward a different light.

"My throat hurts," he managed between swallows. Every movement brought fresh bouts of pain. "Everything hurts."

"Yes, well, you were a naughty boy and deserved to be punished. But I will heal you." Kaldaar covered Zakael's lips with his mouth and forced him to open up for the kiss.

Pressure from a body lying atop him pressed his own body into a soft mattress, and he realized he was lying on his bed—naked. The scent of freshly washed linens came to him, as well as the scented soap he enjoyed in the bath. Someone had bathed him while he was unconscious.

His legs were gently spread apart and a thick cock entered his anus with such tenderness it made him want to weep. Kaldaar was never gentle. Nor did he have a fully realized physical form. Then who was fucking him?

He strained to open his eyes, fluttering his lids until finally they remained partially opened. Kaldaar's face rocked above his, concentration tight in his features. More kisses were planted on his forehead, his cheeks, his neck.

Despite himself, his cock hardened and his blood thickened

with desire. His goddamned body was programmed for lust whether he wanted it or not.

Gradually, with each thrust and grunt from the god, his energy renewed, his thoughts cleared. Golden hair made a curtain to either side of Kaldaar's face and he realized with a start that the god wasn't wearing the cloak he always hid within—and he had hair. Glorious strands of silky sunlight.

But how? How was he fully formed?

"Shhhh, my beautiful boy. Quiet your mind. Let me love you."

"Love?" He scoffed.

"Did you think me incapable of such a pathetic emotion? Yes, *love*. When you were hanging in the balance between life and death, I missed you greatly." He devoured Zakael's mouth in his own, sucking his tongue as if he sucked his cock.

Zakael's belly fluttered and he raised his pelvis to grind against the god. He was loved. Sure, by a deranged god hellbent on destroying Aelinae, but for the moment, he was loved.

They made love for the next several bells, each time bringing Zakael closer to full strength. Although he tried to hide it, with each successive session Kaldaar lost some of his luminosity, some of his physicality.

"How is it you are..." Zakael searched for a polite way to phrase his question.

"Solid?" Kaldaar supplied, and Zakael nodded. "I'm afraid it is only temporary." His gaze slid to the balcony where two bodies lay crumpled in the sunlight.

"Are those the virgins?" Zakael sat up in bed, his flaccid cock sticking to his leg.

"They provided me with what I needed to bring you back." He licked his lips and Zakael swallowed the acrid taste of disgust. "They were delicious. All of them."

"What—" Another splash of bile stopped his words. He

looked away from the women to the floor. "What will it take to make you solid permanently?"

"My darling boy, are you trying to trick me into giving away my secrets?" The god looked glorious as he rested against the headboard of Zakael's massive bed.

Hair the color of spun gold, olive skin that looked kissed by the sun's rays, he wasn't at all what Zakael had imagined the god would look like. He'd envisioned someone more like Rykoto—dark and broody with bloodstained lips. This god could've been Lliandra's twin, except for the dark-brown eyes. He was actually quite handsome in this form.

"Of course not. But if there is any way I can help…" Zakael's eyes razed the god, desire making his cock rise. "I confess, I do enjoy seeing you this way."

A glint of something dark and dangerous lit Kaldaar's eyes. He leaned forward and took Zakael's chin in his strong grip. "As a matter of fact, there *is* something you can do."

Zakael leaned forward, ready to accept his kiss and his command. "Tell me."

"Go to the Sitari Islands and slit the throat of every one of those fucking traitorous women. I will bathe in their blood and be restored."

Zakael hid the tremble in his nerves as he nodded, his mouth already opening. He should've known it wouldn't be something simple. After all, Kaldaar knew his past, knew his penchant for pain. This was just foreplay for the god.

CHAPTER THIRTY

The sky was still dark when Taryn's group gathered outside
the tent. Once Tinsley was safely secured to Rhoane's
darathi, they left the guardsmen and servants with instructions to
meet them in Talaith. Taryn didn't think the small group of travelers would encounter anymore Mohram on the road, but she
wasn't entirely positive either. She left the guards and servants
with several protective wards just in case. Rhoane had added a
few of his own to the mix, as did Khrystina, which surprised the
hell out of both Taryn and Rhoane.

They flew into the coming sunrise at breakneck speed, fast
enough that Kaida had a hard time keeping pace. Yet every time
Taryn offered assistance, she was met with an angry snarl. Taryn
understood all too well the importance of doing it herself and so
she let it drop. Kaida was still young not only in grierbas seasons,
but in Aelan age as well. Taryn chuckled to herself as she realized
Kaida would be about the same age as Tessa if she were Aelan.
The wonderful teenage years. Oh, joy.

Kaida growled at Taryn as if she'd read her thoughts and she
held back the chuckle that threatened. If she needed to exhaust

herself to prove a point, Taryn wouldn't stand in Kaida's way. Even if she was being ridiculous.

Rhoane directed them to the farthest corner of the gardens and they landed with a soft hush between the orchards and the sea wall. Khrystina slid from Taryn's scales the moment her talons touched the ground and raced to help Aomori lift Tinsley off of Rhoane's back.

Taryn wrapped them all in shadows and they made their way to the palace as quietly as five people and a grierbas could. Fortunately, the ground was dry, but unfortunately, the pebbled pathways still made sound underfoot as they traveled along them to a side entrance. Rhoane distracted the guards while she and the others slipped through the door and up a back stairway.

At the intersection where the hallways split into public rooms and private quarters, they turned to ascend a huge staircase that led to Rhoane's rooms. It was early enough they didn't encounter any servants, but once inside, they found not just Alasdair, but Oliver, Hayden's valet. Both men were sleeping soundly in overstuffed leather chairs, an empty bottle and two glasses on the table beside a stack of cards.

Good on them for keeping themselves entertained while their masters were away. Except Hayden wasn't away—he was staying in the palace. Bugger. She'd have to swear them both to secrecy that she and Rhoane were not only alive but had returned under suspicious circumstances.

They placed Tinsley in Rhoane's bed and Taryn dropped the shadows. Aomori twitched and fidgeted, his face pale.

"That was the strangest thing I think I've ever done." He brushed at his shoulder as if shadow still clung to him. "Warn me next time."

"I'll remember that. Stay here and keep Tinsley comfortable." She sometimes forgot not everyone was accustomed to Light and Dark comingling, nor did most people know they could use Dark Shanti the way Taryn could.

"Where are you going?" Panic entered his tone.

"To my rooms to get some sleep. We've been awake more than two days." Even standing was becoming difficult.

"I will stay with him, if you do not mind," Khrystina offered. "I am skilled in healing."

That was a surprise. And most welcome. Taryn touched her and Aomori's temples to allow them access to speak in her mind should an emergency occur. Then she and Rhoane woke both valets, who were indeed very shocked to see them. They explained the situation and asked them to keep their presence a secret.

Once more cloaked in shadow, she, Rhoane, and Kaida made their way to her rooms where she hoped not to encounter any maids or hungover valets. Her rooms were blessedly empty when they entered. And cold. It was as if no one had been in them since she left. She rubbed her arms and shivered, but not from the chill.

Rhoane made a fire in the bed chamber, then the sitting room before returning to her. His arms wrapped around her waist and he pulled her close.

"I sense disquiet within you."

She laid her head against his chest. "Do you think she was sad to learn of my death? Did she cry? Or was it happy news?"

"I think any mother would be devastated to learn of their child's death."

Taryn scoffed and wiped her nose on her sleeve. She hadn't realized she'd started to cry. "Most mothers, but not mine."

Kaida jumped on the bed and made a circle twice before lying down to sleep. Within seconds, she could be heard snoring.

"I envy her the ability to sleep anywhere, anytime, and imme-diately."

"As do I." He nuzzled her head and kissed her forehead. "We can deal with Lliandra later. Right now, we should take Kaida's wise counsel and sleep."

"There's not enough room for the three of us. You go ahead."

She pulled away and walked to the balcony doors. "I want to watch the sunrise."

"Are you sure?"

"I'm fine, mi carae. Get some rest."

Before he could argue, she opened the glass doors and shut them behind her. By then he had already stripped to his small clothes and was climbing beneath the covers.

She sat on the balustrade for a long time watching the sun peek over the horizon. Birds greeted the morning with calls and chirps, their wings buzzing past as they swooped up and down, left to right, without any clear indication of where they were actually going. Story of her damn life, it seemed. Especially lately.

Sounds of the palace waking up came to her, but she stayed where she was even after the sun was long since risen. She heard a door open in her rooms and quietly slipped inside to head off someone finding Rhoane and Kaida in her bed.

In the sitting room, she found Ellie straightening her belongings and tried to enter without giving her a fright, but the girl yelped when Taryn appeared.

"I am so sorry, Ellie. I didn't want to frighten you, but they're sleeping and I had to be quiet."

Ellie burst into tears and rushed to her, wrapping her arms around her waist. "I don't care if you took ten seasons from my life. It's so good to see you." She pulled away, embarrassment clouding her features. "Forgive me, Your Highness. I was overcome with emotion."

"Nothing to apologize for, and it's still just Taryn to you in private." She hugged the girl, holding her a little too tightly. "Gods, I've missed you. How is everyone? Tell me everything."

Taryn swirled her hands above a side table and produced a steaming pot of tea along with enough pastries to feed a giant. While they drank tea and ate their fill of sweets, Ellie filled her in on everything that had happened since she and Rhoane left Menurra.

Ellie and Taryn's other maids were still training, but not with Flik since he'd stayed in the Summerlands. Turns out, King Faisal had insisted Flik's son Ton come with Taryn's maids and train them along with Darius right there in the palace. Lliandra had even allowed Tessa and Eliahnna to join in twice a week.

The news stunned Taryn. Never in all her days did she believe Lliandra would let Tessa, and especially not Eliahnna, near weapons. Well done, Lliandra.

"And you and Darius?" Taryn asked with a smile.

"We are courting." A sweet blush stained Ellie's cheeks. The scar the Shadow Assassin had given her was barely visible, and Ellie hadn't once tried to hide the mark.

Taryn's heart swelled with happiness for her friends, yet she was saddened to hear Tarro and Armando had stayed in Menurra with little Percival. It was for the best, but she missed her little nephew. Happier news was that Iselt now worked in the palace smithy, and that he had a good friendship with Darius.

"Our weekly meeting is this afternoon. Will you be joining us?" Ellie smoothed her skirt before pouring them more tea.

"I need to speak with my mother first. Does she know I'm not dead?"

Ellie shook her head. "With her illness, Eliahnna didn't want to distress her more…" She trailed off, and Taryn filled in what she wasn't saying.

"In case it was true. I don't blame her." She checked the position of the sun and stood to stretch her tired body. The tea had done her wonders, but really she needed to sleep for a month. "I guess now's as good a time as any to let her know that—surprise! —I'm alive." Taryn made jazz hands and a silly face.

Ellie frowned and looked from Taryn to the door. "That wouldn't be advisable at the moment. The, erm, empress is busy this time of the morning."

Taryn sat back down, her interest piqued. "Busy? With a

male suitor?" Ellie nodded, and Taryn pressed, "Does this suitor have a name?"

"Prince Gwainne." Ellie looked apologetic. "He swears he only does it to gain information, but if he's procured any, he doesn't share it with us." She slapped a hand over her mouth and mumbled another apology.

Taryn stifled a chuckle. "I've met him. Kind of a twat, that one. I'll see what I can scrape from his mind when I see him. What time is the meeting in Eliahnna's rooms?"

They made a plan that would allow Taryn time to sleep and bathe without any further disturbances, and once Ellie left, she placed several wards on the doors and windows of her suite. As she climbed beneath the covers, Kaida snuffled and jumped off the bed to lie in front of the balcony doors. Rhoane rolled over and pulled her into him.

If only her mother could love her as easily as Rhoane did. But Lliandra was a complicated woman with issues of her own. Taryn would have to emerge from the dead compassionately and carefully or it might give Lliandra such a shock it sent her to an early grave.

As her eyes closed and mind settled in for sleep, she wondered if that would be such a terrible thing.

CHAPTER THIRTY-ONE

Gwainne kissed Lliandra's forehead and left her in the massive bed he'd once loathed but had come to enjoy. Ever since he cleared her mind of Kaldaar's taint, their love-making had taken on surprising, pleasing twists.

He'd never give her the child she so desperately wanted, but he could give her comfort, and a shoulder to cry on. Literally. It seemed as if since that morning he'd had the vision of Verdaine and healed the empress, all Lliandra did was weep or scream with pleasure. Sometimes, he wasn't sure whether he was hurting her with overenthusiastic lovemaking, or if she was reliving some past trauma that their sexual play eased.

One day, when he was home and could process everything fully, he'd ask his mother about the interesting exchanges he'd had with the empress.

And those weren't only limited to rutting. The empress shared with him state secrets; plans and schemes she'd concocted with her daughter, the late crown princess. There were times he'd longed for the days of her silent recriminations, but as the future laird of Ulla, he tucked her confessions tight in his mind for future reference.

After that first morning when she'd opened her mind to him, he'd shared with Eliahnna and the others Ulla's part in Lliandra's scheme to provide his kingdom with weapons, so long as Ulla provided her with horses and soldiers. But of the rest she shared? That information he kept to himself. It eased his conscience knowing he'd at least confessed to Marissa's deviousness without implicating Ulla too much in the foolhardy bargain his father had made with the late crown princess. Of their dealings with Zakael, he chose not to share those details with Eliahnna's group. They had an uneasy relationship with the new Overlord of the West— why add to their consternation?

Of her second daughter, Taryn, Lliandra never spoke of her. It was as if she'd forgotten the woman existed. He chalked it up to her mourning the loss of the Darennsai, but still it was rather strange. Taryn wasn't even an afterthought to the empress. In life or death, Lliandra didn't acknowledge her feelings for the girl and that worried Gwainne more than anything. Was Lliandra keeping secrets from him? Or did the empress so thoroughly hate her second daughter that she'd excised her from her mind? There was a third option, but Gwainne was hesitant to even consider it— Lliandra didn't loathe her daughter so much as she feared her. And if the Empress of the East feared the Darennsai, Ulla would be wise to have caution where she was concerned.

He hurried through the halls of the Crystal Palace, late as always for their weekly meeting. Princess Eliahnna, the new crown princess and heir to Lliandra's throne, held these meetings in her private rooms each week as a means of keeping everyone informed of what transpired in the kingdoms. He found them cliquey and a bit tiresome, but it gave him intel he wouldn't otherwise be privy to, so he continued to attend.

A maid let him in, and he made his way to the sitting room they generally used, but found it empty. Voices could be heard in one of the inner rooms. Those were Eliahnna's private quarters, and while he might be a cad, he wasn't completely disrespectful.

While he waited, he busied himself with pouring a tipple of dreem into an exquisitely crafted glass. Danurian, if he wasn't mistaken. He made a mental note to get some for himself when he became laird.

"Hello Gwainne," a voice he'd not thought to ever hear again said from behind him.

The informality of the greeting set his teeth on edge. He turned slowly to delay the inevitable. "Novice Khrystina. What are you doing here?"

Her wide smile and eyes full of hope cut him to the quick. Shame slid across him with brutal efficiency.

The smile faltered the tiniest bit. "You left without a proper goodbye and I thought I would come to see how you are. Are you well?" She took in his expensive court clothes, courtesy of the empress, and his polished boots. "You look quite distinguished. Like a proper prince."

"Are you saying I did not look like a prince at the temple?" He tried to keep his tone light, but confusion swirled in his brain. What the fuck was she doing here? And why did she wear that goofy smile with expectation and hope beaming in her every move? She'd denied him at the temple. Hells, he didn't even think she liked him much, and now here she was, thousands of leagues from the Narthvier and her duties? It didn't make sense.

"No, of course not." She twirled a short lock of hair and tilted her head just so. If she wasn't an Eleri novice promised in service to Verdaine, he'd think she was flirting with him. "Are you—I mean, I was hoping you would be happy to see me."

Piss it. She *was* flirting with him. And here he stood, having just rolled out of the empress's bed with Lliandra's stench still on him. Sure, he'd flirted with her at the temple, but he'd flirted with all the other lasses, most of whom were happy to entertain him for a bell or so in their bed. But Khrystina…she'd never once made him feel that she was attracted to him. What was he supposed to do with an errant novice?

"Of course. Yes. I am just a little confused how you came to be at the palace in Talaith. Is Carga with you?" That would explain everything if the Eleri princess were with the novice.

"Carga is still in the Narthvier." Her smile faded as realization dawned in her eyes. "I feel silly now. I thought we—you—well, I thought wrong. I am sorry." She twisted her hair and ducked her head as she turned to go.

"Khrystina, I am sorry if I gave you false hope while I was at the temple. I thought I made myself perfectly clear that I was not there for lasting entanglements." His shame turned to guilt. How could he have been so stupid? He'd taken her timidness and shy demeanor as a challenge, when in reality she had been suppressing feelings for him. It didn't feel nice to realize he'd abused her trust in the most callous way.

She dropped her hands to her sides and then wrung them together. "It is I who am sorry. I should never have hoped you might miss me like I missed you." She dipped a curtsey and stared at the ground.

Gwainne berated himself for the space of two heartbeats. His gaze slid over Khrystina's head to meet the curious gaze of another woman he'd never expected to see again.

"Darennsai." He bowed to her, his mind scrambling to make sense of his conversation with Khrystina, and the appearance of someone he'd believed dead. "You are alive."

"I am. Although, it is not public knowledge. Not yet." Taryn's eyes narrowed, and in that one look he felt he'd betrayed her so violently he'd spend the rest of his days making amends. "I hear my mother is recovered and I have you to thank for her good health."

"I, erm, yes. She is well. You—you look well yourself."

He shook his head, his glance shifting to Khrystina for answers, but she wouldn't meet his eyes.

"If you have no further need of me, Darennsai, I would like

to be excused." Khrystina shuffled closer to the door, but didn't leave.

"I would like you to stay for the meeting, but I understand if it is too uncomfortable for you. Or, if you prefer, we can ask Prince Gwainne to sit this one out. It's your choice." Taryn leaned against the doorframe and crossed her arms.

"You want me to stay?" The novice turned, her eyes wide with eager curiosity.

He'd seen that look too many times at the temple to know that she wouldn't leave. Miss an opportunity for learning? Not her. Whether she would allow him to stay was another matter.

"What about him?" Taryn jutted her chin toward Gwainne and he shifted uncomfortably. It didn't sit well with him how little respect Taryn showed him or his family. Darennsai or not, she was a thorn in his ass.

Khrystina rubbed her chin with a slender finger and studied him a moment. "Do you think he can be trusted? After all, he is bedding the empress. His loyalties seem to be conflicted, but what I know of him is that he is loyal first and foremost to his cock."

Ouch. To have it said so plainly, and truthfully, hurt.

Taryn eased from the doorway, her expression a mystery. "The meeting's about to start. If you're coming, it's this way."

Khrystina gave him a final glance, one full of disappointment and resignation. He'd hurt her without even trying. Instead of following the women, he left the suite. Something in the way Taryn looked at him as if she knew everything he was thinking and feeling made him jumpy and out of sorts. He randomly turned down a hallway and bumped into someone who rushed past. A muttered apology passed his lips even though he wasn't sure the person could hear him.

"Where are you going, Your Highness? The meeting's this way." Hayden pulled him from his dour fog and he blinked to see he'd walked the entire length of the hallway.

"No, I think I will miss today. Let me know if there is anything that requires my attention."

Hayden nodded and moved on, leaving him alone with his thoughts.

"Your Highness," a servant approached, and he glared at them for the intrusion. "The empress is in need of your, ah, special skills."

"'Special skills?'" She had to be jesting. He'd spent the better part of two bells giving the empress his *special skills*. What did she take him for? A common whore?

That was exactly what she thought of him. And he'd allowed it.

"Tell her I am otherwise occupied."

The servant gaped at him—no one denied the empress.

Fuck her. And fuck her haughty daughter, too. What the hell was he even doing in Talaith, anyway? Wasting his fucking time fucking a woman who was batshit crazy, that's what. Well, no more.

He strode to his rooms, surprising his two servants. They tried to hide the fact they'd been fornicating against his chest of drawers, but he'd been too quick to enter and they too slow to notice.

Albie, the valet assigned to him so graciously by the empress, sidled in front of Leonard, the other servant who did whatever it was Albie didn't—honestly, he would never understand all the titles for servants who did shit he could do for himself. The pair wore identical crimson expressions of terror.

"As you were." He waved them off. "I care not whose dick you suck, nor do I care that you did it here. Finish your business and then pack my belongings."

"The prince is leaving us?" Albie cast a concerned glance to Leonard. "Does the empress know?"

"No, she does not know and I do not give a fuck if she finds out. I am done being her whore."

He'd said too much. Dammit, his anger had gotten the better of him and he'd rambled when it would've been more prudent to keep his damn mouth shut. The truth was, he wasn't angry at Lliandra, or even Khrystina—his ire was solely directed at himself.

His gaze flicked to the two men, specifically to Leonard, who was trying valiantly to button up his trousers as inconspicuously as possible. His cock jumped at the sight of an errant button missing its hole. He dragged his glance upward to keep from thinking about the man's cock, only to meet the even gaze of the two servants. An invitation lingered in their eyes where moments ago there had been fear of what he'd do to them.

"Would, erm"—Albie cleared his throat and continued—"would His Highness like a backrub to ease his tension?"

"Or perhaps a bath?" Leonard offered.

The way his cock was tingling and stirring…yes, His Highness would very much appreciate both. Possibly at the same time. It had been so long since he'd allowed himself the company of men that he feared he'd forgotten how to pleasure them.

A brief nod was his answer. As the men approached, he licked his lips in anticipation of an afternoon well spent. Albie unfastened his waistcoat while Leonard untied his trousers. Within moments, a hot mouth was on his cock, and another covered his lips.

A momentary blip of panic threatened his pleasure. He was the heir to the Ullan kingdom and his father had made it quite clear that a laird had only wives to satisfy his needs.

That was fine for Amdi Agnar, but Gwainne Agnar was his own man and would be a new kind of ruler who had not only women but men as his concubines. The days of brutal Ullan rhetoric would die with his father.

He arched into Leonard, shoving his cock as deep as it would go, and groaned against Albie's mouth. Yes, he would have a harem of men and women to love, and who would love him in return. How could anyone not support love?

CHAPTER THIRTY-TWO

Taryn corralled all the courage she could muster and strode down the hallway to her mother's rooms. The reunion with her sisters and Hayden had gone as smoothly as she could've hoped for, which gave her hope that seeing her mother wouldn't be as devastating as her intuition warned. She approached the two guards who always stood at attention, and took a long, calming breath. She could do this. It was as simple as drinking tea. With any luck, her tea would be spiked with dreem.

She stopped at the door and looked each guard in the eye. "I am going to enter these rooms. You are not going to stop me, nor are you going to announce me. It will be enough of a shock to my mother to find me alive that I don't need you giving her a heart attack before I have a chance to explain. Got it?" She held her head high, shoulders back, a withering snarl on her face.

"Yes, Your Highness," one of them said, and opened the door. The other man, she noted, clutched his spear as if he'd like nothing more than to shove it up her ass.

Once inside, she slowed her steps and placed a hand over her rampaging heart. How was she supposed to greet her mother? As if nothing had happened? With a hug? An apology? An explanation? She was swimming in deep waters here and didn't know how to breathe.

At the open doors to her mother's sitting room, she paused to gather her wits. Lliandra stood at the huge windows overlooking the ocean, a cup held in her hands. The steadiness of the fragile porcelain gave Taryn encouragement that her mother was strong of mind and body today. Perhaps this wouldn't shock her as much as she'd feared.

As much as she'd hoped? After all, if she were to faint at the sight of her daughter, it might mean Lliandra had at least mourned her a little.

She dug her nails into her palms to quiet the nonsense in her head. This was her mother. Of course she'd mourned her death.

Except, she knew that wasn't true. Yes, she was Lliandra's daughter, but they'd never been close. Never had the chance to bond or love one another like they should have.

She was stalling. Terrified flutters scraped against her belly, and she took in a deep drag of air to steady her nerves.

She stepped from the doorway into the room and braced for whatever was to come.

"Hello Mother."

The empress turned regally, her cup still steady, her eyes pindots of suspicion. "Ah. Yes. I see you're finally here. Tell me, are you the ghost of my daughter come to haunt me for the rest of my pitiful days? Or are you a phantom wearing the guise of my daughter to torment me to madness?"

"I am neither. I'm your daughter, Taryn, alive and well." She reached for her mother, but Lliandra pulled her hands away as if Taryn were contaminated.

"You lie. My daughter is dead. Myrddin told me so himself."

"Myrddin lied."

The slap came hard and fast, surprising Taryn with its force and vehemence. Of everything she'd imagined might happen, physical violence wasn't on the list. She should've expected it but hadn't, which made it all the more painful. Her hand itched to cover her throbbing cheek, but she kept it by her side.

"Never say that name to me, demon. You are everything that's wrong with my life. Why didn't you die in the womb with your horrid brother?" Lliandra stormed away to glare out the window.

Tears bit the backs of Taryn's eyes, but she refused to let them fall. Not for this woman. She wouldn't give her the satisfaction of knowing she'd utterly, completely, finally destroyed any hope Taryn had of being loved by her.

For a long moment, they neither moved nor spoke. Her mother continued to look out the window, doing her best to avoid Taryn's gaze. Doing what she was best at—pretending something didn't exist so that it might go away.

Well, fuck that.

"Mother," Taryn started, but stopped herself. "*Lliandra.*" Better. If the woman refused to be a mother, then she wouldn't call her one. "I'm sorry you wish I'd never been born. I'm sorry they took me from you when I was only moments old. I'm sorry I am, indeed, the Eirielle. I'm sorry for a boatload of stuff that you'll never know about nor understand—but being sorry doesn't change the fact that I'm here, alive, busting my ass to balance Aelinae just as the prophecy says I'm supposed to. I don't know why Myrddin lied to you, but he did. He lied to all of us."

She went to the empress and stood close enough to embrace, but didn't reach out. Beneath Lliandra's mask of Mari her cheek flinched in irritation. Whatever truths or mistruths her mother was battling, she didn't share them with Taryn.

"Please, look at me." Now she did reach out, took Lliandra's hand in her own. "Feel the warmth of my skin. Trust in what you see."

"Trust? You speak to me of trust? There's no one here I can trust." Lliandra snatched her hand free and stormed to a small table that held several crystal bottles. She poured herself a drink in the teacup she held, not offering anything to her daughter.

This tantrum was beneath her, but Taryn wasn't going to explain how Lliandra herself had created an atmosphere of betrayal and mistrust at the Crystal Palace. If there was no one she could trust, that fault was her of her own making. The courtiers looked to their empress to direct them, and Lliandra was the biggest deceiver of them all.

"I only stopped by to tell you I'm alive, and I have, so I'll be going now." Taryn swung her arms and scuttled toward the door, not really sure what the protocol was when the empress refused to acknowledge her presence.

She was nearly to the entrance hallway when she heard Lliandra's small voice.

"Stay."

Taryn half-turned. "Huh? I couldn't hear that."

"I said stay. It's not a command, but a request." Lliandra arranged herself on a sofa and held the cup to her lips. "If you'd like, that is."

Taryn went to the little table and sniffed all the bottles before choosing a pale pink liquid. She poured herself a healthy dose and sat opposite her mother. "I'm here."

They sat in uncomfortable silence for several minutes, each sipping from their cups. Whatever she'd chosen, it was delicious. It reminded her of a raspberry champagne that tickled her nose each time she drank.

"I lied to him, too," Lliandra stated, unable to meet Taryn's steady gaze.

"Who?"

"Myrddin, and now Gwainne. I've lied to all of them." She looked at Taryn with a softness she'd never seen in her mother. "But most of all, I lied to myself. I told myself that if I kept my heart behind a wall of glass I couldn't be hurt, but that was a lie. Every time Nadra took a child from me, I mourned them, but could never let the public see my misery. When Gavyn was still-born, I shattered inside. And then, out you came like a shining star that I knew—just knew—was the Eirielle. As much as I wished it was true, I didn't want it to be. You were perfect. Huge blue eyes full of curiosity and, dare I say it, hope. Even at only moments old, you had a wisdom and presence that stole my breath. Your little bow lips made a perfect rose, hence your middle name. You were everything I knew I could never be."

Taryn stared at her mother, too stunned to speak. After a longish sip of her drink, she found the words. "Why didn't you tell me? Why act as if you hated me? Why ignore me and call me horrible names?"

"Because, I thought if you despised me, I'd never have to tell you my truth." She waved a hand between them. "I couldn't bear it if you loved me and then discovered what a monster I truly am."

Taryn yearned to go to her, wrap her in her arms and tell her mother she forgave her for everything, but held back. This might be a trick to gain her trust only to destroy her once more. She'd danced that dance before, and it sucked.

"You have no reason to trust me, but if you are what they say you are, all you have to do is look inside my heart. My mind, unfortunately, is a chaotic mess of delusions, misdeeds, and schemes. But my heart—that is where I hold my shame." Lliandra put a hand over her chest and drew in a shaky breath. "I don't like being vulnerable. This…is difficult for me."

"Then why tell me?"

"Because once Gwainne rid her of Kaldaar's taint, her fade came roaring back with ferocity. She has perhaps until Winter-tide, if I am not mistaken," Myrddin said from the other side of the room. He strolled in as casually, as if he'd just come from Lliandra's bedchamber after an invigorating romp.

Taryn startled at his words. The realization her mother would die sooner than anyone expected tore through her anger and distrust.

"What are you doing here, you conniving bilge rat?" Lliandra stood, spilling her drink on her gorgeous ivory gown, but she didn't notice or seem to care. "You have betrayed me for the last time, Alswyth Myrddin."

Taryn rose to protect her mother should the mage do anything devious. He strode to Lliandra and reached for her hands, but the empress crossed her arms.

Undeterred, he smoothed his hands down her arms to her elbows and back up to rest on her shoulders. "I swear to you, my lies were to save you the heartache of learning the truth about me, but once I realized there was no more hiding, I panicked. Kaldaar sent me to kill Taryn, that is true. He needs her still-beating heart to become fully realized, but I couldn't do it. So, I concocted a plan to tell you she was dead in the hopes Kaldaar would believe the lie as well. If he saw you in mourning, truly mourning your daughter, he would stop looking for her."

"You mourned me?" Taryn stared at Lliandra, even more confused than ever.

"Of course I did, you stupid girl."

"When you say it like that, it's pretty hard to believe."

Lliandra's face softened and she pulled Taryn into a rib-crushing embrace. "I have always loved you even when I did my best to hide that fact. I did it to protect you, but I see now that was wrong of me. Someday, when you have children, you'll understand."

A sour pit of melancholy stung her belly. Lliandra couldn't know that Taryn would never have children of her own. Her mother was trying to be kind, even if she was misguided. Still, the truth hurt more than she'd imagined it would.

"We are birds of a feather, my love." Myrddin put his arms around the both of them. "We are duty bound to different ideologies, but with the same results." He pulled back and Taryn disentangled herself from the pair. "I have always loved you, Lliandra. Only you." He ran a thumb down her face and the

Mari mask tightened into place. "You are the reason I have to leave."

"What?" Taryn and Lliandra said in unison.

"I've been hiding from Kaldaar until Taryn returned. I know it is only a matter of time until he comes looking for me, and that would be bad for Aelinae." To Taryn he said, "His latest Shadow Assassin is no more. If you're so inclined, his remains are in the cavern where you found my papers."

Why be so cryptic? Then it dawned on her. Kane or Cashiel or whatever he called himself now was Lliandra's son, her half-brother. With all the emotions swirling around the room, the revelation that yet another of her children had been used by Kaldaar as a Shadow Assassin might send Lliandra into a fit from which she'd never recover. Despite the empress's bravado, Taryn could sense how fragile she truly was. She doubted she had longer than a moonturn, much less to Wintertide.

"Where will you go?" Lliandra looked young and innocent as she gazed adoringly at Myrddin.

They loved each other, this much was clear, and in a different situation they would've married or been life partners, but as he said, they had different ideologies that kept them apart. She was the Lady of Light, and he was the highest-ranking member of the Telraicht Noir Brotherhood. Only Kaldaar outranked him.

"I can't tell you, my love. But know I go with only the best memories of our time together." He held Lliandra's face in his hands, and Taryn turned away to give them some privacy. After several minutes of passionate kissing she tried valiantly to ignore, but failed, he said, "Taryn, I have need of a doorway."

She spun around, confused by the request. "You can't use them any longer?"

He shook his head. "Not since you killed my guardian. You control that realm now."

"What doorway? What realm? What are you talking about?" Lliandra demanded, but they ignored her.

"Seriously?" Taryn stroked her chin, her mind churning with this new information. "I'll grant you passage, but only if you swear on Ynyd Eirathnacht that you will never, ever, ever, ever, and I mean EVER cause chaos again."

"If I do, you will know how to find me." His eyes were full of mischief, and she almost changed her mind.

"Mother." Taryn brushed her fingertips across Lliandra's brow and erased the memory of Myrddin's mention of doorways from her mind. "Thank you for sharing your truth with me. Spend the time you have left with Eliahnna; teach her how to rule with kindness and fairness. Set up a council with the other rulers to meet four times a year to discuss Aelinae's business. They are your allies and should be respected as such. Include Hayden in your dealings. If anything happens to Zakael, he is the heir to the Obsidian Throne." At this, Lliandra frowned, but Taryn went on. "And mostly, take Tessa under your wing. She needs a mother right now more than you'll ever know."

She sealed her words with a light kiss upon Lliandra's lips.

"I have truly underestimated you, my daughter." Lliandra looked into her eyes as if searching for something. "Gwyneira would've been so proud of you. You are so very like her, you know. I wish you'd had a chance to meet her."

Taryn's eyes overflowed with tears and she nodded. "I've met Aunt Gwyn several times and I know she's proud of me. But it's you who she's most proud of. She sees the goodness in you just as I do. It's never too late, Mother."

Lliandra stared at her, tears coursing over her cheeks, through the mask of Mari. A flicker of light came from the window, and Taryn saw the spectral form of her mother's sister drift into the room. Taryn indicated to Myrddin that they should leave, and he led her to a secret passageway connecting to the throne room and the Crystal Palace's portal.

She'd grant his request, with an addendum that he could return to Aelinae only once. After that, he'd be blocked from using the void forever. She almost flipped her hair, so chuffed she was by her newfound position. Who knew "Walker Between Worlds" would turn out to mean she alone controlled those pathways. Well done, her.

Before she shut the door behind her, she blew a kiss to her aunt. She had no idea why Gwyn decided to appear today of all days, but she hoped this would provide the closure Lliandra needed. Gods knew Eliahnna and Tessa needed their mother now more than ever.

CHAPTER THIRTY-THREE

How the hell did Kaldaar expect him to kill every single Sitari? The god had truly lost his mind. If he ever had one to begin with. Zakael stretched lazily in the bed he now shared with the lunatic god. He'd managed to stall his mission by a few days, but Kaldaar was getting restless, and no amount of sucking his cock or allowing him to do what he pleased to Zakael's body seemed to satisfy him lately. Zakael either had to admit he wouldn't go to the Sitari, or he had to do as Kaldaar commanded.

"I cannot use the portals anymore," Zakael lied. "Taryn controls them now and she has cursed them to our presence, so I must travel by other means to the Sitari Islands."

Kaldaar's body trembled slightly at the mention of Taryn's name. More and more of late, he'd noticed the god avoided any mention of her.

"Then fly there. We yet have time. Alert me the moment you've arrived and again when the task is complete." Kaldaar ran his tongue over Zakael's jaw and down his neck to his collarbone. He suppressed a moan, but damn, it felt good. The god certainly knew how to get his blood stirring. "When I am fully restored, you shall be my lover for all eternity. Isn't that what you've always wished for?"

"Immortality, yes, but I never dared hope you might love me enough to want to spend eternity with me." He was going to be sick. Forever with the deranged fool? He'd rather die—but Kaldaar had already proved he wouldn't let that happen. Zakael wasn't sure which was worse: being abused by the dark god, or loved by him.

"I'm just as surprised as you, my beautiful boy." His head lowered to Zakael's impatient cock, and he groaned loudly as Kaldaar took him into his mouth.

The god never tired of Zakael's body. Even when he could barely keep his eyes open, Kaldaar would cuddle and fondle him until his cock was erect. It was the same Zakael used to do to his playmates. In fact, Kaldaar seemed to know every debauched thing Zakael would enact on his victims and happily reenacted them on him. It was the most hideous form of torture because he already knew what to expect.

He came with a shudder, spilling his seed into Kaldaar's mouth. The god slurped and sucked, making grotesque noises and happy little squeaks that made Zakael's balls clench. Before the god could continue, he slid from the bed.

"I need to prepare." Then, on impulse, "If I see Taryn, do you have a message for her?"

This was a dangerous game to play, but he was trusting a hunch. Kaldaar hissed and recoiled.

"Tell her I will devour her heart with great enthusiasm." But the words rang hollow.

It was as he'd suspected—Kaldaar feared Taryn far more than he would admit, even to himself. There had to be a way he could use the information.

Within half a bell he'd bathed and dressed in his typical black trousers, vest, and shirt. It made his life simpler to wear the same style every day. Although, he had thought of wearing a bright-orange tunic on occasion just to see if Kaldaar would notice. The god might be obsessed with him, but he suspected it was only insofar as what Zakael could do for him. What he wore, or what Zakael's desires might be never occupied a moment of Kaldaar's thoughts.

Zakael bid a quick farewell before leaping from his balcony and transforming into a levon. He turned south toward Sitari and flew for a few leagues before banking left and heading north to the Temple of Ardyn.

The Sitari would be there whenever he arrived—there was no need to hurry. But where to hide while he delayed the inevitable? He landed at the temple and within two steps was once more a man. Even before he entered the temple, he knew something was off. His steps slowed, and he gripped the hilt of his sword.

The empty temple was cold and dark, two things it should never be. Rykoto demanded a fire burn at all times. Zakael scanned the area, sensing no one present but himself. The brazier he'd set by the altar was cold, as if there'd been no fire since he last visited. He knelt in front of the altar and called forth his lord, but Rykoto ignored him, or else couldn't hear him.

He paced a circle around the outer pillars, his mind spinning. He could hide here, but it would be the first place Kaldaar would look, and besides, Rykoto might still have a presence here. That the fire was out was bad, very bad, but he couldn't worry about that just yet. First, he needed a safe place to think.

His mind went to the one place he knew Kaldaar would never think to look—the Narthvier. Why he thought of that place in his time of peril, he wasn't sure, but it was the best of a bad situation. He took off again and set a course for the vast forest that took up the entire northern section of the West.

He flew over the tall trees, his levon searching for a nest to steal, but Zakael sought something a little more inviting. A lake shimmered in the sunlight and he flew toward it, unsure how far into the forest he was, and more specifically, how far from the

Weirren he might be. Getting too close to the Eleri king would be even worse than Rykoto's flame being snuffed out.

A woman stood by the shores of the lake, her raven hair cascading down her back. She wore no clothes, only her glorious hair for cover. She bent to retrieve water and stood to pour it back into the lake, her movements fluid, lyrical. He landed on a tree branch high enough she wouldn't spot him but close enough he could hear her incantations as she prayed to her goddess. The sound was music to his heart. He didn't understand the words, but her voice sent a ripple of memory through him. His levon body ruffled its feathers as he shuddered.

The woman set the vessel down and raised her face to the sun. His levon heart nearly gave out when he saw her face. He knew her. Had once loved her. Then forced himself to forget her.

In a fit of wild abandon, he flew to the lakeshore and transformed into himself. She startled but did not scream. Then she recognized him, and her face softened, and the old feelings he'd worked tremendously hard to cauterize reformed—strong, virulent, all-consuming, just as they'd been more than two decades earlier.

"Hello Carga."

She tilted her head and licked her lips. "Hello Zakael."

They stood in silence for a long moment before he finally said, "You look just as beautiful as the day we first met."

"I believe I was naked that day as well."

"Is it a habit with you to go without clothing? Or is this special to me?"

She blushed and giggled. "It does seem to be special to you. What are you doing here?" She glanced over her shoulder and frowned. "If you are found in these woods, you will be in grave danger."

He took a step toward her, but did not reach for her hands as he wished to do. It was as if he were that young lad again, once more besotted with her beauty and intellect. And that glorious body. He clearly recalled the wonderful days and nights they'd lain together. And the heartache that nearly killed him when she no longer came to meet him outside the vier.

"Why didn't you come back?"

"What?"

"You said you loved me and you promised to meet me, but you never came back. I waited." Gods how foolish he'd been then, and if he wasn't careful, how foolish he'd be now. She entranced him. That was it. She was an enchantress set to snare him in her trap once more.

"My father found out about us and I was exiled." She looked at the ground before meeting his eyes. "I thought you were only using me for information about the Eirielle."

It was true, he had interrogated her harshly about Taryn, but he thought she knew how he truly felt about her. She bit her lower lip and that undid him. He closed the space between them to take hold of her head and kiss her on those lovely, luscious lips. She wrapped her arms around him and pulled at his hair, begging him to go deeper, to never let go. At least, that's what he wished.

She pulled away so suddenly, he was left reeling. "I cannot. I am High Priestess now. I serve Verdaine."

"And the High Priestess does not partake of bodily delights?" He unbuttoned his vest and removed it slowly, loving the way her eyes darkened and she rolled her lip between her teeth. Next came his shirt, and finally, his trousers. When he stood as naked as she, he held out his hands. "Let me worship you."

"That is blasphemy."

"I believe if your goddess did not want me to make love to you, she would've popped herself between us and forbidden it. Maybe she knows this is something you want, too."

A blanket appeared on the sand beside him and he grinned as she took his hand and led him to the soft fabric. She laid him back and straddled him like she used to do in the meadows so long ago. When her wet pussy slid over his erection, he sighed with happy contentment.

Her pace was languid as she rocked back and forth on his pelvis. Eyes closed, she arched into him, her breasts lifted proudly. He stroked them gently, loving the touch of her soft skin. He found her rhythm and lifted his arse to meet her movements. They didn't need ShantiMari and he kept his power tightly controlled. He was lost to the sensations tickling through his body, mesmerized by the interplay of emotions on her lovely face. Their lovemaking was tender and heartbreaking. For one mad moment he dreamed he could stay in the vier, making love to her every day for the rest of his life.

When her pussy clenched, his cock responded with a throb. Her rocking increased in speed, and his release was imminent. She moaned and writhed, her face a study in passion. He couldn't hold it any longer, no matter how hard he tried to delay the inevitable, and climaxed with a loud groan. She cried out with her own release, her eyes locked to his. She leaned forward and stroked the sides of his face as she kissed his eyes, his cheeks, and finally his mouth.

They stayed locked together, their bodies trembling and hearts racing. When finally the delicious throbbing stopped, she lifted her head. Her glorious jade eyes regarded him with such intensity, he squirmed against her.

"You have a son, Zakael."

His breath caught and he stuttered a reply. "Where is he? Who is he?"

She sat up but did not roll off him. A knife appeared at his throat and he reached for his ShantiMari, but did not lash out. "You will never know him. Do you understand? He is to remain anonymous. I only tell you because I need your vow that you will protect him. Whatever is to come, you have to promise me you will not let your mad god destroy our son."

Zakael's mind processed this new information while his heart cracked a little. "He is my heir. He will inherit the Obsidian Throne."

She pressed the blade into his flesh and a sharp sting tore his skin. Warmth dripped down his neck. "No, he will never know who his parents are. Do you understand? Not me, not you. Anje can inherit your throne, or his son, but not our child." Another press. "Swear a blood oath that you will never seek him out, but will protect him from Kaldaar."

"How can I protect him if I don't know who he is?" This was madness. How could she demand this of him?

Then he saw it. The desperation of a mother. He recognized in her what he'd often seen in his own mother, and his heart ached for her that she knew of their son but could never be his mother. "I promise." He choked on the words. "I will never acknowledge our son, and I will do all in my power to protect him."

Her Mari swirled around him as the oath was sealed. Tears streaked over her cheeks and she bent down to kiss him one last time. Tenderly, softly, her tears mingled on their lips.

"Thank you."

A moment later, she was gone, and he lay alone on the lake shore, his heart shattered in ways he never thought possible. After all this time, after all he'd done, he had a son.

Just as quickly as the thought came, he cauterized it from his mind. He knew more than most what would happen if Kaldaar discovered the truth. The god could never know.

CHAPTER THIRTY-FOUR

The figure on the bed moaned as he tossed and turned. Taryn stood close by, watching intently as Tinsley's sweat-soaked body fretted atop the light blanket. Rhoane tried to keep his worry from his features, but it had been three days since they returned him to Talaith, with little improvement.

Both he and Taryn had tried everything, but whatever healing they'd done in the tent near Lake Oster wasn't the whole of what was needed. Even the Aelan healer that Hayden had found was stumped. They'd briefly considered bringing Loghan from Ulla, but Aomori had steadfastly refused. Rhoane agreed with the man, but not for the same reasons. He didn't think what ailed Tinsley could be repaired by Ullan healing.

As far as they could tell, all the Mohram poison was cleansed, without a speck left in Tinsley's blood. So what, then? Rhoane glanced at Alasdair and nodded. He'd written a letter to his sister but had waited until he was certain they'd need her assistance before sending it. Taryn tracked Alasdair's movements, her face a mystery. She hadn't outright disapproved, but she hadn't encouraged him to contact Carga, either.

Raised voices and a scuffle outside the bedchamber pulled his attention from Tinsley, and he went to see what the commotion was with Taryn close behind. Gwainne stormed through the room, calling for Taryn. When he saw her, his face turned thunderous.

"You deceiving little bog scrimp. I should have you flogged for what you have done!" His voice rose an octave and Rhoane glared at the man.

"How dare you enter my rooms and assault my betrothed. You have no authority here, Gwainne of the Ullans." He stood ready to attack with ShantiMari if it came to that.

"Shut up, you pathetic Eleri exile. My business is with the princess." Gwainne flicked a hand toward him as if to dismiss him and Rhoane curled his fists. "Why does your mother refuse to bed me? What did you say to her?"

Taryn laughed—an outright belly laugh that sounded out of place in the somber setting.

"I'm flattered you think I have sway over my mother, but I have no idea why she no longer desires you." She pointed to Rhoane. "Nor why you chose to insult my betrothed. I could have you executed for such treason."

"Bullshit." Gwainne crossed his arms and glared at her.

A loud moan came from the bedchamber and Aomori rushed out. Upon seeing Gwainne, he frowned, but turned to Rhoane. "He's weakening. Please, there must be something you can do."

They followed Aomori into the room and indeed, Tinsley looked much worse than he had minutes before.

Gwainne smacked his forehead and chuckled. "Is this the injured man?" He shook his head. "I was so distracted with the empress, I completely forgot. Verdaine said he would arrive soon and that I should seek out someone called Nena. When he did not show up, I thought she was mistaken."

The three of them turned as one to glare at Gwainne.

"You knew how to heal him and you FORGOT? You stupidassfuckwimpbastardmuppet!" Taryn took one step and clocked the prince smack on the chin.

Gwainne tumbled backward, curses flowing from his damaged lips. Blood seeped from his mouth even as he fell against the wall.

"How dare you!" He lunged for Taryn, but lost his balance and slumped back into the wall.

Rhoane and Taryn both drew their swords, stopping any further attack.

"Get out," Rhoane said between clenched teeth. "Get out of my rooms and do not ever set foot in here again. I would strongly suggest you avoid myself and the Darennsai for the next several days." He flicked his sword at Gwainne's privates and tilted his chin toward the door. "Go, before I forget my manners."

Gwainne righted himself and grumbled the entire way out of his rooms. When they heard the outer door slam, Taryn visibly relaxed. Her sword disappeared with a snap.

Aomori stared, fascinated. "Where did it come from? Where did it go?"

Taryn twisted her wrist and the sword reappeared. "Space storage. It's a trick I learned from a friend. I'll teach you after we heal Tinsley. Stay with him until we return." She waved the sword away and looked at Rhoane. "To Nena's then?"

"To Nena's." On his way, he asked Alasdair to hold off sending the letter to Carga. His sister would learn of her son's condition only after Rhoane was certain he would live.

In the hallway, Taryn pulled him into an alcove and pressed herself against him. He cocked his head in confusion.

"This is not an appropriate time for canoodling."

She shook her head and grinned. "Where did you hear that word? Never mind—we don't have time for canoodling *or* dilly-dallying. I'm taking us to Nena's by shadow."

He opened his mouth to ask what she meant, but by the time a syllable was uttered, they were whipped through the city and standing in a doorway near Nena's house. He blinked at his surroundings at then at her. She never ceased to surprise him.

"Space storage, shadow travel…what next, mi carae?"

"Guess we'll find out, won't we?" Her cheeky response made him all warm inside. What next indeed.

At the door to the whorehouse, a burly man tilted his chin when he saw Rhoane and gave Taryn an appraising glance.

"We are here to see Nena. No one else." Rhoane handed him a gold piece and waited while the man spoke with someone through a small window in the door. A moment later they were let inside. "Thank you."

"Sure thing, Your Highnesses." The man's gaze followed Taryn's backside as she strolled past, and Rhoane's eyes narrowed.

The man caught him and laughed. "She's a looker. You're a lucky man."

"I know." He shut the door in the man's face. Oh, how he knew it.

Nena kept them waiting only a few minutes before they were hustled up the back stairs to her room. Inside, Rhoane inhaled the perfumed air and instantly relaxed. Even though they were in the madam's private space where only gods knew what happened, he'd always felt comfortable here. Safe.

"What does Nena do to deserve not one, but two gorgeous peoples in my house?" The busty redhead sashayed into the room fanning herself. "I hope you have come to play with Nena?" She batted her eyelashes and flirted outrageously with them both. "I will never recover from such a time if you do so honor me."

"As enticing at that sounds, I'm afraid we're here on business," Taryn pouted. "Though you are rather fetching tonight. I admit, I'm tempted."

"No! Do not tease Nena. You have love only for Prince Rhoane. I can see it in your eyes, and feel it in your heart."

Taryn gasped and placed a hand protectively over her chest. "You've been inside my tunic? Naughty Nena!"

Rhoane laughed at their antics. He'd never seen Taryn so blatantly wanton. He felt Taryn's ShantiMari as it slid over and around him. She was making a private dome for them to speak, which meant Nena was being watched. By whom? And why?

He is in a house two down from us. Your Empress will not allow him into the palace. You must bring the patient to him. He is waiting. Nena's words brushed his mind. She'd never, in all the seasons he'd known her, used mind-speak with him. Again, he wondered why the caution.

How do you know what we need?

Nena's gaze went to him as she laughed boisterously at something Taryn said. *Verdaine visited me two days ago. She is worried about this patient. Says it is imperative he lives.*

Verdaine? Here? He couldn't possibly envision such a thing. But then again, he'd been here many times without so much as a blush.

We will bring him to the house. Who is waiting, can you say?

I will tell you he can heal your friend.

And nothing else? If Tinsley's life depends on this man, I need to know I can trust him.

Nena bit her lip and slid a glance to the window. She approached with hips swaying and stroked his cheek before she bent as if to kiss where her fingers had left off. *He is a Telraicht Noir practitioner, but he has left the Brotherhood.*

Rhoane struggled to keep his features placid. Like hell he'd let his nephew near one of Kaldaar's dogs.

"Rhoane," Taryn said aloud. "It's our only hope of saving him." Then, silently in his mind, *Verdaine wills it.*

Did he defy his goddess and risk Tinsley's death? Or did he trust one of the Brotherhood? It was an impossible choice, neither of which he wished to make. He inhaled slowly, hoping to clear his thoughts from the rampaging panic that beat against his skull. One of the Brotherhood. It mattered little that this man had left the filthy group. They were never truly free, Kaldaar's dogs.

But he had no choice if he were to save Tinsley. For his sister and his nephew, he would seek out the vermin.

"Which house, exactly?"

Nena gave him a mental picture of where they needed to go, even planting the man's face in his mind so that he would know what he looked like. They thanked the madam and made their way downstairs in silence. The burly doorman had the good graces not to say anything on their way out, probably due to the thunderstorm brewing on Rhoane's features. He struggled to relax his face. It wouldn't do to frighten the healer before the man had a chance to do any good.

"Let's see the house, find the guy, and then I'll go get Tinsley. Sound good?" Taryn said once they were far enough from the whorehouse not to be overheard.

"None of this sounds good, but we must trust Verdaine has a reason for us going to the enemy to heal our kin."

Taryn put a hand on his chest. "You're angry and scared. So am I. But we need to keep a clear head about this. Why the Brotherhood? Why now? What does Verdaine want us to learn from this?"

There was nothing he could learn from the Brotherhood except villainy and deceit.

CHAPTER THIRTY-FIVE

Damn Taryn and her optimism. She always believed the best in people, but Rhoane wasn't as trusting as she. If Verdaine wished for them to learn something from the Brotherhood beyond that they were nefarious scum, then it had better be a damn good lesson because he was not in the mood for trifles. He could at least admit Taryn had made an interesting proposition. One that he would be wise not to dismiss or scoff at too soon. He would go to the Telraicht Noir healer with an open mind and pay close attention to everything the man said and did. If nothing else, Rhoane would be treated to another method of healing he might add to his own skills.

They started off in the direction Nena's image indicated and found the house within a few minutes. An old crone answered on the first knock, surprising them. She peered at Taryn first with a sneer, then appraised Rhoane as vulgarly as the brute outside Nena's house had ogled Taryn.

"In the back." She looked shrewdly at the two of them. "Which one's the patient?"

"He'll be here in short order. Take us to the healer." Taryn stepped into a small parlor and indicated for the woman to lead the way.

In the back room, a man about Ebus's height was crouched over a desk. When they entered, he stood, but that did nothing for his stature.

"Are you of the fae folk?" Taryn asked, and the man looked at her with a little too much interest.

"Are *you?*"

She sighed and rolled her eyes, indicating she refused to play games with the man.

Rhoane got straight to the point. "We are told you can heal a friend of ours. He is in a bad way from a poison that is not found locally."

"Where is he?" The man looked out the door and frowned. "I can't heal someone who isn't here."

"We need to make sure we can trust you. We will be here for the healing, and involved as much as possible."

"Not good. I work alone."

Taryn withdrew Ynyd Eirathnacht and held it loosely in her hand. "You'll work with us, or I'll end you now. I have it on good authority Kaldaar is looking for his brethren. Is there a reason you're hiding in a dark house in Talaith, far from Caer Idris?"

At the mention of Kaldaar, both the man and the crone hissed and shrank into the shadows.

"Do not speak that name here else you draw his attention." The healer's gaze flicked from the sword blade to his desk, and then back again. "Bring the man. I can't promise anything, but I'll do my best."

"You will heal him or you will be dead," Rhoane said in an even tone.

"I can't work under threats."

"Sure you can. I do it all the time. Now get to work." Taryn sheathed her sword and stepped from the room.

"Where is she going? Will she be back?" The healer wrung his hands, his forehead dotted with sweat.

"Prepare a place for the healing. We do not have much time," Rhoane instructed as he mentally asked Taryn if she required assistance. He knew she could bring one other person through the shadows, possibly two, but she'd never taken someone semi-conscious.

She insisted she'd be fine, and though he worried, he trusted her decision. Just as they finished setting up a cot and several candles, Taryn arrived with an unresponsive Tinsley dangling from her arms. The healer jumped and grabbed his chest.

"Where did she come from?"

"The front door, where else?" Taryn laid Tinsley on the little makeshift bed with great care. "What's your name?"

"Names are powerful. I'm not comfortable giving you mine."

"Oh, I was just being polite," Taryn grinned. "I already know your name, the crone's name, and why you're here, but I was hoping you'd be honest with us. Which, to be fair, you were."

"This will go smoother if we have something to call you besides 'Healer,'" Rhoane added.

"Wurnch. Happy?"

"Very. I am Rhoane, and this is Taryn."

Wurnch looked at them as if they were diseased vermin. "Please don't kill me."

"Please do not let my friend die."

Wurnch nodded miserably and sat on a stool near Tinsley's head. His eyes closed and lips moved as he felt all along the man's head. Taryn took a seat to Wurnch's left, and Rhoane sat to his right. They put their hands on Tinsley's torso, ready for whatever came next.

Wurnch mumbled an incantation and Rhoane closed his eyes to better concentrate on what he said. If there was anything nefarious being whispered, he'd stop the man immediately. But Wurnch only said words of healing, coaxing Tinsley to open his ShantiMari to help the process.

Then, suddenly, a swirl of Wurnch's Telraicht Noir Shanti ripped through the young lord's body. Tinsley flinched and rocked, but Wurnch continued. Rhoane saw Wurnch's Shanti coil around Tinsley's power. It bubbled and cracked and blackened as if corrupted. Rhoane glanced to Taryn, alarmed, but she gave a slight shake of her head, her face calm.

How could she be so unaffected? Wurnch had in essence destroyed Tinsley's ShantiMari. That was forbidden, tantamount to murder. Yet she acted as if nothing untoward had occurred. Rhoane's heart stampeded in his chest and his palms grew clammy as he struggled against indecision. Stop the healing? Continue? Why wasn't Taryn more concerned?

There is nothing to fear. Trust in Wurnch, mi carae, Taryn's thoughts brushed his. *What he's doing is good.*

Rhoane swallowed the vile curse he desperately wished to shout out loud at the both of them and forced himself to calm. He cast his thoughts back to what was happening inside Tinsley and saw that now, instead of the blackened strands of power, the threads twisted and bent in on themselves, turning from deepest obsidian to perfect translucence, like a polished diamond.

Taryn had been right. Wurnch was using Tinsley's own power to heal himself, but had first had to break it and twist it with his Telraicht Noir ShantiMari. Effective and incredible. And not something Rhoane would have ever considered. Perhaps there was something to learn here, after all. He caught Taryn's tiny smile as she glanced quickly at him, then back to Tinsley. She'd known—but how?

Wurnch's words drifted and floated on the air between them, lingering for a moment before sinking into Tinsley's flesh. For someone not connected to Wurnch or Tinsley physically, they would see nothing, but Rhoane saw it all as if it truly was happening in the physical world. It was remarkable. And terrifying.

If something went awry, could he stop it in time? Or at all?

His gaze slid to the healer whose brow was streaked with sweat, his hair plastered to his face. His red cheeks puffed with the effort, but he kept his eyes closed, his power focused.

This man, an enemy to the Light and the Dark, worked to heal a stranger. He knew nothing of Tinsley's affliction, nor who he was, and yet he'd done as they asked. Granted, their threats probably helped, but even so, the man risked his life to save the lord's.

A snap of power against Rhoane's skin made him flinch, but he kept his hands firmly on Tinsley's torso. He couldn't tell where the power had come from, but by the grin on his beloved's face, he assumed Taryn wanted him to focus on the healing, not Wurnch's motivations. She was far too comfortable with the amount of Telraicht Noir Shanti that Wurnch was employing to cure Tinsley.

With a shiver, he understood why. He'd all but forgotten she possessed the very same strain of ShantiMari as the healer. If Wurnch were to abuse his power, she could shut him down with a breath.

Knowing Taryn could intervene set his mind at ease. He corralled his wandering thoughts and delved into Wurnch's and Tinsley's power once more.

The clear threads now softly glowed a bluish green similar to the young lord's eye color. Tinsley's breathing evened and his skin tone took on a pinkish hue. He no longer thrashed or whimpered. Rhoane placed a hand on his forehead and felt only cool skin. The fever had broken.

"I have done what I can. The rest is up to him." Wurnch sat back and the crone entered to mop his forehead with a clean cloth.

Her movements were nimble and fluid, more like that of youth than old age. He watched her care for the healer, her attention reminiscent of a lover.

"Does every practitioner have a crone to serve them?" Rhoane asked.

Wurnch blustered and swore at Rhoane, but the woman put a hand on his shoulder to calm him. "I am but four and thirty, my lord. And to answer your question, no, they do not have one, but many. Women are seen only as breeders to the Brotherhood. It is our only value."

"Your value goes far beyond breeding, my love." Wurnch placed his hand protectively over hers. "It is why I left the Brotherhood and hide here in a city large enough I dare hope we won't be found by the Master."

"Are there others like you?" Taryn watched the woman with an intensity that would make a seasoned guard squirm.

The crone looked down and wrung her hands. "Yes, but we are encouraged not to speak about it."

"By whose authority?" Rhoane could guess the answer.

"The Master."

"And who is he?" Taryn demanded.

Wurnch stood in front of the crone as if to protect her from their inquiry. "We don't know. No one does. I suppose the high priests would know, but he is never seen. Only as a shadow."

"As a phantom?" Taryn looked at Rhoane and he understood her meaning.

"How did you know?" Wurnch scooted him and his love closer to the doorway. "I think it's time you leave."

Taryn picked up Tinsley as if he were a child. She cradled him against her chest and sidled through the door. On her way out, she whispered something to the crone, who covered her face and gasped. Tears shone in her eyes as she watched Taryn leave.

Rhoane stopped before the couple and reached for his coin purse. "How much do we owe you?"

"Nothing. Just leave and forget you ever found this place." Wurnch's eyes were filled with worry, his lips a tight white line.

Rhoane took out several coins and put them in the crone's palm before grasping both of their hands. "You have opened my understanding this evening and I thank you from the bottom of my heart, not only for your honesty, but for healing our friend." He squeezed their hands and sent a thread of his Shanti to them. "If you are ever in need of our assistance, you have only but to ask."

"Who are you?" The crone removed her hand from his and rubbed it on her skirts before pocketing the coins. "Nena only said we were to assist if you should call, but your partner, she is… unusual. She bears Telraicht Noir ShantiMari, which is impossible for a woman."

Rhoane blinked in surprise. "You do not know our names?" When they both shook their heads, his confusion deepened.

"Rhoane," Taryn called from the front room. "We need to see to Tinsley."

"Go ahead without me. I will return soon." He looked at the two frightened faces before him and sighed. Verdaine had sent him here for a reason beyond healing his nephew, and even if it took all night, he wasn't leaving until he understood what that was.

In all his seasons as a spy, he'd perfected the art of interrogation, but as he looked at the frightened faces of Wurnch and his crone, he knew a different tact was needed.

"If you would not mind, I could use a cup of tea. Or something stronger if you have it." He pulled up a chair and sat. "Once I tell you of our purpose, I have a feeling you will need some, too."

He was beginning to understand why Verdaine had sent him here this night. Not only to save his nephew's life, or to learn about Telraicht Noir healing, but to understand the plight of those exiled from their given path. If he could learn the exiled Brotherhood's story, then he might be able to guide them to a new path where they could live in safety and contribute to society.

He couldn't save them all, but the least he could do was try.

CHAPTER THIRTY-SIX

Taryn waited for the slap, the verbal berating, the complete freak out, but it never came. Instead, Lliandra gazed out the window with a serenity Taryn had never seen in her mother. Myrddin was no longer on Aelinae; where exactly he had gone, Taryn didn't know. She could probably chase him through the void if she so desired, which she did not. And as far as Taryn knew, her mother wasn't bedding anyone new. So why the peaceful countenance? Usually the empress was in a snit if she didn't have at least one lover to keep her company.

"I suppose this is your life now." Lliandra turned from the window and gazed at them. "Rhoane, I don't think I've ever thanked you for looking after Taryn all these seasons."

"You have, Your Majesty, but I am grateful for the praise all the same." He inclined his head. "We will not be long on this trip, but there are things we must see to that are too important to put off any longer."

"And you must go to the Ullans? Can't this be done from here?"

"No, Mother. Only in Ulla." Taryn approached her mother with caution. "Is there anything we can do before we leave?"

"No, but can you bring me that delightful healer who refused my bed? If he is half as stimulating as his brother, I would be quite pleased." She giggled and fanned herself. "I do not miss Gwainne, or the games he played trying to seduce secrets from me—and I tell you true, I fed him many lies—but his healing. Oh! That was exquisite."

Eww on so many levels.

"Gwainne isn't a healer." Taryn looked to Rhoane who shrugged. "I suppose it's in his blood? I mean, Kaleigh and Loghan are two of the best, so it stands to reason he has some of their talent."

A servant arrived to announce the Ullan prince, and Taryn's stomach twisted. The last she'd seen of him, Gwainne was scampering out of Rhoane's rooms spewing curses aimed specifically at her.

He bustled into the room with all the sanctimonious pomp the twat believed he deserved. When he saw first Rhoane, and then her, his face bloomed red, but just as quickly morphed into a mask of obsequiousness.

"Your Majesty. You look ravishing today." He ignored Taryn and Rhoane to go directly to the empress and clasp her hands.

Lliandra scowled at him. "What in Ohlin's name happened to your face?"

Gwainne lifted a hand to cover the bruise that Taryn's fist had left. "Your daughter assaulted me." At Lliandra's gasp, he continued, "I know! I was equally as shocked as I believed her to be a lady of high refinement."

Taryn openly laughed at that. "You called me a bilge rat."

Rhoane cleared his throat and they all looked at him. "I believe his exact words were 'a deceiving little bog scrimp.' The differences are subtle, but important."

Taryn grinned at her love and turned back to the Ullan prince. "What do you want?"

"What I want," he started, "is for you to apologize and for your mother to punish you publicly for assaulting me."

"No."

They all looked at Lliandra as she crossed her arms.

"No what, Your Majesty?" Gwainne asked, his voice incredulous.

"No. I will not punish my daughter, and she will not apologize. In fact, I will insist that you pack your belongings and leave my kingdom immediately." Lliandra's eyes narrowed and she looked at Taryn. "You're going to Ulla. Can you see fit to deliver him to his kingdom? That way, he will be out of mine all the sooner."

Well fuck. This wasn't how the morning was supposed to go. Taryn sighed and agreed to drop Gwainne off in Ulla. After he left in a huff, she gave her mother a long embrace before she and Rhoane said their goodbyes. Each time it was getting to be more difficult, no matter who the goodbyes were said to.

They found Kaida with Tessa in the library playing a macabre sort of game that involved several desks, two ladders, and an unamused librarian.

"Kaida, we've been instructed to take Gwainne to Ulla. Say your farewells to Tessa." Taryn sat in one of the chairs to wait out the snuggles and cuddles.

"Can't she stay here with me?" Tessa pleaded. "We have ever so much fun and she's the best listener. Aren't you girl?" She scratched Kaida behind the ears and the grierbas raised her head for more. "I wish she was a real girl, though. Like me, with legs and arms that worked right. Then she could hold a sword and fight like a pirate."

Tessa was still playing out the siege of Lliandra's ships, but in her fantasy, she always saved her loved ones. Taryn had heard of her escapades from Eliahnna, and it broke her heart to see her so desperate to reclaim the traumatic experience. It made leaving that much harder.

"I mean, I guess? It's up to Kaida, though." Taryn looked to the grierbas for an answer. She hoped Kaida would say no, but when she nudged Tessa for more scritches, Taryn knew her decision. "That's decided then. Kaida will stay here with you, and we'll go fight sea monsters."

Tessa's face lit up. "Are you jesting, dear sister? Because you know I would love to fight a sea monster by your side."

"I know you would, and one day you will. Just, not today. This sea monster is actually a friend named Xianqin, and we're not fighting her but helping to mend Aelinae's surface."

"That sounds dreadfully boring. I think I'll stay here with Kaida and slay our own sea monsters."

Taryn kissed Tessa's curls and hugged her tight. "Be good while we're gone. We should be home within a sennight."

"Mmmhmm, have fun."

The casual dismissal cut Taryn to the quick. There was a time when Tessa would beg her to stay, but those days were long since passed. She'd left her baby sister too many times for her to trust she'd ever be around for more than a few days. As much as it hurt, Taryn knew it was for the best. Sometime soon, their departure would be forever.

"How are you?" Rhoane asked once they were in the hallway.

"Sad, but I know this is for the best. Tessa needs Kaida right now. Still sucks, though."

"Exactly how I feel as well." He held her hand and kissed her fingertips. "How should we travel to Ulla? I was hoping for a quicker method than horseback, but with Gwainne, I will not be able to fold time. I suppose you could shadow travel us there?"

Taryn grinned. "I've got an idea."

They sent a message to have the prince join them in the far corner of the garden where they would have the most privacy. When he arrived, he was still fuming.

"What is the meaning of this? Where are our horses?" He stomped and sputtered like the spoiled prince he was.

"No horses," Rhoane said before transforming into his darathi.

Gwainne shrieked—actually, screamed like a child—when he saw the great beast.

"Your chariot," Taryn motioned to Rhoane. "Get on, shut up, and don't fall off."

"You must be mad! There is no way I will ride that thing." He half-turned to leave, but Rhoane stopped him with a line of flames.

"I promised my mother I would get you to Ulla and we're in a hurry, so up you go." Taryn used her ShantiMari to lift him by the buttocks onto Rhoane's back. "And please don't scream the entire way."

She chortled at the look of sheer terror on his face. Served the pompous twit right. When she shifted into her dragon, he looked as if he might pass out. Despite her warning, as soon as they lifted into the air, Gwainne's cries took on an animalistic quality and she genuinely feared for his sanity.

He held onto Rhoane's scales with a white-knuckled death grip as they flew over the lands south of Talaith. They avoided the Royal Road and Lake Oster, but that didn't stop her from scanning the countryside looking for more Mohram or other creatures Zakael might've kidnapped from other worlds.

Once they passed the southern end of the Kiltern River where it met the Eastern Seas and crossed into Ulla, they banked north to avoid the more mountainous region of the kingdom.

Up here should be perfect. Rhoane began his slow spiral to land and she followed.

"What are you doing? We are still several days from where my father's camps are located," Gwainne yelled into the wind.

They settled on the dusty ground and he slid from Rhoane's back with more recriminations and curses. Taryn and Rhoane ignored him as they transformed into their Eleri forms.

"What is the meaning of this?" Gwainne demanded. "Why have we stopped?"

"To give you time to think of your choices," Taryn stated simply. "You've been a complete ass not just to us, but everyone at the Crystal Palace, including the empress, and we decided you needed a chance to ponder what your path shall be going forward."

"It is a three-day journey to your father. That should be plenty of time for you to reconsider your behavior." Rhoane tossed him a canvas bag. "In here are some provisions. Enough to get you to the camps if you are not greedy."

"You cannot do this! You would not. My father will have your heads if you desert me."

"We aren't deserting you, Prince Gwainne of the Ullans. We're giving you a chance to see more of your kingdom, and along the way, you just might discover something about yourself you never knew existed." She waved to him and lifted herself into the air, transforming as she did.

Rhoane's wings made a cyclone of dust as he lifted upwards. Together, they flew toward the Jansen Strait and Amdi Agnar's camp. As Gwainne became smaller and smaller, Taryn reflected that some goodbyes came much easier than others. But even this one did not bring her happiness.

CHAPTER THIRTY-SEVEN

Faelara put a protective hand over her belly and asked herself for the twentieth time that morning if she was making a mistake. There was no doubt where Baehlon stood on that decision. He was firmly of the opinion that she was mad to even consider making a trip—underwater—to the sea kingdom. But she knew in her heart it was the right decision not just for her, but Michel, too. And possibly even Baehlon, although she hadn't been able to thoroughly convince herself of that just yet.

It was now or never. She took Michel's hand in her own and nodded toward the water. He splashed through the waves, completely comfortable in his nakedness. Unlike the freedom loving youth, she and Baehlon had decided to wear their small-clothes. Even the lightweight trousers and shifts the Ullans wore might be too heavy in the deep waters and Faelara was leaving nothing to risk.

"You're sure the baby will be fine?" Baehlon held her elbow as he trudged beside her.

"We will all be fine, my love. Trust me." If only she could trust herself. It was only a feeling she had, no hard evidence to support her words.

They stepped into the depths and Faelara turned to wave to Loghan and Kaleigh as they stood on the shore. They'd accompanied them to the strait, more to see Michel off she guessed than for any concern for her or Baehlon. In their time with the Ullans, Kaleigh had been cordial, but not overly friendly. Fae thought they might bond over their pregnancies, but that hadn't happened. Although, they both found it interesting that two older women such as they were had found themselves pregnant at the same time.

Kaleigh had confessed that it was imperative she see her child safely delivered, but she didn't know why. With Amdi Agnar's health improving each day, Fae thought perhaps the Eleri was being overly cautious, but she wouldn't begrudge a mother for doing what she thought best for her unborn child. Hell, if anything, Baehlon would have had them both on bed rest until the day they gave birth.

She turned away from the pair to swim after Michel, who had gotten quite a ways ahead of them.

"I hate this," Baehlon groused. "I like my feet on solid ground."

"Perhaps there is a sandy bottom at King Baldev's palace. Would that suit you?"

"You jest at time like this?" He shook his head and the bells in his braids chimed. They sounded different in the water, more somber, perhaps.

"Are you ready?" She held her hand out for him to take. When he clutched her fingers in his, she dove beneath the surface.

The first few minutes were terrifying, but once she convinced her mind she could breathe underwater, she was fine. Baehlon flailed for a minute more, fighting the sensation of drowning, but Michel swam to him and stroked his face to calm the big knight. They'd bonded wonderfully over the past week, so much so that Faelara was tempted to ask Michel if he'd like to go with them to

Talaith—but his place wasn't with her. Another gut feeling, but she'd learned long ago to trust her instincts.

Once they were all settled, Michel swam deeper and deeper into the sea. His lithe legs kicked hard, propelling him onward as she and Baehlon struggled to keep up. Suddenly the boy stopped swimming and floated in the murky depths.

What is it? Fae looked in every direction, but saw nothing beyond the three of them.

Xianqin, Michel answered, and her heart sped up.

A dark serpentine figure wound around them and from the darkness a face emerged. Blue scales and long tendrils that curled outward from the sides of its face were all she saw through her terror.

"I am Xianqin," the creature said. "I am a darathi eneari, the last of my kind." This was said with a note of sadness. "I have come to escort you to King Baldev. He is waiting."

Baehlon floated as if frozen, his eyes huge, his mouth agape. Finally, he blinked and looked at her. "I thought I'd imagined her. You don't suppose she'll eat us, do you?"

"I don't eat people," Xianqin said with a slight giggle. "Though I've heard you are delicious."

"Xianqin tease," Michel said. "She funny."

"Yeah, a real riot." Baehlon swam closer to Faelara. "Are we supposed to swim to this mythical kingdom?"

"If you like—or you can ride on my back."

Michel immediately swam to Xianqin's back and gripped her scales. "Come!" He held out a hand. "Fast swim."

Fae and Baehlon joined him on the wide expanse of the water dragon's back and held tight to her scales. Xianqin swished and they were off. Michel was right, it was much faster. They practically flew through the water, passing between schools of fish and beneath shadows of bigger beasts that hovered near the surface. Corals and sea grasses were a blur as they were whisked deeper and deeper into the ocean.

They traveled through a short tunnel carved into rock and emerged in what Fae could only describe as a dreamscape. Light drifted down from somewhere above, illuminating a near-translucent palace that looked as if it might break with a strong current. Airy passages led from one space to the next. She hesitated to call them rooms—there was no furniture to speak of, but clusters of plants and rocky beds that made up what she guessed were seating areas.

What amazed her the most wasn't the fairytale turrets and bridges that looked like spun sugar, but the creatures who swam past. They had faces and torsos like hers and Baehlon's, but instead of feet, they had lovely wide tails. Merfolk.

Michel gestured wildly toward an opening and Xianqin turned in that direction. Baehlon's face was a study in wonder as he watched the colorful plants pass. Fish in colors never imagined swam beside the merfolk, who regarded them with just as much curiosity.

In her amazement, she hadn't realized there was no singing. She looked to Michel for an answer, but he merely shrugged.

"Theys quiet today. Upset above." He pointed toward the surface. "No worry, though." His little hand cupped her cheek and he smiled. "Michel take care of Fae."

"I thought that was my job," Baehlon huffed, but there was no malice in his words.

Finally, Xianqin swam into a large area where several thousand merfolk floated from the sandy bottom of the sea to the top of the space. Faelara's nerves woke with a start and her heart fluttered beneath her ribs.

"I have brought the woman as asked," Xianqin said. "If you have no further need of me, I have business elsewhere."

At first, Faelara thought the water dragon spoke to her, but then she saw the great throne made of coral and whale bone. Seated upon the throne was a merman twice the height of Baehlon. His golden hair drifted behind him. Clear green eyes regarded her little group and a smile played on his lips—lusciously full lips that looked as if they enjoyed kissing.

She pulled her attention away from his handsome face, but her gaze landed on his very naked torso and seductively chiseled abs. Holy barnacles, what was happening to her? She was happy with Baehlon and had never entertained the idea of another man, but seeing the sea king, her body trembled in a dangerous way.

Baehlon slid from Xianqin's back and helped Fae to the sandy floor. She gripped his hands a little too hard as they swam toward the throne. Michel stayed a length behind, even when she beckoned him forward.

The king waved Xianqin off with a bored expression. Then he turned his piercing gaze on her and her insides flipped and flounced as if she were a maiden still in braids. What the demon was wrong with her?

"You are with child. Is this the father?" his rough voice bellowed from the throne, and some of her quaking eased.

"I am Sir Baehlon de Monteferron, and this is my life mate. She carries our child in her womb."

"You must be rather proud to have achieved what so few can."

Faelara cocked her head. "What do you mean?"

The sea king undulated as he rose from his seat and it was the sexiest thing she'd ever witnessed in her life. "Only a dozen times in our history has a mermaid conceived with a non-merfolk. Your mother, Nemora, was the first in over a millennia, and now, to have you bear a child so soon after, it has given us great interest in finding the answer why."

"My mother?" Fae's legs began to wobble and the face of a dangerously pale woman entered her mind.

"You've met her several times, but under rather stressful circumstances. For that, I apologize. Nemora is nothing if not impetuous." He held his hand over his heart, or where she guessed his heart would be. "Forgive me, I have forgotten my manners. I am King Baldev." He peered behind them and frowned. "Michel? Is that you? Come forward, boy."

Michel crept forward, his head hung low. "I am sorry, Your Majesty. I did not mean to break your rules, but I have a very good reason for it."

Faelara shared a look with Baehlon as they realized at the same time that not only did they understand the language of the merfolk, they had both just spoken it. She took his hand as a reminder that this was really happening.

"It involves a star, does it not?" Baldev laughed a hearty bellow and waved Michel toward him. "Yes, yes, Xianqin explained everything to me. Did you know, long ago I met this star's life mate and told him the story of the Surtentse and Darennsai."

A sigh came from Fae's left, and she turned to see several young women floating nearby.

"That's my favorite," one of the ladies with blue hair and matching fin said. "It's so romantic."

"I have met him. He's called Rhoane and carries an enchanted sword of light," Michel added hopefully.

"That he does. Did he find his star?" Baldev asked with a gentle tone.

"He healed her and brought her back from near death."

"All because you missed your curfew. What a remarkable coincidence, wouldn't you say?" Baldev looked out into the mass of merfolk gathered in the huge room. "Where is your mother?"

Michel didn't even look before pointing to the right. "Just there."

Baldev beckoned her forward and a lovely mermaid with hair the color of sunset swished from a group of colorful merfolk to her son. A fissure of recognition jolted through Faelara and she stared at the mermaid, struggling to breathe.

"Michel, since you helped the Darennsai and the Surtentse, I will grant you your tail—but miss curfew again and you must stay with the land walkers. Do you understand?"

"Yes, Your Majesty. Thank you." Michel threw his scrawny arms around the king.

Baldev made a swirling motion with his hand and Michel's legs morphed into a lovely amber tail with opalescent fins. Michel clapped and swam a large circle before coming to rest beside his mother. To her, Baldev gave a stern look that would make any soldier shudder.

"You have been too distracted of late and your son paid the price. Do you promise to keep to our borders? No more singing to lure strangers into our waters?"

Singing? Fae's heart pitter-patted with increasing speed.

"I promise." She inclined her head and Faelara saw the smile that lit up her face. "May I see her now?"

Baldev grinned and nodded. "Of course, Nemora. Go and meet your daughter."

Baehlon gasped as if he only just figured it out. Not only was Michel her brother, but the gorgeous mermaid with fiery hair and a tail of jade was her mother.

CHAPTER THIRTY-EIGHT

Kaleigh stared at them as if they'd lost their damn minds, and then burst into laughter. She held her sides and bent double with the prolonged chortling. Of all the reactions Taryn thought they'd get when they told her they'd dropped her son off in the desert, uncontrollable laughter wasn't even on the long list.

"You are not mad?" Rhoane asked cautiously.

"How can I be? He ignored a request directly given by our goddess. He deserved far worse than having to walk a few leagues on his own. If he had been here in camp, I would have made him fight in the arena."

"Harsh," Taryn muttered. "But also, why didn't I think of that?"

Kaleigh's fits started again, much to Loghan's consternation.

"All this jostling is not good for the baby."

"Since when?" Kaleigh challenged her son. "This is the first time in ages I have had a good laugh. Do not deny me this one simple pleasure."

Loghan crossed his arms and stood silently brooding.

Rhoane steadfastly ignored the Ullan healer and spoke only

to Kaleigh. "We will not be here long, but would appreciate a bed to sleep in for the night."

"Not long? But you only just arrived. I thought you would at least stay until your friends return."

"Fae and Baehlon aren't here?" Taryn looked to Kaleigh first and then to Loghan. "Where are they? They're not in danger, are they?" More specifically, was the baby safe?

"Michel took them to the sea kingdom. It seemed very important to Lady Faelara that they go sooner rather than later. Of course, if she had known you were coming, I am sure she would have delayed."

Taryn stared at Kaleigh. "Michel? The little boy who found me on the beach? Why?"

Kaleigh looked to Loghan, who nodded. "Michel is of the merfolk. As is your friend Faelara."

Taryn had known the truth about Fae ever since the day she almost drowned at the cove in Menurra, but to have it said so plainly was still a shock.

"Little Michel? I had no idea. He hid that from me rather well." She chewed on a cuticle until Rhoane gently lowered her thumb from her lips. "Why was he alone?"

"I only know what he shared with me. On a merfolk's naming day, they can come ashore and walk the land, but if they do not return to the sea by sunset, they are doomed to be a land dweller the rest of their life. On the day Michel found you, he made a choice to help, forsaking his watery home."

"Oh." Taryn put a hand over her heart. "What a brave and foolish little boy."

"I am certain Baldev will give him back his tail for helping you." Rhoane stroked her arm and smiled. "I met him once, before you were born. He told me the legend of the Surtentse and Darennsai."

"The story with the terrible ending? That doesn't foster confidence in the man."

"Merman."

"Right." She raised her thumb to her mouth and removed it just as quickly. "Do you think your friend can help with our dilemma?"

Rhoane rubbed his chin. "It is possible, I suppose. We could always ask."

"What dilemma?" Kaleigh's gaze flicked between her and Rhoane.

"We are tasked with repairing a tear in Aelinae's terrarae. That is what the crone was trying to tell me the last time we were here. There's a rip in the land and evil from Dal Ferran is seeping into the sea."

Kaleigh gasped and put a hand over her abdomen. "I have bathed in the sea waters. Do you think my baby is harmed?"

"You and your baby are fine." Rhoane held Kaleigh's hand. "I doubt Loghan here would allow anything to cause you grief."

"Verdaine said this child must survive. It is my duty to see to her wishes." The tattoos on Loghan's head vibrated with his frustration.

"Is there something going on between you two? You seem a little hostile toward each other." Taryn leaned against a bureau and waited for one of them to explain why it felt like they'd rather punch each other than be in the same room together.

After an awkwardly long pause, Loghan shifted and stared at the floor. "I have not been able to forget my feelings for you," he flicked a glance at Taryn, "and therefore, I have also disobeyed Verdaine's orders. I am a disappointment to my family."

"No, you are not," Kaleigh insisted.

"She's right. You're not a disappointment to Verdaine or your family." Taryn put her hand on his forearm and felt the jangle of nerves beneath his skin. "Love is hard. Especially when you have the terrible misfortune of falling in love with someone who cannot or will not love you in return. Your heart is your own,

Loghan. Don't let anyone—goddess or otherwise—tell you who you can or cannot love."

Loghan's face pinched in torment. "I did not expect to see you so soon and thought I would have enough time to forget you."

"Well now, that's just rude. I hope you never forget me." At his look of alarm, she added, "What I mean is, remember this feeling—the good parts at least—and find that in someone who can love you in return." She chuckled beneath her breath. "Funnily enough, there is a lovely woman in Talaith right this minute mourning your brother's lack of love for her. If only she'd met you first, I think you might've hit it off, but instead she had the misfortune of meeting your twat of a brother at Verdaine's temple."

"She is a novice?" Kaleigh's face lit with surprise. "And she is in Talaith? Is she *sheanna?*"

"She left the vier of her own will, but Verdaine gave her blessing." Rhoane explained. "But we could get her if you would like to meet her. She reminds me a lot of you."

"If we are meant to meet, it should be unplanned. I must see to father." Loghan took a few steps before turning back. "Thank you—both of you—for being understanding of my failing."

Taryn shook her head sadly. "It's not a failing to love. Got that? Just, next time maybe don't fall so hard for someone unavailable."

He grinned and inclined his head. "I will endeavor to remember your sage advice, Darennsai."

When he'd left the tent, Taryn asked after Amdi's health and was relieved to hear he was recovering quickly after taking Faelara's elixir. They talked for a few more minutes before sleep beckoned and Kaleigh showed them to a tent close to hers.

There was no healing sex magic this trip, not that Taryn wouldn't have loved to spend several bells wrapped in Rhoane's arms, but she was knackered and needed the rest. When they climbed into bed, she automatically reached for Kaida and once again felt that pit of sadness that her friend had stayed in Talaith.

She fell into a fitful sleep and woke even more tired than she'd been the night before. After a simple breakfast of eggs and flatbread served with the horrid coffee-like drink she detested but sucked down in the hopes it would give her energy, she and Rhoane made their way to the Jansen Strait. It was time to sort out the issue of fixing the rift between land and sea, with a flowing river of lava thrown in just to make things more fun.

They stripped to their smallclothes and dove beneath the waves to swim deeper into the strait. Rhoane handled the transition rather well, all things considered—she felt his panic, but unlike the other times they'd swum, he controlled his fear and kept pace with her.

The only problem now was, where the hell was the tear? She drifted with the current and let her ShantiMari spread out like a radar, searching for something, anything that could help pinpoint where they needed to go. Rhoane's Shanti brushed hers and she saw his Glamour shimmering beneath his skin. She looked at her wrist and sure enough, her runes were sparking as if lit from within. The burn she'd received at Lan Gyllarelle glowed red against her own Glamour.

"I think we're close." She held out her arm for Rhoane to see.

"I feel it as well." He swam to their left and she followed. "Have you figured out how we will heal the tear?"

"Not yet. Do you have any ideas?"

He tilted his head, his hair making a dark halo around him. "I need to see it first, but I have an idea."

Thank the stars he had something because she'd been wracking her brain all day and had come up with nothing. The closer they came to the tear, the more her volcano rune burned, to the point that she had to keep herself from rubbing it. How was it possible to burn while submerged in water?

Then it dawned on her. "Are you thinking what I am thinking?"

His grin said it all. "If you are thinking one of us creates a whirlpool while the other flames the fissure, then yes. The two elements combined should act to seal the terrarae, effectively stitching the ground back together."

"Yeah, that's pretty much what I was thinking, too." She was such a liar. She'd only gotten as far as flaming the tear as if welding to pieces of metal—his plan was much better.

They kept swimming in the direction their ShantiMari led them until they came to an angry red scar on the ocean floor. The burn on her arm flared anew and she gasped at the pain that singed through her. Rhoane cast her a worried glance, and she pointed to her forearm.

"I think we found it and Rykoto is not pleased."

Rhoane stopped swimming and tried to run a hand through his hair, but it was floating in a tangled mess. "Do we repair it as darathi? Or as us?"

"We need flame, so one of us needs to be a dragon." Could their darathi breathe underwater? Xianqin could, but she was a water dragon. What if they could warp their darathi to suit whatever need they had? That seemed impossible, but she'd learned that word only held true if you never tried.

"You are not strong enough on your own to create a whirlpool. And besides, I think once we have the gap sealed, you should use ice just in case. I have yet to master both fire and ice."

How did he know she could? Ah, yes, the runyon tree. He'd been inside of it when she first froze it and then burned it to a crisp.

"Excellent idea. Are you ready, my love?" She didn't wait for an answer before shifting into her dragon. A momentary panic twitched in her belly, but her dragon had no trouble breathing underwater. Her hearing became acute enough that she swore she could hear the fish farting as they passed. She eyed an especially cheeky striped fish, and he swam off with great haste.

She and Rhoane swam in a circle to start the whirlpool. Once it formed, Rhoane settled himself close to the tear. As they channeled their ShantiMari, the whirlpool radiated a brilliant blue light and the scar flared with fiery intensity. Taryn commanded the whirlpool toward the tear as Rhoane blew a flame of controlled chaos. The opposing elements clashed with a breathtaking display of raw energy.

The combined forces of water and fire surged into the rift, pushing against the darkness and stitching the fractured terrarae back together just as Rhoane had suggested. The scar undulated and shrank against their power. In the far distance, she heard Rykoto shouting recriminations and curses. With another surge, the tear vanished entirely, leaving no trace of the malevolent energy that had been seeping into the strait.

Taryn swam forcefully at the now healed spot and blew a glacier's worth of ice onto the soil. Again and again she blew until a thick coating of frozen earth and ice covered half a football pitch worth of seabed. Satisfied it would hold for at least a million seasons, she relaxed and let the vortex peter out.

Her darathi infused her with energy, but once she transformed back into a woman, she was left exhausted and starving. Rhoane swam to her, his face paler than usual.

"I could eat a vorlock."

"Same, but I'd rather not. Do you have the energy to swim to shore?"

"I can help." Xianqin appeared before them, her whiskers unfurling to wrap around their waists. "I could not assist in the repair, but I am permitted to take you safely to shore."

"Thank Julieta for us, will you?" Taryn had wondered if the water dragon would show herself. She'd felt her presence, but had remained focused on her task.

"It is Julieta who thanks *you*. Even now, the waters are clearing of evil that once poisoned our home."

Taryn stroked Xianqin's scales and pressed her head against the water dragon's cheek. "It's good to see you again." A little striped fish swam in front of her and she wrinkled her nose. "Watch out for those guys, they're stinky."

"That is why we call them stink fish."

"For real?"

Xianqin nodded and Taryn laughed at the ridiculousness of it all. Fish that fart, ice and fire healing a tear in the seabed. What next? She dared not ask. The gods just might make it happen. They loved nothing more than messing with her, much to her consternation.

She settled into Xianqin's rapid movements, thinking perhaps a nap would be nice, when it occurred to her they should've reached the surface by now. But they weren't swimming toward the light—they were diving deeper into the dark and foreboding depths.

"Sleep now, Darennsai. We will be with the sea king soon and you need rest."

The hell? What did the sea king want with them? She looked at Rhoane and her heart skipped a beat at the look of alarm on his face. If he was nervous about seeing King Baldev, then this wasn't good.

CHAPTER THIRTY-NINE

The sea kingdom looked like he remembered, with some differences too subtle to make a difference. Rhoane held tight to Xianqin's strong whisker and kept alert to any danger. It had been over sixty seasons since his dream of visiting the kingdom, but he recalled the details with clarity. He also remembered Xianqin's warning to him that day—but that he'd like to forget.

Taryn peeked her head around Xianqin's snout. *What does he want with us?*

Probably to thank us for fixing the tear. At least, he hoped that's why Baldev had the darathi eneari bring them to his kingdom.

Oh. Right. That makes sense. She set her face forward and studied the passing fish and plants that grew at the bottom of the sea.

They swam through an arch of coral and past several open rooms empty of merfolk. He scanned the area, his apprehension mounting. Xianqin swished hard and banked left, nearly knocking him out of his hold. He redoubled his grip and opened his mouth to admonish the beast, but stopped before a syllable was uttered.

All around him, thousands of merfolk drifted and floated, their fins wafting lazily as they watched Xianqin's approach. Rhoane knew this room, recalled it from his dream. His gaze went to the front of the space where a large chair made of coral and whale bone took center stage. To the left of the chair, a huge clamshell sat open. Lounging within the shell was a stunningly beautiful mermaid.

"At last," a voice boomed, and Rhoane's gaze went to a merman floating in front of two people he never in his wildest imaginings thought he would see at the bottom of the ocean.

"Baehlon? Faelara?" Taryn unwrapped herself from Xianqin's whisker and swam to her friends. "What? How? Oh my stars, it's good to see you!" She hugged Fae first, and then Baehlon.

Rhoane joined them and embraced his long-time friends. He congratulated Baehlon with a sly smile.

Faelara and Baehlon shared a look of surprise. "How did you know?" Faelara asked, her hand fluttering over her belly. "We haven't told anyone yet."

"We sometimes see things," Taryn said ominously. "Your secret will not pass our lips. We are happy for you."

"Princess!" a voice called out, and a moment later a small projectile smashed into Taryn's midsection.

"Michel?" She hugged the merboy and stared at him. "What are you doing here? You have a tail!" She hugged him again and pressed her cheek to his head. "It's good to see you."

He babbled at her too quickly for Rhoane to make out, but she nodded as if she understood every word.

"Your mother?" Taryn gaped at Faelara. "And *your* mother? So, Michel is—"

"My brother. Yes." Fae wrapped her arms around the little scamp. "And this is my mother, Nemora." Fae indicated a woman with hair the color of flames, and Rhoane inhaled sharply.

"But she is the one who tried to take you in Menurra." He

desperately wanted to reach for Fae, to keep her from the hostile mermaid's reach.

"It was a misunderstanding. We've had a chance to talk and she's sorry for the way she behaved. I've forgiven her, Rhoane." Faelara's stern look said it would be best if he did, too.

"It's a pleasure to meet you," Taryn said and embraced Fae's mother. Then she gazed at Fae with something akin to awe. "So, you're half mermaid?"

"I am! Trust me, no one is more shocked than me. I do wish my father had told me, but I understand why he couldn't." Her gaze slid to a formidable figure who was gliding toward them. "It's against the rules." She held her mother's arm in hers and Rhoane saw the resemblance clearly.

How difficult it must have been for Brandt not only to raise a daughter on his own, but to know she might never see her mother. And then to repeat that with Taryn. It reinforced his understanding of why Nadra had chosen Brandt to take Taryn away and not Myrddin.

"Prince Rhoane! You have returned to us. And who have you brought with you?" King Baldev smiled, his appraising gaze taking in all of Taryn's lovely features.

"This is the Darennsai, Taryn ap Galendrin." Rhoane cocked his head. "So my memories of this place, of being here with you, they are not a dream? I was truly here?"

"Of course you were. Come, sit, I was just about to tell the legend of the Surtentse and Darennsai. You remember when I told you the tale, yes? Or have you forgotten?"

"I remember." It didn't seem real, being here now, but it was as he remembered. Even the cluster of mermaids to the side, the one with blue hair sighing over her love of the legendary tale.

Rhoane stayed close to Taryn as the king took his seat to begin the story. The gathered merfolk listened in rapt attention as Baldev spoke, their tails making slight swishing noises, the movement causing tiny whirlpools. Rhoane's attention pulled to a gorgeous mermaid who pretended boredom, but he could tell that she, too, listened to the king.

Her sapphire-hued eyes met his and a smile lit her face. She sat up and he blinked with embarrassment at her naked chest. Whereas the other mermaids wore shells or woven seaweed to cover their breasts, this maid proudly displayed her bare torso. Hair the color of palest lavender hovered above her shoulders like a reluctant lover, and he was tempted to remove the offending hairs lest they touch such a magnificent creature.

"I heard it was the Jansen Strait," Taryn said, and he pulled his attention from the mermaid to the king's story. "Not the Summer Seas."

"No, the legend clearly says the Surtentse and Darennsai meet in the Summer Seas. Where did you get this misinformation?" Baldev's yellowish hair snapped in the current, his stern features foreboding, yet Taryn was unaffected.

"At the Temple of Gyllaren. They have a copy of the legend, but it is Ullan in origin."

He crossed his chest like a petulant child. "Well, there you have it. The Ullans are always stealing our stories and making them their own."

"Good stories have a way of making their way into all cultures. Consider it an honor."

This seemed to mollify the king, and he settled into his great chair to take up the tale once more. Rhoane avoided looking at the seductive mermaid, instead admiring the architecture of the palace. It was unlike any he'd seen in all his seasons, but then again, all those structures were built on land.

An uneasy disquiet settled in his gut. Something was off here. The smiles were too forced, the current snapped with unspent energy just looking for an outlet. He looked to Xianqin, who lay curled like a dog with merfolk snuggled against her scales. Even she appeared content, but he couldn't shake the sense that something was not right. He recalled how Faelara's mother had sneered at him with sharpened teeth, and just as quickly appeared to have pearly straight teeth. Were they all demons in disguise?

It is the tear, Xianqin said in his mind. *It has affected us all like a poison, seeped into our scales and disfigured us. We are part of the malevolence now.*

Can we fix it?

Would you? Of your own free will?

Of course.

Xianqin lifted her head, upsetting several merfolk who dozed there. *Then we should try.*

The merfolk clapped and Rhoane realized the king had finished his tale. He swam from one side of his dais to the other, accepting the applause like an attention-starved child. He definitely didn't recall the king being so flamboyant. Or attention seeking. And there hadn't been a seductive siren at his side, either.

Rhoane kept his voice low and said, "Mi carae, Xianqin and I believe we are needed still."

"Are we in danger?" Faelara asked, her gaze loitering on the king.

"It is just a feeling, but I do not think so." To Baldev, he said, "Your Majesty. With your permission, Xianqin and I would like to perform a ceremony of gratitude for your wonderful retelling of the legend."

"A ceremony?" The mermaid in the clamshell sat up. "Does it involve dancing?"

"Hush, Salaria. My wife," he added, as if she were an afterthought.

"Your queen," Nemora sneered.

"Now, Darennsai." Rhoane held out his hand for Taryn to take and kicked upwards.

Why the alarm?

Something is not right and it is getting worse. Xianqin says the merfolk have been poisoned by the tear, and this far down, it will take quite a while before the waters are cleansed naturally. We are going to speed up the process.

Taryn gazed at the king, her eyes soft, as if she was looking at something particularly delightful. Baldev strutted across his dais, his flabby belly bouncing with each swish of his tail.

Xianqin joined them and they swam in a wide circle just as they had to make the whirlpool outside the scar. This time, they didn't take on their darathi forms. It made the work harder, but neither he nor Taryn felt it would be safe for them to shift.

Below them, the merfolk twittered and chattered, but Rhoane tuned them out. Faelara clung to Baehlon, who in turn held Michel in his big arms. Nemora crouched behind the knight, her eyes huge with caution.

They had to get this right not only for the sea folk, but every living creature in the oceans. Rykoto had been poisoning them for ages, unbeknownst to everyone who lived on the land. There had to be a way to get the kingdoms communicating with each other in the future so that there would be no more ugly surprises.

He swam harder, his kicks making little vortexes of their own behind him. Xianqin whipped past, her long tail trailing into the circling water. Taryn raised a hand and light blasted from the surface to the depths, its brilliance cleansing. He added his Eleri ShantiMari, touching all the flora and fauna with his healing. Xianqin's scales glowed as if she had Glamour and shards flew in every direction.

Shouts erupted from below—encouragement or commands to stop, he didn't care. They were close now to purifying the water; they had to continue.

His legs shook with the effort to keep swimming and his head was close to bursting. His vision clouded as if an inky substance had been dropped in his eyes, and he saw the poison Rykoto had spread. It incited madness and delusions in its victims. And beneath those, a fissure of hatred. Rhoane took in the poison as his own and lit it from the inside, burning every vestige from the seas and oceans of Aelinae. Not just where they were, but the rivers and streams, the lakes—everywhere Rykoto might've touched, he sent his ShantiMari.

Taryn's power joined his, and then Xianqin's, and their ShantiMari spun out like a star, creating a light that made daylight of the depths. Rays traveled in every direction, through the seas, over the land, to the skies. Together the three of them destroyed every last remnant of malice that had leaked from the tear.

The spinning stopped and their power dimmed. Xianqin lowered them to the seabed where the merfolk moaned and stretched as if waking from a difficult night's sleep.

Queen Salaria rose from her clamshell and swam to her husband. He blinked and looked at her with love and adoration. "My love. What happened?"

She stroked his face and kissed his lips. "My heart is clear and I feel alive once more."

"Yes, alive." Baldev turned his attention to Rhoane and Taryn. "How can we ever repay you?"

The poison must've been infecting them for many seasons for them to have lost sight of their true selves. Rhoane sagged with exhaustion, grateful they had been able to clear the waters and restore the merfolk.

He voiced his thoughts, hoping the king didn't dismiss them as ridiculous. "You can meet with the other kingdoms. Tell them of your travails, discuss with them ways to better Aelinae. The seas are as much part of this world as is the land."

"Yes," Taryn gripped his hand. "A council of united kingdoms, if you will. With summits once or twice a season, where the rulers of each kingdom will have a voice, so too will the delegates from each province." She turned to Faelara. "And if the rulers can't make it, they send ambassadors to speak on their behalf. Someone wise who understands the nuances of what Aelinae needs most."

It was a radical idea that would take some finessing, but

Rhoane saw clearly it was the only way Aelinae would maintain peace. Every kingdom represented, every ruler an equal say. Could it be done? As he watched Taryn animatedly explain her ideas, he believed it could.

They only had to convince the rest of Aelinae. As Taryn often said, no problem. Easy peasy.

If only.

CHAPTER FORTY

Taryn gave Faelara one last squeeze before turning to leave. They'd had three glorious days with her and Baehlon before reality reminded them they were on a ticking clock and there was still much to be done. Healing the tear in the Jansen Strait seemed to be the last element to Amdi's healing and the laird now strutted through his camps like the egotistical asshole he was. How Kaleigh put up with him, Taryn would never understand.

Love made people stupid sometimes. There was no other reason for it. It's what drove Khrystina to travel outside the Narthvier, the only home she'd ever known, and profess her feelings to an uncaring prince. It's what made her and Rhoane travel to the depths of the ocean to rid the waters of a mad god's taint. Stars, but she was glad that was over.

She glanced over her shoulder and waved to the little group standing outside Kaleigh's tents. Gwainne glowered behind them, unpleased with his mother's agreement of Taryn's decision to drop him in the desert. He'd arrived the night before spitting mad and swearing vengeance on her, her family, the entirety of Aelinae for what she'd done. Kaleigh would have none of it. She'd risen from her overstuffed pillow and calmly slapped her son across the cheek.

The entire tent had gone silent. Taryn giggled remembering the look of astonished disbelief that had crossed the Ullan prince's face. He'd stormed out and went straight to his father, who would hear nothing of his son's whining. It seemed their healing had garnered Taryn a fraction of good will with the laird. She and Rhoane thought it best to leave Gwainne's future in the hands of his parents and make a snappy getaway before things got even more tense.

Faelara and Baehlon would leave later that morning and travel by horseback to Talaith. Taryn and Rhoane had offered another way, but Faelara had turned green at the prospect of flying. Since Nikosana and Fayngaar were in Talaith's stables, and Amdi wasn't inclined to give his saviors new horses, they were left with few options.

"What shall it be, then, portal or flying?" Rhoane had led them to the outskirts of the camp and a little farther still to make certain they weren't followed.

"I could do with wind beneath my wings. It might clear the cobwebs lingering from our time underwater."

"There are no spiders in the sea kingdom."

His honest response made her laugh. "True, but my brain is muddled all the same. Too much thinking about your proposition of the kingdoms meeting. I think it's a great idea, but how are we going to convince not only my mother, but your father?"

"We will find a way. We always do." He stretched his neck and loosened his shoulders. "Ready?"

They shifted into dragons and flew west over a mountainous region of Ulla where she hoped no snipers lay in wait. Her fears were unfounded as they continued across the kingdom unscathed. Instead of banking north, they turned to the south and skimmed over a large bay that lay between swamplands and the desert. The Stones of Kaldaar were ahead and for one mad moment, she almost suggested they fly there to destroy the stones.

But she knew it wasn't yet time. Kaldaar would know they'd been there, and as yet, they'd managed to avoid the lunatic. She caught sight of several pockets of what looked like camps of makeshift tents stretched between trees.

Are you seeing this?

Rhoane's stunning green darathi nodded and they headed toward one of the larger camps. The swamp reminded her of Enghor's home world and her heart stuttered at the memory of those Zakael had slain. It'd been a brutal attack that had no meaning, no purpose other than to satisfy some ghastly craving of her half-brother's.

They landed a short distance from a copse of trees, alert to danger. After their experience in the Hben Firn, she no longer trusted jungles or forests unknown to her. These swamps were too close to the Stones of Kaldaar for comfort.

Movement came from their left, and a few minutes later from their right. They were being tracked, but thus far, not challenged. She kept her hand close to her sword, ready.

"Stop where you are," a voice called from directly in front of them.

Rhoane lifted his chin and glared at the trees. "By whose authority?"

A man, Aelan by the looks of him, stepped out from a large bush with leaves the size of a small child. "By King Zakael's authority."

King Zakael? Taryn snorted. It fit with his delusions of grandeur.

"Well, that is too bad because you are on soil that belongs to the Empress of Talaith. I have heard she does not take kindly to trespassers." Rhoane rested on his leg, hip cocked as if he were relaxed, but Taryn knew otherwise. "This camp, what is it for?" He peered between the trees. "If I am not mistaken, there are Mohram living here. Is this also by the king's authority?"

"Never you mind who or what lives in these swamps. They are controlled by Kaldaar himself and need no permission from you or the empress." The man spoke with authority, and despite herself, she was impressed with his control of the situation.

"Are these Mohram here by choice?" Taryn asked. "Because I know how Zakael procured them, and I gotta say, I don't think they really want to be here." She counted at least two dozen of the beasts hiding in the trees.

"*King* Zakael." The man crossed his arms over his chest. "I could have you executed for that slip."

"Yeah, see, he's not my king, never will be, and is a fool to think otherwise. You, however, strike me as a wise man who knows what's good for him. And right now, that's letting us into the camp to see for ourselves if the Mohram are being treated well." Taryn kept her tone light, her focus on the leader, all the while listening to the whispers coming from the trees.

"I said never mind what we have here. This is none of your business."

"Taryn, he will not see reason." Rhoane pulled Claidholm Solais from its scabbard and held it in front of him. A soft green glow came from the blade. That was new.

Instantly, several dozen soldiers emerged from the grasses and bushes, surrounding them.

"Drop your weapon."

"No."

The man waved a hand and the soldiers advanced. Taryn groaned and pulled her sword from its scabbard. Three relaxing days of no fighting, no having to save the world, nothing but food, wine, and good conversation. That's all they were afforded before they were thrust back into the mayhem.

Thundering footsteps sounded and a moment later, perhaps one hundred Mohram broke through the trees. One of them faced the man in charge. "We want to hear what they have to say." He pointed to Taryn. "She knows things."

Taryn fluffed her hair and snickered. "It's true. I do know things."

"Shut up." The man turned on the Mohram. "Get back in the trees before I slit your throat myself."

"Oh, now that's just rude." Taryn cocked her arm as if she were throwing a baseball and lobbed a fireball at the man. It hit him solidly on his temple and he flew sideways. A loud squish sounded as he hit the marshy ground.

"Here's how it's going to be," she directed her words to the soldiers crouched in anticipation of an attack. "Rhoane and I are going to very nicely ask all of you to back the fuck up, and then we're going to have a chat with the Mohram. Any Mohram who wishes to return to their home world, we'll provide safe passage. Those that wish to stay, well, good luck with that, but I can't protect you from Kaldaar's insanity."

She glared at the soldiers, and then into the trees to anyone who might be spying on them. The soldiers waffled for several minutes, talking amongst themselves about the correct procedure. She was certain this wasn't in any training manual they'd ever had to study. Nor was guarding ram-ape men.

The Mohram looked to their leader and he held up a hand, cautioning them to hold off on any sort of attack. At least, that's what she hoped it meant.

"What is your plan?" Rhoane asked.

"Exactly as I said. If there are any Mohram who want to go home, we open a portal and send them back. They didn't ask for this. You saw what Zakael did to their friends, their families. This isn't their war."

"You know what the pale man did?" A Mohram stepped between the soldiers, ignoring the sharp look his leader gave. "You have been to our jungles?"

She sheathed her sword. "We have. We are sorry for what

Zakael did." Her gaze slid to the soldiers. "Not all of us are like that."

The Mohram pounded his chest and roared, scaring the wits out of her, and was joined by many others. She held steady, but only just.

"I should like to go home."

"As would I."

"And me."

More and more Mohram came from the jungle, overwhelming the soldiers who prudently chose to back away. Hundreds and hundreds gathered in the clearing, and Taryn's heart broke with each new face that emerged from the trees. Zakael had taken whole villages, entire cities of the beasts. She only hoped he hadn't slaughtered their women and children. Seeing his carnage in one village had been enough to scar her forever.

Rhoane guarded her while she opened a portal wide enough for five Mohram to cross through.

"How do we know this is not a trick like the pale man?"

"One of you go through and come back," Rhoane suggested.

Their leader strode forward, clearing a path through the others. "I will go. If I do not return, kill them all." He stepped into the swirling blackness and disappeared. A collective gasp went through the Mohram. A minute later he reappeared with a huge smile on his ram-like face. His horns glowed amber. "It is our home. She tells the truth. Come, let us away!" He directed the others to the portal.

They rushed forward, trampling each other to get home. She held the portal, her arms shaking with the effort until every single Mohram who wished to leave had disappeared. When finally the leader stepped into the darkness, she closed the portal and rested her hands on her knees, her breathing ragged.

"What about those that stayed?" Rhoane scanned the trees where sounds of shuffling feet could be heard.

"They had a choice, and they chose to stay. We can't save them all."

His face softened and he took her hand in his. "I wish we could."

A small group of Mohram, perhaps thirty in all, approached. One who was at least half again as tall as Rhoane stepped forward. "We have no homes to return to. Our village was destroyed, our families killed. We will stay and fight for you." He pounded his fist on his chest and roared like the other Mohram had, but this time it didn't frighten her.

She looked to Rhoane, but he only shrugged. Her thumb made its way to her teeth and she gnawed on a cuticle. They could use the manpower, but where could these creatures live so that they and the citizens of the land would be safe? Zakael had chosen well to hide them in the marshes. It was similar to their home, and no one dared travel there for fear of sinking into its watery pits.

"Fight for us, and when the battle is ended, we'll find you a suitable home. As long as you don't kill anyone, we promise to keep you safe." Taryn said. The Mohram pounded their chests in assent. "Travel northwest to Talaith. I will meet you on the road south of the city in ten days. Do you know how to get there?"

They shuffled and shook their heads. "We only know these jungles."

Rhoane reached for the speaker's hand. "I will show you." He used his ShantiMari to draw a map of sorts on the beast's palm. "Go west to the coast and follow it north. Avoid the cities if you can. We will see you ten days from now." He lifted his chin and looked to the trees. "If there are any others who wish to join this group, the same deal applies. For those of you who stay, I will only say this: Kaldaar is not to be trusted, neither is Zakael. Whatever promises they have made, you will not live to see them honored. That goes for the soldiers and lieutenants as well."

"Please, what name shall we ask our gods to protect?" the one with the map asked.

"Trust me, your gods know who we are, and I'm not entirely sure they like us." She clapped him on the back and turned to go. "Ten days, my friend."

Once she and Rhoane reached Talaith, she'd have her mother send a squadron to meet Faelara and Baehlon to escort them safely to the city. They'd already been through too much with the Mohram; she couldn't risk those that stayed going on wild hunts and her friends getting caught in their snares.

She and Rhoane shifted into their dragons and lifted into the air. They'd found these camps, but were there others? How many lives had Zakael destroyed in the name of his god?

CHAPTER FORTY-ONE

A knock at the door sent her maids into a tizzy and Taryn went all warm and fuzzy inside. It reminded her of her early days at the palace when she'd newly been crowned and her maids made such a fuss of her gowns, her hair, her everything. They were more than maids now, more like personal guards trained in hand-to-hand combat, but who could destroy an enemy with a comb just as easily. Her bosomed swelled with pride in their accomplishments.

She rose from the chair she lounged in and went to see who had disturbed their quiet morning. Hayden made his way through the women, offering apologies and compliments along the way. The ladies did look especially lovely this morning. Taryn had insisted if they braided her hair, they must also braid each other's.

While she waited for Hayden to stop flattering her maids, she busied herself looking for the crystal she'd found in Mount Nadrene after Brandt died. Nadra's tear. Thus far, she'd searched through her garments, her bed chamber, the dressing room, and two sitting rooms, but had yet to find it, or Myrddin's looking glass. She remembered hiding them, she just couldn't place where.

"Cousin!" Hayden greeted her enthusiastically with a great hug. He'd been embracing her more and more of late, as did his father, Duke Anje. "Are you ready?"

"Are we going somewhere?" She couldn't recall anything being on her diary, and their daily meeting wasn't until later.

"To the Mohram. Rhoane insisted today is the day."

The Mohram? She mentally counted backward and Rhoane was right. She'd thought it was tomorrow, but today was indeed the day. They left her maids and met the others in the stables. Half the palace wished to join them, it seemed. Already seated in their saddles were Tessa, Eliahnna, Eoghan, Anje, Darius, Timor, Carina, Khrystina, Sabina, and Iselt. Nikosana stood idly waiting for her and a groom brought out two saddled ponies. Taryn gave Rhoane a curious glance. A moment later, her unspoken question was answered when Ebus and Gian came trotting out of a palace side door.

"Are we forgetting anyone?" She kept her tone light, but the idea was to welcome the Mohram, not terrify them on their first day here. Kaida padded to her side and nudged her hand. She buried her fingers in the soft fur and immediately her rampant heartbeats slowed.

"Lliandra is still against this plan of yours but gave the others permission to come along," Rhoane explained once they passed the palace gates.

She nodded, her attention on Khrystina and Carina. "What happens to an Eleri woman who falls in love with another woman outside the Narthvier?"

Rhoane watched the two for several minutes. It was obvious to everyone at the palace that an attraction had formed, one that went beyond friendship, but the two women were as yet pretending otherwise.

"She would be *sheanna* and exiled."

"Hmmm. And what if the Eleri goddess approved?"

"I suppose then it would be up to the woman to proceed however she wished. Verdaine lifted Kaleigh's *sheanna*, but she remains in Ulla with her hair short. If Kaleigh, or another Eleri woman should decide to return to the vier, I suppose a conversation with the king would be in order. His chuckle was low and deep and sexy as fuck. "Although, I get the feeling Khrystina does not wish to return to the vier. Ever."

Taryn nodded in agreement. "Eliahnna's already offered her a position here as a chancellor. I'm not sure what that means, but Khrystina was humbled by the offer."

"It is a very high position in the court." He reached for her hand and kissed her fingertips. "More matchmaking?"

"Nope. This one is purely organic." She was happy for her guard and the Eleri. If they asked permission to court, she would grant it without hesitation. "I mean, I had thought she and Loghan would be a good fit, but it appears Khrystina and Carina are even better. Just goes to show, sometimes even the *Darennsai* gets it wrong."

"And that is why you are the perfect person for the job. We are here." Rhoane pulled her attention from the women to a block of warehouses south of Talaith's city walls. "Keep an eye on Eoghan. He claims he welcomes the Mohram, but he witnessed the attack and I worry for my brother."

She understood Eoghan's concerns. None of them were comfortable having the Mohram stay inside the city, at least not until they proved they weren't murdering beasts. The warehouses were empty when they arrived, so they took the remaining time they had as an opportunity for an impromptu meeting.

Since returning from Ulla, Taryn and Rhoane had met with Lliandra and the highest-ranking officers in her army. Plans were made and adjusted, with backup plans made just in case it all went to shit. They were ready for an invasion, but Taryn insisted in the end they would have to take the battle to Kaldaar.

According to Ebus and Gian's reports, the god didn't travel far from Caer Idris, and only then to feed off the souls of those who refused to leave the city.

The reports told of empty city streets and overflowing graveyards. Caer Idris wasn't a pleasant place on the sunniest of days, so she could only imagine the horror it had become since Kaldaar arrived.

As they discussed the scheme to convince the empress to move forward with sending the army west, they also sketched out the "council of united kingdoms" idea Rhoane had suggested while they were in the sea kingdom. Eliahnna had of course been quite keen to investigate this avenue, as was Hayden. Taryn was confident they would convince the other kingdoms and provinces to join.

In private, she'd met several times with Hayden to discuss ways she thought ShantiMari could improve the lives of those on Aelinae. Without getting too specific, she'd talked about wind power and energy and universities. He'd loved every idea she presented and even had a few of his own that surprised her, such as steam-powered ships for faster ocean travel.

She and Rhoane had discussed at length whether they should tell the future rulers about the portals and decided it best to keep that secret. Aelinae was still under Nadra and Ohlin's protection. If they wished anyone else to know about the portals, it was up to them to share that information.

The sound of several dozen feet stomping the ground ended their meeting, and Hayden quickly rolled up the scrolls they'd been studying. He slid them into his tunic just as the Mohram entered the warehouse. It had been set up with sectioned-off rooms for sleeping and relaxing, and contained a kitchen area and separate bathing facilities. This warehouse was one of five they'd revamped for the Mohram's use.

The Mohram Rhoane had made a map for saluted him with a chest thump. "Well met this day."

The saying sent a spiral of dread down her back. The saying sounded too much like Myrddin for her comfort.

Rhoane introduced everyone to the Mohram, and they shared their many names. Each one had at least five, it seemed. Taryn stood back while they discussed the particulars, noting how each would put their thick hands together and touch their lips. It was reminiscent of the Eleri touching a thumb to their forehead, then their lips, and finally their heart. Different races, different species, even, all worlds away—yet some things the same.

The exchange was polite and respectful. None of her group showed outward anxiety, but she sensed it from not just Eoghan, but Eliahnna as well. Yet they kept their questions focused, never making accusations or laying blame for the attack at Lake Oster. From what Taryn could discern, they didn't even know there had been a squad of Mohram sent to harm her friends.

Once satisfied the Mohram were comfortable in their living quarters, Rhoane touched the leader's temple and she saw threads of ShantiMari pass between them.

"If you have need, call me." Rhoane gripped his forearm. "Darius and Iselt will stay here to make sure you are safe. Friends of ours were gravely injured by your kin, and people are not as quick to forgive these days."

"We will endeavor to change their opinions of Mohram. We welcome your kin to our home." The leader pressed his palms together and kissed his fingertips.

On the way out, Taryn touched Iselt's and Darius's sleeves to let her know she appreciated what they were doing. It took a great amount of trust for them to stay with the Mohram. They'd seen Tinsley when he was first brought to Talaith; they understood the risk. She just hoped she wasn't making a colossal mistake.

The ride back was full of chatter about the Mohram, but no one called them by that name. They said "guests" or "new friends" to keep their identity a secret. Eoghan especially was fascinated by the ram-ape men and had asked for a sample of their poison for Faelara to study. Not only had they agreed, they promised to have it ready in two days.

Taryn looked back toward the direction they'd just come and a pit formed in her belly. This group was excited, but what would Faelara and Baehlon think? Or Tinsley and Aomori? No one had had the nerve to tell the two men about the secret guests staying in the warehouses.

Carina and Khrystina approached and Taryn held in a bubble of excited expectation.

"Your Highness," Carina started, but Taryn interrupted her.

"Yes! Yes, ohmygod, yes."

Carina's face scrunched into confusion and she looked to Khrystina for an answer, but the Eleri only shook her head. "We thought you should know, Lady Faelara and Sir Baehlon are returned.

"What?" That was not what she'd thought Carina would say. She'd assumed—wrongly—that her guard was going to ask permission to court the novice. Her face flushed with embarrassment, but there was no time for shame. "Are they well? Were there any issues?"

"We do not know details, but they are waiting for you," Khrystina answered for the guard.

"Rhoane, did you hear? Fae and Baehlon arrived while we were gone."

His expression said it all. The relief they felt knowing their friends were home, and hopefully safe, spread from them to the group. "Then let us not delay." He reached for her hand and she gripped it with a huge grin on her face.

The last of her concerns were settled. Well, not entirely, but for the moment, she would bask in the happiness she felt.

A guard rushed up to them, one Taryn recognized as Lliandra's personal attendant. He bowed to her, to Rhoane, to Carina and Khrystina and everyone he passed. A buzzing started in her ears and she dared not breathe for fear she might scream. She knew his next words, could read them clearly on his flustered features.

"Your Highnesses, the empress has commanded the armies to ready themselves. At first light tomorrow, we march for Caer Idris." With those few words, her happiness was ripped asunder. It was what they'd planned for, had discussed ad nauseum, but through it all, she'd held hope that somehow, they could avoid it.

The war for Aelinae had begun.

CHAPTER FORTY-TWO

The Sitari Islands sat at the southernmost tip of the Summer Seas, apart from the Summerlands yet close enough there was never a shortage of men to lure ashore. Zakael flew over the islands twice, his amazement growing with each pass at the two smaller islands that seemed to float above the larger island. Waterfalls flowed from one to the next, and a larger fall splashed into a lake far below.

How was this even possible? His levon brain hurt trying to think of how islands could dangle in mid-air. His gaze shifted to the lush green of the jungles that covered the main island. That, he could comprehend. Trees, vines, shrubs, sandy beaches—those made sense not just to his levon, but to him.

He spiraled twice more, concern for his mission growing with each beat of his wings. Kill all the Sitari. Kaldaar knew they were fierce warrior women, their scarred faces said to be self-inflicted. Their blue skin was a curse given by Mallaqai. The Sitari lived alone on the island, all women. Any males born to them were either killed, eaten, or sent to live on the mainland.

His feathers ruffled with his anxiety. Slit all their throats? Kaldaar was truly beyond reason.

He'd delayed enough. With a final beat of his wings, he glided down to the beach and turned into a man the moment his talons touched sand. His boots crunched as he made his way to the jungle proper, his eyes scanning the trees, his ears primed for any sound.

Yet the jungle was quiet. Only bird calls and animal cries came to him. More than strange was that there weren't a dozen pikes at his throat. Sweat ran in rivulets down his temples and he regretted the clothing he wore, but he dare not strip here and give the Sitari bare flesh as a target. At least the sturdy wool he wore provided some protection against their weapons.

It was impossible to tell how long he walked, or even if he walked in a straight line. Trees with broad leaves and vines dangling from one branch to the next blocked most of the sunlight. Instead of providing cool shade, they made the interior of the jungle a steamy mess. This was ludicrous. He should leave at once and tell Kaldaar to fuck off.

"Are you lost, my lord?"

He spun around to see a lovely woman with scars slashed into her pale cheeks. Flesh-toned, not blue. "Who are you?"

There was an etherealness about her that intrigued him. She appeared alive, yet he didn't sense a presence. She was truly a conundrum.

"I am Mallaqai."

Nothing else. No explanation followed to give him a clue how a witch believed dead stood before him.

"You are Mallaqai's spirit."

"Potayto potahto. Either are delicious."

"Why are you here?" He didn't have time to bicker over potatoes. Besides, she was right.

"Why are *you* here?"

"Not to play games, that's for damn sure. Tell me where I can find the Sitari." His mind was fuzzy with the heat and he stripped off his coat, followed by his vest, and unbuttoned his shirt.

"What do you want with them?"

"Look, woman, I'm not here to be trifled with. I've been sent by Kaldaar to slit their throats. Since you once served his brother, I think you know how important it is that I complete my task."

Mallaqai's face crumpled for only a mere moment before she blinked at him, her eyes wide and pure with innocence. "I thought when I cursed them Rykoto and his wretched brother would leave them alone. Why do you think I marked their faces and turned their skin blue? I believed if I made them hideous, they would be safe." She covered her face with her hands and he heard soft sobbing coming from the witch. "I was trying to save them, but all I did was make it worse. And now your pathetic god wishes to use them to restore himself? I'll not have it. You'll have to go through me to get them."

Zakael digested her words, the pieces falling into place at last. "And the dragons? Were you saving those as well?"

She nodded miserably. "I exiled them where the gods would never find them."

"Have they been found?" This information might help if he failed to kill the Sitari. Kaldaar was desperate to control the dragons, but other than Taryn and Rhoane, they'd not been seen for ages.

A dozen women stepped from the trees, deadly spears held at chest height. To a one, their blue-hued faces were scarred and marked with tattoos. What little clothing they wore showed it wasn't just their faces that bore the heavenly blue shade.

"The Sitari, I presume?" He ogled them out of habit, but they didn't frighten him. In fact, they intrigued him, and his cock twitched in anticipation. What else was blue?

Dammit man, focus. There were a dozen pikes ready to run him through and he was thinking about fucking. Bad habits were hard to break. But perhaps a few days with them would eradicate the memory of Carga and her sweet kisses.

"And you are the Lord of the Dark, if I am not mistaken." A

woman with white spiked hair and a fierce glare held her spear high, near her face.

"Guilty." He placed a hand over his heart and inclined his head. "I was sent here by Kaldaar to kill you all."

A sharp intake of breath came from several of the warriors. His gaze took them in one by one. Some didn't look as committed to wishing him dead as their leader.

"But you have reservations?" The leader lowered her spear and leaned on it as if it were a walking stick. "Why? Why not slaughter us all and finally be rid of our scourge?"

Why not, indeed? He could do it. Just a thrashing of his Shanti and every woman there would be dead—but that was too quick for Kaldaar. He said he wished for Zakael to bathe in their blood, which suggested something more intimate. Maybe it was a test for him. Kaldaar was testing him to see if he had the balls to commit such an atrocity. One more test out of the many he'd failed.

Mallaqai watched him with a curious expression that he couldn't decipher. He had the sense she was waiting for him to discover something, but what more was there left to uncover? He'd been stripped bare emotionally, mentally, and physically in the last few moonturns. There was nothing more to learn.

"Are you sure about that, Your Majesty?" she giggled, and it was the same caggle that he'd heard at Caer Idris.

"It was *you* spying on us at the castle." He pointed a finger at her as if to punctuate his irritation. "Why didn't you reveal yourself?"

"Why haven't you?"

The heat became unbearable and he removed his shirt so that he might feel a cool breeze, but there was only thick air where he stood. The warriors appraised him appreciatively, a few openly showing their lustful desire, but he was too damn hot to care. It took all his will not to tear his trousers from his legs and race to the water.

"Is there somewhere not as stultifying where we can talk?" He swallowed against a dry mouth. "And perhaps have a drink?"

"Go to the floating islands and swim in the pools there. You'll find they are cooling and full of surprises." Mallaqai pointed above them. "Start on the lowest island. When you've found what you need, come back to us and we will discuss your terms."

His terms? They would surrender to him? The warriors stepped back into the jungle, disappearing between the leaves. Mallaqai watched him with the same expression as before. It was that curiosity that made him transform into a levon and take to the air. It was indeed cooler this high up, but still overbearing. He landed on the first island and shuffled out of his trousers, leaving him naked.

He plunged into the small pool, the refreshing cool washing over him and clearing his mind. He dove and swam for some time before exploring the rest of the tiny island. There was nothing to see except a few palm trees, a boulder or two, grass, and the pool. Whatever Mallaqai wanted him to find must be in the water. He returned to the pool and this time dove deeper where he discovered a cave. Taking a deep breath, he kicked hard and swam into it. On and on it went until he was certain he'd lose the air in his lungs.

Finally, he saw light ahead and swam harder, kicking with all his strength. He surfaced in a cavern lit by small windows. He pulled his naked body out of the pool and stood dripping as he surveyed the area. His gaze traveled over a desk with papers scattered beneath what looked like black sand, and then to a cot shoved into a corner.

His balls shrunk as he stared into the unseeing eyes of his one-time lover Kane-turned-Cashiel. Bile splashed the back of his throat, and he choked it down with a stern reminder that he was Zakael, King of the West. He was not a schoolboy discovering his first dead body. He was a seasoned killer.

So why then, did seeing the decapitated body of Kaldaar's latest Shadow Assassin turn his blood to ice?

Because he knew this could have been him.

Gathering his wits, he inspected the wound that had severed the head from the body. No weapon had done this, but someone strong in ShantiMari. His gaze went to the desk and he stood to inspect the papers there. They were written in a flowing hand, in a language he didn't recognize, though the script was familiar. He cast his memory back to the papers in his father's study. Yes, some of the writing could have been by the same person. But who?

Myrddin. He looked with renewed interest at Kane's body. Myrddin had been tasked with killing Taryn but had instead disappeared. Kaldaar had assumed he'd gone to another world, but what if he'd been hiding here the whole time? That meant Kaldaar hadn't been able to see him in this cavern. Zakael's heart beat wildly. He could stay here in safety. But for how long? He'd lose his mind in this prison.

His fingers rested on a page that had illustrations of circles and more circles, but they meant nothing to him. Whatever Myrddin was charting, it was of no use now. If he wasn't here, and had left Kane dead, then most likely he had left Aelinae for good. Which is what Zakael should have done ages ago. It's what he should do now.

But he couldn't leave. Not yet. Not until he knew Kaldaar had been defeated for good. Aelinae was his home and he wouldn't leave it to the deranged god to destroy. He left the cavern and returned to the little island where he tugged on his trousers over damp skin. As uncomfortable as it was, he couldn't return to the Sitari naked. Although, he could fashion himself some of the loose trousers the Summerlanders wore. For half a beat he considered it, but decided he'd look a fool. Desperate, destroyed, and downtrodden as he was, he'd not allow himself to ever dress ridiculously.

As he flew above the trees, he heard Mallaqai and one of the women having a heated discussion. Rather than interrupting them, he hovered and eavesdropped.

"We should kill him before he has a chance to destroy us all."

"Shandris, think about what I said. He can help us. Help you. I feel the disquiet in him. He is not the same man he was a season ago."

He peered through the foliage to see Shandris, the spiky-haired leader, pacing a tight line. "Did you truly wish to save us with your curse?"

Mallaqai dropped her head. "I did. I was desperate. I knew Kaldaar would come for you. A village of beautiful virgins, how could he not wish to claim you as his vessels? I saw firsthand the crones he made of other women just like you. So I marked your skin and sent you here. My plan was to release you from the curse once the other gods destroyed Kaldaar and Rykoto, but I was killed before that happened."

"Do you think once they are destroyed the curse will be broken?" another warrior, this one tall with a willowy frame asked.

"I don't know, Beilis, but I hope so."

Shandris looked up to where Zakael hovered. "You can come down now. We will not harm you."

Surprised they knew he was there, he fluttered to the ground and landed as a man. "You have excellent eyesight."

"And hearing. Even as a levon, you breathe heavy," the one called Beilis snorted.

"What now?" Shandris asked Mallaqai. "Does he kill us? Do we kill him?"

"No killing." The witch looked to him with a twinkle in her eyes. "He doesn't wish it; in fact he would not mind staying on a few days to see if the rumors of your skills are true."

Zakael cleared his throat and grinned. "There are some interesting stories told about the Sitari. I would be remiss if I didn't do due diligence to disprove them."

Beilis ran a finger down his bare chest and grabbed his crotch. He stifled a surprised grunt and watched her intently.

"I should like him first. I, too, have heard stories and I would like to see if they are true. It is rumored you like pain."

A delirious tremor ran the length of him. His eyes flashed to Mallaqai. "We still have the issue of Kaldaar wanting their blood."

"Satisfy the women, do not kill them, and I promise you on the day the battle begins, the Sitari will be there." Mallaqai spread a ghostly hand on his chest and sighed. "Where were you when I was living?"

He ignored the compliment. "You would have them fight for Kaldaar? But he will destroy them and feed off their souls."

Mallaqai caggled again, her face lighting up with mischief. "I never said who they would fight for." Her gaze went to Shandris. "It is your choice whose side you'll support."

Shandris straightened her shoulders and slammed her fist against her chest. "The Sitari will fight for Taryn."

A cheer went up through the women and traveled far up into the trees where hundreds more of the blue-skinned women must've been hiding. He would've cared more if Beilis wasn't removing his trousers.

He'd find a way to let his sister know of the turn of events, and where to hide the Sitari, but that would happen later. Much later. Thoughts of war were the farthest thing from his mind as a hot mouth covered his already hard cock.

CHAPTER FORTY-THREE

Sunrise was but moments away, its rays peeking over the horizon to announce the coming of the light. Talaith's army was ready, with soldiers shifting in their armor and horses nickering their impatience. Rhoane surveyed the area, a frown pulling his brows low.

No one there had seen battle in their lifetime, not even him. They might be trained soldiers, but a sustained war was something completely different from what they'd been taught. At least he and Taryn had gotten a taste of what was to come when they'd fought the vorlocks, but even then, the skirmish had lasted but a bell. There was no telling how long this fight would last.

Lliandra's voice came to him from where she readied herself in her tent. She had insisted on traveling with her army, sometimes riding in her carriage, sometimes on horseback. With over ten thousand soldiers in all, it had taken them two weeks to travel from Talaith to the plains north of Gaarendahl. Rhoane's gaze drifted to the north where his father's armies should have arrived by now. He was to meet Stanton and Paderau's army at the Dierlin Pass. Neither army had come through the mountains and he despaired something terrible had prevented their crossing to the east.

Kaldaar knew they were coming—Taryn had seen to that—but would the god show up? Would he take the bait and arrive at the plains as they'd hoped? Rhoane stood sentry for another bell, scanning the landscape for signs their efforts hadn't been in vain.

When the sun was a small wedge above the horizon, he heard the unmistakable sound of a mass of footsteps trodding upon the hard soil. He motioned to a soldier who stood guard outside Lliandra's tents. He disappeared, and a moment later, bells rang out in the camp alerting everyone to Kaldaar's approach.

Taryn rode up to him, looking resplendent in her silver-edged leather armor. She'd refused to wear steel plates, insisting she was more powerful without the added bulk. Nikosana nickered and pawed the ground, impatient for action.

"Have you seen them?" she asked, a bit breathless, as if she'd rushed through her preparations.

"Not yet, but I hear them." He closed his eyes and concentrated on the footsteps. "A few hundred Mohram, at most. But there are others whose steps I cannot make out. Some shuffle, while others stomp, but all seem lighter than the Mohram."

"More aliens? I was hoping it would just be Aelans but looks like I don't get my wish." She scanned the landscape as he'd done, her lips tight. "Zakael is with them."

"We always knew it was a possibility." He too had hoped Zakael would forsake the god.

Taryn glanced toward the Sitari tents. "After what Shandris said, I really thought he'd turned from Kaldaar, but I guess when you're the son of Valterys, some loyalties are harder to break."

A horn sounded from the north and Lliandra's army moved forward to set up a line on the plain. The Sitari came next, followed by several hundred Ullan soldiers. Amdi Agnar rode with them, with his son Gwainne at his side. In truth, Rhoane had been surprised when they showed up at Talaith's gates, but happy for whatever assistance they could give. The few Mohram who had chosen to stay and pledged their loyalties to him and Taryn brought up the rear of their forces.

The Summerlanders were still enroute. King Faisal had sent a message that he wished to be with them, but storms in the Summer Seas had slowed their travel. As for the dwarves of Haversham? They'd never accepted Taryn as Darennsai and chose to stay neutral in the war. They had, however, left mass crates of weapons at the Ruins of Mallaqai that Taryn just happened to "find" on a random whim to scout the area.

Miracle or not, those weapons would come in handy.

Faelara, Loghan, and Kaleigh had set up several healer's tents and stayed behind to see to those who got injured. Rhoane prayed to all the gods—elder, younger, and those not yet made—that the deaths be few, the injuries not catastrophic.

A cloud of dust preceded the arrival of Kaldaar and his army. Rhoane peered at the soldiers, surprised at how few Aelans there were. They'd heard the rumors of how Kaldaar had decimated the city of Caer Idris, but he'd underestimated just how thorough the god had been. He could see no Geigan or Danuri forces. They courted Kaldaar's wrath by sitting out the battle, a risky decision on their parts, but one Rhoane couldn't fault. If Kaldaar succeeded today, he'd march on their cities and destroy them as viciously as he had the northern cities.

"What the hell are those?" Taryn pointed to a large group of lizard-like people who shuffled to Kaldaar's left.

"I have no idea. If they are as brutal as the Mohram, we have an even tougher fight on our hands."

Next to them, shortish men with long pointed ears and furry feet stomped toward the field; behind them, vorlocks and the Helben men who controlled them brought up the rear. The Helben rode their sturdy ponies and brandished weapons coated in poison.

"Are those vorlocks?" Taryn groaned. "Great. More poisonous

assholes coming to the party. I suppose we should get down there and greet our guests."

He pulled himself into Fayngaar's saddle and nudged his horse forward.

"Rhoane, look." Taryn pointed toward Kaldaar, who grew substantially until he was the height of one hundred men.

"Bring me the Eirielle!" Kaldaar boomed across the plains. "Bring me the one prophesied to balance this miserable world."

"Do you suppose he means me?" Taryn laughed, but Rhoane heard the nerves in her voice. "I'm here, you miserable maggot," she called out in a voice loud enough to be heard in Talaith.

They made their way down the small slope and rode out to the middle of the plain. As soon as Kaldaar saw them, he blasted a ray of power directly at the pair of them without warning. So much for rules of engagement. Rhoane blanketed them in a shield of ShantiMari and Taryn did the same. Even with both of their powers combined, he felt the sting of Kaldaar's rage—and an insight into his motivations.

The deranged god wasn't there to win the battle—he was looking to destroy all Aelinae. The land, the seas, and especially those who called the planet home. Rhoane turned to share his discovery with Taryn, but she kicked Niko hard and galloped toward Kaldaar. A moment later, she lifted herself into the saddle and leapt, shifting into her darathi mid-air.

Kaldaar shrieked and cursed her, his power arcing to hit his target. She swooped and dove, avoiding his assault while throwing large fireballs of her own.

As if that were a silent signal, Kaldaar's armies rushed forward and Rhoane found himself alone on the battlefield facing an onslaught of hundreds of alien beasts. He raced into the melee, passing Niko, who had wisely chosen to return to camp.

In a heartbeat, he was flanked on all sides by Ullans and Talaithians, their weapons drawn. He broadcast his thoughts to the soldiers and captains, informing them that the Mohram and vorlocks used poison in their attacks. Whatever good the warning might do, he hoped to help spare his forces of the agony of what Tinsley had suffered. To his right, he saw his nephew ride past, his face set in grim determination. He'd been nearly dead only three weeks past but was hearty and hale now. It was truly a miracle. One he had an ex-member of the Brotherhood to thank for.

Rhoane nodded to the man and veered right to cover his flank. The sound of metal meeting metal rang out, the battle well and truly underway. Streaks of ShantiMari whizzed past his head and cries from the alien creatures scratched his hearing, but all he could do was focus on one fight at a time. Some called out that the lizard-like people with their snub noses and smooth skin had prehensile tongues and to be cautious of them. Another person warned of the goblin-like aliens' speed.

Rhoane's vision and hearing heightened as he cut down his first victim and sped to the next. He tuned out any unnecessary distractions and became one with his horse and sword. All that mattered was reducing Kaldaar's army so that they couldn't attack his friends.

How long he slashed and bashed, he couldn't say. All around him cries and whimpers could be heard between grunts and attacks. He looked for Taryn and saw her in her womanly form now, braids flying wildly, her face smeared with blood and mud. She battled a Mohram with Tessa and Hayden by her side. Kaida raced in to rip the Mohram's tendons from the backs of its legs.

Then he saw Tinsley again, this time running on foot toward Zakael, his sword held high for an attack. Time slowed, but not by his doing. All around him the battle raged, but for Tinsley, Zakael, and himself, they were caught in a time slip.

Suddenly Carga was there, rushing to prevent Zakael from bringing his blade down on Tinsley's neck.

"Zakael, stop!" she called out, her eyes huge with fright.

Zakael blinked as if seeing a ghost and halted his sword.

Tinsley slid to a stop, his sword missing Zakael's head by a breath.

From the corner of his vision, Rhoane saw Taryn on the edge of the folded time, her attention fixed elsewhere and yet he knew she saw what happened. Felt her presence in the small bubble.

"What are you doing here?" Zakael grabbed Carga to him and kissed her forehead before holding her at arm's length. "You promised to stay away."

"And you promised not to harm…*him*." Her quick glance at Tinsley told Rhoane everything he needed to know.

"This is him?" Zakael asked, his eyes growing misty.

"What the devil is going on here?" Tinsley demanded. "Why are we in some kind of tunnel?" He poked at the air.

Carga brushed his forehead and kissed his cheek. "You will forget this, but know that you were always loved by your mother. Always." Then she pushed him out of the time slip and turned to Zakael. "He can never know. You promised."

"And I will uphold that promise, but if Kaldaar finds out, he is as good as dead."

"If we do not end this, we are all dead."

They both turned to look at Rhoane.

"Brother, Kaldaar cannot be stopped by mortal weapons. You know what you need to do."

"No." Rhoane shook his head, not ready to believe what she implied.

"How can Glennwoods end this?" Zakael demanded.

"He and Taryn are the balance bringers. Their deaths are the only thing that can stop Kaldaar now. He's grown too powerful."

Zakael looked at Rhoane as if he'd grown six heads. "You? But Taryn is the Eirielle."

"That is only one part of the prophecies." Carga stroked Zakael's face. "There is yet time to make amends." She rose on tiptoe and kissed him full on the lips. "I never stopped loving you, *mi carae.*"

And then time resumed its normal pace and she was gone. Rhoane looked around wildly, but Carga was nowhere to be seen. Nor did he see his father's army. Tinsley wobbled a few steps, holding his head. Rhoane called out for him to seek the healer's tents and he nodded.

Zakael turned on Rhoane. "You? But you murdered my mother."

"And you ruined my sister." Rhoane shook his head to stop the old arguments and aggressions. "I am sorry for what I had to do, Zakael. It was for Aelinae, but that does not absolve me of the crime. I hope one day you can forgive me. Without her death, Aelinae would not have had Taryn and Kaldaar would have gone unchecked."

Zakael spun to gaze up at the god who was consuming Aelans as if they were candy. "Can you truly stop him?"

Rhoane nodded sadly. He could explain how, but what did it matter? If they didn't stop Kaldaar soon, all would be lost.

"Did you love her? Did you love Carga?" It was a futile question, but Rhoane had to know.

It was Zakael's turn for circumspection. "She was the only woman I ever loved besides my mother." He flicked a glance toward Taryn. "And perhaps my sister."

Without another word, Zakael sped toward the Kaldaar. Taryn's cry drew Rhoane's attention and he followed her horrified stare to see Lliandra—hair glowing, her armor gleaming in the sunlight—throw a thunderbolt at Kaldaar. It would've decimated an entire squadron, but it barely affected the god. He snatched her from the air and held her in front of his face while laughing a hideous laugh that made Rhoane's insides recoil.

"You are no match for me, Empress of Nothing. None of you are! I am Kaldaar. I am a god, and you are nothing."

He drew in a breath and Rhoane watched in horror as Lliandra's life force was sucked out of her. The power she held as Lady of Light flowed in waves of blue to the god and he moaned in ecstasy. Taryn flew to him, her darathi pulling at his glorious golden locks, her talons scratching his head, but he ignored her.

A dark light cast a shadow over the battlefield and suddenly Myrddin was there, shouting for the god to release his love. Kaldaar laughed in Myrddin's face and dropped the dead empress. Rhoane shifted into his darathi and caught her before she hit the ground. He flew with her to the tents and set her down gently before flying off to assist Taryn with the deranged god.

By the time he returned, Kaldaar had sucked out Myrddin's power and held the mage's corpse between two fingers. The god moaned and smacked his lips as if enjoying a delicious meal.

"Who is next?" he called to the surrounding area.

"Kaldaar!" Zakael roared, and ran toward him, sword raised.

Kaldaar flung Myrddin to the side and Taryn rushed after him the same as Rhoane had done for Lliandra. Zakael screamed and Rhoane saw a Mohram slam his head into the Lord of the Dark, not caring who he was or what his title might be. Without a moment's hesitation, Kaldaar hissed and kicked the Mohram into the air away from Zakael.

Shocked by the god's behavior, Rhoane drifted to the ground and transformed back into a man. When he was two steps from Zakael, Kaldaar bent low and swiped a finger across Zakael's face so viciously it left a gaping wound.

"I should kill you, my beautiful boy, but I cannot. The Mohram poison will do what my heart won't allow. Leave my sight before I change my mind." Kaldaar rose and lifted his fists to the sky. "Bring me more!"

Zakael turned toward Rhoane, and Rhoane gasped at the flap of skin that hung from where Zakael's cheek used to be. "Do not trust his mercy. He will give no quarter. He will leave no survivors. It has always been his goal to destroy Aelinae to punish the elder gods. You must stop him." He limped away and Rhoane let him go.

Kaldaar grabbed a passing Mohram and ripped his head off before shoving the beast into his mouth. Not even those who fought for him were safe from the god's terror. Rhoane searched for Taryn and spotted her on a small rise overlooking the battlefield. When their eyes met, he knew he could deny his destiny no longer.

It was time.

CHAPTER FORTY-FOUR

All was not lost, and yet, as Taryn looked around the battlefield, she couldn't help but despair. Kaldaar grew in strength with each fallen soldier. It wasn't enough he'd siphoned Myrddin and Lliandra's power to restore him to full godhood. For him, it would never be enough. She saw that now, as clearly as she saw the path she and Rhoane needed to take to defeat him. The time was now, before the god slaughtered every last person just to soothe his ego.

Hell, he'd murdered half his battalion just to feed off their souls. He cared nothing for the people of Aelinae, or the creatures he'd had Zakael kidnap from other realms. She wished those who had stayed had listened to her and Rhoane. Instead, they'd believed Kaldaar's lies and now lay dying on a world that wasn't theirs.

"Sister," Zakael rasped. A sword hung from his bleeding hand and a gaping wound marred his handsome face. He was dying, that much was obvious from the greyish tint to his skin, the slack jaw and empty eyes. It would be nothing to heal him, to restore his features to what they were before all of this, but she hesitated.

"I am done for."

She watched him, confused by his slow movements, by the way he held the sword as if it were more for support than a weapon. Only moments earlier he'd been fighting vigorously against Kaldaar, yet the wound on his face was not caused by a weapon. She stared at it and saw tiny flickers of ShantiMari at the edges. The deranged god had disfigured Zakael out of spite.

That kind of wound was personal. Kaldaar had known Zakael would die, and instead of ending him with mercy, he'd damaged him out of vanity. As if he were a lover scorned. Odd to think Kaldaar could love anyone but himself, but as she saw Zakael struggling to keep his head steady, she realized it was not only possible, but a reality. Kaldaar loved Zakael. Enough so he couldn't kill him even though Zakael held as much power as Lliandra. Or had he stolen Zakael's power without killing him in the process? Her gut told her no, and she desperately hoped she was right.

"I can heal you." She reached for Zakael, but he shook his head.

"Kaldaar has seen to it I cannot be healed. Not by you, not by anyone. I only wish I'd had more time."

"Time for what?"

Sounds of fighting came to her and she knew she should be down there with the others, but she stayed with Zakael.

"To tell you how wrong I was." He slumped to his knees. "You were right about everything. Me, Marissa, our father, your mother, Kaldaar, every damn thing I fought so hard to believe in, you saw the truth of. Maybe that's because you were raised far from us, away from our influence, I don't know. Can you ever forgive me?"

She knelt in front of him and brushed bloodied hair from his forehead. "That you are asking tells me all I need to know. You are not the same angry man I first saw in the cavern. You've grown, Zakael, and become wiser."

"For all the good it did me." He chuckled and opened his

coat where his blood-soaked tunic clung to his skin. "One of the creatures I brought from another world got me. Poison, if I'm not mistaken." He pointed to his head. "They coat their horns in it."

She knew all too well the dirty tricks the Mohram used. She'd spent too many bells ridding Tinsley of the deadly stuff. "Kaldaar's wrong, you know." She placed her right hand on his bloody tunic above his heart and her left against his forehead. The runes shimmered and shifted just as she'd hoped they would.

"What do you mean?" His eyes fluttered with his coming death.

"I can heal you."

"It will kill you."

"Nothing can kill me now." Except Rhoane.

He tilted his head back to look at her, his steel grey eyes full of something she'd never expected to see in them—hope.

"Now shush and let me do my thing."

"Heh. Your thing." But his bravado was all but extinguished.

She closed her eyes and channeled as much love and care and healing into him as she dared. Too much might expedite his one-way trip to Dal Ferran. Too little and he'd be left little more than a fleshy husk.

Her power infused his blood, cleansing the Mohram's poison, and eradicating Kaldaar's taint. From far away, she heard the god scream into the wind, cursing her seven ways left of midnight. Zakael chuckled again and suddenly his Shanti swirled with hers, strengthening, supporting, inviting. She'd been right—Kaldaar hadn't stolen his power. Curious. But then, doing so would've killed his lover. It was sweet, in a way, that a mortal man had stolen the heart of a god, but it was too little too late.

"You are amazing," Zakael rasped.

Now it was her turn to chuckle. "I tried telling you that, but you never listen."

"I'm listening now."

His forehead burned with fever and he moaned against her healing, but she held steady. She'd been through this before and knew what to expect. When he turned his head to vomit, she was already seated away from the spray. When his body convulsed and trembled with the last vestiges of the poison, she held him tight and infused more of her power into him. A wound on her hand seeped blood into his skin and she encouraged it to mingle with his.

Kaldaar shrieked her name, commanding her to stop, but she ignored him. Rhoane's shout silenced the god, and Taryn's heart beat with passion and love for her life mate.

"Your bond," Zakael gasped, "it is unbreakable. It is admirable."

"You will have a bond like ours. Once you've learned to love yourself, only then can you love another."

He scoffed, and that started a wracking cough that ended with more convulsions. "I have a son, but I think you already knew that."

Unsurprised Carga had told him, she nodded and blinked against the tears that stung her eyes. "He is kindness and goodness. He deserves to be happy, Zakael, and so do you."

"After all I've done? I deserve death."

She held his face and stared hard into his lovely eyes. "You might've been set on a path of darkness, but you have a chance for redemption. It's yours, Zakael, if you want it. But you have a lot of work to do before you get there. Are you willing to do the hard work?"

He blinked at her, his face taking on a more natural shade. "A second chance?"

"More like a fifth chance for you, but yes. I am granting you a chance to learn, to do better, to *be* better."

His fingers touched the gaping flesh on his face. "Will I be scarred?"

"Do you want to be? It would look mysterious and sexy on

you." It was strange to jest with him. To act as if they were truly brother and sister. To be allies.

"I'm already hideous enough on the inside, it's only fitting my outside matches."

"Very well." She smoothed her fingers over the wound, healing it so completely there wasn't a mark remaining.

"Didn't you hear what I said?" He stood on wobbly legs and glared at her, but there was no bite in his demeanor.

"I did. And one day, you'll see the same person inside that I do." She rose and faced him. "Are you ready?"

"For what?" His gaze went to the battlefield. "I have seen enough death and destruction to last several lifetimes. I cannot kill anymore today. If ever."

"That's exactly what I was hoping you'd say." She spun her wrist and created a small portal. "I'm sending you somewhere to heal, but also to learn about yourself. It's a world where ShantiMari is dying, sadly. You'll understand your path soon enough, but first, you'll meet a friend of mine. Her name is Sam and she needs your help figuring out who she is."

He blinked at her and shook his head. "I truly don't understand."

"That's part of the fun." She pressed her hand upon his chest, cleaning his tunic of the blood. "I'll check in on you from time to time, so don't disappoint me. Oh, and you won't have access to your ShantiMari. Should be exciting to see how you fare without it."

She winked and laughed at his look of horror. Zakael without his power. What a marvel that will be. She stretched to kiss him on the cheek, lingering long enough to feel the warmth of his skin. He would recover, and learn, and eventually love. It was as it should be.

With a shove, she sent him through the portal. A grunt of surprise was followed by shouted questions that were silenced when she closed the spinning black hole. He was on his own now; the answers to his questions were his to discover.

Rhoane approached and slipped his hand into hers. "Where did you send him?"

"Earth. It's a few years—seasons—later than when we were last there, but I have a sense he'll be fine."

Rhoane held her shoulders and gazed into her eyes. She tried not to see the sadness lurking in their mossy depths, but it was impossible to ignore.

"Kaldaar is too powerful. He is at his full strength, and I am afraid you and I together cannot fight him."

It was always going to come to this. She'd realized long ago that they couldn't defeat Kaldaar until he was fully recovered, and she hated that it had taken so many deaths to get here.

"I know, my love." She unsheathed her sword and listened to the song that had been playing in her mind for the past week. "I know the words now. I know what they mean."

Tears pricked her eyes and her face flushed with what she knew was coming. She kind of wished Zakael would be here to see it, but his time on Aelinae was complete. There was nothing more he could learn from her or the others. It was time he took what he'd learned and used it for good.

Rhoane held his sword beside hers and the words inscribed on his blade shifted.

"'From the heart this song is sung. From the heart this mortal coil is undone. Sing, sing, sing this song as one. Only then, who you shall be, you will become.'" He looked at her, confusion etched in the furrows of his brow. "I do not understand."

The tears she'd held back for far too long coursed over her cheeks and she sniffled. "Yes you do, mi carae."

She gripped his hand and placed the tip of his sword at her heart before nestling her sword tip against his.

"No, I will not." He jerked Claidholm Solais away and turned his back to her. "I. Will. Not. *Cannot.*" When he turned back to her, his cheeks were wet with tears. "Do not ask this of me. Anything, please, ask of me anything else, but not this."

"It's the only way."

"But what if it does not work? What if we are not gods? If we go through with this, we could die."

"We *will* die, Rhoane. This mortal coil cannot serve us any longer." She replaced his sword at her breast. "You have to believe, mi carae. Truly believe. I have never once doubted who you would become." That wasn't entirely true; there were many times she'd doubted many things, but right then, her belief was steadfast. This was the only way to stop Kaldaar and save Aelinae.

The swords sang in harmony, repeating the words Rhoane had spoken. Her fingers shook as she adjusted the tip of Claidholm Solais to where her heart thrummed like a drug-addled speed freak.

"I cannot." He hung his head, his tears racing off his nose to drip on the ground. Where each drop landed, a tiny crystalline flower bloomed, but he didn't notice.

"This is your final betrayal." She lifted his chin and he looked miserably at her. "Not all betrayals are bad."

"This is far worse than bad. You are asking me to kill you."

"No, I'm asking us both to have faith that this isn't death. This is a rebirth."

He glared at the sky. "I hate all of them right now."

"So do I, but that changes nothing."

She held Claidholm Solais's blade against her breast and aimed Ynyd Eirathnacht at Rhoane's heart. Her knees wobbled and her mind screamed at her to stop. Nothing about this was normal. She shouldn't have to kill her beloved to save a world. It wasn't fair. None of this was fair.

But it's what needed doing.

"I love you." She snuffled against a rush of emotion and blinked against the flood of tears that spilled from her eyes. It was just as well she couldn't see him clearly because if she could, she might run screaming toward Kaldaar and let him end it all.

"You are my life, Darennsai."

"And you are mine."

Before she could change her mind, she shoved her sword into his flesh and pressed forward onto Claidholm Solais.

Pain unlike she'd ever felt before tore through her, shredding her thoughts, weakening her resolve. The swords' song rose in volume and she heard Kaldaar shriek from somewhere close. He was coming for them.

She felt Rhoane pull away and wrapped them in her Shanti-Mari. All four strains held them, cocooning them in a swath of love and protection. Then Rhoane's power joined hers and he pulled her close, impaling them fully on the blades.

A cry of pain—hers, Rhoane's, she wasn't sure—tortured her hearing. Agony upon agony washed over her in terrible waves that seemed never-ending.

Rhoane's lips claimed hers and she opened to the kiss as if it were their last. The last she'd ever know of his sweet touch, his loving embrace, his scent and smell that made her knees weaken and heart stutter.

Through her tears she saw him not as the Eleri he'd been, but as the Surtentse. Branches stretched from his skin, and leaves formed a canopy above them. He was her Surtentse and she his Darennsai, united at last for forever and all time. The terrarae didn't erode, nor did the night sky darken. The sea king had the story wrong all this time.

Their togetherness would create life above and below the surface of the worlds they would bring into existence. Their love would nurture the creatures and the people who would call their worlds home. She saw it all so clearly now. They were so close to becoming who they were always meant to be. Rhoane saw it too —his thoughts were hers, his heartbeat hers. They were united by the blood and the blade. *She* was the tear of Aelinae. She was Nadra's greatest creation and biggest remorse.

"The gods couldn't save Aelinae without destroying everything, but we can. I see it now, what you always saw. The goodness, the villainy, the balance in everything. I see it all and it is beautiful." Rhoane's gorgeous moss-hued eyes looked at her with heartbreaking love and devotion. "I am ready. I believe."

"Stop!" Suddenly Kaldaar was there, shouting and waving his arms maniacally. His words were lost to her, as was his anger. She was with Rhoane, that's all that mattered. His heat warmed her, his love infused her, his body protected her.

Buzzing started in her ears and she claimed his mouth to deepen their kiss. If this was the end of it all, she wanted her last memory to be of Rhoane and nothing else.

Tiny motes of dust and glitter swirled around them, of stars and bark, of moondust and moss. She was jerked violently away from Rhoane, her connection shattered, her mind torn asunder. She gripped her sword as if her life depended on it and glared at the one responsible for interrupting her precious moment, from stopping their deaths.

Bloody fucking Kaldaar.

She raised her sword as if to attack, then stared, amazed, at the tiny flickers of shimmering light that shone through her transparent hand. First her sword, then her wrist, followed by her arm dissolved to nothing. She looked to Rhoane, terrified at what she might see, but he, too, was dissipating into a swirl of motes. His eyes locked with hers, awe and wonder filling them.

She reached for him, but he was gone.

And then, nothing.

CHAPTER FORTY-FIVE

*D*arling, *it is time to awaken.*

Darkness shrouded her. There was no sound, no senses, no feeling of anything. It wasn't the void, or was it? Had something else happened to the walkways between portals? Or was this death?

"Taryn darling, come back to the light." Nadra's soft voice brought her out of the nothingness, and she blinked through a haze.

"Where am I?" Even as she asked, she saw the brilliance of the other gods as they hovered in a half-circle around her. And there, just beyond them, still in physical form but glowing like a tiny star, was Brandt.

Her breath caught. "I'm on Dal Tara."

She looked at her hands, but no limbs came from her, nor did she have a body. She was a cluster of stars—a nebula of her own making.

"Where is Rhoane?" She glanced at the others—the elder gods she knew, and younger ones she'd never met.

"I am here, mi carae." Rhoane's voice came from beside her,

but like her, he wasn't a physical shape, but pure light and flickering stars.

"Darlings." Nadra morphed into the physical form of a woman and drifted closer.

Ohlin and then Verdaine, then Julieta, and the other gods all took on human-looking shapes. It was to make them more at ease, she was sure of it, but all it did was confuse her. Were they dead? Had Kaldaar interrupted something important?

"You are not dead, and yet you are." Nadra motioned to their masses of light. "This is your pure essence, how you exist as a god. But you can make yourself appear any way you wish." She suddenly became a fierce ogress with tusks and horns. A moment later, she was a flittering hummingbird. Finally, she became the woman Taryn had first met in the cavern, with flowing white hair and the face of an angel. "Your sacrifice has earned you the destiny that was foretold at your births."

Rhoane became Rhoane again and he knelt at the goddess's feet. "I am honored you found me worthy."

"My dear young man, we all found you worthy, but you had to believe in yourself to make it true." Ohlin placed a hand upon Rhoane's head. "There is still more work to be done." His gaze went to somewhere behind Taryn and Rhoane.

She looked over her shoulder, surprised to realize she'd shifted into her woman form. In the distance, she saw the battle on Aelinae. Saw Kaldaar striding across the terrarae in search of more victims to slaughter. A speck of white caught her attention and there, a short distance away, Kaida rushed toward the god with Tessa sprinting beside her. The dagger she'd gifted her sister glinted in the sunlight and a strong battlecry came from her lips.

"No," Taryn shouted, "not Tessa." She turned to the gods. "You must stop him."

"They can't, Taryn." Brandt emerged from the group and held her hands in his own. She could no longer smell his scent of cigar and aftershave and a part of her mourned her mortal soul.

"They've given you these gifts to do what they cannot. If they entered the battle now, all Aelinae would be ripped apart." He embraced her with arms that felt solid and kissed her cheek. "You know what you need to do—do not hesitate. Trust yourself."

He was right. She knew what to do, had always known, but that didn't make this any easier. Rhoane took her hand in his and squeezed.

"It is time, Darennsai."

"You know what we have to do?"

"We must kill a god. It does not bring me happiness to say so, but you were right all along. It is the only way."

"Do you have the crown, Rhoane?" Nadra asked, and they turned to see the other gods watching them intently.

"I, erm, it was enhanced by a queen in another realm." He flicked his wrist and the crown appeared out of nothingness. "I hope you do not mind."

Ohlin took the crown and whistled. "Ingrid did a cracking job with it. I daresay we chose well."

"That we did, my love." Nadra placed her hand over the crown. A spark flared from the gold tips of the headpiece, and she handed it back to Rhoane. "As we know you will, too."

"What am I to choose?" Rhoane asked as he settled the crown upon his head.

"You will know when the time comes. Now, go save your home world. We will be waiting for your return." Nadra gave them a gentle push and an encouraging smile.

Rhoane gripped Taryn's hand and together they flew like comets back to Aelinae. They landed like superheroes on the ground, in a sort of half-crouch, half-sprint. The terrarae vibrated with their arrival and a hush fell over the battlefield.

Whatever she and Rhoane looked like to the others must've been terrifying because every face that turned toward them had wide eyes filled with a silent shriek. Taryn muted her glow and searched for Kaldaar, finding him thirty paces away closing in fast toward Tessa.

"Stop!" she cried out, and he slowed his steps, his face turning toward her with a sneer that quickly morphed into a gaping maw.

"No!" he shouted. "I will not have it. Mother! How could you?" He raised his fists to the sky and the ground shook with his rage.

Taryn and Rhoane darted to him quick as a carlix, she in front, Rhoane circling behind the god. Now that the moment had come, she hesitated. It was what needed doing, but still—she'd hoped it could end another way. Any other way besides this one.

Taryn, we must, Rhoane urged. *You cannot redeem him as you did your brother. He will never change, mi carae.*

I know. It's just—he's a god.

As are we.

Oof, that hit hard in the solar plexus. They were. She was. Holy fuck.

Ready? She held her sword gripped tightly in her hand. Her runes glittered and shifted just as they did when she was mortal. In a way, it comforted her to see that tiny detail of herself. Godhood was new, but being a badass? She understood that well.

"You measly upstarts are no match for me. I don't care what Mother and Father think, you cannot defeat me." Kaldaar raised his hands as if to bring the very stars crashing upon their heads.

"Shut up, you pretentious twat." Taryn nodded to Rhoane, and together, they shoved their swords into Kaldaar's body.

Instead of funneling her power into him, she concentrated on only one thing: kindness.

Kaldaar shrieked and writhed, but their swords held him trapped. He couldn't manifest his godly form, nor could he use his formidable power. Rhoane's head cocked to the side as if he were studying what was happening.

Their swords burst into song, filling the air with their melodies. It was the song of redemption and rebirth they'd heard in Lan Gyllarelle. A new verse started and Kaldaar shuddered against the words.

> *Rebirth of the spirit, a symphony untold,*
> *Through trials and battles, our destiny unfolds.*
> *With hope as our armor, we'll rise above the strife,*
> *Seeking peace eternal, in this enchanted life.*
> *In the depths of despair, a flicker ignites,*
> *A chance for redemption, to make things right.*
> *Through battles we've fought, scars etched on our skin,*
> *But the fire within us won't let evil win.*

"We are the Light, we are the Dark, we are Eleri and Telraicht Noir. Don't you see, Kaldaar? We are everything you could never be, not because you were exiled, but because you chose a path that limited you to this pathetic excuse for a god." Taryn twisted Ynyd Eirathnacht with more savagery than she intended.

"You will exist no more." Rhoane shoved Claidholm Solais deeper.

Their swords emitted a bright light, pure radiance that stretched from inside Kaldaar's fading body to the sky. Taryn held firm, her resolve set, her conscience clear. Rhoane glowed as bright as the sun, just like he had on the bank of the Kiltern River when Rykoto was trying to kill her. She glanced at her hands and found she, too, was shining like a star in the night sky.

Kaldaar shrieked one last time before his godly essence shattered and sparked into a million flames that dissolved into nothingness.

She and Rhoane collapsed to the ground, their arms shaking from the effort it had taken to hold the god.

Kaida rushed up to them and licked first her face and then

Rhoane's. Then Tessa was there, hugging them both, squeezing her little arms as tightly as she could.

"You glowed," Tessa said with wonder. "I saw you shimmer like a star in the night sky." She looked from Taryn to Rhoane. "Both of you. But you were like the rays of the sun."

"Tessa," Taryn started, but choked on the words.

"My son." King Stephan approached, his face a mix of grief and awe. "Is he gone? Truly?"

Taryn wasn't sure if Stephan meant Rhoane or Kaldaar.

"Kaldaar is no more, Father." Rhoane stood and embraced his father. "But there is something more I must do."

The others were crowded around now, talking in excited voices. Eleri, Aelan, Danuri, Geigan, even the Mohram were there, all waiting, wondering, watching. The battle had ended, but what did that mean for Aelinae?

Taryn knew what was coming, but even so, she held her breath as Rhoane lifted his hands to the sky. A great portal opened, a swirling blackness that terrified those on the ground.

"What's he doing?" Tessa slipped her hand into Taryn's, her grip tight.

Taryn kissed the top of her sister's head. "He's bringing Aelinae's darathi home."

"The darathi?" Stephan asked, his eyes full of hope.

"Yes, Your Majesty. And, someone very special who's waited a very long time to reunite with her love."

He looked to her with a question burrowed in his frown. Before she could answer, a great roar came from the portal followed by Gilchrist's gleaming scales. Jinnipher came next, the only darathi with a rider on her back. Beside her, Ahmbra blew flames from her snout and a great whoop went up from the crowd. More dragons than had ever been in the wasteland came through the portal and she realized some of Aerithilyn's darathi had chosen to join a fight a war that was not theirs, to aid darathi they hardly knew. But that's what friendship was—taking a risk for those you love.

Stephan stared at the single rider, his expression a mystery. Finally, he looked to Rhoane. "Is it true? Or do my aged eyes deceive me?"

Rhoane grinned and nodded. The darathi were home at last, and with them, the Eleri queen.

CHAPTER FORTY-SIX

Campfires dotted the battlefield with makeshift tents providing shelter. An uneasy peace settled around them, but the future was as yet unknown. It was a new world. A better world. A balanced world.

Taryn drifted between the gathered groups listening to their conversations, tending to their wounds—physical, emotional, and mental—as she passed. They didn't see her walk among them, but a few lifted their heads as if they could.

The dead had been cleared and the ground cleansed by all who possessed ShantiMari. It was a unified spiritual cleansing that had spontaneously happened without her encouragement, and for that, she was hopeful. In their suffering, the people of Aelinae had found something in common with those they'd been told were their enemies. Even the Mohram had assisted in burying the dead, and now supped with the Aelans they'd fought only bells before. The Sitari had joined the others as well, their scarred blue faces lit by firelight and looking more beautiful, more ethereal than ever.

It was a start.

But there was more work to be done.

She floated to where Rhoane sat with his mother and father. Bressal and Janeira were there, too, but Eoghan sat with Eliahnna and her family.

"Mi carae, it is time." She held her hand out for him and he nodded.

"Are you to leave us so soon?" Aislinn grabbed her son's shirt in a desperate attempt to delay the inevitable.

"Not yet, but there is something we must do." Rhoane kissed his mother's cheek. "We will return shortly."

They walked several paces away and shifted into their darathi forms. A great murmur went up from those gathered on the plain. Most of them had never seen a dragon before today, and certainly didn't know Taryn and Rhoane possessed darathi souls. She spied Tessa and Eliahnna gazing at them with wet cheeks, their arms around each other. Eoghan put a strong arm around their shoulders and held them close. Tessa's family was smaller now, but she would know love and acceptance and kindness. All the things a growing child needs.

Taryn pulled her gaze from her friends to focus on the task at hand. The other darathi joined them and together they flew north toward Caer Idris. Once they confirmed the castle was deserted, she and the other dragons flew in a circle, speeding up as they went to make a powerful vortex. They blew flames from their snouts and flapped their wings hard enough to break stone from mortar, to crumble the castle walls and demolish its dungeons.

Where the runyon tree once stood, the icy charred ground gave way, disintegrating to dust as if fell into the ocean below. They flew faster and faster, around and around again until the castle ground to bits of rock that whirled in their vortex.

In the center of it all, standing calmly alone, was a woman. Taryn motioned to Rhoane and he followed her to the ground where they shifted into their physical forms. The woman curtseyed low, almost to the bits of rubble that were all that was left of Caer Idris.

"I have waited a long time to meet you." She stood before them as solid as they were.

"And I have so many questions for you, Mallaqai," Taryn quipped.

Rhoane grunted and crossed his arms. "So you are the trickster witch who enchanted Saeko on the ship? What did you mean 'two truths and one lie?'"

"Hey, I said I have questions! That doesn't mean you get to ask yours first." Taryn's hair blew around her in a cyclone to match the vortex that whirled dangerously close.

"That's your riddle to solve, Surtentse, but you have plenty of time." Mallaqai giggled and it sounded a little like a cackle.

"The wall in the Narthvier, was that your doing? If so, why is it tearing?"

"I put that there to keep the Eleri from seeing the darathi. Once I realized the dragons could see into the vier, I knew it was only a matter of time before they would try to cross the canyon, or the Eleri would try to rescue them. It was for everyone's safety."

"Is that why you exiled them?" Rhoane asked the question on Taryn's lips.

Mallaqai nodded, her eyes full of sorrow. "Rykoto was going to steal their power. I couldn't let that happen." She looked up at the ghostly forms spiraling above them. "I at least owed them that for my betrayal."

"They are home now, and your penance is at an end. You are free of the shackles holding you to Aelinae." Taryn waved her hand and sent a thread of her power to unlock the invisible bonds.

Mallaqai drew in a deep breath and lifted her face to the sky. "I have waited eons for those words. Thank you. Before I go, may I ask a favor?"

Rhoane crossed his arms, eyes narrowed. "What is it, Changeling?"

She chuckled. "Yes, I am a changeling, but then, so is your beloved." Rhoane glared at her, but she was undaunted. "An Aelan becoming Eleri? Whoever heard of such a thing? If anything, she is the greatest changeling of all. As are you." Mallaqai poked him in the chest. "You woke up an Eleri prince and now you are a god. Powerful stuff, don'tcha think?"

"She's right, you know. But you had a favor to ask," Taryn prodded. Time was ticking and there was still much to be done.

"The Sitari. Will you open your hearths and homes to them? They've been punished enough."

Rhoane heaved a sigh and flopped his arms to his side. "Is that all? Stars, but I thought you were going to ask for something outrageous like an entire planet to call your own."

"You can do that?" Mallaqai grinned cheekily. "I mean, if that's on offer, I wouldn't mind."

They all had a little chuckle at that, then Taryn said seriously, "I will protect the Sitari. I'll even go so far as to give them the option to keep their blue hue or lose it, but it has to be their choice."

Mallaqai grabbed her hand and bowed. "I was afraid to ask for too much, but that would be wonderful. Thank you."

Even as she spoke, her body started to dissipate into a cluster of glitter and motes of dust. She raised a hand in farewell and then she was gone. Taryn took a long drag of air and looked to the heavens. She hoped Mallaqai was on Dal Tara with Brandt, but that wasn't her call to make.

The vortex sputtered out and the darathi landed where Caer Idris once stood dark and brooding upon the clifftop. Everything had been demolished and destroyed. Everything except Gwyn's garden. Amid the torn soil and pits where the dungeons once were, row upon row of glorious roses bloomed, a riot of colors and perfumes.

Taryn walked to a patch of upturned soil and stuck her hand deep into the dirt. She channeled her power into the ground and a moment later, tiny green shoots rose to curl around her forearm. She stepped back to watch as a large bush formed, then a trunk that grew straight and tall. Branches spread from the trunk with broad green leaves casting shadows in the evening light.

Dotted among the leaves were glittering crystal flowers with petals as large as a dinner plate.

"A gllanaed tree." Awe and wonder filled Rhoane's voice. "The physical embodiment of the Surtentse and Darennsai."

"A reminder to all those who need it that where evil festered, goodness can bloom. And, a happy ending for King Baldev's fairytale. I always hated his version of the ending."

Rhoane reached a hand to touch the trunk and she felt his ShantiMari infuse the tree with his blessing. In seasons to come, this tree would be a symbol of hope and healing, of restoration and rebirth, and of remembrance.

Hayden and Sabina would build their own palace somewhere in the West, and eventually Caer Idris would be known for something other than the hideous violence that took place here. In time, Aelinae would be healed. For now, this tiny corner of the world wasn't more than an enchanted tree and roses that were planted with love.

"It's a start," Taryn said, her gaze traveling to where the battle had taken place. "But now we need to plan a wedding."

"Whose?" Ahmbra asked excitedly.

"Ours," Rhoane answered. "Did you not say you wished to be married when we were in London?"

Her gut swirled with sorrow of all that she'd lost. "I did, but after all we've been through, I don't need a grand party where we make devotions of love in front of our family and friends. I think perhaps we're beyond that."

"Then who is getting married?" Ahmbra looked at them, confusion on her shimmering gold-scaled face.

"Eliahnna and Eoghan," Rhoane answered as understanding dawned. They didn't need a public spectacle, but the new empress did. "Yes, it is as it should be."

"I'll meet you there." Taryn kissed him briefly before stepping away from the darathi.

That gave Rhoane pause. "Rykoto?" he asked, sadness cloaking his eyes.

"Yup. He's the only thing left that can destroy what we've fought for."

"And you need to go alone?" His tone said he didn't approve.

He didn't understand—this was her path. Rykoto was her responsibility. After all, Mallaqai never would've hidden the dragons if Rykoto hadn't known about the prophecy. He had planned to use the darathi to tear worlds apart looking for her. She remembered the warding and returned to Rhoane's side.

"Change your mind?"

"Remembered something." She stroked Gilchrist's snout and reached for Jinnipher's ruby scales. "Your ancestors warded these magnificent creatures. It's time we undo the damage they did."

"What?" Rhoane stared from her to the darathi. "They would do no such thing."

"They have, Your Highness." Jinnipher nudged him gently. "We learned many things in the elven kingdom. Chief among them was that we not only have ShantiMari, but that it is our duty to use our power to maintain the balance on Aelinae. It was never meant to be Taryn's duty, but always ours. When Mallaqai betrayed us, Aelinae lost that protection."

He stumbled backward, knocking into Ahmbra and she wrapped her tail around him for support. Jinnipher's words had shocked him violently. She felt his confusion and shame.

"We can remove the wards, mi carae." Taryn held her hand out for him to take. "Together. The darathi will only follow the one who wears the Crown of Awakening, and only you can fully free them of their restraints."

He touched the crown, seeming a little surprised that he still wore it. "I am sorry for what my ancestors did. We will right those wrongs and make it permanent, so that you will never be chained to any race ever again. You will be esteemed as you should always have been, and your counsel respected."

"It is the least we can ask of you, Surtentse." Gilchrist breathed out and a waft of warm air sent their hair flying. "I believe it was also these wards that weakened us. We needed Aelinae to thrive and flourish. Without the wards and living once more on our world, we shall grow stronger and multiply."

Taryn kissed first Gilchrist's chin, and then Jinnipher's. They'd suffered so much.

She and Rhoane joined hands and closed their eyes. Their power swirled through each darathi, even the ones who had come from Aerithilyn. With each one, they removed all wards and taints from previous Caretakers. Some had been kind, while others were not. To them all, she bestowed her grace, as did Rhoane.

By the time they finished, she and Rhoane glowed softly. The more they used their power, the stronger it became. She'd almost forgotten they were divine beings now, but the way her hands sparkled was reminder enough.

When certain the darathi were cleansed, she promised to see them soon and transported herself to the bowels of Dal Ferran, where a solitary figure stood in the middle of death. He turned his bloodied eyes on her and laughed.

"Come to finish me off, too? I saw what you did up there. Kaldaar was a fool to underestimate you. I as well."

Taryn strode to him, her battlefield garb shifting to a flowing white gown. "No, Rykoto, I'm not here to gloat or to punish you. That was never my path. But I'm sure these two might have something to say about it."

Two bright lights lowered from the ceiling to materialize into the forms of Daknys and Julieta. Rykoto went to his knees and sobbed, begging forgiveness from the goddesses he so cruelly betrayed.

She kissed them both full on the lips before stepping back. "Whatever you choose to do, I support fully and with all my heart."

Julieta gripped her shoulders. "Thank you, Taryn. You have freed me from my suffering." Her eyes were no longer full of sorrow, but of something close to joy. The shells embedded in her skin fell off and only a beautiful shimmering remained.

"I am glad of that." Taryn hugged her tightly. "You deserve all the happiness in all the worlds."

And she did. They all did.

She waved as she ascended to the terrarae. The last thing she heard was Daknys quoting a line from one of the swords' songs. Then Rykoto was silenced forever.

CHAPTER FORTY-SEVEN

On a perfect summer day, at precisely sundown, an Aelan empress and an Eleri prince vowed to love, honor, and support each other until their dying breaths. It was a day of new traditions. Never in the history of the empresses of Talaith had any married. And definitely none of them had shared their throne with their partner. Eoghan would be Emperor of Talaith, an Eleri co-ruler who held as much power as his wife.

Taryn sat with Rhoane, her eyes shining with unshed tears and a lifetime of happiness. Not only for Eliahnna, but for her cousin Hayden who wore a magnificent obsidian crown that was the exact counterpart to Eliahnna's diamond crown. Lingering above the wedding goers, the elder gods floated on tufts of air, their physical forms glowing with love. They had come to give their blessing not just to Eliahnna and Eoghan, but to all the people of Aelinae, with special attention to the new rulers, including Hayden and Sabina. Taryn blew the gods a kiss and inclined her head to acknowledge their presence.

The star crown she wore cast glittering rainbows over the wedding guests as the swags of diamonds shifted with her move-ments. It was still the most ridiculous crown she'd ever seen, but since it was a gift from Nadra herself, Taryn thought it important she wear it this day, of all days. Once the ceremony was finished, she'd return it to her private space storage where she kept the sword, and other mementos of her life on Aelinae. Her time there had been short, but she'd lived it balls out, as Dony would've said.

In the months since the Battle for the West, as it was now called, they'd buried Lliandra and Myrddin in the crypt beneath the Crystal Palace, and welcomed several babies into the family. Hayden and Sabina made frequent trips to Talaith while their palace was being built on the western edge of Aelinae south of Caer Idris. They had yet to name their new home, as that proved to be more difficult than naming their firstborn.

Her, they called Galendra after the star Taryn was born under. Taryn watched her cousin fuss over his daughter, pride swelling her bosom. He would make an incredible king, and Sabina a formidable queen. Aelinae was lucky to have them. But more importantly, they would be remarkable, devoted parents.

Sitting beside his son, Duke Anje tickled his granddaughter's chin and cooed to her with the sweetest, most content expression on his face. Some thought he should take the throne in the West, but he'd refused for personal reasons.

Valterys had been the cause of Anje's deepest unhappiness, and some wounds couldn't be healed with a crown.

Her gaze slid to Faelara and Baehlon. The big knight held their newborn son, who was tiny in his arms, and gazed adoringly at his lifelong love. She beamed up at him, pride and affection oozing from her in waves. Their son bore the name Glennan, named after Rhoane ap Glennwoods al Narthvier. Without him, they told anyone who asked, they would not have met. It wasn't exactly the truth, but Taryn loved a good romance with a happily ever after and never corrected them.

She squeezed Rhoane's hand and flicked a glance at the

Crown of Awakening he wore. "Have you decided on a worthy heir?"

His cheeky half-smile made a delicious twist in her belly. "I have, and I think you will approve."

"Oh? And are you going to tell me who will be the new Darathi Vorsi Prince?"

He leaned over and kissed her cheek. "No."

Such a tease. She'd find out soon enough. It was one of the more difficult decisions they'd had to make. Their godhood was new enough they still felt grounded to their physical forms, but theirs was a future of many worlds, not just Aelinae. And those worlds needed nurturing that would divert Rhoane's attention away from the dragon prince's responsibilities. So it was that they decided he would choose a worthy heir to become that which he was no longer suited for—someone who could travel between worlds, finding dragons.

Carga finished her proclamation that Eliahnna and Eoghan were now husband and wife, life partners, and co-rulers of the East. A thunderous applause broke out and even King Stephan had tears rolling gently down his cheeks. He sat with his queen, Aislinn, their hands entwined. Bressal and Janeira sat beside them, both beaming with joy.

A swarm of well-wishers crowded the couple and Taryn took the opportunity to slip away to the orchards where it was less chaotic. Tessa joined her, walking in lockstep beside her, and Taryn found she missed her little sister's rib-crushing hugs. She was a young woman now and very aware how uncool it was to show affection.

"You'll be leaving us again, won't you?" Always perceptive, Tessa had never taken their absences well.

"We will." Taryn tilted her head to the sky where a few stars blinked against the dusky light. "I was never meant to be here long, but that doesn't make this any easier." She wrapped her sister in her arms and kissed the top of her head, which came nearly to Taryn's chin. She'd grown so much over the past season. "I am only ever a wish away. If you need me, I'll be here."

Kaida padded up to them and sat, her tongue lolling to the side. Rhoane was a step behind.

"With Eliahnna married now, I won't have any friends left." Tessa narrowed her eyes. "And don't say I have Faelara or Baehlon. They have a baby now, and eww. Babies are stupid. They don't know anything."

Taryn laughed at that. She wasn't wrong. "You have Gian." She looked into the trees to see if he was spying on them. "Where is he, anyway?"

Tessa jutted her chin toward the palace. "Filling his gullet with wine. He'll retch like a sailor in the morning, but that's his own damn fault." She wrung her hands and looked at the ground. "I want more than this," she waved at the palace grounds. "After everything we went through, I long for adventure. And friends."

"You have Kaida," Rhoane offered hopefully.

"She's just a dog. She doesn't even have opposable thumbs."

"Tessa! That's not nice. Kaida's been there for you through everything. You owe her your gratitude."

But she is right, Darennsai. I am just a grierbas. I do not have thumbs at all, opposable or otherwise.

Rhoane shared a look with her and she grinned. It was outrageous, but what good came of being a goddess if she couldn't use her powers to make someone happy? She nodded, and together they knelt in front of Kaida. Rhoane asked her permission, and the grierbas barked her answer. They wrapped their arms around their most loyal and trusted friend, and together, granted her and Tessa's most secret desires.

When they pulled back, a young woman knelt in front of them, her shining white hair and golden eyes unmistakably Kaida. Instead of fur, she wore a gown of palest blue.

She held a hand in front of her and flexed her fingers. Next, she felt her face, her lips, her throat, and finally her small breasts.

"Is that Kaida?" Tessa asked with incredulity. "She's…a girl."

"She was always a girl, but now she can be whatever she wants. Aelan, dragon, grierbas, cat—it's her choice."

"Remarkable." Tessa bent down and stroked Kaida's glossy hair. "My friend, is it truly you?"

Kaida smiled and laughed. "It is. And look, thumbs!"

The pair embraced and laughed and cried.

"We are going to have some wicked adventures," Tessa promised the grierbas-turned-human.

"We shall have remarkable shenanigans."

Taryn looked at Rhoane with a knowing grin. "We've created a monster."

"A pair of them, I would say."

They left the two to conspire together and walked hand in hand to the far reaches of the garden. She reached for Kaida and a pit of sadness swirled in her belly. She would miss all her friends, but Kaida had been with her nearly from the beginning, sharing her bed, her secrets. It was time the grierbas had her own life, but even so, Taryn would miss the companionship and safety she had given her without asking for anything in return.

"We did good." She meant with Kaida, but also balancing Aelinae.

"Aye, we did. And we will continue to do good." Rhoane wrapped his arms around her and nuzzled her neck. "We will create worlds and races that will thrive."

"We'll have to decide how involved we'll be."

"That is a question for tomorrow's tomorrow."

Several darathi flew toward them and landed in a semi-circle. Ahmbra bowed to them and snorted a flame into the air in greeting.

"Your Eminences, we have a request." She glanced at the other dragons—seven in total, including two from Aerithilyn.

"We have flown over the entirety of this world and we have seen a lone darathi eneari in the seas." She faltered, and one of the Aerithilyn darathi nudged her to continue. "We would like to become like her. Darathi eneari."

Rhoane cleared his throat and Taryn saw the shimmering in his eyes. "You would give up your wings to swim in the dark seas the rest of your days?"

"We would," Ahmbra answered for the group, and all of them nodded in agreement. "We have spoken about this at length, and even asked permission from Gilchrist and Jinnipher. They gave us their blessing, but only you can make it happen."

Her golden scales glittered in the fading light. She was the first darathi born in the wasteland and had survived more than two hundred seasons of strife.

"You will make a wonderful companion to Xianqin. She is very wise and can teach you many things." Taryn turned to Rhoane. "Why does it have to be either-or? Why must they lose their wings to gain fins? Xianqin has wings, at least I swore I saw them, but I was nearly dead so I might be wrong."

He rubbed his chin and took off his crown to study the dragon eggs embedded in the gold. "You can be whatever you wish, Ahmbra. All darathi can choose—water, fire, air, terrarae, space, male or female, it is your choice. This is what I decree as the Darathi Vorsi Prince."

The crown shimmered and the eggs sparkled like gems. The oath was set. Xianqin would have companions and all darathi could choose their own paths. Taryn gave each of the dragons an embrace before they took off toward their futures. Ahmbra lagged behind and Taryn stroked her golden scales.

"Did you have another request?"

"Could I choose the color of my scales?" She snuffled the ground and sneezed at a particularly long weed that tickled her nose.

"You can be any color you wish. Or *all* the colors. Go wild."

Taryn pressed her face against Ahmbra's. "You are the future of darathi."

"That is a big responsibility."

Rhoane stood beside Taryn. "One we know you can handle."

Ahmbra sucked in a long breath and grinned. "I will make you proud."

"You already have. Now, fly, beloved. Make your heart happy." Taryn gave her a slight nudge and the gorgeous dragon took flight.

As she spiraled into the air, her scales turned from radiant gold to a riot of color, settling on a rainbow effect. She whooped and looped against a backdrop of stars and Taryn waved with both arms.

She and Rhoane watched the darathi until they were tiny specks in the distance, neither wanting the day to end. When night fell around them, they knew it was time. Time for new adventures. Time for new worlds. Taryn turned to Rhoane and held both his hands in her own. Tears coursed over their cheeks and where they dropped, tiny buds blossomed from the grass.

"One last flight?"

"This is not the end, Taryn. We can always come back."

"Yes, but everything will be different. Today was the last day we were just us."

Rhoane chuckled and wiped a tear from her cheek. "We were never 'just us.' We have always been who we are now. It took us a while to realize."

She glanced toward the palace. "They'll be fine without us?"

"They will live and love and thrive, mi carae. Now come, it is time." He led her to the seawall and they scrambled atop the old stones.

Hundreds of dragon wings sounded above them and they looked up to see Aelinae and Aerithilyn's darathi flying in a wide circle.

"They have come to see us off." Rhoane inclined his head in respect.

As one, they jumped from the wall and shifted into their darathi forms. First they circled the palace where the wedding guests waved and blew kisses in their direction. After several passes where they blew breaths that produced glitter-like confetti as a farewell gift to the delighted guests. With heavy hearts, they flew over the lands of Aelinae. From the Summer Seas to Haversham and Danuri, up to the ruins of Caer Idris, and over the Narthvier. All along the way, the darathi flew beside them, snorting flames from their snouts and roaring their happiness. They passed over the Ullan desert and the swamps south of the Stones of Kaldaar where only a season earlier Taryn had vanquished the phantom.

If they'd known then what they knew now—but then, if they'd known everything at once, they might not have become who they were meant to be.

One last pass over the Crystal Palace, where their loved ones stood on the seawall and waved to them, and then they turned north toward Mount Nadrene where everything had begun for Taryn. They said farewell to Aelinae's dragons and landed on the ledge where she'd gotten her first glimpse of her home world. Rhoane took her hand and gazed at the valley below. She felt his emotions as if they were her own. It was bittersweet to be here again.

Yet, she reminded herself, there were new worlds to create, more family to discover. She used shadows to speed them to the cavern. Waiting inside were the elder gods.

Nadra clasped their hands and beamed with pride. "My darlings, we thank you. Truly. Aelinae is at peace thanks to you both. The darathi will thrive, the kingdoms are unified. It is more than we could have asked for." She kissed their cheeks and stepped back.

One by one, the gods gave them their blessings and expressed their gratitude. It was heartwarming and overwhelming. Taryn accepted every kiss, each embrace with gratitude. She and Rhoane belonged here, with the gods. In time, that wouldn't feel so strange, but for the moment she let the enormity of what they'd done sink in.

Finally, Brandt stepped from behind the gods and Taryn gasped a sob. "Baba." She rushed to him and threw her arms around the man she'd always known as her grandfather. "Will I see you again?"

"Now more than ever, I would presume." He no longer smelled of tabac and aftershave, but of starlight and joy. "I am so proud of you." He reached for Rhoane's hand. "Of you both. I look forward to seeing what you do with yourselves now that you're free, truly free to choose your own paths."

He released them and stepped back to where the gods watched, contented smiles etched on all their faces.

Rhoane took her hand and led her to the very same spot she and Brandt tumbled through on her return to Aelinae only a few seasons past. Together, they made a portal, their powers sparking silver and moss green around the opening. That was new, and unexpected.

"Where to, mi carae?" Rhoane asked.

"We'll figure it out when we get there."

With a final wave to Brandt and Aelinae's gods and goddesses, they stepped into the portal. The future was theirs to create. Together.

Their time on Aelinae was at an end.

Interminable darkness. No sound. No light. Nothing. It wasn't the in-between, nor was it the void. It just was. He didn't know how long he drifted—it could've been a bell, a day, a week, or four thousand seasons. In this space, he didn't see others; it was just him and his thoughts. So many thoughts. So many questions. First among them: what the fuck was Taryn thinking?

Zakael landed with a hard thump on something soft yet unyielding. He gripped his sword and looked for his sister, but she was nowhere to be seen. A stern face hovered above him, and a second face joined the first. A hand thrust toward him and he flinched out of habit.

"Need a hand up, mate?"

They spoke a language different to Elennish, yet similar. He'd heard it somewhere before, or had Taryn given him the ability to understand?

He tentatively took the man's proffered hand. At least, he thought he was a man, but the stony expression he wore was puzzling. As their skin touched, the man's features softened and he looked completely Aelan.

"Where am I?" He rubbed his chest where the Mohram had

rammed him with his horn. Then, remembering the gash Kaldaar had given him, his hand went to his unmarked face.

"You're in London. Where do you suppose you're supposed to be?" a female said, and he whirled around to see a petite woman standing with arms crossed. Her features also made him think of stone and he shuddered.

"I, uh, I don't know. Taryn didn't say."

"Taryn?" The woman's face relaxed with her smile. "We have not seen Taryn for, what has it been Silar? Twenty years?" She didn't wait for a reply, but the man nodded anyway. "If Taryn sent you then you're exactly where you need to be." She held out a hand. "I'm Donyatella, but you can call me Dony. These are my boys, Silar and Gage. Don't upset them or it'll be hell for you." She motioned him to a table surrounded by a wooden box and upholstered seats. "Sit here, I'll get you something to take the sting off."

He slid into the box and the two men stood at the end of the table as if guarding him. His head pounded and the air was hard to breathe. It was either too thin, or his throat too tight, but whatever the reason, he found it hard to catch his breath.

"You're having a panic attack. Here, drink this." Dony handed him a fat glass filled with something that resembled watery mud, and sidled into the seat opposite.

He tasted the brown liquid and grimaced. "This is revolting."

"It's Taryn's favorite. Now, drink."

He chugged the foul liquid and set the glass down. "She and I always did have different tastes."

"Yes, so tell me how you know her." Dony leaned forward, her eyes narrowed. "And how you came to crash-land in my pub."

Crash-land? Yes, that's what he'd done, he supposed.

He rubbed his head, enjoying the wooziness the drink had brought on. "I don't even know where to start."

"How about at the beginning."

"That would take an age." He motioned to the glass. "May I have some more?"

She motioned to the men, and one strolled to a counter several paces away.

"Thank you. I, eh, Taryn is my sister. Half-sister, technically."

Dony sucked in a breath. "You are Zakael?"

He sensed rather than felt her power whirl in a protective shield around her and her boys.

"I am. But don't worry, Taryn made certain I could do no harm while I'm here. She blocked me from my power. I don't know what she was thinking other than she said I had to help someone."

Dony sat back, her ShantiMari diminishing. "Who?"

"I don't know. Someone called Sam. Do you have another boy with this name?" A glass was set in front of him and he drank it in two long gulps. "Thank you."

Dony folded her arms and for a moment she looked like a stone statue. "I don't know anyone who goes by Sam. Did she say what he looks like?"

A commotion at the front of the pub drew their attention. A very pretty young woman stumbled into the dimly lit room, her black hair bouncing with her movements. Zakael stared, fascinated with the way the light glistened off her deep brown skin. She looked touched by faeries, but that was impossible. Taryn had said ShantiMari was all but dead here.

Except, Dony had scads of it.

His gaze slid to the young woman. Yes, he sensed something in her, deep, hidden, dormant.

"Hiya. I'm looking for a flat to let and I, weirdly enough, received this card today with this address on it. But there's some mistake, right? I mean, this is a pub. Or, do you have flats above? And possibly one empty that you would be willing to let to someone with not a lot of money, but buckets of charm and a work ethic bar none?"

Silar took the card from the woman and whistled long and low. He handed it to Dony, who read it with a placid expression. She tapped it to her cheek a moment before asking, "What are you called?"

"Me? Oh, erm, Samantha, but my friends call me Sam."

Dony slid from the box and handed the card back to the girl. "You're in luck. I do happen to have a flat for let, but this gentleman also needs a place to stay. It's a two-bedroom, so you could share the rent. That's the best I can do for you."

Sam fiddled with the card a moment before looking at Zakael with an appraising glance. He scooted from his seat and bowed to her. Old habits were hard to break.

"I'm Zakael. If I had any friends they would call me Zakael."

To his utter surprise and delight, Sam laughed. The sound was like nothing he'd ever heard. Pure. Full of joy. It reminded him of his sister. Of her kindness and her optimism.

A funny feeling started in his belly. Not enough to alarm him, but he was apprehensive all the same. If Taryn were there, she might have told him what he felt was love. But then, she always was hopelessly deluded.

Not hopelessly deluded, dear brother. Hopeful.

Zakael chuckled to himself with a smile. Yes, hopeful.

CAST OF CHARACTERS

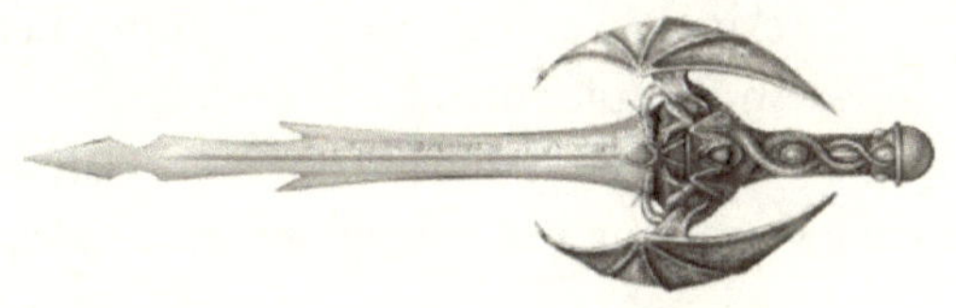

Acelyne (Ace-lynn) ~ Faerie. Witch believed responsible for kidnapping and imprisoning creatures into glass prisons. Deceased. *Part of the Aetherverse and introduced in the Fatal Fae books.

Adesh ~ Summerlander. A spice merchant in Talaith. Tabul's brother.

Ahmbra (Amm-brah) ~ A golden darathi vorsi living in exile. She was the first darathi conceived and born in exile. She gave the other darathi hope for the future.

Aislinn al Glennwoods ap Narthvier (Ay-s-lynn) ~ Queen of the Eleri. Aislinn purportedly perished in a ShantiMari accident when Rhoane was a young man. She did not die in the accident, but lived with the exiled darathi in the wastelands as their Caretaker.

Alasdair (Alice-dare) ~ A faerie servant in the service of Rhoane. Brother to Illanr and Carld.

Alswyth Myrddin (Alls-with Mere-din) ~ Mage with exceedingly long life. Myrddin is the advisor to Empress Lliandra and is often far from court on assignments from the crown. No known children or spouses. No known House.

Amaleigh (Ahm-a-lay) ~ Dragon mage living in Eidyn on the world of Nasus. Amaleigh found two dragonlings on Cilachaem and brought them with her to Nasus. They currently live with the other darathi in the kingdom of Aerithilyn. Married to King Gwilym of Eidyn. *Part of the Aetherverse and introduced in the Chronicles of Eidyn books.

Amanda ~ Aelan. A young woman from Talaith with dubious ties to Adesh the spice merchant. Deceased.

Amdi Agnar ~ Laird of the Ullan tribes. He claimed Kaleigh as his consort. Has two sons and a daughter with Kaleigh. House Agnar.

Anje ap Paderau (Ann-jee ap Pah-der-oo) ~ Duke of Paderau, father to Hayden, husband to Gwyneira (now deceased). Anje is cousin to the Lord of the Dark, and second in line for the Obsidian Throne. His father was brother to Valterys's father. A prince in his own right, Anje renounced his Dark heritage to live with his wife in the Light. Descendant of House Djeba.

Aomori di Monsenti (A-more-ee di Mon-scent-ee) ~ A young Danuri lord fostering with Lord Tinsley in Paderau. In a committed relationship with Tinsley. Descendant of House Monsenti.

Arianna (Arr-ee-ana) ~ Faerie. Daughter to Queen Eirlys. Was once imprisoned in the same glass vial as Rori. When Rori broke free, Arianna did not wake up. *Part of the Aetherverse and introduced in the Fatal Fae books.

Armando ~ Summerlander. Lover of Tarro. Previously worked as a whore in Nena's house, and was Marissa's favorite. Currently lives in Menurra with Tarro and their son.

Ashanni (A-shawn-ee) ~ A mare Duke Anje gives to Taryn.

Baehlon de Monteferron (Bay-lohn de Mont-fair-on) ~ Danuri and Geigan knight employed by Empress Lliandra, sworn to protect Taryn and her House. In a committed relationship with Faelara kaj Endion. Descendant of House Monteferron.

Baldev de Deistra (Ball-dev de Des-tra) ~ King of the Seas. Baldev lives within a vast complex at the bottom of the ocean. Merfolk are believed to be legends as they are not often seen. Once a year, on their naming day, merfolk have the option to walk among the other races on Aelinae. It is unknown if Baldev has ever honored the tradition. Married to Salaria. Father to several daughters and sons. Descendent of House Deistra.

Beary ~ {Master} Unseen character in book one. Advisor to Taryn on household matters.

Beilis (Bay-leesh) ~ Sitari. Second in command to the Chieftess Shandris. Does not trust outsiders.

Bornu (Bore-new) ~ Summerlander. A young boy who works for Adesh.

Brandt Kaj Endion (Brant) ~ Aelan. High Priest of Talaith and advisor to Empress Lliandra, Brandt was commissioned with Taryn's safety when she was born. After his death, Nadra took Brandt to Dal Tara, (home of the gods), which allows Brandt to communicate with Taryn. House Arran.

Bressal ap Narthvier (Bress-all) ~ Eleri. Second Son to King Stephan and Queen Aislinn. Heir to the Weirren Throne. Possibly betrothed to the warrior Janeira.

Carga ap Narthvier ~ Eleri. Daughter to King Stephan and Queen Aislinn. High Priestess to Verdaine.

Carina (Ka-reen-a) ~ Aelan. A member of Taryn's personal guard. Currently living in the Summerlands and training with Flik.

Carld (Car-uld) ~ A faerie maid in the service of King Stephan. Sister to Illanr and Alasdair.

Cashiel (Cash-eel) ~ Second son to Lliandra, fathered by Esna fei Garrith. Given name is Kane, but now goes by Cashiel. Killed by Rhoane at the Ruins of Mallaqai. Is now Kaldaar's latest Shadow Assassin.

Cassie ~ Elf. Princess on Nasus who helped Taryn and Rhoane escape. Asked for help with dragons.

Celia ~ Aelan. Minor noble and Marissa's favorite until she perished at the Stones of Kaldaar. Descendant of House Deltanna.

Cian MacNair ~ Faerie. Brother to Rori. Also a known assassin and spy.

Cora ~ Aelan. A maid in the service of Empress Lliandra assigned to Taryn upon her arrival in Talaith.

Crone ~ Ulla woman who gives warning to Taryn in Amdi's tents. She is killed for her efforts.

Cynda (Sin-dah) ~ A mare Rhoane provides for Taryn.

Daknys (Dak-niss) ~ Elder Goddess. Daughter of Nadra and Ohlin, she is worshipped by the Light and Dark in the central area of Aelinae.

Darius (Dare-ee-us) ~ Artagh, Eleri and Aelan. One of Taryn's guard. They met in Celyn Eryri, but currently Darius is living in the Summerlands and training with Flik.

Darrew (Dare-oo) ~ Danuri lord, Chief Councilor to the Steward of Danuri.

Delarainne/Rainne (Rain) ~ Elf. Lady living at Elvenwood as the betrothed to Prince Theo. She hints at a past secret. Knows the entire history of Cilachaem, including Taryn and Rhoane's role in the world.

Denzil de Monteferron (Den-zell) ~ Danuri and Geigan. A mercenary hired by Lliandra to patrol Talaith's docks. Brother to Baehlon.

Deshan Agnar (Day-shawn Ag-nar) ~ Ullan. Deceased laird of the Ullans. Brother to Amdi Agnar.

Donyatella/Dony ~ Until recently, believed to be Taryn and Brandt's landlord in London. It was discovered that Dony is part of an elite group of immortals knowns as Stone Guardians. She's been tasked with guarding over Taryn since her arrival in London as a baby. *Part of the Aetherverse and introduced in the Fatal Fae books.

Ebus (Ee-bus) ~ Race unknown. Spy employed by Taryn and

Rhoane. Can see the Shadow Assassin.

Eiodian (Eee-dahn) ~ Elf. Healer at Elvenwood. Bears a remarkable resemblance to Baehlon.

Eiric (Err-ic) ~ Danuri. Lover of Zakael. Deceased.

Eirlys (Air-liss) ~ Faerie. One of two faeries queens living on Cilachaem, Eirlys is queen of the Seelie court. *Part of the Aetherverse and introduced in the Fatal Fae books.

Eliahnna Tjaru (Ee-lahn-ah Shar-U) ~ Aelan. Daughter of Lliandra. Her heritage is much debated since Lliandra has never publicly named her father. She is third in line to the Light Throne. Descendant of House Nadrene.

Ellie ~ Aelan. A maid in the service of Taryn. Currently living in the Summerlands and training with Flik.

Enghor (Ain-gore) ~ Mohram. Beast forced to fight Taryn in the Ullan arena. With the legs of a man, chest of an ape, and head of a goat, he is not a creature from Aelinae.

Eoghan ap Narthvier (Eee-gan) ~ Eleri. Third Son to King Stephan and Queen Aislinn (now passed beyond the veils).

Esme Daj Valen ~ Faerie. Lady living at the Seelie Palace. Is remarkably familiar to Taryn and Rhoane.

Esna fei Garrith (Ez-nah fay Gare-eth) ~ Danurian. Minor noble who attracted Lliandra's attention. Fathered a son with the empress and Marissa, the crown princess. Was executed for trying to poison the empress. Descendent of House Garrith.

Ezra ~ Elf. King of Aerithilyn on the world of Nasus. Father to Cassia, husband to Ingrid. King Erza and Queen Ingrid care for the darathi on Nasus. *Part of the Aetherverse and introduced in the Chronicles of Eidyn books.

Faelara kaj Endion (Fay-lara) ~ Aelan and mermaid. Daughter of Brandt, an Aelan and Nemora, a mermaid. Lady-in-waiting to Empress Lliandra. In a committed relationship with Baehlon de Monteferron. Lady Faelara's Healing skills are legendary, as were her father's. House Arran.

Faisal dei Tarnovo (Fay-sal) ~ Summerlander. Sabina's father and the king of the Summerlands. House Tarnov.

Fayngaar (Fain-gar) ~ Rhoane's stallion.

Flik ~ Summerlander. Master swordsman who works for King Faisal training guards, spies, and assassins. Doesn't suffer fools.

Gagoiru/Gage ~ One of the fabled Stone Guardians of lore. Protected Taryn her who life and continues to protect her and Rhoane while they are in London. Has a special affinity for Kaida. *Part of the Aetherverse and introduced in the Fatal Fae books.

Galendra ~ Aelan and Summerlands. Daughter of Hayden and Sabina. Princess. Named after Taryn ap Galendrin.

Gameson ~ {Master} Aelan. Head tutor in the service of Empress Lliandra.

Gayvn ~ Taryn's twin. See 'Shadow Assassin'. Deceased.

Gian ap Brenbold (Jawn) ~ A faerie found in Valterys's dungeon. He has a life debt with Taryn, but refuses to say what that means. Employed by Taryn as a spy. Apprentice to Ebus.

Gilchrist (Gill-krisst) ~ Elder darathi vorsi living in exile. Mate to Jinnipher.

Glennan – Geigan, Aelan, and Merman. Son of Baehlon and Faelara. Named after Rhoane al Glennwoods ap Narthvier.

Gris ~ Aelan. A kitchen boy in the service of Duke Anje.

Guillermo (Ghee-er-moe) ~ Human. Head chef at the pub below Taryn's flat in London.

Gwainne Agnar (Gw-ayn) ~ First son to Amdi Agnar and his Eleri wife Kaleigh. Heir to the Ullan Laird.

Gwilym ~ King of Eidyn. Gwilym has a dragon soul, rare in the kingdom due to their turbulent history. Married to Amaleigh.

Gwyneira Tjaru ap Paderau (Gwin-eera ap Shar-U) ~ Aelan. Sister to Empress Lliandra, wife of Duke Anje, mother to Hayden. Gwyneira died after childbirth when Hayden was a young man. Houses Nadrene and Djeba.

Hanan ~ A Summerlands spice merchant living in Menurra.

Hayden ap Valen ~ Aelan. Lord Valen, Marquis of the province Valen, son of Anje and Gwyneira. Hayden is cousin to the heirs of the Light Throne and the Obsidian Throne. Descendant of House Djeba. Newly married to Sabina dei Tarnovo.

Helena ~ Elf. Queen of Elvenwood kingdom on Cilachaem. Wife to Thane, mother to Therron, Thaddeus, and Theo. *Part of the Aetherverse and introduced in the Fatal Fae and Court of Stars books.

Hensen ~ Elf. Librarian at Elvenwood who met a grisly end.

Herbret ~ Aelan. A minor noble in Talaith's court and one of Marissa's favorites until he perished at the Stones of Kaldaar. Descendant of House Gilfroy.

Illanr (Ill-an-or) ~ A faerie maid in the service of King Stephan. Sister to Carld and Alasdair.

Ingrid ~ Elf. Queen of Aerithilyn. Mother to Cassia, wife to Ezra. Queen Ingrid and King Ezra care for the darathi on the world of Nasus. Ingrid was tasked by the god Ohlin to improve the Crown of Awakening if and when she was to ever meet Rhoane. *Part of the Aetherverse and introduced in the Chronicles of Eidyn books.

Iselt (Ee-selt) ~ A blacksmith at Celyn Eryri with secrets and a past he's trying to hide. He is half Artagh and half Eleri. Currently living at the palace in the Summerlands at Taryn's request.

Ishnara ~ Faerie. Unseelie queen whose ghost is lingering at Elvenwood due to a curse. Deceased.

Janeira (Juh-nair-a) ~ An Eleri warrior of great standing, excellent skill, and deadly capabilities. Possibly betrothed to Bressal.

Jayved dei Tarnovo (Jay-ved) ~ Summerlands prince. Heir to Faisal and Prateeni. Brother to Sabina.

Jinnipher (Gin-i-fur) ~ A darathi vorsi living in exile. Mate to Gilchrist.

Julieta ~ Younger Goddess. Daughter of Rykoto and Daknys.

Kaida (Kay-da) ~ A grierbas Taryn rescued in the Narthvier. Companion to Taryn ~ they have the ability to speak with each other in their minds. Kaida can track the Shadow Assassin.

Kaldaar (Cal-dar) ~ Elder God. Son of Nadra and Ohlin, worshipped by inhabitants of the Southeast until his banishment after the Great War. Kaldaar hasn't been seen in Aelinae in over five thousand seasons.

Kaleigh al Fyrnwood ap Agnar (Kay-lee) ~ Eleri. Sheanna living among the Ullans. The sworn concubine to Laird Amdi. Kaleigh has two sons and one daughter with the laird. One of the best healers of all Aelinae, she and her son Loghan have perfected the art of Ullan healing. Favored of Verdaine. Friend to Taryn and Rhoane.

Khrystina (Christina) ~ An Eleri novice studying at Verdaine's temple in the Narthvier.

Kragor (Kray-gore) ~ Geigan. A brutish man Rhoane fights in the arena.

Lliandra Tjaru (Lee-on-dra Shar-U) ~ Aelan. Empress of Talaith, Lady of Light. Mother to Marissa, Taryn, Eliahnna, and Tessa. Lliandra is directly descended from the goddess Nadra. She is thought to be a just ruler who thinks of her subjects in all matters. House Nadrene.

Loghan Agnar (Logan) ~ Ullan prince. Second son to Amdi Agnar and his Eleri wife Kaleigh. Acclaimed healer. His entire body is covered in tattoos that are meant to aid in his healing.

Lois Tranton ~ Human. Works at the museum in London. Was an associate of Taryn and Brandt's.

Lorilee ~ Aelan. A maid in the service of Taryn. Sister to Mayla.

Lucitan (Loose-eh-tahn) ~ Rhoane's Ullan stallion, given to him by Amdi Agnar.

Mali ~ Darathi vorsi. Dragonling found on Cilachaem and

taken to Nasus by Amaleigh. One of two dragonlings Taryn and Rhoane meet when they visit Aerithilyn. *Part of the Aetherverse and introduced in the Chronicles of Eidyn books.

Mallaqai (Mal-ah-kai) ~ Aelan. A witch who once lived on the plains of the East. She is responsible for the disappearance of Aelinae's darathi vorsi. She's called a Changeling because she was one of the rare Aelans who had a darathi vorsi soul. Deceased.

Marissa Tjaru (Shar-U) ~ Aelan. Was once Crown Princess of Talaith, heir to the Light Throne. Daughter of Lliandra and Esna. Lover to both Zakael and Valterys. Mother to Percival, only a few know of his true parentage. Descendant of House Nadrene. Deceased.

Mayla ~ Aelan. A maid in the service of Duke Anje. Sister to Lorilee.

Margaret Tan ~ Geigan. Seamstress to Empress Lliandra, she often travels with the court. Her tailoring skills are said to be admired in all the kingdoms.

Marina ~ Summerlander. A maid in the service of Marissa.

Matilde ~ Aelan. Amanda's mother. Lives in Talaith with dubious ties to Adesh the spice merchant.

Meg ~ Faerie. Witch living on Cilachaem. Helps Taryn and Rhoane get into the Seelie Palace.

Micha Askell (Mike-uh Ask-elle) ~ Aelan. Baehlon's intended wife. Daughter of Lord Askell. House Askell.

Michel (Michael) ~ Merman. Young boy who found Taryn on the shores of the Jansen Strait. Believed to be an Ullan foundling, it was discovered Michel is a merman and brother to Faelara. Son of Nemora.

Nadra ~ Mother of Aelinae, Great Mother of all Creation. Along with Ohlin, Nadra created Aelinae. Mother to Daknys, Rykoto, Kaldaar, and Verdaine.

Nemora ~ Mermaid. Faelara's mother. Lives in the Sea Kingdom.

Nena ~ Race unknown. Owner of a house of prostitution in Talaith.

Nikala St. James ~ Businesswoman Taryn and Rhoane meet in London. She's part of a larger conspiracy that tangentially involves Aelinae. Appears to be an ally.

Nikki ~ Sitari. Companion and beloved to Shandris, Chieftess of the Sitari. Healer.

Nikosana ~ Black and tan Ullan stallion given to Taryn at the Light Celebrations by Duke Anje.

Ohlin (O-lynn) ~ Father of Aelinae, Great Father of all Creation. Along with Nadra, Ohlin created Aelinae. Father to to Daknys, Rykoto, Kaldaar, and Verdaine.

Oliver ~ Aelan. A servant in the service of Hayden, Lord Valen.

Percival ~ Marissa and Armando's child. He was born in secret and only a few know of his true parentage. Since male heirs are unwelcome at the Crystal Court, Taryn gave him to Armando to raise.

Phantom ~ An unknown entity manipulating Celia, Herbret, and Marissa. The phantom is thought to be an agent of Kaldaar.

Pora (Pour-ah) ~ Cat. Companion to Rainne, Pora is keeping a secret.

Prateeni dei Tarnovo (Pruh-teen-ee) ~ Summerlander. Sabina's mother and the Queen of the Summerlands. House Tarnov.

Rainne (Rain) ~ Elven. Lady Delarainne Dequette. An elven lady once cursed to become an ogress each night. Lives in Elvenwood with her betrothed, Prince Theodonys. Friend to Taryn and Rhoane. House Dequette. *Part of the Aetherverse and introduced in the Court of Stars books.

Rhoane al Glennwoods ap Narthvier (Rone) ~ Eleri. First Son of Stephan, King of the Eleri, and Aislinn, Queen of the Eleri (now passed beyond the veils). At birth Rhoane was prophesied to be the Eirielle's protector. When he was old enough, he took an oath forsaking all others and devoting his life to upholding Verdaine's prophecy.

Rori MacNair ~ Faerie. A faerie spy and assassin Taryn once met in a vision. They meet again in London, and then on the world of Cilachaem. Rori's ties to Taryn are unknown, but their paths continue to cross. *Part of the Aetherverse and introduced in the Fatal Fae books.

Rykoto (Ree-ko-toe) ~ Elder God. Son of Nadra and Ohlin, worshipped by inhabitants of the Northwest and of the Dark. Rykoto was imprisoned in the Temple of Ardyn after the Great War.

Sabina dei Tarnovo ~ Summerlander. Daughter of King Faisal and Queen Prateeni. Currently fostering with Empress Lliandra in Talaith. Sabina's ShantiMari was unlocked after the ordeal at the Stones of Kaldaar. Descendant of House Tarnov. Married to Hayden ap Valen.

Saeko (Say-koh) ~ A maid in the service of Taryn. Currently living in the Summerlands and training with Flik.

Samantha Taylor ~ Human. Taryn met her at the museum. She has ShantiMari, but it is latent.

Shadow Assassin ~ Taryn's twin brother Gavyn. Stillborn, he was stolen from the Crystal Palace the night Taryn was born. His master raised him to hunt Taryn. He is used as an anchor to the god Kaldaar. Deceased.

Shandris (Shawn-driss) ~ Sitari. Chieftess to the Sitari. Skilled warrior and benevolent leader.

Shailana (Shay-lana) ~ Unknown species. Mate to Enghor.

Sheila ~ Bitch who nursed Kaida when she was a puppy. Lives at the Weirren and produces excellent hunting dogs.

Shen ~ Darathi vorsi. Dragonling found on Cilachaem and taken to Nasus by Amaleigh. One of two dragonlings Taryn and Rhoane meet when they visit Aerithilyn. *Part of the Aetherverse and introduced in the Chronicles of Eidyn books.

Silar (Sy-lar) ~ One of the fabled Stone Guardians of lore.

Protected Taryn her entire life without her knowing, and continues to protect her and Rhoane while they are in London. *Part of the Aetherverse and introduced in the Fatal Fae books.

Stanton ~ Duke Anje's Captain of the Guard.

Stephan ap Narthvier ~ King of the Eleri. Direct descendant from Verdaine. Married to Aislinn. Father to Rhoane, Bressal, Carga, and Eoghan. Stephan firmly believes the Eleri are stronger on their own, away from the other races of Aelinae. He opposes Verdaine's prophecy regarding his son, Rhoane.

Sulein ap Lorn (Sue-lain) ~ An Artagh living in Talaith.

Tabul (Tah-buhl) ~ Summerlander. Spice merchant from Paderau.

Tarro (Tare-O) ~ Danuri. Assistant to Margaret Tan. Lover of Armando.

Taryn Rose Galendrin (Tare-in) ~ Daughter of Lliandra, Empress of Talaith, Lady of Light and Valterys, Overlord of the West, Lord of the Dark. Raised on Earth, Taryn grew up unaware of Aelinae, believing Brandt was her grandfather and only family. House Galendrin.

Tessa Tjaru (Shar-U) ~ Aelan. Daughter of Lliandra and Razlog (not named in books one or two). She is fourth in line to the Light Throne. Descendant of House Nadrene.

Thaddeus/Thad ~ Elf. Son of King Thane and Queen Helena. Status: Missing. He is believed to be trapped in a glass prison. *Part of the Aetherverse and introduced in the Fatal Fae and Court of Stars books.

Thane ~ Elf. King of Elvenwood. Currently believed to be possessed by an evil presence. Husband to Helena, father to Therron, Thaddeus, and Theo. *Part of the Aetherverse and introduced in the Fatal Fae and Court of Stars books.

Therronysus/Therron (Ther-ahn) ~ Elf. Elf living on Cilachaem in the kingdom of Elvenwood. Heir to the throne, but Rhoane sees another path for Therron. Has a dragon soul, but is unaware of this fact. Son of King Thane and

Queen Helena, brother to Thaddeus and Theodonys/Theo. *Part of the Aetherverse and introduced in the Fatal Fae books.

Theodonys/Theo ~ Elf. Youngest brother to Therron, son of King Thane and Queen Helena. Interested in astrology. *Part of the Aetherverse and introduced in the Court of Stars and Fatal Fae books.

Timor (Tim-or) ~ Aelan. A member of Taryn's personal guard. Currently living in the Summerlands and training with Flik.

Tinsley Alcath (Tins-lee All-koth) ~ Aelan and Eleri. Hidden son of Carga and Zakael. Tinsley has no knowledge of his parents' identities. Believes himself nothing more than a young lord with business ties to Duke Anje. Often visitor to Paderau Palace. In a committed relationship with Aomori. Adoptive descendant of House Alcath.

Ton ~ Summerlander. Flik's son. Trains Taryn's maids in the art of self-defense and spying.

Troyanna Djeba ~ Aelan Wife to Valterys Djeba, mother to Zakael. House Djeba.

Tug ~ Giant. Lives on Cilachaem near the Seelie Palace. Helps Taryn search for seals. *Part of the Aetherverse and introduced in the Fatal Fae books.

Tudyk (Too-dic) ~ Aelan. Sword Master in the service of Empress Lliandra.

Valterys Djeba (Val-terr-iss D-jj-ay-ba) ~ Aelan. Overlord of the West, Lord of the Dark. Father to Taryn and Zakael. Valterys is directly descended from the god Ohlin. He ruled his kingdom with a tight grasp on its economy and trade. His subjects think of him favorably. House Djeba. Deceased.

Verdaine (Vare-dane) ~ Elder Goddess. Daughter of Nadra and Ohlin, she is worshipped by the Eleri in the Narthvier.

Wurnch ~ Telraicht Noir healer living in Talaith.

Xianqin (Shhawn-kin) ~ Darathi Eneari. Thought to be the last of her kind, most on Aelinae believe her to be a mythical beast and not real.

Zakael Djeba (Zah-K-ay-el D-jj-ay-ba) ~ Aelan. King of the West. Son of Valterys and Troyanna. Favorite to the god Kaldaar, half-sister to Taryn ap Galendrin. House Djeba.

GLOSSARY OF TERMS

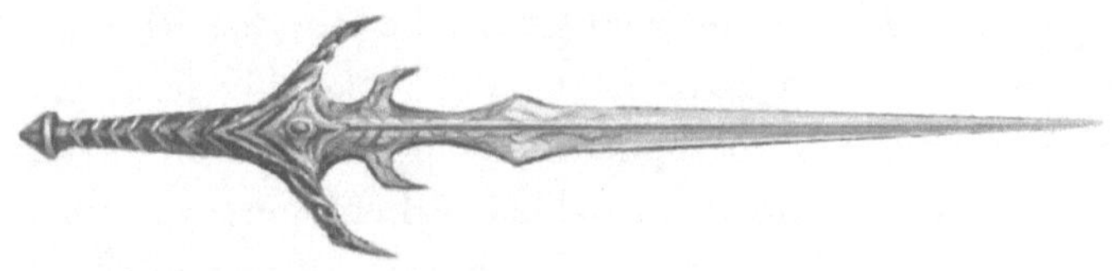

Aelan (Ay-lan) Any person born of Aelinaen descent. These are usually men and women descended from the Elder Gods: Nadra, Ohlin, Daknys, Rykoto, and Kaldaar. In modern times, Aelan refers to those not of another race.

Aelinae (Ay-lynn-ay) A world created by Nadra and Ohlin. It is disk-shaped with waterfalls at the edge of the world, and volcanoes beneath it.

Aelinaen(s) (Ay-lynn-ee-an) Of or having to do with Aelan culture.

Air Faerie Winged Faeries who call on the elements of air for power.

Artagh (R-tah-g) Related to the Eleri, Artaghs lack the Eleri Glamour, as well as the sophistication of the ancient race. They are rumored to be the best at making weapons and working with metals, especially the fabled Godsteel found only in the Haversham Mountains. Outsiders are often distrusted and it's rare to find Artaghs far from their caves.

Atharrach (Ath-ah-rock) A term Taryn found written in Myrddin's papers. Meaning uncertain, but she believes it is a name given to one who wishes to usurp Rhoane's position as Surtentse.

Bells Aelinae's form of time telling. One bell is one Aelinean hour.

Caer Idris (Care Ee-dris) The ancestral home of The Overlord of the West. Currently, Zakael, Lord of the Dark, name calling himself King of the West sits on the Obsidian Throne.

Carlix A sleek, winged feline who makes her home in the mountains known as the Spine of Ohlin. One of the first creatures to inhabit the planet of Aelinae. Often referred to for their flexibility and quick responses, the number of people who have actually seen a carlix is few.

Celyn Eryri (See-lynn Air-ee) The mountain home of the Empress of Talaith. It is here the Light Celebrations take place every Wintertide.

Cere City in Faerie with a Shoogly Dragon. Located close to the Seelie Palace.

Cilachaem World Taryn and Rhoane are believed to have created. A peaceful world where elves and faeries rule their kingdoms, but tensions are rising between the races.

Claidholm Solais (Kleeve Solish) Sword of Light. Ohlin had this sword made for his daughter Verdaine during the Great War, but she refused to use it.

Cllynellren (Clen-elle-aren) Ancient name of the great tree where the Weirren resides.

Crogall An alligator or crocodile like creature living on Enghor's world.

Crystal Court The accepted nickname for the court of the Empress of Talaith.

Crystal Palace The accepted nickname for the palace in Talaith where the Empress rules. It's fabled walls are made from a thin layer of rock clear enough to see through, yet unable to be penetrated by weapons or ShantiMari. No one knows who built the great palace, or where the stone came from.

Cynfar (Sin-far) The Eleri name for a talisman given to someone. Usually a pendant, it can also be a bracelet, earrings, or even a small stone. It must be kept close to the recipient for maximum benefit, hence the use of jewelry.

Dal Ferran (Dahl Fair-en) The fiery pits of hell beneath Aelinae's surface.

Dal Tara (Dahl Tar-a) A celestial resting place for the Gods and those they deem worthy. It is located in the second quadrant of the Meirdia Nebula.

Danuri A Province located in the West. The second largest city to Caer Idris, Danuri is widely known for their wine and ale making skills.

Danurian Anyone of Danuri descent.

Darennsai (Dar-en-sigh) An ancient title given to Taryn by the Eleri. Most don't know the true meaning of the word, thinking of it as nothing more than an honorific bestowed upon her by the Goddess Verdaine. Only a few know the word means, Daughter of the Sky. Less an oath than a promise that one day Taryn will sit at the side of Verdaine, as a goddess in her own right. The Eleri reject this idea.

Dark The part of ShantiMari that is derived from the sun. Only men are skilled in the ways of the Dark, except for the anomaly. To have Dark powers does not automatically make one bad, or evil. There are many men who use their Dark Shanti for good.

Dark Master A highly skilled practitioner of Dark ShantiMari.

Dark Shanti The male side of ShantiMari.

Darathi Eneari (Dah-rahth-ee Ehn-eer-ee) Fables water dragons of Aelinae. Found mostly in the Summer Seas, their kind have not been seen for many millennia. Only a few on Aelinae have seen the sole surviving darathi eneari in person: Faelara, Rhoane, and Taryn.

Darathi Ostgur Shoogly Dragon. The name given to pubs

located on worlds across the universe. Inside each pub is a doorway, or portal that can be used to access any other Shoogly Dragon. A network of pathways between worlds.

Darathi Vorsi (Dah-rahth-ee Vor-see) Aside from the carlix, *darathi vorsi* are the oldest creatures on Aelinae. Several thousand seasons ago they disappeared from the planet, but the Eleri hold the belief that one day they will return.

Delante (Day-lan-t) A dance performed with a group of people.

Dreem A whisky-like drink that ladies don't usually partake of.

Drossfire Light or flaming balls made from ShantiMari.

The East A geographical location on the map indicating all lands, properties, kingdoms, etc east of the Spine of Ohlin. Includes the Narthvier, Ulla, Talaith, and the marshes near Kaldaar's Stones.

Eirielle (Air-ee-elle) The one of prophecy. Said to be the destroyer or the savior of Aelinae, depending on which prophecy you read. Only one Eirielle is ever said to be created, but that doesn't stop those of the Light and Dark from trying to make one. The Eirielle is rumored to possess all the strands of Shanti-Mari: Light, Dark, Eleri, and Telraicht-Noir. Although, the last is only known to the Brotherhood.

Eiriellean Prophecy A collection of prophecies that record various oracles' visions and ramblings about the Eirielle. Throughout history, there have been those that decried the prophecies, and those that touted them as truth. Nearly everyone fears either version coming to pass.

Elennish (Elle-enn-ish) The oldest language on Aelinae still spoken in the East and West.

Eleri (Ee-ler-ee) A mysterious clan of elf-like men and women who live in the Narthvier. They stay within the borders of their forest and don't like outsiders coming on their land. The Eleri share a collective conscious, in that they can call on the wisdom of past and future Eleri in times of duress. The oldest race on Aelinae, they and the *darathi vorsi* share a common bond. Thought to be caretakers of the beasts, when the *darathi vorsi* disappeared, it was a time of great mourning for the Eleri.

Fadair (Fah-d-air) The name Eleri have given to anyone not Eleri. It is meant to be used as a way to signify someone not of Eleri descent, but often it is used as a disparaging slur against non-Eleri.

Fade The natural progression of those with ShantiMari. A fade can last anywhere from a few moonturns to several seasons. With the fade comes a weakening of power.

Faerie Cakes Small cakes light in texture, but filling. Made with sponge cake and jam, these are Taryn's favorite. Don't ever leave a plate sitting around or she'll eat them all.

Feiche (Fee-ch) A large black bird similar to a raven, but faster and a bit bigger. They hunt in packs and are capable of taking down a small horse if so inclined.

Frost End The time between Wintertide and Summer. On Earth, it would occur around April.

Gaarendahl (Gare-en-doll) An older castle located between the Spine of Ohlin and the Summer Sea. It belongs to Valterys's family, but Zakael uses it most often.

Gargoyles Mythical immortals known as Stone Guardians. They take on the appearance of humans. Powerful, not believed to have ShantiMari of their own, they are endowed with other gifts.

Geigan (Guy-gan) A warrior race of people. Dark in coloring, they are rumored to be the source of mating with the Sitari.

Glamour A slight shimmering beneath the skin. Found only on Eleri.

Godsteel A metal forged by the Artagh of Haversham. Stronger than any other metal, godsteel is unbreakable. Long ago, only the gods could wield weapons made of godsteel (hence, the name), but at least two swords have made their way into mortal's hands. Rhoane's and Taryn's. But there are rumors that a few other swords have been tainted by Telraicht-Noir ShantiMari. Their owners are unknown at this time.

Grhom (Gr-om) A spiced drink made by the Eleri. It has healing properties and gives strength through the many ingredients used to make it. Taryn likens the taste to a thick chocolate mixed with chai. Occasionally, the Eleri will add alcohol to the drink.

Grierbas (Greer-bah) A large, wolf-like animal that makes its home in the Narthvier. Wild and territorial, grierbas keep away from civilizations, even avoiding the Eleri.

Gyota (Gee-o-tah) In Eleri, *gyota* means 'destroyer'.

Harvest The months during the season between Summer and Wintertide. On Earth, this time is referred to as Fall.

Haversham A mountainous region where Artagh mine for gems, minerals, and the necessary metals to make weapons. Highly guarded, outsiders are not welcome in Haversham.

Helben A city north of Caer Idris. That far north, the city is covered with snow for most of the season.

Hben Firn Jungle forest on the outskirts of Menurra in the Summerlands. Usually a peaceful place full of blooming flowers and luscious plants.

Hildgelt (Hill-d-gel-t) A Danurian ornamentation made from thin layers of blown glass.

House The family name by which most Aelans associate themselves. Every House has their own color and insignia. It is by these outward displays members of nobility and the court can recognize another's importance.

House Galendrin Ohlin created this House for Taryn on her crowning day. This is the highest honor anyone could hope to achieve and has only been granted once.

Horiscus Tree Tree found on the beach near the Crystal Palace. Legend tells of a princess who was nourished by the tree for seven days and seven nights.

Kitka An animal from Faerie. A cross between a fox and a carlix, the kitka lacks the ability to fly, but is commonly regarded as one of Faerie's fastest animals. Nocturnal. Not often seen by others.

Lan Gyllarelle (Lahn Gill-a-rell) A vast lake located in the Narthvier. Its waters are rumored to hold healing properties. The Eleri often hold ceremonies on the banks of the lake.

Lake Oster Located between Talaith and Paderau, Lake Oster is often used as a stopping point for travelers. Fresh water and an abundance of fish refresh stores between the two great cities.

Larell A flower found on the banks of Lan Gyllarelle. Is rumored to have healing properties.

Levon (Le-von) A sleek black bird. Faster than any other birds, the levon is a favorite form of transportation for those competent in transformation.

Light A strain of ShantiMari found in females born on Aelinae. Not all women exhibit traits of the power, but are able to pass on Light ShantiMari to their daughters. Eleri females have Light ShantiMari, but their powers will differ from the Fadair's in that they use nature as a catalyst and Fadair use the air and sky. The Lady of Light is able to manipulate weather and has slight control over the sea.

Light Celebrations A week long event featuring competitions of physical prowess. The celebrations began as a way to offset the dreariness of Wintertide.

Light Throne The ancestral court of The Lady of Light, otherwise known as the Empress of Talaith. Also referred to as the Crystal Court. The actual throne is made of ancient oak from the Narthvier. Woven into the planks of wood is a thin layer of crystal.

Looking Glass A clear orb used for scrying. Can also be used to spy on someone. Ranges in size from a small marble to a large boulder. One of the lost arts, but still used by some with powerful ShantiMari.

Lycan A wolf/man hybrid creature Taryn and Rhoane encountered at Elvenwood. His ShantiMari had been brutally stolen from him and he was close to death.

Mari (Mar-ee) The female side of ShantiMari. Also referred to as Light.

Mallaqai's Ruins An ancient castle now in ruins. Mallaqai is believed to have made a vortex during the Great War and forced all of Aelinae's darathi vorsi into exile.

Menurra Capital city of the Summerlands.

Mi Carae An Eleri saying that means 'My heart, my truest love'. It is not spoken lightly, and acts as a bond between two people. When *denilithia* is added, it translates to 'Cherished love of my heart'. Usually spoken between a parent and their child.

Mind-Speak A form of communication used between two people within their minds.

Mount Nadrene (Mount Nay-dreen) The holiest place on Aelinae, Mount Nadrene is where Nadra sent Taryn through a portal to Earth. It is also a cavern filled with glittering crystals and a large lake. Some believe the cavern is the birthplace of all the gods and goddesses of Aelinae.

Nadra (Nah-d-rah) The Mother Goddess, she and Ohlin created Aelinae.

Narthvier (Narth-veer) A vast forest covering the northeast portion of Aelinae. The Eleri make their home in the Narthvier, or vier as some call it. The Eleri are protective of the forest and use veils to dissuade unwelcome visitors. Only the Eleri know how to raise the fabled veils.

Obsidian Throne The ancestral home of the Lord of the Dark. The actual throne is made of the same oak planks as the Light Throne. Within the wood fibers is woven obsidian granite.

Ohlin (Oh-lynn) The Great Father, he and Nadra created Aelinae.

Paderau (Pah-der-oo) A vast city ruled by Duke Anje. Paderau sits between the Narthvier and Talaith, which makes it a busy port city for trading goods.

Paderau Palace The home of Duke Anje and his family.

Privy Council A body of advisers to the Empress of Talaith. The council is made up of senior members of the highest Houses. On occasion, as with Hayden and Duke Anje, a junior member can represent their House in council. Also included in the privy council are the High Priest, and captains of the guard or military.

Ravenwood The less formal home of the Duke of Anje. When in residence, he oversees the local businesses.

Runyon Tree A black, gnarled tree with sharp thorns embedded in its trunk and branches.

Sabinth Aarendhi Seventeenth Vessel – mentioned in papers found in Talaith's library, this vessel is needed to propagate Kaldaar's followers.

Scyver Magic Hunters found in London.

Seal of Ardyn Seals created by the Elder Gods to keep Rykoto imprisoned in the Temple of Ardyn.

Season Aelinae's term for the passing of one calendar year. The difference in time between a season on Aelinae and a year on Earth is approximately one season equals nine months on Earth.

Shanti (Shahn-tee) The male side of ShantiMari. Also referred to as Dark.

ShantiMari (Shahn-tee Mar-ee) Two halves of the same whole. ShantiMari is a power found in all things on Aelinae. Within men and women, it manifests itself in varying degrees from no visible signs, to extremely powerful. Those in positions of great power will have more ShantiMari than those born to the lesser clans or Houses. ShantiMari is often referred to as Light and Dark, or female and male. Within the confines of Shanti-Mari are rules, or etiquette. The power can be culled from the smallest pebble to the stars themselves. Wielding more power than one is capable of controlling often leads to a painful death.

Shadow Assassin Neither alive nor dead, Shadow Assassins were the elite force of Kaldaar's army. Only a powerful Master can create the demons.

Shadow Spawn, Shadow Soul Nicknames given to the Shadow Assassin.

Seelie Faerie term. On Cilachaem there is the Seelie and Unseelie courts. The exact differences between the kingdoms has been lost to history, but the current queens can be differentiated in the ways they rule their kingdom. The current Seelie queen believes she is more rational and dignified than the current Unseelie queen.

Sheanna (Shee-ahn-a) An exiled Eleri. When an Eleri is *sheanna*, they are required to cut their hair and live outside the borders of the Narthvier until a certain amount of time has passed. Once they return to the Narthvier, they must complete the purification ceremony before they are considered to be Eleri once more.

Sitari (Sit-ar-ee) Blue skinned warrior women who live in a community devoid of men. Their island sits at the southernmost edge of Aelinae. It is rumored their preferred mates are Geigan males. Sitari women can be found in other kingdoms of Aelinae, usually scouting for the strongest to procreate with. Once coupling has been achieved, the Sitari return to their island. Male offspring are said to be sacrificed to their goddess.

SIRE Business in London where Brandt purchased the Seal of Ardyn before he and Taryn returned to Aelinae.

Spine of Ohlin The range of mountains stretching from the Temple of Ardyn in the far north to the Summer Seas in the south.

Summerlands An island kingdom located south of Talaith in the Summer Seas.

Summer Seas The body of water covering the entire southern area of Aelinae.

Surtentse (Sir-tants) An ancient title meaning 'Son of the Terrarae'. Verdaine gives this honorific to Rhoane.

Sword of Ohlin Also known as Ynyd Eirathnacht. Ohlin had the sword made out of godsteel for his daughter, Daknys. The bearer of the sword must be pure of heart and worthy of the weapon.

Talaith (Tal - eth) The capital city of the East. Ruled by the empress, also known as The Lady of Light.

Telraicht Arts (Tell-rah-ckt) A twisted version of ShantiMari that binds one's soul forever to the banished god, Kaldaar. Practitioners can be either male or female, but females become barren once they invoke the Oath of Fealty. Because of this, they are viewed as Brothers alongside the men.

Telraicht Brotherhood (Tell-rah-ckt) The oldest, most secret religion in Aelinae's history. Much of the Brotherhood is unknown to any except those who are counted among the members. Once a practitioner is invited to join the Brotherhood, they are challenged to a series of tests, many of which require virginal sacrifices. See also Vessel. Membership is often passed from one family member to another, but the terms must be satisfied before being accepted. Those who do not satisfy the requirements, or are not deemed worthy are destroyed.

Telraicht-Noir Shanti and **Telraicht-Noir ShantiMari** (Tell-rah-ckt Nwaarh) Also called simply Noir. See also Telraicht Arts. This form of ShantiMari uses chaos to fuel its power. External and internal sources give practitioners their strength. They pull their power from the world around them, or the inner conflict people try to conceal. The use of Telraicht-Noir Shanti-Mari is shunned by the Light and Dark, but there are those who have found a way to manipulate the strands of light and shadow into a woven tapestry of devastation that cannot be traced. These are Masters that even the Telraicht Brotherhood fear.

Temple of Ardyn (Ar-din) Rykoto's temple and source of

power. He was imprisoned here by Daknys and the Elder Gods after his defeat in the Great War.

Terrarae ~ Aelinean name for earth, or ground. The substance upon which life is built.

Treplar (Treh-p-lar) Round apple-like, spiky fruits from the Summerlands.

Trisp A thick alcoholic drink.

Ulla (Oo-la) A kingdom located in the far East of Aelinae. The Ullans are a tribal people, following their herds throughout the season. Ullan horses are of the finest stock.

Unseelie Faerie term. On Cilachaem there is the Seelie and Unseelie courts. The exact differences between the kingdoms has been lost to history, but the current queens can be differentiated in the ways they rule their kingdom. The current Unseelie queen follows the custom of providing a learning experience of sorts that involves pleasures of the flesh.

Verdaine (Vehr-d-ane) Daughter of Nadra and Ohlin, goddess of the Eleri.

Verdaine's Prophecy When Rhoane was born, Verdaine prophesied that he would be exiled from his people until the *gyota* returned. His fate would be tied to the one who is and who is not for all time.

Veil A mysterious barrier preventing outsiders from entering the Narthvier.

Vier ~ Nickname of the Narthvier.

Vorlock A huge, lizard-like creature with heavy scales and a wide frill around its head. Vorlocks contain a poison that can kill a man or woman instantly.

Weirren (Weer-en) The ancestral home of the Eleri King and Queen.

Weirren Court The gathered nobility of the Eleri live among the many buildings interwoven through the ancient tree that makes up the Weirren.

Weirren Throne Built into the oldest tree on Aelinae, the Weirren Throne is a living, breathing seat.

The Shallows Geographical area located to the west of Danuri. Swamplands and marshes.

The West Geographical area located to the west of Ohlin's Spine. Includes the kingdom of the Overlord of the West (now called King of the West), Danuri Province, and Haversham.

Western Seas The body of water located off the Western Coast of Aelinae.

Woodland Faerie Faerie folk who make their home in the forests Aelinae, most commonly found in the Narthvier. Woodland faeries grow to be around three feet in height, although some are taller. They are the exception. Woodland faeries share a special bond with nature and can cultivate new species of living plants or animals.

Ynyd Eirathnacht (Inid Air-ath-nack-t) The name of Ohlin's sword, currently in the possession of Taryn Rose Galendrin.

AUTHOR NOTES

Every ending is bittersweet. I'm excited Taryn and Rhoane finally have their happily ever after, but I'll miss our adventures. Naturally, they'll pop up in other books within the Aetherverse, and I'm sure I'll see them around the Shoogly Dragon, but it won't be the same living day to day without them constantly nattering at me to write one more adventure. One more story. One more villain for them to defeat.

Never say never! They might be gods now, but they're still full of mischief and I fervently hope our paths cross again.

I do hope you've enjoyed their shenanigans as much as I enjoyed writing them. There are so many people who helped or supported me along the way, far too many to list here, but they know who they are, and they know they have my eternal gratitude.

First, last, and always among them is my husband David. Without his patience, his kindness, and his love, none of this would be possible. Thank you for loving me. You're my favorite. Always.

ABOUT THE AUTHOR

Tameri Etherton is a *USA Today* Bestselling and award-winning author of fierce scorching fantasy and paranormal romance. She grew up inventing fictional worlds where the impossible was possible.

It's been said she leaves a trail of glitter in her wake as she creates new adventures for her kickass heroines, and the rogues who steal their hearts.

She lives an enchanted life traveling the world with her very own prince charming and their mischievous dragon, Lady Dazzleton.

Read More from Tameri Etherton and explore the Aetherverse at
www.TameriEtherton.com

9 781941 955499